ANSARILAND

J. Alan Veerkamp

A NineStar Press Publication

www.ninestarpress.com

Ansariland

Printed in the USA

ISBN: 978-1-64890-370-0

First Edition, August, 2021

Also available in eBook, ISBN: 978-1-64890-369-4

CONTENT WARNING:

This book contains sexually explicit content, which may only be suitable for mature readers. Depictions of kidnapping/abduction, murder, dubious consent, past trauma, medical procedures, death of a prominent character, and graphic violence/gore.

Corporations control every sector of society from law enforcement to automated manufacturing. The economic and social divides are chasms.

Jobs are scarce for an undocumented slug like Arad Ansari, and life on Earth's Grey District A-5 colony is even harder. With no other options, he plies his youthful looks to hustle enough money to stay fed even without a roof over his head. So when Captain Torrins of the *Midas Ascending* offers him employment as his personal cabin boy, Arad takes the opportunity despite his reservations. Because what other choice does a desperate, poverty-stricken man with no prospects have?

When corporate military forces demand payment for Torrin's and the crew's sins, Arad is left alone and adrift in unknown space. After years of smothering on the crowded streets of Grey District, a ship of his own should be an unexpected windfall, but it doesn't take long to discover what—or rather, who—were originally being smuggled on board.

More than human, more than an animal, Roku is a blend of both, a marvel of genetics and highly illegal. His past is a mystery, even to himself, a story told only through his nightmares. Despite a dubious introduction, an unspoken bond forms between him and Arad while they try to repair the ship before supplies run dry or corporate forces track them down.

Time is not on their side.

Overcoming their pasts and learning to trust one another are the keys to Arad and Roku's survival, and they have to succeed to find their place together in the universe.

To Mom: You never read my books because the potential for sex scenes leaves you squicked out, but you still encourage my efforts and never suggest I stop. Ever.

Chapter One

It was too early for bright lights. Even once they'd breached dawn, it would be hours before the sun rose above the towers choking the sky and illuminated the district through its near-permanent cloud layer.

Traffic beacons swept the corporate work zone, directing the shuddering mechanical beast to the landing pad. The ground quaked as it set down, metal legs straining. Its great mouth opened with a hydraulic release of breath, and it spit out another load of hopeful people to join the rest nearby. The last person had barely exited when it closed its mouth and roared off into the sky once more. Mustard-tinged exhaust choked the air in its wake.

Expandable fencing corralled the crowd like the livestock his parents used to talk about before cloned meat became necessary. Scarcity had driven the price high enough only the wealthiest elites could afford it.

It had been a long time since Arad Ansari had tasted actual meat.

"A little breathing space, please." Bracing his shoulder, he nudged at the woman trying to press past him on the left. Everyone on this planet made him appear miniature, but he was wiry and didn't allow anyone to push him aside.

Not anymore.

Pulling his collar closed, Arad shivered, lacking enough layers to keep him warm in the chilly morning. More people than he'd hoped stood ahead of him in the claustrophobic queue leading to the Grey District A-5 tech yard after camping overnight in the nearby alley. Manufacturing was automated, leaving tech jobs scarce among the self-made engineers in the factory slums. The token he'd lifted off a wayward tourist allowed him to visit the bathhouse, so he'd be sure he was clean and appeared ready to work. He wouldn't risk giving them any excuse to turn him away.

A chorus of boots clunked along the steel causeway in practiced unison as the mass of people shuffled forward, invading Arad's personal space in all directions. Whether intentional or not, he kept a tight grip on his shoulder bag even though it was latched tight, keeping his few possessions safe. The crowd funneled into a line aimed at the guard wall entrance, but the man big enough to be a hybrid DemiShou blocked Arad's view to see how much farther he had to travel. The sea of workers thrummed with anticipation and a hint of desperation yet plodded along at a cautious pace.

Above the crowd, a smooth electric hum drew Arad's attention. A clutch of security drones hovered, lasers scanning everyone present with their unnatural eyes, maintaining order. The red pinpoint beam stopped on one person, then the next. Arad held his breath when it targeted the back of his neighbor's head.

The project was a big deal if they'd gone to the expense of hiring a security force, and apparently word had gotten out given the number seeking positions. They would move along and keep to themselves because no sane person would be willing to lose wages spending the day dealing with District Authority.

Arad nudged the tall stranger next to him, trying not to cringe when he felt more bone than muscle beneath the man's sleeve. "Are they actually doing anything yet? Or are we waiting to trample each other?"

"Naw, they're checking people. It's just slow as hell. How early did you get here?"

"Late last night." Peering over his shoulder, Arad couldn't see where the mass behind him ended. "Didn't want to be in the back half when they filled the quota and sent us all away."

"No shit. Good luck, kid."

"Thanks. You too."

The crowd inched along as a sluggish wave. Stretching around the human wall before him, Arad spied the attendant reading his handheld against the scan results, passing some through the gate and sending others on their way. With too many people and not enough work, the whole labor force was built around a lottery. Supposedly, everyone would get their turn. At least, that was the official corporate spin. A flawed and dysfunctional system, but all the slugs—poor bottom-feeders like himself—could hope for. He'd arrived early, but there were still so many in need and not enough work to go around.

Finally reaching his turn, Arad pressed his finger to the attendant's screen and waited for the gruff man to verify his details.

"Not authorized. Next."

All the ambient noises faded away as a bubble of focus closed around Arad. "What do you mean not authorized?"

Weathered with facial lines giving him a permanent air of exhaustion, the man sighed in frustration but never raised his eyes. "You're not on the work list."

"No, no, that's not right. Davis confirmed this yesterday. He said I'd have a spot for once."

Using the scanner, he impatiently pointed at the group milling alongside the wall outside the work queue. "Take it up with him. Next."

"No, no, wait a minute! I'm supposed to be on the list!"

"Not my problem. Next."

Before he protested further, the bony man shoved Arad out of line. The bubble popped and sound rushed back in. Feet skidding on gravel, he managed to catch himself, only to spin around and find the waiting slugs had filled the gap he'd left behind. No one looked his way. The crowd continued as if nothing mattered. As if he didn't matter.

Hands curled into fists, he dug his fingers into his palms and clamped his jaw tight to keep himself from shouting. A security drone floated nearby. Long-practiced habits aimed to stuff down the growing panic. Since the day he first wound up on the street, he had learned meltdowns were a privilege he no longer possessed. However, it didn't stifle his confusion and a bit of outrage. Davis had promised him it was a done deal. How could this happen? Grilling the attendant would be useless. He had a job to do and less reason to care than most.

No, Arad needed to hunt down his so-called buddy and shake some answers out of him. It didn't take long, since the attendant had all but pointed him out.

Taking a drag off a cigar, Davis stood waiting for the shift to start. A true Caucasian, his pale skin and dirty-blond hair made him easy to spot. A rare occurrence for his genetic line to survive in the breeding soup of the current population. At least on the poor side of the city, most people were all various shades of brown and gold. Pure races of any type were hard to come by. Arad's family had managed to maintain their dusky tan heritage through careful selection, but it hardly mattered since he hadn't laid eyes on them in so many years.

When Davis caught sight of Arad approaching, he cursed to himself as he carefully stubbed out the smoke to salvage his precious vice.

"Davis, they kicked me out of line. What happened?"

The scruffy foreman hesitated, pocketing his dead cigar in his stained coveralls and avoiding Arad's piercing stare. "Sorry, kid. Management went a different way. They gave the spot to a wolf DemiShou this morning."

"Why? You said the job was mine."

"He's got a wife and kids to feed."

"So, because the wolf-human hybrid is married and has kids he can't afford, he gets first dibs?"

Shaking his head, Davis shrugged. "It's a quota thing. Politics. Way above my pay scale."

Arad sidestepped in front of him when he started to turn. "You couldn't get me into the general selection? There's still people being selected."

"I tried. I really did. But you're off the grid, and that's all sorts of red flags."

"That's not my fault."

"Maybe not, but they don't like hiring folks they can't track a history on, and they don't have time to figure it out."

"I'll take less money. I'll take anything."

"Company policy won't let them. They're afraid of corporate blowback. Everyone's afraid for their jobs 'cause everyone's replaceable as far as they're concerned."

"Maybe I should let someone experiment on me and then maybe I wouldn't have to slave for wages."

With a firm clamp on Arad's arm, Davis pulled him aside. "Don't say stuff like that. Someone might hear you."

Too many rumors that might not be rumors circulated of desperate people selling themselves for corporate experiments. Most were probably rubbish, but a slug had to be careful. More than one street drug had been designed using test subjects who wound up dead.

Dirty steam billowed out of a nearby service vent, and Arad deflated. "I really needed this, Davis."

"I know, kid. I'm sorry. I tried. Really." As Davis released Arad, regret colored every inch of his husky frame. It helped soothe the rolling frustration but didn't extinguish it, since one look told Arad the man wasn't prone to missing meals.

"Yeah. Thanks. I have to figure out what to do now."

Dragging his fingers through his dense thatch of wavy black hair, Arad tugged hard enough to remember not to place so much faith in one single thing to survive in the future. He'd allowed Davis's word to change his usual strategies. Normally, he kept plans within plans, multiple options, always trying to think three or four steps ahead where possible. This time he'd let the excitement cloud his judgment, and now here he stood outside without another option, thankful it wasn't raining. He wanted to be furious with Davis, but in the end, this situation was as much his own fault as anyone else's.

Dropping his hands to his sides, Arad sighed. It wasn't the first time he had to start from nothing. It likely wouldn't be the last either.

Brow arched, Davis glanced around and ducked his head. He spoke out of the corner of his mouth in an almost comical effort to be secretive. "I know it's not much, but you know...you could stop by after shift end. It'll be another week before I can get home. I'd like the company."

"You're not serious?"

Opportunistic prick. Even if it wasn't the first time he'd exchanged funds for favors with Davis, Arad wanted to tell the man to go to hell. But he'd lost the job he needed—was counting on. He didn't have any wolf Demi welfare to rely on, and those wages might have fed him for a month.

"C'mon. It's not like we've never done it before. We have a little fun, let off some stress, and you get some credits in your pocket. Everyone wins." Davis smiled, which gave his smudged and unshaven face a certain charm. He wasn't a slug on the bottom of the food chain like Arad. While hardly an elite, Davis didn't need to scrounge to feed and had a real roof over his head.

"You've got some balls on you, Davis."

Rolling his shoulders, Davis puffed his chest. "One of my best features, from what you said. You were right gentle with them even."

"That was pillow talk."

"And that's not a no. C'mon. What do you say?"

The ongoing murmur blanketing the area swelled into a raucous noise behind them. Arad turned to find a stout man trying to push into the job line. Probably a reject like Arad.

"You can't do this to me, you bastards!"

Shouts rang out on all sides and tempers flared as he refused to quit. New people in line defended their place, and the attendant leaned out of the fray, his hand reaching for the alarm button that would end the whole employment lottery. Arad had seen it happen before. Screaming and shoving escalated between everyone involved. The reject was sturdy and determined enough to keep the fight going. Tensions already strung tight, threatening to break.

A security drone swooped in behind the man, its red laser focused on the base of his neck. A few people tried to run but were trapped by the crowd. The first wave of frightened cries began. A sharp crack fired from the drone, driving a thin cable to the man, who jerked from the pain and stumbled into the barrier. Sparks arced off his hands, racing through the fence, shocking anyone in contact. Curling wisps of smoke spun off his hair and skin as an inhuman, guttural shriek spewed out of him. People screamed, unable to escape, but others would rather risk being killed in a stampede than lose their spot in line.

The taser retracted into the drone with a snap, and the reject collapsed to the ground, half moaning, half sobbing. Returning to its general scans, the drone ignored the pacified man. The disrupted crowd gradually quieted, no one daring to move.

Chest heaving, the attendant settled himself in place. "Next."

A brave woman lurched ahead of the line, taking advantage of the lull. A soft chime signaled the scan approved, so the attendant sent her through the doorway to work. Spell broken, the rest went back to the routine before they lost their turn. Rejects stepped over the downed man, knowing better than to protest.

Arad's stomach growled, gnawing at him with ceaseless hunger and anxiety. He didn't have to check his shoulder bag to know there wasn't enough cash left to buy even the smallest morsel of food.

"I'll think about it."

The money always became more intriguing when reminded about how little he had and how few options he had to acquire it.

Davis patted Arad's shoulder and walked off. "You know where to find me."

Arad watched Davis leave until the rumble of an incoming transport split the air, no doubt full of another batch of hopeful slugs like him.

"Yeah. I always know where to find you."

Chapter Two

"Stay the night."

Davis brushed his knuckles along Arad's shoulder. Holding back a shudder, Arad smoothed his hair, still damp from the shower. The dingy, once white sconces embedded in the wall were calibrated in automatic night mode, bathing the one-room flat with a meager level of illumination. In the poor light, Davis's pleading eyes were dilated with barely any visible color left. He meant the words now, but when the drug wore off, the morning would be painfully awkward for them both.

Like every other time.

"I need to go."

Davis's shoulders sagged as if sadness were a physical thing. "You always say that."

A strobe of harsh light from a passing trawler swept through the window slats, highlighting Davis's sturdy, naked body in moving stripes of brightness. While not fit and pristine like a holographic advertisement, his skin shined with sex and sweat, covering a meaty frame built for power.

Arad had to turn away. "Because it's true."

It wasn't the first version of this exchange. Temptation was a seductive creature. Having a bed to sleep in, being a kept man with access to funds, food, and shelter made for a powerful enticement.

But the price...

Arad didn't need reminding of how they'd spent the last few hours, rutting in a Syn-fueled frenzy. PnP was Davis's preferred scene, giving his appetites a voice he wouldn't have otherwise. His addiction for companionship outweighed his decency. Arad shouldn't have followed through again, but in the end, credits were credits and jobs were hard to come by. He didn't have any more leads, since getting into the tech yard this morning fell apart.

Davis was always more emotional until the Syn wore off. It lowered inhibitions and induced a nice sexual euphoria, making for a fun time. It was also cheap enough for even a slug to get their hands on. Tricks often liked it, but Arad left it alone. It wasn't a case of judgment. Stoned hustlers were likely to be rolled, raped, or worse.

The script played out the same each time. Arad would prepare to leave. Davis would beg. Arad would politely refuse, holding out his hand, waiting for payment. Like now. Brow crinkled in embarrassment and frustration, Davis slipped the fund tokens into Arad's hand. For a moment, he hesitated, like he might take Arad's hand and make some kind of overt gesture but drew back instead.

"Be safe out there. Let me know if you need anything."

Shirt barely buttoned, Arad slung his satchel over his neck before he did something stupid, like change his mind. Davis would never be an option for one glaring reason.

"Tell your wife and kids I said hello."

And there was the price.

He heard the soft gasp, picturing the hurt flinch. Stepping onto the landing, Arad didn't look back, knowing Davis would be standing there, high and undressed in the doorway, oblivious to his neighbors, until he was out of sight like all the times before. It might have been a cruel jab, but Arad couldn't afford to get too close to Davis for far too many reasons, and the man needed a dose of reality. Arad was many things, but he wouldn't be the tool to break a family, purposefully or not. Also, the nagging whisper Davis had tanked him to set up this encounter in the first place wouldn't get out of his head. A near lifetime of distrust and suspicion on the street would never let him forget it.

In the end, Davis had to be a customer. No more, no less. Nights with Davis were business, not romance. He vowed not to land in Davis's bed again. Even if everything turned hopeless.

Once at ground level, he moved a block down the street to be sure Davis hadn't followed. Each step twinged with the promise of a furious ache in his backside tomorrow morning. With a stuttering exhale, he stopped and slumped against the nearby warehouse until his forehead contacted the cold metal wall. Life fed his weariness, from its trials to his own choices. Arad was educated and handsome enough most people usually saw it under the grime. If he made more of an effort, he'd rake in far more credits than he did. There were plenty of offers. But by accepting, he'd have to face himself, and it was hard enough with what few men he hustled now. Multiplying the resulting shame would do him no favors. Arad scoffed. World's oldest profession? He was a part-timer at best. This wasn't the life he was born to, but it's what he had, thanks to his parents, and he refused to wither into nothing.

Leaning back, he cast his gaze up the wall, admiring its construction. Square panels of mismatched texture and purpose had been welded together into a symmetrical grid. A touch of aesthetics inside part of the world most ignored. All it needed was a little color to turn the pattern into an oversized chessboard.

Oh, he missed playing. Calculating each move, thinking several possible steps ahead, and anticipating your opponent became life tenets as he grew older. The game became something to pore over when the family had other interests. Chess was elegance and discipline, an honored tradition of intellect and skill. Arad loved it. Talk of competitive tournaments had even sprung up before his life showed its true face and kicked him into the dirt. Games were far and few between these days.

Pushing off, he set back on his path, making the long trek to...where again? Not home. He didn't have one of those.

It was late, yet Arad wasn't sure of the time. Like every other slug, the cost of the tech implant that linked to the world server was outside of reality. The bioware in his wrist had been rendered obsolete on the day life declared checkmate and sent him away. The street was devoid of people, and buildings reached upward to such impossible heights. Few stars showed themselves once the cloud cover parted. Random vehicles floated between sleek towers dotted with vulgar brilliance all the way to their peaks. The world up there was active and vibrant, and here he stood—far, far away from it—cast in shadow.

So he walked. The farther from the district's center he traveled, the more dilapidated the environment. Ground level was hardly well maintained, but his destination could be mistaken for a scrap heap. These machine docks had long since been abandoned by their corporate owners. Maintenance panels along foundations and site barriers were out of position or missing, their valuable parts long since scavenged.

Slugs like himself—the disenfranchised with nowhere else to turn—had taken over the derelict area, scrounging enough materials to build rickety shelters and tents. Sometimes they would share fires built inside of old cargo crates when the seasons brought in winter, but not much else. Wounded by society, it wasn't much of a community. People existed within proximity of each other, yet few were trustworthy because living on the edge of survival bred recklessness, and not everyone was well.

Arad was spent. A makeshift shanty might be all he had, but it was shelter, and he needed sleep. Feet and body aching, he almost wished he'd taken Davis up on his plea to stay. Almost.

As he approached, a commotion rose, slowing him to a halt. Noises that didn't belong here grew in volume, similar to the incident at the tech yard when the reject had tried to force his way into line, except somehow backward in its direction and intensity. As if coming this way instead of rushing in? Angry overlapping voices and chugging machinery had no place in this dead facility. Movements broke out between the aisles separating shelters. A smattering of people appeared, scuttling away from the ragtag community of slugs and their only refuge. They ran in random directions like vermin spilling out of sewer ducts during a flood. One woman caught sight of Arad and rushed at him.

"Arad! Go back! Go back!" She fisted his shirt, shoving at him in her panic. In the dark, he didn't recognize her until the searchlight of a series of security drones swept the area.

"Mareth? What's going on?" Arad grasped her wrists to keep the burly woman from knocking him over. Her eyes were wild and wet, ready to overflow. A broad smudge nearly camouflaged a fresh bruise blooming on her cheek.

"Go back! You have to go back!"

Her manic words continued to loop, and he struggled against her hysterical strength. This wasn't like her at all.

"What are you talking about? What's happening?"

Mareth gasped as the first tears fell. "They're destroying everything."

Arad jerked away from Mareth and ran around her into the chaos, finally skidding to a halt as he cleared the tall building obscuring his view. Dust kicked into the sky, clouding the air around the mammoth transport. Its spidery legs bit splintering cracks into the pavement, mooring it to the dock. Alarms blared and the three-story face split open. Search beacons reflected through the fog, scattering the light into a dangerous haze as a line of machines exited the vehicle. Mechanical leviathans at least fifteen meters tall rose between the buildings, crushing makeshift shelters between their hydraulic jaws. Each step was thunder and wrenching metal all in one.

Frightened screams competed with the layers of noise as people fled their only sanctuary. Children were dragged to safety. Hopefully. The clamor stole part of Arad's sanity, and he drove deeper to make some sense of the danger. Off to one side of the transport he found a few sporadic humans standing alongside the machines.

Traitors.

Arad ran to the closest man, trying not to notice his military-like garb complete with body armor and riot helmet. The guard caught sight of Arad and raised his hand.

"You need to leave. Now. It's not safe."

Another shanty being crushed jarred Arad's spine. "What are you doing?"

"This area is under order for demolition."

"For what purpose?"

The guard glanced at Arad and immediately averted his eyes. "Corporate reconstruction."

Yards away, Shaky Jake—the only person here who played chess with Arad in spite of his hand tremors— barely avoided being smashed under the rusted metal shed as he scrambled to retrieve his few meager belongings. The machines weren't hesitating, ignoring the people present and treating them as less than obstacles as they performed their duties. Corporate reconstruction at its finest. After all this time, the company was reclaiming its property, and woe to anyone caught in the crossfire while they used mercs to do the dirty work. Fewer witnesses that way if things went wrong.

"I want to see your permit." Fists at his side, Arad refused to leave.

The guard barely glanced his way. "Do you have some kind of magistrate order to stay the work?"

"People live here."

"Not anymore. They're trespassing." The guard's mouth was tight, and his words were clipped. He didn't even raise his head this time, maintaining focus on the com-pad in his hands and making an obvious effort to ignore Arad. Almost as if he had issues with this job.

"Someone's going to get killed."

"Not if they get out of the way." The comment was some kind of pleading order not given to the crowd at large. Had there been any warning before the destruction began?

"What do you expect them all to do?"

The guard shrugged, his voice impatient and exasperated. "I don't know. Get jobs like the rest of us."

Outraged, Arad circled in front of the guard, throwing out his arms to demand his attention. "How can you say that with a straight face? Are you seriously that dense? If there were jobs to go around, do you think anyone would live like this *on purpose*?" Arad swung his arm wide, showcasing the decrepit conditions of both the demolished and undemolished zone. How did he not understand?

No one chose this existence. Circumstances and financial inequities forced this upon them all. When the machines did the work themselves, what use were the people who once did the work? Even here, in their plan to reclaim the area, only a small number of men ran the operation.

The guard stalled. For a moment, a calculating light brightened his eyes. A glimmer of recognition hinted at the truth of Grey District's social dynamics at work, but he shook his head and the sympathy flickered out. He raised a hand and spat out a response. "Look, I've got work to do. Go earn a living and quit begging for a handout. Lazy fucking slugs."

The fresh venom left Arad aghast. Everyone present was being upheaved without the slightest notice, all for the love of profits. If you didn't create it, you didn't matter.

"We don't want handouts! We just want a chance to survive!"

"Survive somewhere else."

"We don't have anywhere to go, you bastard!" Arad flung himself at the guard, oblivious to their size differences. Burning anger swallowed his better judgment. He was no fighter. Years of being smaller than average had curtailed that impulse, yet here he was attacking someone who could easily break him. Flailing wildly, he grabbed and punched at the armored panels attached to man's uniform, unable to get purchase on the slick material.

"Step off!" Snarling, the guard stiff-armed Arad in the chest, knocking him to the ground.

The texture molded into the plasti-crete pavement for traction dug sharp lines into his back. Spasms froze his breathing into short, erratic pulses, but Arad jumped to his feet and advanced on the man again. He didn't make half the distance before a security drone dove between them, its pacifiers armed and sparking. The new threat quashed his rage. Hands raised in surrender, Arad inched backward as one would from a rabid animal, not trusting the bot wouldn't strike him from behind if he tried to run. Who knew if a person was behind the controls or an algorithm? Neither one was a guarantee of safety.

A pair of arms latched around him and pulled him away. His heels dragged twin lines in the dust as Mareth's familiar worried voice hissed in his ear. "I told you to go. You can't win this. None of us can."

This time, he didn't resist, because Mareth was right.

At a safe distance, she released him and continued on, leaving Arad behind to watch the heartless erasure of his haggard community. The people who used these docks scattered like insects and would be treated as such by the population of whatever street whose alleys they next huddled inside of. Constant relocation was a way of life for them. Permanence was a fiction for slugs in Grey District A-5. A series of shanties collapsed under a tech behemoth's foot as another scooped up the debris and shuffled it into a garbage scowl waiting in the landing zone. Steel screeching vibrated up Arad's spine. So much gone in such a short period of time. Many of the fleeing slugs would be left with nothing. Arad clutched his shoulder bag that much tighter. It was all he had in the world. He was fortunate not to lose much in the destruction, but it didn't make the impact any less profound.

Arad slumped against a dirty half wall, his strength and resolve bleeding out in combination with an extended, defeated exhale. He stretched his gaze up again for the few stars visible through the skyline, jealous of their position so far, far away from this wretched planet.

Chapter Three

Two drinks maximum would tap his budget, and the bottom of number one came closer no matter how much time Arad dragged out between sips. The lager had warmed a while ago, but he didn't mind. He wasn't actually here to savor the cheap alcohol.

Almost a week had passed since the dock reclamation had ousted him and the others. Six days of walking the streets looking for suitable shelter each night, holding tight to what little he owned. Word was Mareth had stowed away on a transport, following a rumor of a job lottery in District A-6. It took some effort to get more information because of the expected awkwardness, but Davis told Arad the chance wasn't any better there than here, so Arad hadn't followed. Loyalty barely existed among most of the slugs, and he wouldn't see her again.

Arad liked this tavern with its simple, low-tech atmosphere. Filled with locals and outliers alike, the pricing brought in wealthier clientele, but not beyond Arad's ability to blend in. After a trip to the bathhouse, anyways. His seat at the bar was well suited to keep sight of all the current patrons, to watch them come and go as he quietly nursed his drink. Suppressing the frustration when someone approached was difficult. The aura of booze drifting off the middle-aged, decently groomed man turned Arad off as he sidled close.

"Looking for a little company?" Words on the verge of slurring confirmed Arad's disinterest.

"No, thanks."

The man edged closer, scrubbing his chest against Arad's shoulder. "You sure?"

"Yeah, I'm sure."

"C'mon. I got a place 'round the corner."

The drunken attraction almost made Arad want to take Davis up on his offer two weeks ago. Strangers under the influence often couldn't be trusted for safety or credits because there was no telling what they were on. Some combinations created dangerously unpredictable risks. Arad cursed under his breath. He didn't need this hassle. The trick would be getting the jerk to bugger off without causing a scene, and the longer this went on, the less chance there was.

A sudden shadow blanketed them. Paired with a hostile snort, it caused the pushy man to pale.

"He said no. Get the fuck out."

The drunk backed off and left the building at an unexpected casual pace, leaving Arad only partially relieved. The new, hulking bartender blocking the light unnerved Arad enough he'd avoided him most of the night.

His facial structure and the ring looped through his wide nostrils pegged him as a bull DemiShou. Smooth, black fur covered his skin, making the oversized arms spilling out of his short sleeves shimmer in the minimal light. Two broad horns protruding from his temples had been cut close to the skull, leaving the black bone flat and harmless. Which was ridiculous given the fearsome muscles found on most DemiShou.

DemiShou had originally been engineered for the military well over sixty years ago as first settlers during terraforming efforts. Their human-animal hybrid physiologies were spliced to be better suited for the hostile extremes on undeveloped planets. Once the planets were suitable for regular people, there wasn't much need for them, so they were folded into the population. At least, that's what Arad understood. Most DemiShou he'd encountered were laborers, security, or penniless slugs like himself. A wolf DemiShou snatched the job he'd been promised last week, but he didn't harbor any ill will. Being at the bottom of the food chain didn't give him any illusions about being better than anyone else.

"I was surprised you told him no. I figured you were here to make a little money."

Arad gave the bartender a flat glare. He didn't appreciate his perceptiveness. This place was a refuge he didn't like hustling, even if that was exactly his plan. He was trying to be subtle about needing more cash, once his other moneymaking options had busted. Arad had spent the first drink sizing up potential marks, but he wasn't running off with just anyone. The bartender may have been a big beast, but he wasn't stupid.

Arad took the last swallow of number one and pushed the glass across the bar. "I'll take a whiskey. Well version, not top shelf."

The bartender collected the glass and stowed it under the bar. Lacking censure, his non-human gaze never wavered, drifting over Arad with...appreciation? Surely, he was imagining it.

"There are better ways to make a living."

Arad had no intention of giving the bartender the satisfaction of being right. "Are you offering me a job?"

The bull chuckled. "I wish."

"Then pour."

The bartender filled a rocks glass higher than normal and slid it over to Arad. Their hands brushed when Arad reached for it. Leaning in, the bull shared his quiet rumble with Arad alone.

"A man like you shouldn't have to demean himself. If you were mine, you wouldn't have to. Ever."

"I...I don't know what you're talking about."

Spoken—or rather, stammered—like a guilty man, Arad had difficulty thinking. He'd never been approached by a DemiShou before, and he didn't know how to process his reaction. Indecent ideas surfaced as his face grew hot. He wasn't attracted to the bartender, but the bull bulged everywhere, from his arms to his shoulders to his legs...and between them. Everything about them was oversized. Whispered rumors and jokes ran rampant about DemiShou mating instincts, their appetites and sexual prowess, but Arad had never considered it. Not in any real capacity.

Flustered, Arad dug into his shoulder bag, scrambling to find money and end this conversation. Where the hell were those tokens?

Out of nowhere, a dark-haired man with a perpetual tan and broad shoulders pushed forward, becoming a wall between Arad and the bull. He slapped the bar, cash in his hand.

"Save your money. I've got this one." The stranger stared at the bartender. A silent challenge, but subtle enough someone might miss if they weren't paying attention.

"I don't need you to."

The swarthy gentleman turned to Arad, his grin confident and disarming. "Call it my good deed for the day."

"You sure?" Arad hated needing to be saved, even if only from his own embarrassment, but he'd yet to find the last of his tokens.

"I'm sure."

The bartender frowned and took the cash, apparently not caring who paid in the end. All business, he nodded at Arad's savior. "A'right. What'll ya have?"

"I'll have whatever he's having."

The bartender's mouth tightened in obvious disappointment. The new man collected his drink, his voice positively gloating. "I think we should find a better corner to sit in."

He swept an arm around Arad's waist and ushered him away from the bar. His touch was light without being overbearing, as if there were no doubt Arad would follow. Allowing himself to be led, Arad hazarded a glance at the bull, who snorted in disgust and went back to his work. Arad would have to do the same.

"I'm Torrins. Since I bought you a drink, I figure you at least owe me your name."

Knowing when to play his part, Arad leaned slightly into Torrins's hand. "You might be right. I'm Arad. Thanks."

As they walked deeper through the bar, knowing gazes followed their every step. Torrins's hand never left the small of Arad's back. The public display marked him as chosen to every man present, leaving Torrins as Arad's only option for the night.

Perhaps Arad should have been thankful. Torrins had forced him to choose, an unsavory task that often stalled if it took too long. The real trick would be convincing the man to purchase his time for the night. Well-kept work clothing, groomed dark hair with a whispering of grey, and a rugged charisma all spoke of a man who rarely would be refused, let alone be willing to pay for a smutty tumble. It might not be easy. Confident men like Torrins often needed subtlety and to believe all ideas were theirs in the first place.

Their short trek led them to the last booth under poor lighting, where a man with amber locs knotted over his head sat waiting.

"You didn't even bring me a round?"

Arad schooled his expression even as his chances to hustle Torrins dwindled. Men with friends rarely solicited company—not in front of them, at least—unless everyone present was interested. If that was the case, Arad would walk. No amount of money was worth the risk. He'd been told enough stories of rent boys without pimps disappearing after entertaining a gathering of men. Arad had no interest in pimps, and the authorities didn't care enough about slugs to provide justice when bad things happened.

Torrins pulled out chairs for them both and ran a gentle caress down Arad's neck and shoulder as they sat. A claim confirming Torrins's interest for anyone watching, but especially for his buddy. Now, Arad needed to turn that to his advantage.

Snorting, Torrins gestured to the dark-skinned man. "I got mine for the night. Get your own. Arad, this is one of my crew. My helmsman, Franc."

Franc nodded as he swept his gaze over Arad, his eyes bright in contrast against his natural color.

Arad returned the greeting. "Nice to meet you. Crew? Helmsman? I guess that means you boys aren't locals." This was fortunate. Visitors raised the chances of either man looking for a sure thing. And nothing was more sure than paid company. Given the space between their chosen seats, Torrins and Franc likely weren't lovers. The night wasn't over yet.

"Nope. We don't stay in any one place for too long." A teasing grin played across Franc's features. "So...how do you know Torrins?"

Creating awkward moments for his own pleasure appeared to be Franc's game. A trickster, for sure. Arad wasn't about to fall prey to that nonsense. A wild story formulated in his head, a tale worthy enough to show Franc that Arad was no one's prey, but Torrins beat him to the reply.

"I saved Arad from the pervert Demi bartender. Can't believe he had the nerve to hit up on you like that."

Franc rolled his eyes. "Yeah. The nerve of the guy trying to hook up at a bar."

"Better me than the furry freak. I don't mind them working alongside us and all, but they shouldn't be mixing with us like that. He had Arad cornered."

Arad shook his head. "I don't know. Cornered might be a little strong."

"You weren't actually going to take him up on his offer, were you?" Torrins's words were served as a joke, but Arad picked up a hint of offense.

Arad chuckled, hoping to defuse any of Torrins's doubts. "Oh no, that wasn't happening. I wasn't interested. He just caught me off guard. I don't have strong feelings toward Demis one way or another. Although some people think I should since I lost a job to a wolf last week." Mentioning the wolf might grant Arad a touch of sympathy.

"What kind of job?" For all of his mischievous appearance, Franc appeared genuinely curious.

"A friend tried to get me in as a repair mechanic at the tech yard during the last job lottery."

Torrins's brow quirked. "Really? So, you know your way around machines?"

"It's a requirement in this zone. There aren't many other options."

"So, you live around here?"

The question caught Arad unprepared. Since the dock reclaiming, his stock answers for where he lived had fallen apart. It was easier to hide the truth when the truth was woven through the lie. Trying to find a new response left an uneasy pause between them.

"Well...yes."

Torrins and Franc shared a brief look.

"Ah. I see. Don't stress over it. Times are tough all around," Torrins said.

With barely a word, Arad was convinced both of them knew his status on the street. What was it about men in this bar being so damned clever? He read their faces, a mix of pity and something else out of place that said it all.

Arad took a larger swallow of his drink than he had all night, shuddering at its potency. Damn bull gave him a seriously stiff pour of cheap booze. It didn't dull his apprehension as Torrins and Franc continued staring at one another. A silent conversation waged between them that Arad was at the center of. A sly smirk curled the corner of Torrins's mouth.

Franc's face flattened and he narrowed his eyes. "No."

"What do you mean no?" Torrins appeared equal parts confused and affronted by Franc's refusal, whatever it was about.

"You know exactly what I mean."

Franc's dark gaze locked onto Torrins, and the two resumed the unspoken communication, which took on a new intensity and flared into an unheard argument. A test of wills, helmsman challenging the captain. Were they going to share their ideas or continue to share body language and psychic data streaming? Although Arad had the impression neither man was wealthy enough to have the requisite hardware installed or would allow themselves to be connected to any corporate network in such a fashion. They didn't seem the type.

A strobe of red and blue caught Arad's eye. Through the nearby window, a sector authority officer tackled a running man, slamming his quarry against the wall. Security drone lights swept back and forth, their harsh spotlight flashing into the tavern, distorting the interior's colors. Disquieted murmurs from the establishment's patrons flitted between booths and tables. Arad shuddered at what might have prompted the overzealous arrest. Neither Franc nor Torrins gave the scene the slightest attention.

Torrins shook his head and took a swig of his drink. "I don't see what your problem is."

"This isn't what we talked about." All of Franc's earlier playfulness had vanished. Left over was an unerring sharp edge aimed at Torrins, and it brought up a cautious warning in Arad.

"He's perfect." Torrins leaned in his chair, leaving his arm resting on the back of Arad's. His fingers cupped the join between Arad's neck and shoulder.

"You don't know that."

"He fits everything we need." Torrins began a deliberate massage with his thumb, working up to Arad's nape. The move underscored Torrins's interest, and under better circumstances it would have settled Arad's worries. It did not. The contact failed to rise any revulsion, building on his sense of wariness instead. There was far more going on than he understood, but he managed to gather at least one thing out of the veiled discourse.

"Excuse me. I'm assuming you're talking about me?" Arad tried to stare each man in the eyes, to no effect.

Franc reached out to find his empty glass, which only renewed his scowl at Torrins. "The crew won't like it."

"Why?"

"Too many people knowing isn't good. We'll lose our privacy."

Torrins stared at Franc's glass and taunted him by taking a slow sip of his own. "Not everyone has to see and know everything."

"There's not enough room on board."

"We have plenty of space if we get creative. We were prepared for that."

"Daiko and Serene will have a shit fit. You know they didn't want anything to happen unless they had a say in it."

"Well, in the end, it's my ship, and I'm gonna hold on to my supreme veto power, if you don't mind."

Arad waved at each man in turn. "Hello. I'm sitting right here."

And again, they continued talking as if Arad weren't even present or speaking out loud. Heat built along the edges of his ears at the insult. He may have been a slug, but he had some pride, even as low as it had become recently. Outside, the officer ignored the man's pleas and requests for the charges as restraints were lashed around his wrists. Dust swirled around them as the sentries hovered close. Another officer joined in and grabbed a fistful the man's hair, drawing his head into a painful angle. They clamped a gag around the man's jaw, stifling his outcries.

"You're asking for a mutiny. We all have a stake in this," Franc said.

"And you'll all get paid like normal. Shit, Franc. I'd think you'd back me up a little here. It's what we're here for in the first place, remember?" Torrins gave Franc a knowing grin. "You know, you stand to benefit in a lot of ways too. I'll make sure of it."

Franc glanced at Arad and away just as quickly. "I don't like this at all." He rubbed his face with both hands in frustration.

"Fat payment cards will make it all better. Now's not the time to get squeamish when what we need is right in front of us."

Outside, the authorities dragged away their suspect as he kicked and squirmed, protesting their handling. They heaved him into the security trawler, which had flown in during the scene and brought down the solid metal door. The searchlights vanished, leaving the tavern in its standard level of bland lighting. Everyone else in the tavern went back to their booze, meager snacks, and whispering, pretending their lives wouldn't be affected by the violence out there but knowing it could at any moment with one wrong word or one wrong move.

Arad kicked back his chair and set his drink down hard. Drops of cheap alcohol splashed onto his wrist, chilling as they evaporated. Abruptly, Arad stood, dislodging Torrins's hand from its perch.

"You know what? I think the two of you have some serious issues to sort out. I'm going to go. Thanks for the drink. You boys have a nice evening."

Torrins and Franc both finally shut up. Interrupting their discussion gave Arad a small sense of satisfaction, even if the night had turned into a complete disaster. Nothing had gone as planned, no matter how flimsy a plan he'd started with. So very, very unlike him. At this point, Arad should have been shacked up in a motel earning the credits to feed himself, but no...he had to take way too long to choose a mark and run into these two.

With a snug grip on his bag, he turned and stepped away, only to halt when Torrins spoke up over the room's din.

"Arad, come on and finish your whiskey. If you leave now, how are you gonna get paid?"

Arad turned slowly, glaring at Torrins. "What's that supposed to mean?"

"I'm still willing to pay for your time. And the way I walked you here pretty much killed any other choices for you." Torrins held out the whiskey Arad had left behind. "You might as well finish it. I imagine it'll be a while before you get another."

"I'm not a drunk." Arad took the drink but stayed standing, silently noting the closest exit.

"Didn't think you were. But simple luxuries are hard to come by for some people. How long have you been living on the streets?"

"I never said I was."

The comical tilt of Torrins's head showcased his disbelief. He looked ready to start laughing. "I've been watching you for a few hours now. Your clothes are worn, and you only had enough on you to scrounge up two drinks."

"That doesn't mean anything."

"You're a little rough, but you're still a looker. If you only wanted some dick, you'd have had that ten times over. No, you've been scoping the men in this bar and ignoring them all while sipping a drink that's long gone warm. Almost like you're holding out for the right target. Maybe someone with enough funds to be worth your time. On top of that, you're honest."

Arad sipped carefully, not wanting to waste any more than he already had. "How can you be sure of that?"

Taking a quick swig, Torrins patted his thigh. "If you were a pickpocket, I wouldn't still have all my stuff. And the way that bartender eyed you over, you could have fleeced him for everything he owned and then some."

"There's no guarantee of that, so why approach me?"

Torrins's head tilted, a smug gesture at best. "I got curious. Plus, you're my type. I've been around enough crooks to know how to handle them. It's nice to be surprised."

"If you want my time, I don't do parties." Arad glanced at Franc. "No offense."

"He wasn't invited." Torrins tossed a gloating smile at his helmsman. "No offense."

Franc's brow flattened, and he flashed Torrins his middle finger.

"So, my time is all you want?"

Torrins chuckled softly. "And then some…"

A frisson of annoyance escaped Arad. "You know what? I've only known you for about ten minutes, and I'm already tired of being talked about like I'm not in the room. Spit it out or I walk. Money or not."

Gaze locked on Arad, Torrins nodded. "I need someone who can help do mechanical work on my ship."

"Let me know which landing bay it's in, and I'll take a look."

"I mean while we're traveling. I don't have anyone working on my baby that's not part of the crew, and we spend a lot of time off planet."

"What kind of business are you running?"

"We do freelance trading."

"With a little smuggling on the side?"

A broad grin curled Torrins's lips. The mark of a man impressed with Arad's deduction. "I did say freelance."

"So, you want me to what, live with you on your ship?"

"You'd be working."

"As a mechanic." Brow raised in doubt, Arad dragged out the words.

Franc broke into the conversation, his voice laced with mischief. "Wait for it..."

Torrins shrugged. "And other things. I've always wanted a cabin boy. Sometimes we're out for weeks at a time. I don't like waiting that long."

"Are you serious?" Arad had to tone down his volume at Torrins's boldness. Most men weren't so direct with him, but perhaps he'd always aimed for guys with something to lose. Torrins didn't appear to have such insecurities.

The eye roll was so subtle Torrins managed not to look disgusted. "It's nothing you haven't done in some way before, is it?"

Arad pondered the scenario with another sip. "What if I was on board and changed my mind?"

"I bring you back where I found you. We come to Earth pretty often."

"Why me?"

"I have a need, and my gut says you fit my needs." Torrins grinned, displaying a fine set of teeth. "In more ways than one."

Arad didn't want to show his worries, but the frown gave him away. "I don't know."

"It'd be an adventure."

"It's a huge step."

"Tell me you have something waiting for you here, and I won't say another word. But if you say yes, you'd earn a percentage, have a roof over your head, and never wonder where your next meal comes from. Tell me you have—or will have—a better offer in the near future. There's nothing safe about the world you're living in."

"At least I know this world and what's expected of me here."

Torrins pointed a thumb over his shoulder. "I bet that guy the cops roughed up and dragged off outside thought the same thing. I get the feeling that sort of thing happens often around here. Maybe a little too often. It's not right. I believe a man should choose the way he lives."

"I do too." Arad averted his eyes. Torrins's gaze was too piercing, digging into truths Arad didn't like to face.

"There's a lot of folks like you in this district. Too many scratching in the dirt to make their way. What are your chances without my help?"

Arad didn't know how to answer. He stared into his drink as if the poor amber fluid did more than dull his senses. Torrins's argument had merit, but so did the cautious twinges that had kept Arad alive for the past several years since landing in the district as a penniless slug. Luck had never been Arad's companion. He survived on his wits and assessing his options. Nothing held him in Grey District other than funds because geography didn't inspire any loyalty.

What was the downside? He didn't see it, but it was there, hiding in the dark corner.

After an appropriate pause, Torrins slugged down the rest of his drink and stood. "Tell you what. I've said my piece, and I'll consider the topic closed. You want the job and everything included, you come find us at Landing Bay Theta 6-Delta tomorrow at eleven hundred hours."

"That's all the time I get to decide?"

"Yep. I don't believe in wasting time." Franc stood and followed as Torrins pulled a fund token out of his pocket and dropped it on the table. "That's for your time. Don't forget, there's more where that came from if you want it."

Chapter Four

Everything Arad Ansari owned fit in one half of one drawer.

Lifting the flat metal latch, he pulled the panel from its seat flush within the rusted wall. It made a painful screech as it stuck halfway open, but a quick tug forced it the rest of the way. Dull red paint flaked off the rusted metal walls everywhere in their cramped quarters except inside the sleeping berth large enough for two. It was still a far cry better than the shelter back home. He'd lived in worse places.

"Use this drawer," Torrins said. *"When you bring up the rest of your stuff, we'll figure out how to squeeze it in."*

Arad tugged on the strap crossing his chest. "This is everything."

Torrins's brow creased. "What do you mean this is everything? One shoulder bag full?"

"It's all I own."

"That won't even fill half the drawer. How can you own so little?"

Arad shrugged as he emptied his satchel. "It's only safe to keep what you can carry."

"Why?"

"Keeps you from being a target." One by one, Arad stowed away the sum of his life into the deteriorated space.

"From who?"

"Thieves. Gangs. They leave you alone if you don't look like you have anything." Scraping his fingers inside the bottom of his bag told Arad he was finished. A quick study of his work left him with plenty of room to spare.

Torrins scanned the contents of Arad's half of the drawer. "You don't have much of anything."

"See? It works. It's even easier to keep up the image when you can't actually afford to have anything."

"How long have you lived like this?" The peak in Torrins's voice bordered on an accusation. Did he think Arad might be lying? It nagged at Arad, making him face the captain with an incredulous stare.

"How long? When haven't I?"

The last comment hadn't been entirely true. Arad hadn't always been on the street. It only felt like it some days. Besides, Torrins had acted so smug when he'd deduced Arad's social status when they first met at the tavern. By the next day, he was disturbed when faced with some of the gritty details? How strange someone so worldly would be so squeamish. It served him right. Years of living destitute had washed out most traces of Arad's shame. Reality was reality.

Arad scrubbed the gritty disposable towel over his wet skin. He hadn't planned on taking a second shower today, but Torrins had requested a maintenance check in the filthiest section of the ship at the last second. Arad protested, but Torrins insisted, reminding him who was in charge. If they were on planet, Arad would swear Torrins was trying to get rid of him to invite his mistress over. Which was absurd. None of the crew would sleep with him.

The chill overtook the leftover warmth of his shower, so Arad dressed like it was a race. He rubbed the towel through his hair, hoping it wouldn't disintegrate before the chilly water dripped down his spine. An old exploration cruiser, the *Midas Ascending* comfortably housed a crew of six and was a piece of junk. Arad was only an assistant to the engineer, but he knew the ship could run warmer. Little held off the absolute cold of outer space seeping through the walls, but the environmentals' running at 15°C was Torrins's doing. Stingy bastard. Regardless, the shower system produced more than sufficient hot water, so Arad held his tongue, like always. Growing up in poverty made a man know all too well how to appreciate such a luxury.

Thankfully, Torrins preferred his men younger but legal—like most of Arad's clients—and was willing to make space. Arad shouldn't have been surprised when Torrins announced they'd share his quarters. There wasn't a spare room on board. It wasn't the worst arrangement, and Arad didn't have any better options. Do grunt work on the ship, get paid, and play cabin boy. Another kind of grunt work. Arad liked handsome, authoritative men, so he was hardly compromising his standards. At least the captain lacked any alarming kinks for the most part. Torrins liked regular servicing and occasionally to watch as he shared his boy with Franc of all people.

Arad hated thinking of himself as the captain's boy. It was meant to be an act of trade that would elevate him above the status of a lowly slug, but such a feat would require more than a simple change of venue. He also couldn't deny the situation he'd placed himself in.

Two months had passed since Arad had joined the crew, but memories of the day after their meeting was as bright as yesterday. Once Torrins and Franc had left him in the bar without a viable customer, he'd only spent a few hours deciding, ignoring the clamor of warning in his head. It wasn't a choice. Arad had nothing and no prospects. The internal argument was short-lived. Torrins's offer, while dubious at the least, was an opportunity he couldn't pass by. So, he found himself at the landing bay far ahead of the deadline with his limited possessions stowed in his trusty messenger bag he never left without.

Torrins's possessions were a different kind of creature. The drawer's left side was stacked with Torrins's folded thermals, a few phase pistols, and spare ammo cells. The captain had more weapons than anyone Arad had ever known. Stashes were hidden in every drawer and cabinet. Everything from guns to knives and a few items Arad only guessed at, and they all had to be lethal. It made him wonder what kind of trouble Torrins was preparing for or if he was simply paranoid. Perhaps a touch of both?

It wouldn't be the first time Arad had known a man who wasn't completely stable. Look at Davis. At this rate, it wouldn't be the last one he'd know either.

Arad took a quick glance at the cracked time panel above the door and frowned. It was too early to say the day's work was done. As captain, Torrins had the power to declare otherwise, but Arad would need to check in first. Could he manage the rest of the day off? Well...he was the cabin boy. A nice smile and a better offer to distract the captain might make his day easier.

Smoothing his damp hair with his fingers, Arad hoped he hadn't showered for nothing. He straightened his clothes, ignoring the frayed seams, and headed out. At this hour, Torrins should be found on the bridge.

It was an effort to step lightly and not make a commotion. The rattling clang of boots on the metal floors brought up too many images of the corporate mechs dismantling the shanty village on the docks. On occasion, he thought of Mareth and the others and what became of them. It wouldn't be easy, but he told himself they would be fine. They were survivors. Thinking anything else while he lived under this roof would ply him with guilt for ages.

Shuffling down the hall, he reached out, brushing his fingertips along the cool walls. Scuffs and scratches covered the once pristine surfaces, giving away their age. He skimmed invisible trails over the worn paint and metal seams until he passed over the hand reader connected to the cargo bay's door. A defiant chime blared out of the device as faded red text flashed across the panel.

Arad Anasri - Rank: Private Third Class

ACCESS DENIED

The rude noise and message brought him to a halt. Arad couldn't care less what was inside the cargo bay. He'd hammered the word *smuggling* out of his vocabulary the day he boarded, knowing it was most likely in his best interest. Plausible deniability would serve him well if anything bad happened. And something bad always happened eventually.

Honestly, now he was only curious enough to open the door because he'd been told no. Testing its functionality, Arad placed his hand fully on the palm panel and received another loud rejection. A quick examination found the key port to open the panel casing and override the lock manually. He was rummaging in his head if any of his tools were up to the job when a hard series of footsteps approached. A hand slammed against the wall, barring him from a closer view and further brainstorming. Following the arm—muscles visibly twitched under the thermal sleeve—brought Arad face to face with its owner, the main mechanic, Serene.

"What do you think you're doing?" Bracing and hostile, Serene's name couldn't be more ill-fitting. Not once since he'd arrived had she behaved like her namesake. Serene leaned forward into Arad's personal space, menacing as ever. The heavy dark braid pulling her hair tight to her head accented her sharp features.

"Nothing. Just playing around." Being casual was difficult when faced with Serene's natural ability to unnerve people.

"You don't have permission to be in there."

Arad had learned enough to know the ship's OS was retired military grade with rank-based access to each area. This had been the first time he'd seen it at work. Up until now, he'd never been denied access to anywhere he'd wanted to go. Granted, he'd never tried to enter the cargo bay before. Usually, when confronted with the crew's cold reception, he'd mind his own business, but Serene's attitude made him feel insubordinate.

"That sounds...mysterious. What's in there?"

"It's private. And none of your concern." Serene stepped forward, attempting to herd Arad away from the door.

For years, Arad had dealt with slug squabbles, occasional fights over food and necessities with people who desperately needed them. He was hardly going to be pushed around by one abrasive crew member, even if she was bigger than him. Arad stood his ground and waved his hands, shooing at her. The gesture forced Serene to lean back to avoid being slapped in the face.

"Sorry. I'm just curious. No need to be so salty."

Serene's snarl deepened. It appeared to be a permanent feature. "Don't think that because you're shagging Torrins, you're something special. You're not actually part of the crew. If it was up to us, you wouldn't be on board."

Arad crossed his arms over his chest. "I know. You all find a way to remind me every day."

"That's because we see what Torrins can't...or won't. You're extra weight we don't need."

"Maybe. But I am here. And as long as I am, I plan to do what I came here for."

"I can handle the ship fine. I don't need your help."

Arad dropped his arms to his side and slumped his shoulders. His voice softened. "What do you expect me to do?"

"Exactly what you're doing. On the next dock, no one would think twice if you took your pay and moved on. Don't worry about Torrins. He'll find another boy."

Putting on his best urchin-face—the kind he used when snatching produce from the market—he peered up at her with wide eyes. "You're probably right. This is quite a mess I've gotten myself into. If you were me, what would you do? Do you think I should disappear without saying a word?"

"It might be for the best," Serene said in her best attempt at a motherly tone as she laid her big man-hand on Arad's shoulder. The delivery was so insincere Arad cringed as he cocked his head and narrowed his eyes.

Arad swept her hand off his shoulder. "Do you think we should ask Torrins what he thinks of your brilliant plan? I'd be curious to see who he thinks he needs more." Arad shifted forward into her space. "Are you so sure he'll choose you?"

If such a thing were possible, Serene's expression became more severe as her hand curled into a fist. Arad waited to see if she'd raise it. She didn't.

"Yeah. I didn't think so. For your information, I'm here to earn my keep, and that's it. I know Torrins brought me on without asking your permission, but I don't think he needed it. I'm sorry I set foot in your territory, but stop pissing on my feet already. You don't even have to talk to me. After this cuddly moment, I'd prefer it. Whatever you guys have going on has nothing to do with me. I don't care what's in storage."

Arad turned and walked off, trying not to hyperventilate. There was still a chance she'd beat his ass or slit his throat. That woman was crazy, and he'd shined her on like she was another slug marking her zone. Either he'd impressed her by not falling to his knees, or he'd upgraded her dislike into future malice. Better not to wait around and see which. Keeping his footsteps quiet, he managed not to start running, and she didn't follow. One small win.

Arad had done his best to avoid the crew, considering their open hostility for his presence. He hadn't even tried to be friendly enough to offer playing chess. If they knew how, they'd probably refuse. In his typical arrogance, Torrins believed none of them would cross him, meaning Arad's safety relied on his staying on the captain's good side and his cabin-boy status staying active. Being next to the captain was more sensible than ever. No more side trips.

The closer he came to the bridge, the easier he breathed. Hard starlight spilled into the hallway through the open port, bringing any and all structural flaws to life in shadowed relief. Voices echoed off the metal walls, giving them a tinny, distant quality.

"Franc, charge the space fold and enter coordinates." Torrins's tenor was unmistakable.

"Are you sure they're still going to be there? We've already lost Go."

Questions slowed Arad's approach. Only the ship's acoustics allowed him to hear the hushed conversation. Were they planning a space fold? To where?

"We've already lost Go."

Why did that seem significant? Go? What was Go? What were they talking about?

Chapter Five

The moment Arad stepped onto the bridge, all conversation stopped.

Soft chimes from the instrument panels became background noise in the uncomfortable silence. Franc, Torrins, and Daiko sat in their respective seats. As he stepped across the threshold, three sets of eyes followed him. Sometimes, walking in the hallway was noisy. The short trek was downright deafening as he found his place next to Torrins. It wasn't the first time his appearance had quieted the room, but he refused to give them the satisfaction of knowing how unnerving it was.

"Am I interrupting something?" Pretending he hadn't overheard them beforehand would likely be for the best. Arad had no idea what they'd been talking about, and asking questions usually resulted in more animosity. If they wanted to include him, they would. Being treated as less than by others was common enough for Arad to be less aggravated than he should be.

Daiko swiveled his chair to face front without answering. The usual cool reception. As Serene's other half, one would expect drama from the dark-eyed man as opposed to the calm disdain he normally exuded at Arad. Apparently, opposites did attract in the real world.

"We have some business to attend to." Torrins snaked his arm around Arad's waist and brought him closer, snugging him against the captain's side. Arad resisted the urge to pull away. After two months, Arad should have been used to Torrins's public demonstrations—half affection, half possession—but he still found himself off guard with crew members who questioned his role on the ship. Which was pretty much all of them.

Franc cleared his throat. "Should Arad be in here for this?"

"Set coordinates, Franc. I'll deal with it."

With a disapproving look, Franc returned to his console and tapped at the control screen. When they'd first met, Arad hoped he might have a comrade in the dark-skinned helmsman, but like the others on board, he ran standoffish one minute and Arad's best friend the next. Usually if he wanted something. Such as a night with the cabin boy with the captain's permission. It was difficult to know if Franc's mood swings were simply an attempt to keep in the crew's good graces, but it told Arad that he shouldn't be trusted any more than the corporate mercs dismantling the shanties in Grey District.

Arad tilted his head to get a better look at Torrins. "So...I need to be dealt with?"

"Poor choice of words, my boy. What brings you up here?"

"I did the maintenance and cleaned up."

Torrins leaned in and sniffed a blatant line up Arad's stomach and chest. "Mmm, yes. You are smelling awfully fresh."

A shiver born of equal parts arousal and embarrassment prompted Arad to playfully push Torrins's head away. "Stop that. I didn't have anything else to do, so I came looking for you."

A brilliant yet lusty smile lit up Torrins's face. "That's what I like to hear."

"I didn't mean to disrupt your meeting. Should I go?"

"No. I like you where you are right now." Flexing his arm, he gave Arad a gentle squeeze. The move was as much a distraction as foreplay. If things were different and their ranks not cabin boy and captain, Arad might have taken a proper shine to the man. But things were not different, and instead, he found himself growing more and more suspicious.

Something odd was going on. In the beginning, he'd told himself to be blind to Torrins's schemes, but enough little things had been adding up to trigger Arad's exit strategy. Arad wanted more information. He may have been feeling bold after standing up to Serene earlier, but dealing with Torrins required another tactic. Demands were rarely met with success. Getting the captain to share required an offhand approach.

"Setting coordinates? Does this mean you're charging up for a space fold?"

"We are."

Arad frowned, almost pouting. "Do we need to? Can't we ride straight through?" There was no joy in bending space for instant travel. Since he joined the *Midas Ascending*, they'd only done it twice, and he wasn't aching for a repeat performance. It was a wrenching ordeal no one appreciated. After his first jump, Arad had puked all over himself and passed out for hours. The crew found it hysterical.

"We don't have that kind of time, and sometimes it's better to get right to business." Torrins patted Arad's behind.

Flexing his bottom under Torrins's hand, Arad reached up and toyed with the small hairs at the captain's nape. Arad knew how to play this game. "Where are we going?"

"No place in particular."

"Will you warn me before we jump this time?"

"I'll consider the request."

"I hate throwing up. I won't be in any condition afterward for *anything*."

"Duly noted."

Torrins was normally full of himself and flirtatious, so short answers were always a sign he was hiding something. The man liked to hear himself speak, but now he avoided the topic of the fold, which meant he was steering the conversation away from their destination. On top of that, even though both men were facing front, there was no doubt Franc and Daiko were listening with full intent.

What required so much secrecy? True, the ship's dealings weren't 100 percent legitimate. Torrins had all but admitted that the night they met. What was happening here was far more than the typical reaction he'd received on the ship.

Curiosity could be damning. Arad had seen more than one slug vanish for asking too many questions in the past. Even so, the tension floating in the manufactured air left him craving information. Arad searched for parts of the conversation he'd accidentally overheard.

"Are you sure they're still going to be there? We've already lost Go."

"Are we meeting one of your business partners? You never said who—"

Torrins interrupted him with a finger pressed to Arad's lips.

"Shh. Everything's fine. Don't worry your pretty little head about it."

How long would Torrins indulge Arad? There were limits to the man's patience, and he was edging around them. Time to be penitent instead of inquisitive.

"I'm sorry. I shouldn't be asking. I'd like to help if I can. That's what I'm here for."

Arad dipped his head to peer through his brow like an apologetic urchin, keeping silent, just short of begging. Two months by his side gave Arad as much insight as Torrins was capable of gleaning when he tried. Torrins paused, calculating. The captain's eyes softened, almost as if he might bring Arad into his confidence for the first time, when Franc broke in, his voice lacking his normally collected tenor.

"Torrins. We're getting a hail."

Silence more severe than Arad's arrival blanketed the bridge as a massive vessel, all dread metal and force, drifted in front of the ship. A weathered military insignia marked the hull, dwarfed by its pristine supporting corporate logo. Even at this distance, the beast blocked the entire viewport, cutting off the hard light from the nearby sun. There were plenty of stories about single ships like this having enough firepower to wipe out whole fleets.

"Unidentified vessel, this is First Commander Hyland Bard, *Alpha One Flagship*. Respond at once."

Torrins's arm, which had been wrapped around Arad, relaxed and fell away. Fresh tension drew lines through the length of his body as he stood and stepped forward, staring at the warship without blinking. "I thought you said this star's radiation field was supposed to hide us from sensors."

"It should have. It appears this ship is better equipped than most." Daiko's annoyance was as strong as his visible discomfort.

"Shit. Patch me through."

Daiko and Franc exchanged agitated glances. With a few taps on the console, Franc nodded, signaling Torrins the comm was open.

"This is Captain Torrins of the *Midas Ascending*. How can I be of assistance?"

It may have only been audio communication, but Torrins stood tall and smiled, throwing on his most persuasive persona. The bearing of a born actor. This was the charismatic man who had convinced Arad coming on board would be a grand adventure. He was having second thoughts.

"Captain Torrins, you are in possession of stolen corporate property. Stand down at once and prepare for reclamation." Bard's voice, riddled with arrogant contempt, made Arad want to run for cover. Nothing scared him more than the determination of an official used to stomping out obstacles in his path. The lack of compassion. Flashbacks of the arrest at the tavern where he'd met Torrins shined bright in his head. He'd never known of a good interaction with corporate-sponsored military. A lack of accountability hovered over these people when profits were involved. A slug didn't need to be part of the government to see corruption running rampant inside it. Running a warship that size had to bleed insane amounts of credits, so Torrins must have smuggled something worth a fortune to warrant such a spectacle.

"What? Stolen property? There must be some kind of misunderstanding." Torrins's denial was award worthy. Arad almost believed him, despite knowing better.

"The only misunderstanding I see is your interpretation of the law. Refusal to comply will be treated as an act of aggression in full accordance with my authority."

"There's no need for aggression. Honestly, Commander, I don't know what you're talking about. How about we chat a bit and sort this out?"

Bard appeared immune to Torrins's charms. "We're not here to discuss anything. You will simply do as you're told, or I will be forced to act."

"And what exactly are you asking us to do?"

"Transmit your ship's override codes immediately. You will be boarded and towed planetside, where you will face the corporate magistrates."

The unflinching demand bristled Torrins. "If you'd be good enough to show me your warrant—"

"I don't need one. Act fast. My patience is thin, Captain."

The comm connection went dead.

The confidence holding Torrins's façade eroded in minuscule amounts. Fear weakened his expression, and his shoulders slumped a fraction. The atmosphere on the bridge thickened into soup, becoming unbreathable.

Arad stepped up to the captain and placed a hand on his arm. "Torrins, what did you do?"

"Be quiet. I have to think." He dislodged Arad's touch with a hard shrug. Scrubbing a hand over his head, Torrins paced in a tiny circle. "Franc, can we fold?"

Franc shook his head. "The system still isn't charged enough."

Lurching forward, Torrins gripped the back of Franc's seat, neck stretched to read the display over Franc's shoulder. "How long do we need?"

"At least five minutes. Maybe more."

Jerking away, he returned to circular pacing. "Okay, okay. We need to stall them. Franc, keep your eyes on that screen. The second we have minimum charge, bounce us out of here."

"Shit. That's gonna hurt."

"Give me another option."

Arad was in total disbelief. "Are you kidding?"

Seconds passed as an eternity waiting for something to happen. All four men were frozen in place, the universe daring anyone to make the first move. Arad prayed it wouldn't be the *Alpha One Flagship*. Atheists should know better than to pray.

Daiko's normally stoic tone cracked with terror. "They're locking their weapons systems on us."

A subtle tremor raced through Torrins's hand as he wiped at his mouth and jaw in frustration. "It's a bluff. They're not about to kill us and destroy their property."

"Are you sure about that?" Arad's voice pitched upward to the point of shrill and his chest grew tight. In Grey District, this would have been the point he would have cut through the streets, dodging people and police, and found a place to hide deep enough where no one would find him. Where he would be safe. That option didn't exist now.

Torrins didn't answer. "Patch me back in."

"I'm waiting, Captain Torrins." The delay hadn't improved the chill from First Commander Bard's tone. Arad's spine was icing fast and his hope was fleeting.

Clearing his throat and squaring his shoulders, Torrins tried to buy some time. "I'd like to discuss the terms of our surrender."

"There are no terms." Bard was incensed. "I made one simple and specific request, and you couldn't even do me the courtesy of that. I warned you, Captain. I don't appreciate having my time wasted."

The channel died again.

Arad stopped breathing. Torrins's gamble held on by the thinnest cable, and it was fraying to the final strand. He stared fixedly on the flagship, its presence echoing First Commander Bard's gift at oppression. They needed to do something, and they needed to do it quickly before they ran out of time.

Daiko's shout broke the fragile impasse, shattering the silence.

"Shit! They're charging weapons!"

The universe stalled, refusing to move forward.

Daiko shouted, and everything rushed forward. "They're going to fire!"

Torrins braced against Franc's chair. "Evasive maneuvers!"

Franc's hands flew across the controls, and *Alpha One Flagship* spun and dipped in the viewscreen. The maneuver still wasn't fast enough to hide the flare of the warcraft's particle cannon. The *Midas Ascending* lurched as a violent tremor shook the framework, throwing Arad to the unforgiving metal floor. The power flickered, dimming the lights and equipment displays for a moment. Alarms blared and the emergency warnings flashed in every monitor.

Franc righted himself in his seat. "Main engine is down!"

"Get it back up, damn it!" Torrins's desperation matched Arad's.

"It's not responding to a restart, and we're drifting into the star's gravity well."

"Can we fix it?"

A new schematic on Daiko's screen scrolled a litany of text at his fingertips. "Damage report shows emergency bulkheads are down. They breached the hull. Better yet, the engine's venting and it's pushing us out of orbit toward the star. We've already drifted past the gravity well's safe point."

"What about thrusters?"

Panic seeped into Franc's response as he frantically beat on his console. "The damage to the engine is affecting them too. Even if they were working right, they're not enough to escape the warship or keep us from burning."

"Fuck!"

Unsure of the next step, Arad sat on the floor, rubbing the ache out of his shoulder. "What do we do?"

The comm flared to life, the audio of First Commander Bard's voice distorted with static. "Captain Torrins, I am under orders to bring back the contraband property or erase it if we cannot. I don't particularly care which option you choose."

Torrins snarled in disgust. "Kill that comm."

As Franc slapped the control, Torrins resumed pacing, scrubbing furiously at his jaw. Arad swore the deck showed signs of wear.

"Franc, talk to me. How much time do we need?" The lights dimmed briefly, and everyone scanned the bridge. Hopefully it would hold together long enough.

"At least another five minutes."

Daiko's sharp inhale had physical weight. "They're charging weapons again. Time is a luxury we don't have."

Torrins stopped pacing.

Blinding light filled the bridge as the star they'd been orbiting entered the viewscreen, forcing everyone to avert their eyes. Shadows fled in the intensity, giving Arad a glimpse at an afterlife he wasn't sure he'd earned. The brightness made him teary. He shielded his face until the ship turned far enough to move the star out of view once again.

Blinking the light out of his eyes, Torrins turned, sweeping his sad gaze over every nut and bolt in the room. Pain, rage, and loss etched lines into his face, each one entangled with the others. The dread pooling in Arad's gut told him the captain was making a silent goodbye to an old friend in the middle of the chaos. Seconds stretched into forever as Arad joined him.

Stomping to his chair, Torrins growled as he punched the panel on the armrest. "Emergency evac! Abandon ship! Abandon ship! Drop everything and head for the shuttle!"

The command carried into the hallway, echoing and overlapping, building like the anxious swell in Arad's chest. It continued to repeat, becoming part of the alarms.

Daiko and Franc scrambled out of their seats and sped out the door.

With a ragged inhale, Torrins headed for the hallway, ignoring Arad as he bolted. Arad jumped to his feet and followed because he was not about to be left behind if there was any chance of survival. He'd come too far for this to be the end. The evacuation order continued over and over, mixed with the sirens. Arad winced, trying to block out the noise as he raced to keep up with Torrins. For the first time, he would have welcomed the clatter of footsteps.

Lungs burning from fear and exertion, Arad managed to shout at Torrins over the bedlam. "You're going to get in a shuttle and escape? That's insane! What makes you think you can outrun a military vessel of that size? It's big enough to block out the sun!"

"The shuttle's cloaked. They'll never see us until we're long gone."

Arad had doubts. The warship had found them even when Franc said it shouldn't have. "How can you be sure?"

"Staying on board isn't an option. We'll end up in prison or the morgue before that commander is done. I choose none of the above."

They turned a corner to find Tank allowing Nixta to enter the mini airlock to the shuttle first.

"Cap, what the fuck is going on?"

"Corporate warship found us."

"Son of a bitch." Tank dipped his head, turning his body to step through. It was the only way his bulk would pass the threshold. The crew were strapping themselves into sturdy chairs with Franc and Daiko already at the helm, powering up the lifeboat. It would be a tight fit for all of them, but Arad wasn't picky by habit.

Serene caught sight of Arad, and her standard discord flared. "Torrins? What do you think you're doing?"

"What?"

"There's only room for six." Her piercing stare rooted Torrins in the doorway.

Franc glanced Arad's way and turned to the front along with the rest. The disconnect grew larger than ever. The captain paused in a moment of indecision.

"Torrins, get a move on! We don't have time for this bullshit!"

With a tight-lipped growl, Torrins spun to face Arad. The captain's brow creased hard. His entire frame quaked with the unsteady stance of the guilty man. Regret stained his words in ugly colors.

"Sorry, kid. You were fun, but this is what we hired you for."

Torrins gave Arad a hard shove, pushing him clear of the hatch. Arms pinwheeling, he stumbled backward and landed on his ass. The solid door swung closed with a loud clang, leaving Arad on the other side, trapped on the wounded ship.

Torrins's evacuation command continued to repeat through the ship, the urgency heightened by the blaring alarm loud enough to signal the end of days. Metal shifted behind the walls as the airlock cycled. The crew were about to escape and leave Arad behind, sitting dumbfounded on the deck.

He wanted to kick himself for not seeing it sooner. He should have seen it coming. Bits and pieces of their original meeting became clearer. Torrins had brought Arad on board for a purpose beyond a hired bedmate, and now here he was, fulfilling that role.

"He fits everything we need."

Stupid, stupid, stupid not to see it sooner. Enough signs were laid in front of him, but Arad had let having a roof over his head and money in his pocket overrule his better judgment. Enough. He'd punish himself later. The corporate flagship still had its guns aimed at the *Midas Ascending* while Torrins and the rest were going to flee in a cloaked ship, leaving him the sole occupant.

The word *scapegoat* came to mind. Or *sacrificial pawn.*

This might have been the pinnacle of bad scenarios, but sitting there and doing nothing wouldn't save Arad. Scrambling to his feet, he raced to the bridge. Like any authority figure under a corporate contract, First Commander Bard was the devil, but prison was preferable to being blown into charred debris floating through the airless wastelands. Living was always the better option. Dead people had none.

On the bridge, the stars swept to the side as the ship continued to spin. He needed to think, and quick. Time was not his friend, but the endless alerts filled his ears and dulled his mind. He stumbled to the captain's chair and started pressing buttons.

"Shut up already!"

The noise abruptly stopped. He wasn't sure which control worked, but he'd have to be thankful for the quiet as the *Alpha One Flagship* drifted in front of the ship once again.

Arad needed to contact them, convince them to stand down. Surrender. He could do that. Slugs did that better than anyone. Survival was everything. As long as a man was alive, he had a future. Franc had shut down the hail before at Torrins's order, so the controls must have been at his station.

Through the viewer, a cloud of steam emanated from the *Midas Ascending*, probably from the damaged engine. A mix of frost and smoke, it caught the starlight, leaving a gossamer nebula between the two vessels. The haze parted as if something unseen pushed through the veil, opening a pathway on a vector away from both ships. The warship started firing at the distortion. The third particle blast stopped short in a burst of phosphorescent sparks, causing the once-hidden shuttle's cloak to fail, revealing it to anyone watching.

The shuttle tumbled in a lazy roll from its leftover momentum. Its running lights sputtered out, the craft dead and useless. Torrins and the others weren't going anywhere if the ugly scorch down the side was any indication.

A swell of smug satisfaction warmed Arad's chest, right up until the moment the burn scar marring the shuttle's hull ruptured. A geyser of freezing oxygen, debris, and human beings billowed out into the vacuum. Six figures glided out of view, each face frozen in recognizable horror, clothes flowing in their wake, marking them as ghosts.

Torrins. Franc. Daiko. Serene. Tank. Nixta. All gone. Head fritzing, Arad didn't know how he should be reacting. The six of them had left him behind, but did they deserve this? Regardless, his animosity for the motley crew paled before the disgust Bard's voice crackling through the new audio feed sparked in him.

"*Midas Ascending*, my scans show there's only one life sign left on board. How very noble to go down with the ship, Captain Torrins."

"Don't shoot! I surrender!" Panic forced Arad's shout into the air, counting on the channel to send the message.

Breathing quickened as the seconds passed and Arad's pulse spiked, pounding in his ears. Bard said nothing in return. The readout on the display read *RANK UPDATED*. What the hell did that mean? There wasn't time to consider it.

"Bard! I surrender!"

"Respond, Captain. I'm waiting…"

This wasn't a game he was playing. Men like Bard expected a response and ignored any word they didn't want to hear. Arad pounced on Franc's dashboard, desperately hunting for the comm controls. "I'm not Torrins! Torrins was on the shuttle you just blew to hell!"

The commander sighed. "I'm growing bored playing this charade. I'm only going to ask this one more time. Send me the override codes so I can take command."

Arad didn't know the codes. Torrins would never have trusted him with such things. If he did, he'd have transmitted them long ago, saving himself from this insanity.

"Where's the on switch? Where is it? Where is it?"

"Salvaging the stolen property is preferable, but it's within the scope of my mission to treat you as hostile if you don't comply. If I have to wait much longer, you'll join your crew out the airlock."

"Shut up, you moron! I'm trying to surrender!" Arad's fingers flew as he spun the screen menus, hunting for anything that might help him.

"The timer is counting down, Captain." Bard's fraying patience was audible. If Arad didn't find a way to contact him, he was no better off than Torrins and the rest. Explosive decompression in a wave of fire and destruction was not in any version of how he imagined dying.

Having zero success with Franc's terminal, Arad scanned through Daiko's station as well. His eye caught a prompt on the right-hand monitor:

***SPACE FOLD CAPACITORS ACTIVE

MINIMUM CHARGE ACHIEVED***

Did that mean it was primed to use? Arad backtracked through his memories like a madman. Hadn't Torrins had Daiko enter the coordinates earlier? A holographic icon labeled *ENGAGE* hovered on the screen, begging to be touched.

"You had your chance, Captain Torrins. It's a shame you have no sense of self-preservation."

Time's up. One last chance. Act now or lose forever.

"Please be ready." Arad tapped the control, and a dialog box with additional buttons popped up on the screen, pulsing in red.

WARNING

Performing a space fold within a star's gravity field can cause unexpected results.

Do you wish to continue?

YES ***NO***

"*Are you kidding me? Yes!*" Arad shrieked at the monitor.

"Goodbye, Captain."

Arad punched the button. Light and vibration ignited the *Midas Ascending*, growing bright and noisy, filled with otherworldly sensations. And with a snap, the universe turned itself inside out even as the flagship fired. Arad screamed alongside reality. Crushing his eyes closed, he prayed for a miracle he'd never seen slugs receive.

Chapter Six

The first thing Arad noticed was the deadly silence of outer space, yet oxygen curiously filled his lungs. The telltale chirp of tech coming to life broke through the dark, shining light on his face. It brought the past into the present, leaving him wary. He was afraid to open his eyes. No one wanted to find their internal organs on the outside for a change. Heaped on the bridge deck, he patted his chest and around his torso, as well as his head and face. Everything appeared to have stayed where it belonged. Thankfully, he had not been turned into one of those cubist paintings from the museum archive kiosk.

It's not to say he didn't ache in unfamiliar places.

How long had he been out? The space fold had been brutal—more than usual—and he'd passed out. His pants were chilly and damp but not soaking wet. At least he hadn't woken lying in vomit. A small victory. All he wanted was to strip down and get clean and warm again, but other priorities took the lead.

"Ugh...this is so nasty."

Groaning, Arad dragged himself to his unsteady feet and hobbled over to the helm while trying to ignore the clammy material gripping his legs and bottom.

It took some time, but he managed to navigate Daiko's station for more information. Queueing up the damage reports confirmed all external sensors were off-line. Internal systems, including life support, were fully operational, but engines and navigational sensors were zeroed. The ship may have arrived at the preprogrammed coordinates or, given the sketchy jump conditions, wound up on the other side of the galaxy. Beyond looking out the window, there was no way to know where they were, for all the good that would do. Arad didn't recognize any constellations in the distance, but why would he? Back home, Grey District's skyscrapers eclipsed the horizon so badly stargazing wasn't a popular hobby.

"Where the hell are we? Arad, what did you do to us?"

From the way the stars in the distance crept across the viewscreen, the *Midas Ascending* hadn't lost its earlier momentum from the venting engine. The military warship was nowhere to be seen, and it had no reason to hide. If it wasn't outside waiting to shred the ship into debris, the jump must have been successful. Possessions of jump drives were restricted. It was common knowledge following a ship that folded itself into a getaway was impossible. No wonder a smuggler's ship had the necessary upgrades to do so.

"Well...looks like we won't be dead so soon after all."

The communications array was also down. Without the pressure of a warship bearing down on him, he found the comm control on Franc's console far too easily. All of this nonsense might have been avoided if he'd gotten a grip on himself and returned Bard's hail. How stupid was he? If anyone found him now, he'd die of embarrassment.

That sobered him faster than avoiding arrest.

Torrins and the others were in no position to see anyone. Ever again.

Taking a brief moment of silence allowed him to say a quick prayer for the crew like his parents used to do. Arad wasn't sure why he bothered, because no higher power shined on slugs, and for the most part, Torrins and the crew had proven to be awful, dishonest people. For some reason, he'd lost the ability to grieve. Torrins had hired him as the one to take the fall if his schemes went sideways and the authorities caught up to them. The rest of them were in on the joke too and treated him like scum so they wouldn't have to feel bad if his role played out. Worse, he'd never know for sure whether First Commander Bard wouldn't have killed him the moment he boarded the ship and took control had Arad managed to surrender. Torrins's plan was determined to fail, and it was blind luck Arad had survived.

Even so, the prayer was the right thing to do. He would have lit a candle if he had one.

"Sorry, Torrins. You should have played your hand better."

With a meager salute into the air, Arad continued looking through the command panels for more information. A sub-command on the damage report menu caught Arad's eye.

CREW CONDITION.

"What have you found for us here? Curious."

Having a conversation with himself wouldn't be considered the healthiest way to manage his situation—especially if he kept using plural pronouns in the process—but the intense quiet underscored the current catastrophe in ways he wasn't ready to disassemble yet. Only the insane or hopelessly intoxicated did such a thing in Grey District, and it marked a person to be avoided at all costs. Well, Arad wasn't drunk. The rest was up for debate.

A touch to the graphic header pulled up a new window on the screen. In nice, neat rows sat a list of the entire *Midas*'s crew with name, rank, and life-sign percentage. Torrins, Franc, Daiko, Serene, Tank, and Nixta were marked as *RANK N/A, LIFE SIGNS 0%*. Last on the list was Arad, his readout making no sense whatsoever.

ARAD ANSARI, CAPTAIN, LIFE SIGNS 100%

Captain?

He blinked at the display more than once, expecting the fevered mirage to fade. Testing the theory brewing in his head, he tapped Torrins's name, which brought up a scan box.

Press for Permission Scan

Arad touched his finger to the field. The box flashed and confidential details, including medical records no one should have access to other than Torrins himself, sprang into view. Other than a high-ranking medical officer—which they didn't have—only the captain would have such a privilege.

This shouldn't be right, but it was. The military-based OS must have been keeping a bio-scan locked on all crew members. A little creepy, but Arad appreciated knowing he was battered and bruised at 100 percent in spite of feeling like crap. The shuttle must have been in sensor range when the flagship blew it out of space. With everyone else killed in action, the protocols must have automatically updated the ranks. As the only surviving crew member, it appeared Arad had been promoted to the highest-ranking officer on board. If he understood this correctly, he now had total access to every square inch of the *Midas Ascending*.

The ship was his.

A throaty laugh welled up from deep inside. Arad was lost, adrift in space in an unknown quadrant. The sole occupant on a ship going nowhere with no way to contact another living soul. No authorities to give orders. No suffocating crowds or foremen to beg for work or pay. No clients to make demands of him.

"This is so awesome!"

For a change, the universe finally favored a slug.

The first thing Arad did as newly crowned emperor (after showering and changing) was rename the ship.

Ansariland had a nice ring to it.

But to make it official on the operating system, he had to open the ship's technical files and find the correct protocols, many of which had been restricted. Which didn't seem to be a problem anymore. Schematics of every system were at his perusal. A tech's wet dream. The first day he did little more than read up on all the areas he'd been barred from up until now.

Swarthy jazz pumped through the hallways via the ship-wide speakers as he dropped a noodle packet into a bowl inside the cooker. Torrins had an excellent selection of music in his audio library. Arad hummed along, not knowing the words, but he found the tunes strangely familiar. Maybe the songs were something his parents had liked back in the day. Pulling the memories was more effort than it was worth. Far too much time had passed since he'd last laid eyes on them, and he strove to forget them for the most part. It was the least they deserved.

Tapping his feet to the eclectic beat, he squinted through the tiny window, willing the dish to heat quicker. "Come on. Faster, faster, faster. I'm hungry."

Torrins had stashed enough rations on board to feed them all for several months if necessary. No doubt to be prepared in case they were avoiding the authorities for an extended period. With the crew complement down to one, Arad had enough to last for years before he had to get nervous. Plenty of time to learn how to repair enough of the ship to seek the outside world again.

But no need to rush.

With everyone gone, Arad was safe. His world was his to define, and currently his needs were met. Or were about to be, if his tasty dinner ever finished.

The cooker beeped and he pumped his fist in victory. "Ah, yes. Come to papa."

Collecting his food, he stirred up the steamy ramen with a pair of metal chopsticks and inhaled the spicy scent. He slurped up a thick line of noodles and groaned happily. Not as good as street fare but a decent substitute. The crew always complained about the rations and made fun of Arad for enjoying them, but they didn't know how good they had it. A common problem with people whose daily requirements were always met without fail. They often didn't see anything beyond their own myopic interests. How did that work out for them?

"A bunch of selfish bastards, the whole lot."

Torrins and the crew had everything they needed. A roof over their heads, work, and funds to spend, and they never wondered where the next meal would come from. In the end, they lost it all, including their lives, out of sheer greed. Maybe his slug-based viewpoint was a bit simplistic, but now all of this was Arad's, and he had never once asked for it. He'd earned it through sheer survival skills.

It was about time he'd explored the spoils.

Bowl in hand, Arad stirred up another mouthful of noodles and headed for the crew quarters. Head bopping to the piped-in music, he was still chewing when he arrived at Daiko and Serene's door. As he reached for the access panel, the hallway jazz morphed into something more ominous—filled with dread-bearing percussion and jarring brass. Far too appropriate for the room he was attempting to enter.

Pausing, he swept his gaze upward. "If you're up there watching me, Torrins, your sense of humor is probably why you're dead. And, Serene, your lack of one...same thing."

With no one to hear him, Arad giggled out loud as he pressed his thumb on the scanner, which chimed with the words *CAPTAIN OVERRIDE* on the display. The door slid open with a hard, mechanical grind.

First glance of Daiko and Serene's room garnered little of interest. It was a whole lot of what he'd already seen on board: metal surfaces, chipped paint, and a space too cramped for two people at once. It was difficult to rummage through the storage drawers with his food in one hand, but he managed. Inside the drawer next to the bed sat an odd bottle filled with little squares of paper. He'd lived long enough to recognize someone's drug stash. Only a tiny number of drugs were processed like this, but the only affordable type on the street these days was Syn. And Arad didn't think any of the crew had the spare income to deal with the expensive stuff. It was made the same as every batch he'd ever laid eyes on. Arad didn't want to understand why these two kept a bottle of Syn next to the bed. Or, better yet, he'd rather not picture Serene under its influence. Shudder. He opened the closet, and a glint of sparkle caught his eye, deep in the shadow.

"You have got to be joking."

He almost missed the deeply buried skimpy minidress. Its threadlike shoulder straps barely held to the hanger, and the sequins managed to reflect the room's meager light into megawatt voltage. The weave was so sheer it wrapped around his fingers in an indiscreet way. Too narrow to fit Daiko, it had to be Serene's, which made no sense whatsoever given her harsh, no-nonsense manner. Surprises lurked in every corner under the right circumstances, apparently. Perhaps, from time to time, she liked pretty things.

Arad set the noodle bowl down long enough to throw the garment on over his T-shirt and pants. The fabric hung askew off one shoulder and bunched around his waist, caught on his empty belt loop. Laughter spilled out of him at a reckless rate. He looked ridiculous in Serene's dress, but in all fairness, so would she.

This would be the beginning of many excesses he planned to indulge in as the *Ansariland* captain.

Ansariland. Yes, that definitely sounded good to his ear.

Properly adorned in garishness, he continued to look for any other items worthy of his attention. The limits had been lifted. Every corner was his to explore. Every item was his to covet. Everything and everywhere belonged to Arad.

It was a rush to have full access to information and parts of the ship he hadn't previously had sufficient rank to enter. If Serene found him in here like this, she would lose her mind and rage all over him. Like she had at...the cargo bay.

Hmmm...

Arad tossed and turned, unable to sleep. The time panel's bleak glow was the only light source in the bedroom. Its dull holographic numbers changed in aching succession with the third number left jagged by the cracked display—it mocked his inability to sleep.

It wasn't the darkness, the ship's silence, or the isolation. He'd welcomed all of these given the clamor and chaos he'd lived with beforehand. The previous night had been a blissful sleep with the bed all his own. The crew used to bitch about the mattresses and lack of luxury, but they'd never slept in an alley, huddled in a corner, praying they wouldn't freeze to death before dayfall. They were scoundrels but swam in privilege.

"Well, they did swim. Past tense."

Every effort to get more comfortable had been made. The temperature had been set to a cozy level. The pillow had been properly punched into submission. Nothing helped. He'd even worn nothing to bed. Not for the feel of the sheets against his skin. No, it was for the first time since boarding that he didn't have to wonder if Torrins would see it as an invitation. Sometimes, the captain's lusts challenged Davis's Syn-soaked benders for a horny decathlon trophy. At least Torrins took pride in making Arad enjoy their time together as well.

"Fine. You weren't totally horrible. Just when you were leaving me on a ship to die."

No need to risk Torrins haunting him. He had his own brain doing the dirty work now.

None of the above reasons had anything to do with why he couldn't settle this evening. His curiosity had been sparked, and no matter how much he'd meant it when he told Selene he didn't care about it, the niggling idea continued to burrow into his brain. Arad wanted to ignore it and prove he wasn't a slave to the mysteries that had likely created the whole situation he was in.

The clock moved forward one minute.

"Well, crap. We're not going to get any sleep until we go look, are we?"

Throwing off the sheet, he stomped out of bed. He raised the lights enough to see, and as he forced the drawer open, it made a wrenching noise.

"Oh, yeah. We're oiling you first thing tomorrow."

Arad grabbed a set of Torrins's clothes. Shirt and pants were both several sizes too big, making him feel like a kid dressing up. The pants wrapped under his feet like child's pajamas. He endured it because he hadn't spent enough time going through the crew's old quarters to scrounge for another pair of boots. Why was he worrying about being clothed? It wasn't as if anyone else would see him. Except maybe the ghosts of Torrins and the others.

"No peep shows tonight, you perverts."

Internal lighting in the hallways had been set low for the hour, increasing the shadow and amplifying the quiet. But no matter how carefully he walked or cautiously he peered into the dark, nothing jumped out. Nothing surprised him. The short trip to the hold was largely uneventful.

Hand above the security panel, Arad paused. Did he really want to know what the crew had hidden inside the cargo bay? A stupid question. Of course he wanted to know. Would it be worth it? Whatever lay inside, they were willing to abandon him to the corporate authorities who didn't hesitate to kill the crew rather than risk being caught possessing it.

That wasn't ominous at all.

He placed his palm on the panel, and this time it chimed with bright letters across the screen. For once the new rank didn't tickle him enough to arrest his growing apprehension.

ACCESS GRANTED CAPTAIN

Hydraulics hissed and metal scraped as the dense hatch lumbered open. Light panels flickered on, and the door finished opening with a weighty thunk. Inside, a wall of crates loomed nearly to the ceiling. How much stuff was in here? The inventory blocked the way not even three meters in.

"This can't be packed this tight, can it?"

His gaze swept the barrier, and far along, all the way to the right edge, a gap appeared. Following it only led to a new path between another row of crates that opened on the far left this time. Another hairpin turn greeted him. *They built an indoor maze? Who has that kind of time?* The ridiculous number of containers formed a tight channel weaving deeper into the cargo bay. What kind of product had Torrins stolen that needed to be hidden inside the locked storage area that required special permission to enter? The idea boggled Arad enough he shuffled aside the idea that all the stuff in these boxes was his. He'd sift through the new hoard of riches soon enough. Something special and maybe even potentially dangerous lurked within the bay's confines. Unearthing the secret that had almost cost his life might seem like a dumb move, but if he didn't, he'd never fall to sleep tonight. He deserved that much.

Continuing through the labyrinth, Arad was finally greeted by light reflecting around a makeshift corner. From there he exited into a vacant area he pictured being the far end of the bay. Segregated from the rest of the clutter sat a cluster of four medical capsules—the kind used for quarantine critical conditions—each with its own series of active computer terminals and screens attached. A gentle chorus of humming wafted from the devices. These were not the recycled tech of a former military craft turned smuggler's vessel. Exquisite and high-end, the term *machinery* didn't do them justice. This was art.

"Oh...you're so pretty."

Entranced by their elegance, Arad tugged his pant legs higher to shuffle forward for a closer look without tripping himself. The construction was immaculate. Four pristine and unblemished pods with near-invisible seams. Whoever had created them deserved an award. Even the adjoining computers were beautifully designed, matching everything in perfect sophistication.

First Commander Bard had accused them of possessing stolen property. No kidding. These devices had to be worth a fortune. They were actively running a simulation of some kind...medical data? What were these being used for?

Behind their glass faces, each capsule had a murky interior. A phosphorescent fog obscured the shadowed contents. Something was definitely inside. Reflections off the room's severe task lighting left hard glares in bright spots, making it impossible to see without getting right on top of them. Ducking his head to protect his eyes, Arad stepped within arm's reach and gasped.

Sleeping soundly inside three of the four berths were different types of DemiShou. And from as best as Arad could tell, they were alive.

"Oh, man. Torrins, what did you get yourself into?"

Chapter Seven

Each DemiShou floated in a foggy liquid in its capsule, except the last one, which was dry and empty.

Where had they come from? Amber text on the monitors read like health data—heart rate, blood oxygen, and other stats—along with...bio-chrysalis percentages? None were at 100 percent. Did that mean they were works in progress? That shouldn't be possible. Public newsfeeds were always filled with archives of the days when politicians spouted slogans to protect human rights by ending the breeding programs every time some kind of DemiShou controversy reared its head. Test-tubing new DemiShou was highly illegal.

Not that corporation ethics aligned with statutes and legislation on a regular basis. The rules were reserved for everyone beneath their social tier.

It certainly explained the corporate interest in retrieving their property at all costs. If word got out some company higher-up had ordered the manufacture of DemiShou—of any kind—stocks would plummet and ruin them. The military connection was also disturbing. Did they know what cargo they were assigned to collect or were they just following orders?

Now Arad understood why Torrins, who normally exuded endless self-confidence, had to marshal his nerve when confronted by First Commander Bard. The game had become dangerous. Somehow, he and the crew had smuggled these containers on board, no doubt intending to sell them for a profit hefty enough to ignore the hazards involved, all without Arad noticing a thing, including his being set up as fall guy to authorities if they needed a backup plan. A complex plan, but with too many future moves to guarantee checkmate.

"I'll give you credit, Torrins. That was a pretty bold scheme, no matter how stupid."

Careful not to touch anything important, Arad slid his fingertips over the sleek surface of the nearest incubator. The faintest, almost imperceptible vibration tickled his senses, the mark of engineering excellence. He wanted to kiss the outer shell for its beauty, but the fact there were people inside held him off, leaving him unable to be sure whether he should be awestruck or horrified. Curious fascination won out, stomping down the creepier side of things. The capsules made him think of life-size dolls packaged for sale to the highest bidder. A niche brothel back home served bizarre role-playing scenes like that and more.

However, there was nothing playful about the slumbering beastmen.

All three of the DemiShou bodies were dotted with tiny pieces of tech on every major body part: temples, neck, chest, arms, and legs. They wore no obvious breathing apparatuses, so the fluid must have been oxygenated, right? Denser than water, it hazed the view and dulled their coloring closer to monochromatic. Their chests expanded and contracted in an exacting, controlled rhythm.

If the display didn't confirm their heartbeats, he might have believed they were androids or anatomic simulators. However, if he waited long enough, he would catch involuntary twitches, parting of lips, curling of fingers. The kind of motions no one would bother to animate.

Were they grown from scratch DNA? Clones? People allowing medical experimentation for money? Too many unknowns. Arad needed more details about his guests, if only to stave off irrational theories and prevent nightmares. If only there were more information to see beyond peering into each capsule and reading its monitor's matching data.

Designation: Hachi. The bull hybrid reminded Arad of the bartender at the tavern where he'd met Torrins. Dark skin, thick neck, and short horns defined a face with bovine features less pronounced than the bartender's. Would that change? When he pressed close to the glass and looked down far enough, he had a better idea of what he'd have been in for had he accepted the bartender's offer. It had probably been for the best. Arad liked bigger guys on principle, but there were body parts he wouldn't know how to manage. Hachi was huge, like all the DemiShou, but his scale dwarfed the others. Good thing someone planned ahead to make the tubes large enough to accommodate his freakish size.

Designation: Shichi. Everything about him was a contrast to Hachi. Even as his facial features were smoother with a smaller nose and thinner lips, his dusky skin held some kind of pebbled texture. Almost patterned in neat rows like scales. Would that make him a lizard hybrid of some sort? Arad wasn't sure through the milky haze. Again, his physique was fantasy material. Arad had to give credit to the choice of men used in this project. Shichi may not have been Hachi's size, but he was still impressive. Although, he found something about him a little unnerving.

Designation: Roku. Powerfully, near-pornographically muscled like the others, Roku had a wide, elongated nose that reminded Arad of a cat. Maybe a tiger. Faint stripes lined his skin in defined, almost geometric patterns. Definitely influenced by the hand of man rather than nature. His ears were pointed, riding higher on his head than normal. Like the others, his head was shaved, but his skull appeared softer, as if covered in a fine layer of fur. It may have been a trick of the light, but his chest and abdomen appeared lighter than the rest of his body. His body parts and proportions were arousal inducing.

Growing up, Arad had had a cat despite his mother's protests. She claimed she had allergies, but he suspected she didn't like taking care of anything beyond herself. Fat, lazy, and standoffish, that cat did little more for him than bat his chess pieces onto the floor. He preferred the one in front of him better.

Designation: Go. This capsule sat empty and lifeless. The tube seams were pronounced, as if opened and poorly closed. Darkness hid most of the tech lining the walls, and a dingy film crusted over the glass's interior. Perhaps left behind from dried-up fluids? No energy flowed through this machine. It was dead, and the tube held too many comparisons to a coffin for Arad to handle. The screen displayed no active data other than the text *ABORTED* in bold. Why?

"We've already lost Go."

A swell of sympathetic grief grew inside him in a way he hadn't felt over the loss of the crew. Something had happened. Had Go died? Most likely. Arad shivered at the idea of drowning in the tube, but it shouldn't have happened if the rest of them breathed the fluid, right? Right? Had he woken as it happened? Arad didn't want to know. Not really.

Obviously, when faced with a dead DemiShou, the crew treated him like damaged cargo because to them it's all he was. A product to be bought and sold that was cracked and worthless. They were hardly altruistic. Timelines ran through Arad's head. He pinpointed the most likely opportunity to bring the DemiShou on board during their last planet-side docking a week ago. Torrins had sent Arad on a number of errands, no doubt to keep him occupied while they sorted the cargo bay. He recalled some additional tensions on the ship starting a few days ago. Perhaps that's when Go had died? Arad had been working on the maintenance Torrins had insisted on out of nowhere, giving Torrins the ideal opportunity to dispose of the evidence and keep his secrets from the cabin boy. Maybe ejecting the body so it would be incinerated by the local sun? Go had been thrown out like garbage.

The idea made sense—the whole order of events did—and it sickened him.

Arad tipped his head and shouted at the ceiling. "Whatever I said before, Torrins, I was wrong. You were *absolutely* a horrible person, and every single one of you deserved what you got. I'd pull the trigger on you myself if I had the chance."

Piecing Torrins and the crew's scandalous plan together absolved Arad of any lingering survivor's guilt he had of the encounter with Bard. They had hatched an unforgivable scheme, and to top it all off, they intended to leave him behind as a sacrificial goat while they dumped their cargo and made off to thieve another day.

"Yeah, it didn't work out that way, did it?"

Go may have been lost, but Arad had no intention of allowing anything of the sort to happen to the rest. He understood being cast aside, treated as an object with no value. A slug's existence. No living being, human or otherwise, should live that way only to be abandoned out of convenience.

Old memories came to mind, and Arad forced himself not to give them much time to roam. There were better ways to spend his time here.

The surviving three deserved a better fate than Go's. Arad had no idea what he was in for, but he would do what he could to help them. There was no way to know if they were willing participants or victims. If anyone discovered their origins, they would be designated as contraband and confiscated as government property. What would become of them? The authorities would let them rot in jail first and ask questions later. No, Arad was determined to welcome them to the *Ansariland* and find them a safe place to call home.

Now he only had to figure out how to do that.

Arad crossed his fingers as he attempted to download the ship's schematics onto the handheld computer he'd found in Franc's old room. Years on the streets hadn't given him near enough opportunity to work with operation code, and he had to guess and experiment to get this far with the unfamiliar equipment. He tapped on the screen with an impatient finger, yet gentle enough not to jostle the progress bar graphic.

"Come on. You've only wasted seven hours doing this today."

The device chirped and its status updated. Arad blinked at it more than once to believe the readout. *UPLOAD COMPLETE.*

Arad pumped his fist and shamelessly gyrated his whole body in success. "Yes! I never thought I'd get it right."

A chime echoing down the hall halted the victory dance.

His head perked up with a tiny panicked yip. Gripping the tablet tight, he sprinted to the galley, keeping the heavy blanket over his shoulder from falling. Running full speed, he nearly skidded out of control as he bounced through the doorway. Once he saw it, he sighed in relief. His noodle bowl was safe in the cooker, ready to go.

Arad patted the appliance and retrieved his meal. "That's a good boy. Daddy like."

The food wasn't actually going anywhere, but so much time spent in the past procuring meals had left him a little paranoid on the subject. Arad was secure enough to admit that.

Tucking the tablet under his arm, he spiked a pair of chopsticks into the noodles and carried everything—bowl and all—down the hall to the storage bay. Even though he had access, the door had been left open. Locking the bay's tenants in the closet was unacceptable now that he knew they were here. Traversing the maze of cases was still necessary. At some point, Arad needed to dismantle the barriers and pull up the inventory to see what actually was hidden inside, but it could wait for now. He had other priorities.

"Hi, guys, how did you sleep?"

The DemiShou floated in silence, not replying. Arad shrugged the blanket to the floor and kicked it into a rounded pile in front of the cryotubes.

"I hope you don't mind. I always heard you were supposed to talk to coma patients. Not sure if that's to help them wake up or prevent brain damage or something. A lot of the medical stuff I learned in Grey District was a little sketchy, so bear with me. Plus, I'm not sure if I'm ready for any of you to wake up yet. Either way, I have to find someplace safe when you guys hatch, but I can't do that if we're floating in space blind, now can I?"

Refusing to give up the bowl and handheld, Arad carefully squatted down until he sat into the piled blanket cushion. He managed not to drop or spill anything either.

"As much as I like drifting about, at some point, we'll need supplies. I can't do that with the ship busted. So, I need to learn as much about the *Ansariland's* systems as I can because I think I'm stuck being the only one who can fix anything."

Arad propped the tablet on his knee and thumbed through the ship schematics, slurping his noodles at the same time. Ooh, spicy. He settled in, eating and reading, looking for anything to help teach him the repairs he needed for the *Ansariland*.

The sudden alarm startled Arad, making him lurch off his seat. The tablet and bowl clattered on the metal deck, noodles and red kimchi sauce splattering in a violent arc. Chopsticks bounced end over end into a corner, dotting the path with a trail of spice. Hachi's cryotube emitted a piercing alert as the bull seized and convulsed inside.

Arad shook himself into moving and rushed to the station. The control screen flashed, and the siren knifed into his spine worse than when First Commander Bard had crippled the ship. What was going on?

Hachi's health data reads were erratic, the gentle rhythmic lines having turned into snarling holographic barbed wire. Arad didn't have a clue what the different details meant, only what he was seeing was bad. Was that his heartbeat going all crazy? Hachi continued to flail, thumping against the tube's walls. Was this what had happened to Go? Arad's chest tightened in pulses matching the alarm's cadence.

A series of controls ran down the screen's right side. Under the *PAUSE SEQUENCE* button sat another labeled *ABORT*.

"I'm not a doctor! What am I supposed to do?" He was afraid to touch anything in case he made things worse. But could it get worse?

The tube was active and Hachi was in distress. Could aborting hurt him? What were the chances it would kill him? The health telemetry became wilder, his thrashing louder, more pronounced. Hachi's mouth sagged open like he was screaming. Did Arad have a choice? Would Hachi die if he did nothing? Could he live with that? Arad's hand hovered over the *ABORT* command as he said a silent prayer to higher powers that had never given him anything.

Before he touched the button, the alarm silenced. The data leveled into its standard pattern, and Hachi quieted.

Arad stepped backward and scanned the group. All three DemiShou slept in their capsules as if nothing had happened. The only proof was the bass pounding of Arad's heart.

Rubbing his hand over his neck and head, Arad surveyed the area, mourning his lost meal. The spray of noodles and red sauce made him think of a crime scene he'd snuck into a few years ago. Blood had stained the whole area. The shopkeeper had been gunned down, gory burst-open chest, face a rictus of agony. Arad had overheard the cops processing the scene. All this hardship over a handful of credits.

So much misery over greed. A common theme.

Arad's appetite flattened into non-existence. If this was what had happened when Go died, none of them were safe from another seizure. Time wasn't Arad's friend. Picturing a repeat of this scene only reinforced the work he needed to do.

"I'm going to clean this up and get back to my research." With a near-bottomless inhale and exhale, he turned and pointed with a shaky hand at the unconscious DemiShou. "Don't do that again."

It took several uneventful hours with no additional DemiShou alarms before Arad was satisfied enough to pry himself from the cargo bay. Even so, he still peeked over his shoulder and stretched his hearing as he cleared the crate maze and crossed the threshold. Worry lingered in his chest, but it sat hushed, dulled enough to prevent the impending panic over the chance something horrible waited to happen at any second.

Dulled, but not extinguished. Arad's medical knowledge had all the skill of a beginner chess player. If another emergency came up, he needed to know what to do. Catching the eye of a local medic to keep himself healthy was no longer an option. No one's sympathies could be counted on. Arad needed to be better prepared, and he only had one source for it.

Quick steps rushed him down the hall to the closest thing the *Ansariland* had to a sick bay.

In all honesty, the infirmary was a glorified janitorial closet with a first aid kit and exam chair mounted to the wall, dominated by a high-end automated medical bed looking way too pricey for this ship. He'd only ever seen one in newsfeeds and entertainment vids through store-front windows. This sleek model was out of place among the rusted yet functional aspects of the *Ansariland*.

Arad circled the bed and its tech, another beauty he never believed he'd see up close, let alone touch. A proper reverence warmed him as he brushed his fingers over the glossy, hygienic surface. "Man, Torrins. I always wondered if you smuggled this on board or if you sold someone's firstborn to a workhouse to get ahold of this."

Humor rushed out of Arad faster than a storm drain. Some things shouldn't be joked about no matter if a person survived the experience or not.

Arad shook himself to bring him back to the present with a hard shiver. Hachi's seizure had stretched his tolerance for bitter memories into tattered mesh. Blocking the sieve was a necessary skill born from years on the streets. If he bogged himself down in the unchangeable past, he'd have no chance to help Hachi, Shichi, and Roku. Survivors didn't wallow.

With no one to shake a disapproving finger at him—mostly Serene, but the rest also had taken their turns keeping him in his place—Arad was free to explore. The portable first aid kit released from the wall with ease. Inside, the contents appeared well stocked and mostly untouched. Many of the items were unfamiliar. Hopefully, instructional files were included with the med bed.

The bed's translucent surface gleamed in the artificial light as a gentle glow brightened it from within. Too hard to be plastic, too soft to be metal. Arad marveled at its construction. Much of its appearance bordered on design and aesthetics rather than function, marking it as an item of excess. Something not intended for the likes of him. Quite a score for Torrins and crew for sure.

The cryotubes had similar characteristics. Unnecessary perfection for an illicit machine. What a shame that those with wealth and power would waste such splendor.

Well, it was in his hands now, and he planned to make use of it.

It took several minutes to dig through the monitor's menus to find the medical library. Navigating a piece of tech so complicated was something he might have excelled at years ago—before his fall from grace into slugdom. Now he struggled with unfamiliar systems, an awkwardness built from disuse.

But Arad would persevere.

He found the search function and pulled up everything the bed was programmed for regarding the care of DemiShou.

ERROR — FILE NOT FOUND

Arad's heart sank. "You have to be kidding me!"

Only fleeting references to DemiShou existed inside the encyclopedia of data. No specialized medical profile to cover the three in the cargo bay in case of emergency. Even if he found a way to drag them into the machine, the bed was powerless to help them. Welcome to Go's fate.

Arad remembered what it was like after being ousted from the condemned workhouse so many years ago.

One hand on the scanner pad, he stood before a med kiosk in the pouring rain, trying to navigate the device's diagnostics program through the fever haze cooking his brain.

"Your diagnosis is...double pneumonia."

No surprise given the shoddy conditions he'd lived and worked in for so long. Barely able to breathe through painful, wet coughing fits, he stopped pretending this might pass.

"To dispense treatment, please insert currency."

Arad had fed the last of his meager credits into the machine because starvation would be a slower death than the one brewing from his current condition. And far kinder.

"Accepted. Thank you for choosing GalatiCorp. Have a nice day."

He curled up in an alley behind a dumpster, shivering against the deluge. Creating what little shelter he could manage from a discarded metal sheeting as a makeshift roof, he waited for his meds to kick in and the ache in his chest to ease. No job. No money. No home.

Hope circled into the sewer faster than the gutter's runoff as he learned life's most important rule.

Corporations didn't care about people over profits. Nothing personal, just business, of course. The giant excuse for unethical behavior on a global, if not universal, scale. If they hadn't already, it was a harsh lesson Hachi, Shichi, and Roku would learn the moment they set foot on solid ground once again and were forced to make their way.

Assuming they survived long enough to find out.

"Dammit, Torrins! You brought them on board for a quick score and had no secondary plan if something went wrong! You're just like my idiot parents! I'm glad you and the crew are dead!"

Arad punched the bed twice, three times, leaving no mark on its lavishly durable shell. Fist aching, he pulled back. He needed to calm down before he really hurt himself. This was why he hated dwelling on the past. Only shame and humiliation lived there. Living for the future was how he continued moving forward, no matter what.

"Okay. I'm not glad. But I'm not sad about it either."

With a deep breath, he dug into the directory for first aid instructions. If the bed was useless to help the DemiShou, he would have to do it himself. Add it to the growing pile of things to learn along with the engines, communications systems, and everything else.

He'd never envied people with enough money to pay for implants to instantly upload everything into their brains before now.

Chapter Eight

Throwing his arms wide, Arad slumped backward on the mattress and allowed the tablet to tumble out of his hand and to the floor.

"No more today, guys. I can't look at another schematic."

Six straight days studying the *Ansariland*'s mechanical systems had turned his brain to mush. It's not that he didn't find it all fascinating. There was just so much material to get through. The first day overloading on emergency medical procedures had been bad enough. He should have paid more attention in biology. Academics came easier before he had ended up in the workhouse. Arad used to complain so much about school, and now he almost missed it.

Almost.

Most of his time was now spent in the cargo bay standing watch while he scoured the databases. He'd even gone so far as to drag Franc's mattress out of his room, dropping it in front of the cryotubes for a more comfortable vantage point, because the hard metal floor beat his ass after the first day. He almost unbolted a couch from the rec room, but he guessed he'd never be able to drag the steel-framed sofa down the hall without help. So the mattress made a better choice.

In the end, it wasn't a big deal. Franc didn't need it anymore.

An unfamiliar chirp from one of the tubes startled Arad. "What was that?"

After rolling to his feet, he sprinted the short distance to the capsules, barely noticing how he kicked the tablet aside in the rush. Starting with Hachi, Arad scanned the slumbering DemiShou, his container, and the attached control screen, searching for any sign of distress. The bull floated in peace, oblivious to Arad's concerns. Finding nothing, he repeated the process with Shichi and Roku. None of them moved, clearly not caring about Arad's state of mind. The status line under Roku's health data had changed from *BIOLOGICAL* to *SYNAPTIC*.

His panicked breath stalled as Arad stared at Roku, waiting for something to explode.

Long, long minutes passed, and nothing happened.

Roku continued to sleep like the other two with no more movement than the rise and fall of his chest and the occasional muscle twitch, amounting to a whole lot of nothing.

He wished he understood the DemiShou process. There was no way to know if any part harmed them, and no available data file existed to teach him about the past week's changes. A fine pattern of iridescent scales covered Shichi's body, the pebbled texture now defined. Hachi's skin had grown darker, and Roku's geometric stripes were richer and deeper in tone. All of their animalistic facial features and details were more pronounced. Roku's face and nose had flattened into more of a cat's muzzle, but not completely inhuman. What more was in store? How likely was another seizure, and would it end as uneventfully as the previous one?

Scrubbing a hand through his hair, Arad stepped backward. Frustration over his lack of knowledge was such an understatement.

"I gotta take a break. You guys relax. I'll be back later."

With one last fleeting look of concern at Roku, Arad left the cargo bay. Stepping into the hall did little to ease the constant state of tightness in his chest. If he didn't start managing his stress, overseeing the DemiShou would send him to meet Torrins and the rest.

"Forget it, Torrins. I'm not getting buggered by you in the afterlife."

Too much information and worry and uncertainty flooded his mind and left him more adrift than the ship. Focusing on one thing was near impossible when all sides of the situation competed for equal time. Arad wasn't sure which portion deserved the most attention.

The resulting sigh echoed down the corridor, amplified by the emptiness. He probably should have left the music running, but the background noise pulled him out of his studies too easily. Street noise he ignored, but not Torrins's eclectic playlist. And Arad needed to learn about all the ship's areas he'd never had access to before the crew got popped because there was too much riding on it now.

Why couldn't he be like Torrins and not give a shit? Life would be so much easier if he were like so many others he'd met over the years. So selfish, sacrificing everyone around them in order to survive came naturally. Arad understood the appeal, but no matter how hard his life became, people still mattered. He hadn't given up on the universe simply because it had turned its back on him. He was only somewhat jaded.

Middle finger raised, Arad waved his hand at the ceiling.

"I'm gonna figure this out no matter how hard you jerks made this."

Half in a fugue state, Arad wandered the halls, looking for something, anything to distract him. Shuffling about between the crew quarters, he ambled into Tank's old room. It didn't take long until boredom moved him along into another and he wound up in Daiko and Serene's.

Without any real intent, he wrenched open various drawers, hardly flinching as the metal scraped. The noise did little to jar the fuzziness of his mood. He thumbed through their closet for the thousandth time, barely finding anything of interest. The weight on his soul muddied him into boredom.

Had he skipped his last meal? It was possible given how much energy he'd thrown into the ship schematics, but finding the momentum to deal with food was harder than it should have been. Too much weighed on his shoulders. Too many dilemmas in his head. If he didn't get a handle on it soon, he was going to have a spurting, bloody stroke all over the ship, and with his luck, he'd be crippled and still have to clean up the mess.

He'd give anything to spend a little time out of his own head. But seriously, what kind of options did he have?

Arad slumped down onto the bed and fell on the mattress, refusing to harbor images of how Daiko and Serene had spent their intimate time on this potentially seedy surface. Shuddering, he rolled to his side and bumped his knee against the first storage drawers he'd opened when he came in.

"Ow!" Arad rubbed out the ache, oddly proud to remember his first aid studies. "If you drew blood and I need a tetanus booster, I'm gonna rip you off the hinges."

Peeking into the drawer, he spied Daiko and Serene's bottle of Syn.

A tiny thing, it easily fit in the palm of his hand. His parents would be aghast he had any knowledge of it, let alone allow it in their presence. Value existed in escaping the dark parts of the world. Being cast in shadow, people on the bottom half understood it. Anything that brought light into their lives—even if only for a brief moment—had an allure whether they indulged or not.

Arad stared at the nine or ten tiny squares of paper inside. Each one had an identical stamp marking the maker so the buyer knew where to get more.

Syn was based off an obsolete synthetic drug called LSD. Still a hallucinogenic, it centered on the pleasure centers of the brain, making everything feel good. Severe overuse left a person *corrupted*, leaving them in a perpetual state of uncontrollable sex addiction.

Arad had seen enough of it after Sketch had found him recovering from pneumonia in the alley. He'd taken pity on Arad and let him crash with him for a few months. Sketch made and dealt the Syn—it was easy enough with a basic lab—but he didn't use. He explained Syn and its construction in endless detail while insisting Arad keep clean as well. The last thing he wanted was a corrupted burnout in his flat. Sketch was kind and didn't ask for any favors in return. He said Arad was far too young.

The few months together were an odd blessing compared to living in the workhouse, but it couldn't last. Sketch had used his expired pharmacy certificate to steal the ingredients from a corporate chemical storehouse, and the authorities managed to trace them and raided their home. Sketch was arrested, but they pitched Arad into the street—literally face-first—because his identity had been scrubbed and was undocumented. Corporations didn't care about slugs. He never saw Sketch again.

Lost in old memories, he rolled the bottle in his fingers, watching the illicit swatches tumble.

Concentrations varied from dealer to dealer, but paper this size only soaked up so much Syn without visible discoloration. These looked fine. All encounters with Davis included Syn, so Arad had an up-close-and-personal history with its effects. There was little risk of being corrupted with a single dose. Davis wasn't an addict, and he usually took two hits at a time. When he did, for a few hours, every aspect of his grim life in Grey District would shine and sparkle and become fabulous.

An exhausted sigh made Arad's shoulders sag. "Oh, I could use some of that right now."

He'd lost count of the number of men and women who lost themselves to chemical escape over the years. Stealing small moments in a life of drudgery was common, and for some, the hunt became downright dangerous. Arad had made a point to avoid the trap. When the high faded, all the crap of the world still existed.

But sometimes a little distraction was appropriate.

He flipped open the stopper with his thumb. Carefully using his fingernails, he picked a single square from the bottle, trying not to touch the rest. Syn didn't absorb through the skin, but its potent residue on users' fingers often gave them more of a dose than planned on. He dropped the tab on his tongue, letting it soak before swallowing it down. After closing the bottle, he tossed it onto the bed. Now he only had to sit back and wait for it to take effect.

When the chipped red paint on the wall started looking especially luscious ten minutes later, it had begun. Colors appeared more vibrant, each detail crisper. Serene's glittery dress sitting in a heap on the floor was sad, unable to shine.

"Starting to see what Davis saw in this stuff."

Was the room temperature climbing? Warmth spread through his body and his skin tingled. It felt good. *Really* good. Arousal ramped up in a gradual incline, and Arad found himself thumbing his nipple through his shirt. Each little stroke built a charge that flooded his battery and threatened to overflow. His clothes had never been so confining. Restrictive. Arad attacked his belt. Completely stripping himself from the waist down, he dumped his pants on top of the glitter dress. The recycled air on his bare ass and legs was a blessing.

"Oh, wow. My cock's hard enough to do the work of a crane! That's awesome!"

Swollen and jutting out like a flesh-covered spike, his dick had never been so rigid. He had a fleeting idea to tie a cord around the end and see if he could lift things with it. But no, that was the Syn talking. The color and stiffness were impressive. Arad took a light grip to better examine his organ and was gifted with a hard, pleasurable shudder that quaked him to the core. Never had the sensations been so amazing before. So fantastic, so addictive, he didn't let go as his flesh swelled and pulsed in his tightening fist.

Davis used to make the weirdest, uncontrollable noises in their sessions, and Arad did the same as he made an exploratory stroke. So much glossy fluid dribbled out of the slit. He spread it around, making each slick movement peel away a new layer of his inhibitions. A pantsless, horny onion. Three or four strokes were enough to throw the idea of stopping out of the airlock. Eager and needy like never before, he launched into his task with a new vigor.

Near mindless in ecstasy, he kept pumping until he came loud, crying out at the top of his lungs, and all over Daiko and Serene's sheets. Spraying his DNA to mark the bed as his own made him preen even as his moans echoed in the room's tight confines. He wondered what it would be like if they were still here with him—

"Nope. Full stop." Arad shook that traitorous thought out of his head with a vengeance. "That is definitely the Syn talking."

Several long, tedious minutes were required to calm his breathing. He scooped up the bottle, dumped it in the drawer, and kicked it shut with a scraping bang. "So glad Torrins didn't ever get the nerve to dose me with this junk. Who knows what he would have talked me into? Ha! You missed out, Torrins. Sucker."

The heat still simmered under his skin, but the intensity muted after his orgasm. His cock continued to do its impression of a third leg, but the burning need to couple and rut was gone. A touch of euphoria elevated his mood above normal, lifting the stress from his bones. Now that the edge was off, he'd go back to work. The DemiShou and *Ansariland*'s issues were still waiting to be resolved.

Refusing to glance at the bed's condition, Arad stepped into the hallway and headed to the cargo bay.

Plodding barefoot across the cargo bay's riveted metal floor was oddly comforting instead of outright painful. Every little sensation brought him a touch of joy and pleasure, a sure sign the Syn lurked under the surface. He twisted as he walked to cause his shirt to shift against his skin, the fabric unusually silky. The air circulating brushed through his hair, a caress of his scalp. Audible medical beeps and chimes became a sultry bit of music. Arad found himself evaluating the DemiShou in an entirely inappropriate way. Not that he been blindsided before, but he was slightly obsessed with how the cryotubes' transparent faces allowed near-complete peep show views of their inhabitants.

Hachi's fearsome size continued through every part of his body, including his flaccid junk's prizewinning length and girth. If all bulls were this well hung, it was probably a good thing he'd turned down the bartender the night he met Torrins. Even so, his gaze lingered much longer than it should.

Shichi's scales sat in rows and rows of coarse, serrated nubs covering every inch of his body. Including his now textured dick. Oh my. What an interesting option. Would they score patterns into another person's bare skin? Internally or externally? Strangely, Arad's rampant curiosity kept coming back to that feature until he forced himself to move on. Stupid drug.

Roku's endowment, while more than ample, elicited far less terror. It suited the fine hair covering his perfect musculature that made his body appear so silky. Arad found every centimeter of his physique alluring even as Roku started...to twitch?

The alarm blared as Roku's movements progressed into full seizure. He jerked and flailed, thumping over and over against the container's sides. His muscles swelled in relief, contractions increasing the definition with each pulse. Ropy veins pushed to the surface, threatening to explode at any moment.

All arousal fled, replaced with razors of panic. Arad's heartbeat spiked as he tried to keep it together, knowing he would be useless if he freaked out. The incessant electronic cadence tugged at the braided thread binding his nerves together, making it difficult to concentrate. His attention flew between Roku and the screen, his hand millimeters over the *PAUSE SEQUENCE* and *ABORT* controls. Last time, Hachi's seizures had resolved themselves and everything was fine—

Abruptly Roku slumped in the cryotube, and every health data readout flatlined. The alarm condensed into a single shrill tone reserved for the dying.

"No no no no no..." This wasn't supposed to happen. It's not what happened with Hachi. He was supposed to have time to learn how to save them all.

Not knowing what else to do, Arad slapped the *ABORT* command.

Arad jumped backward as the capsule split open, the top and bottom halves separating like a cracked egg. Chamber fluids gushed out in a wave, splashing the floor and rushing toward the built-in drains nearby. When the tube opened far enough, Roku crumpled and tumbled out into an unseemly heap, arms and legs bent at odd angles. Arad rushed to him, ignoring the pooling liquids splattering his shins and ankles.

"Roku! Roku, wake up!" Shaking the unconscious DemiShou did nothing. Dead weight refused to move. No, not dead. He wasn't allowed to be dead. Arad grabbed a shoulder and heaved with all his might to roll Roku onto his back.

"First aid, first aid, first aid." The myriad of instructions whirled in his head, and there wasn't time to hunt down the tablet somewhere in the cargo bay and confirm them. Arad needed to do this right. And now.

Roku's chest didn't move. It didn't rise and fall like a living man, and Arad couldn't find a pulse at his neck. Hopefully he was checking the right spot. He'd practiced finding his own often enough while he studied. Light glinted off the fluids filling Roku's slack mouth.

"Oh, man, you're drowning." With a grunt, he rolled Roku onto his side and tipped his head, allowing his mouth to drain. "You breathed this stuff fine in the tube. Why not now?" Once the flow stemmed to a faint trickle, Arad slapped him. "Come on! Please! Wake up!" Arad slapped him again.

Nothing happened.

Scrubbing at his face, he cried out in desperation. No higher power would help him now. He had to do the work himself. Arad reached up and grabbed fistfuls of his hair as he raced through the procedure in his head. He could do this. He shoved Roku onto his back and knelt alongside him, praying he had the correct position.

Arad's exhale stuttered. "I hope I'm doing this right."

With one hand over the other, he pumped at the center of Roku's chest, making a wish he was using enough power to do the job. One at a time for a count of thirty. He grabbed Roku's head and sealed his mouth over Roku's. It wasn't easy with his tiger features and thin lower lip, but Arad managed. He blew steadily and with enough force to make Roku's chest rise. Two, one, then repeat.

Over and over, he ran through the steps, praying he had them right. He only stopped as water gurgled up in Roku's mouth, forcing him to turn his head and drain it once again. His arms burned and his eyes blurred with only his grunting efforts filling the room. What he wouldn't give for the alarm to distract him. He'd worked too hard for it to end this way. Arad refused to give up, even though his patient did nothing on his own.

The only thing stemming Arad's tears was the rhythm of two breaths, thirty compressions, two breaths, and cracks were forming in the dam. He wasn't sure how much more stamina he had left. His strength was fading along with his determination to survive. The one thing he'd always held dear and it was failing him.

"I'm so sorry, Roku."

Suddenly, Roku lurched, bucking Arad off with a yelp. The DemiShou rolled over and heaved, spewing all the fluids trapped in his lungs until he gave out a ragged, weakened gasp. The first breath of a newborn. He coughed and sputtered with his face on the wet floor, too weak to hold himself up higher.

Tears laced with relief finally tore free from Arad. He carefully crawled closer, not wanting to startle the groggy DemiShou on the floor.

"Roku, can you hear me?"

Roku swayed back and forth in minuscule movements. His lidded eyes stared at nothing, unfocused and groggy.

"Can you hear me?"

Arad risked reaching out to touch Roku's head, trying to get some response. Roku allowed the contact but barely reacted, almost unaware of it as well. The soaked fur glided between Arad's fingers with the touch of luscious velvet, begging to be stroked. Dense muscle danced underneath the surface.

The medical tech attached to his skin popped off one by one when Arad brushed his hand against them. He traced the unnatural stripes decorating Roku's body with his fingers. They ran down his arms to merge with his neck and back, all the way down to his meaty buttocks. Arad snatched back his hand and averted his wandering eyes. He was perving over a possibly injured man while hunched over Roku with his bare ass hanging out. He convinced himself it was the Syn influencing his behavior, but either way it was damned inappropriate.

Tugging down his shirt hem, Arad stood and stepped backward, trying to maintain a crumbling air of decency. "Um... Hold still. I'll be right back and get you a blanket."

With a jerky, awkward movement, Roku reached out and caught Arad's ankle in his grasp. Uncoordinated his grip might have been, but it was made of unforgiving steel. He gave a sudden pull and Arad lost his balance, dropping to the floor.

Still holding Arad's ankle, Roku shifted forward in a clumsy shuffle, barely sufficient to be called a crawl. Nose flaring, he snorted and sniffed his way up Arad's shin, thigh, and into his groin.

"Whoa! Whatcha doin'?"

Roku's inhales grew stronger, more urgent. A feral yowl seeped out as he opened his jaw and wetted Arad's cock with his wandering tongue.

"Oh, shi—" The word caught itself short as shocks surged through his body and brain, all centered on Roku's lazy but intent slavering. Arad's dick responded instantly, the Syn having turned his normal recovery time into nothing. The drug used to fuel Davis's marathon sex binges. A cycle of excitement, plateau, orgasm, and limited resolution to be repeated until his body gave up. Arad had taken half of Davis's usual amount and assumed the effect would be far less. Perhaps not.

"Don't..."

A fluttering of unease captured his splintered inhibitions. This should not be happening. Arad grabbed at Roku's head, but instead of shoving him away, he found himself pulling the DemiShou closer, rubbing his swollen, eager cock all over Roku's mouth and face, desperate for more.

Fevered rushes struck hard, far faster than rubbing one out earlier. Without warning, he peaked and toppled. In a wordless shout, every muscle seized as he came. Streaks of semen coated his shirt and Roku's face, and it did nothing to slow things down for either of them as the Demi licked up the mess.

Roku lifted Arad's leg as he rooted deeper, his snout and tongue forcing Arad to turn over on his stomach to avoid being folded in half. The new position allowed Roku to push forward and separate the halves of Arad's buttocks with his free hand and face. With unfettered access, he wasted no time digging deep, lapping the tender iris into a center of quaking need.

"Stop..." Arad's pitiful plea was unconvincing to his own ears as he pushed backward like a desperate two-credit whore.

Sex had always been a transaction for Arad, no matter how pleasurable. A way to afford food. A roof over his head for the night. Acts of trade of any variety. Hooking up with someone exclusively to chase a sexual high? Never. It had always been an exchange of services. Always. How was he supposed to handle walking through this foreign territory?

Or handle the disappointment when the treatment ended?

Roku stopped long enough to climb Arad's body, still stumbling and groggy until he clamped his jaw over Arad's collar and shoulder. Sharp teeth didn't pierce his skin, but when Roku's steely arms circled Arad's chest and arms, he knew Roku didn't want him going anywhere. The rest of the DemiShou's body settled on top of Arad, with an obviously large and hard penis landing between his spit-slick cheeks. With a shift of his hips, Roku's solid member humped the wet channel between Arad's haunches at a maddening slow and frustrating pace.

Arad should have been scared. Roku was a fierce stranger with all the power. The unforgiving metal and rivets in the floor should leave him in pain. But the Syn morphed all of it into heady sensations, and the more he got, the more he craved. And the more he urged it on.

"Don't stop..."

Canting his hips on each upstroke, Arad hoped to capture the slippery knob and force it inside to no avail. Held down tight in feral arms, he lacked the clearance to do much more than feel each juicy slide rub across his opening and moan uncontrollably. The slow stroke allowed his feverish mind to map out each ridge and vein, teasing him into a frenzy.

Roku's speed didn't increase, but each rut strengthened. The growling against Arad's shoulder vibrated deeper through his body, meeting his crushed cock until everything swelled into climax. Roku squeezed Arad tight and, with a muffled roar, went rigid. Searing fluid shot up Arad's lower back and flooded between his buttocks, ultimately dripping down his sac in hot rivulets. All the conflicted feelings and ramped-up tactile sensitivity triggered Arad again. He cried out as he came, smearing the floor beneath them.

Without releasing Arad, Roku's huffing reduced to normal breaths until he fell asleep with Arad still trapped in his arms. Then he began to...purr?

The guttural chainsaw reverberated into Arad's shoulder and chest. It lulled him, drowning his anxiety on the harsh metal floor. Exhaustion dragged him into sleep, and he allowed it because he was sure Roku wasn't letting him up anytime soon.

And strangely, he felt safer than he should have.

Chapter Nine

Arad's eyes fluttered awake. Had minutes or hours passed? Roku's mass and iron embrace still pinned him to the floor. Two rows of teeth continued to gently rest around Arad's drool-soaked shoulder. Rucked up from earlier, his shirt was chilled and clammy from wicking moisture off the DemiShou's fur, hopefully meaning too much time hadn't passed. None of the sensations were morphing into weird arousal, so the Syn must have worn off.

All kinds of things told him he should be terrified, but the extra weight was less like a cage and more like a warm, dozy shelter. Roku's powerful arms restrained him without constricting him, only tightening with an unhappy rumble when he tried to wiggle free, like someone taking a treasured possession away from a child. On odd analogy, but the only one that came to mind.

Arad should have been more alarmed by his predicament. If this were Davis, he would have elbowed himself free right away, safety be damned. Instead, he found himself basking in the afterglow of the first sex in ages where he'd enjoyed it more than the other person involved. Not exactly a stellar example of good mental health.

The opportunity to assess his wayward brain ended as Roku shifted and woke with a gasp, probably from stuck-together body parts peeling apart. His jaw released Arad as he straightened his arms against the floor, lifting his weight. With a confused, inarticulate grunt, he lurched backward and away. A chill rushed over Arad's skin as he rolled over, taking all the warm feelings he'd woken up with it.

Roku sat on his feet, corded muscles twitching as his wild eyes fixed on Arad. Distressed, feral noises rumbled out of him. Now able to see Roku unhindered, Arad saw the bestial side hidden during his hibernation, the dangerous unknown in his midst. It stoked Arad's primal urge to run. To flee. But even slugs were smart enough not to run from a predator.

However, the longer Arad stayed put, the less enraged Roku appeared. The tiger's skittish gaze grew glossy with each passing minute, his face sagging. His broad shoulders weren't hunched, poised to pounce. They shivered as if struggling to hold the weight of his huge arms.

Roku was somehow monstrous and vulnerable at the same time. Shattered. Lost.

Like curling up behind a dumpster in the rain, waiting for the meds to kick in.

The tables were turned, and now he was Roku's Sketch. Stamping down his unease took practice, a necessary skill for even a part-time hustler. It didn't vanish, but he smothered it long enough to paste on a façade of confidence. They may have been trapped on board together, but he wasn't letting go of the promise he made to help the DemiShou. Someday, Arad's ethics would be the death of him.

Raising both hands, Arad tried to project calm. "It's okay, Roku. Everything's all right."

"Who are you?" Roku growled. He clasped a hand to his own throat. "What's wrong with my voice?"

"Oh! You can speak!"

Annoyed ridges crinkled Roku's snout. "What? Why would you say that?"

"Sorry. It's been a weird week. You've been through a few changes."

Feeling abruptly stupid, Arad tried to maintain a casual tone. The tiger hybrid was spooked enough. No need to add to his anxiety.

Roku's baffled gaze swept to the ceiling, the walls, and Arad again yet hadn't turned far enough to see the cryotubes behind him. "Where am I?"

"Oh, man. That's gonna take some explaining."

"You called me Roku. Why?"

"Um…long story. What should I call you?"

Roku opened his mouth to speak and paused. His eyes lost focus as he searched himself, brow creasing as he dug deeper. Arad waited, watching Roku's feline features darken into a growing despair as if he came up with a big fat nothing. From his expression, more than his name was missing.

"You know, it's okay. You can be Roku until you come up with something better."

"What's wrong with me?"

The last status on Roku's monitor before the seizure had read *SYNAPTIC*. That meant brain cells. Or neurons firing. Or something else Arad should have paid closer attention to in biology class. The capsule had processed his body and had been in the middle of processing his grey matter? The idea made him a little queasy. Did something go wrong and give him amnesia? Or were they scrubbing him and starting over? No option springing from Arad's fertile imagination was good.

Roku wrapped his powerful arms around himself, curling forward as if trying to shrink and escape. Every glance and every movement screamed out his disorientation.

Marshaling his nerve, Arad covered his concern. "You just woke up. Give it time."

"Your voice. It's familiar."

How many hours had he spent watching over the sleepers, sometimes reading the manuals out loud like a storybook to pass the time and keep it interesting? More than Arad wanted to admit.

"I talked to you a lot while you slept. Didn't know if you heard me."

"Was I sick?"

"I'm not sure. You were in a kind of coma, I guess."

Roku opened his mouth to say more but stopped, suddenly fixated on his hands. He raised them for a clearer view, lightly stroking his fingertips over the sheer fur. Spreading his fingers wide, he followed the unnatural stripes running up his arms, rolling them slowly to see as much as possible. His breath stuttered into a soft gasp, one step away from shedding a tear. It wrenched at Arad's heart.

"What happened to me?" The shiver in Roku's voice unnerved him.

"I wish I knew. I don't understand what was going on."

He raised his head to stare Arad in the eyes. "Do we know each other?"

"Sort of? Maybe?"

"How?"

The word *biblically* came to mind, but it wasn't completely accurate, so he struck it down as poor phrasing. "I'm not sure how to answer that."

Roku cast his gaze down at himself and paused, as if finally aware of his nudity. He scratched at the dried fluids around his groin and smelled his fingers. When his attention came around, he sniffed in Arad's direction.

"You smell like... Did we...?"

"You don't remember?"

Roku's eyes widened as he took in Arad's lack of pants and the stains on the shirt. Recognition flashed across his tiger face, and there it was. That terrifying moment when a person wakes up and the drugs have worn off, and they're forced to realize what sleaze they'd been up to the night before.

"Oh, no."

"Okay... Yeah...you remember." Mildly humiliated, Arad fingered his shirt hem, tugging it lower as if a hooker could make himself decent. He tried to be nonchalant, but Roku was paying attention.

"Did I hurt you?" Only the cargo bay's acoustics allowed Arad to hear the fragile, horrified whisper.

"No."

"But I scared you."

Scratching his head, Arad's face burned as he tried to find an answer. "That's not how I'd describe it. I wasn't exactly sober at the time, and I'm pretty sure I egged you on. I don't think either one of us was in our right head."

"I...I...don't understand."

The questions and Arad's conflicted thoughts made the awkward scene heavier still. They needed a chance to get settled. Somewhere without the evidence and memories of their first encounter getting in the way. Roku needed a touch of stability.

"Right now, it's not important. I don't know about you, but I don't usually run around with my junk hanging out when I have guests over. As if I have guests. Let's go get cleaned up and see if we can't find you some clothes." Arad stood and offered his hand. "Roku? C'mon."

Tentatively, Roku took Arad's hand and allowed himself to be pulled to his full height with a featherweight tug. Averting his eyes, Arad took care not to ogle Roku's rather robust physique. The DemiShou appeared meek and confused, if lacking even the barest shred of modesty. Barest. An accurate word. With his free hand, Arad attempted to pull his shirt down over his goods without being obvious.

At a cautious pace, he led them through the container maze and out of the bay. Emerging into the hallway didn't lessen Roku's disorientation or his wandering gaze.

"Is this a spacecraft?" Roku asked with a timid stammer.

"Yes. Welcome to the *Ansariland*. I am your captain, Arad. It's a pleasure to have you on board." In Red

District, holographic brothel barkers would try to entice people with their carnival sales pitches into their establishments to pilfer what little funds they had. Arad had refused to work for any of them. Imitating their upbeat manner and programmed speech patterns wasn't his greatest skill, but the mood needed lifting, and Roku radiated misery. More since their raunchy introduction skirted the boundaries of normal consent. "We'll do a complete ship tour soon enough. For now, we both need a turn in the bath. Follow me, sir."

Without saying anything, Roku shuffled along, staying close and keeping pace with little urging. Arad continued to jabber as they walked, pointing out items of interest. Anything to fill the uncomfortable quiet. It made him feel like an idiot, and he breathed a sigh of relief when they arrived.

Torrins had told him he'd removed the wall between the modest gym and lavatory to make the space larger. End result: an absolute lack of privacy outside of the three toilets and three shower stalls. Typical pervy behavior he expected from the original captain.

Like everywhere else, Roku scanned the room, but this time, he froze as he caught sight of himself in the mirror over the sink.

His hold on Arad's hand firmed as he locked eyes with his own reflection. Arad waited for him to reach up and touch his face to inspect the changes, but instead he only stared at himself as his eyes widened, becoming wetter with every passing second. A tremor built along his feline jaw.

"C'mon. Shower time." Arad patted Roku's shoulder hard enough to interrupt his attachment to his reflection.

Roku turned away from the mirror, cringing subtly as he peeked from the corner of his eye.

Arad closed Roku into one of the shower stalls and, when the water was running, stripped off his shirt and claimed one of his own. The steam built quickly into familiar rolling tendrils. Arad dunked his head under the spray, trying to drench the chaos ricocheting in his skull. Hopefully it would also wash away the tacky physical evidence of his and Roku's encounter. His scalp was beginning to scald when Roku's frustrated murmur drifted between the stalls.

"Why won't it wash off?"

Reaching out with his hearing only brought the sound of their showers to Arad's ears. The unease rose into his chest.

"Roku? Are you okay?"

Pause.

"Roku?"

Pause.

"I'm fine," he mumbled.

Hardly convincing, it spurred Arad to finish first.

He scrubbed himself clean and exited, wanting to be available when Roku was done. The second shower stopped, and Roku emerged. The fine fur slicked to his skin clung to every substantial muscle and sinew except for the matted patch on his forearm, like he'd scrubbed the hell out of it. Arad passed him a towel from the dispenser and went about drying himself instead of mapping the black bands on Roku's limbs and back. Now was not the time to notice that the pattern reminded him of an abstract circuit board. Definitely deliberate design.

"Let's get you some clothes."

Leading Roku into the corridor, he soon landed at Tank's old room. He let himself in with his all-access rank pass and rummaged through the drawers. He'd never been allowed inside before, so he had to start somewhere. It was much tidier than he would have expected.

"I'm not sure if anything will fit, but this is our best shot."

Roku drifted inside, his bulk dwarfing the room. "Who's room is this?"

"It was Tank's. He's gone. There's no point in making this a shrine when we can make use of what's left behind."

"How did he die?"

"Same as the rest of them. Shot by corporate military squad while being a bunch of backstabbing pricks."

Roku didn't ask for more details, and Arad was thankful. He'd revealed more than he had intended. Torrins's double cross still chafed, but settling Roku into some clothes took a higher priority. The drawer next to the closet squealed open, revealing a stack of kilts. Jackpot. He sifted through the pile, searching for the largest, and held it out to Roku.

"Hope you don't mind, Tank only wore kilts. Which is probably for the best because you're still bigger than him, and he was huge. If he wore pants, I don't think they'd fit, and you'd be stuck running around naked." Arad found himself needing to clear his throat. "Which would be bad."

Roku took the kilt and wrapped it around his waist. It rode shorter than normal, but at least he was on the road to decency. Before Arad hunted down a shirt, Roku dragged the oversized blanket off the bed and threw it over his shoulders, forming it into a makeshift robe. With the edges brushing the floor, the blanket covered every inch of his body like the nun from the Saints of Seven Sins on Bleacher Street who shouted damnation from atop an upside-down bucket at any and all who took pleasure or profited in *sins of the flesh*. She targeted Arad a lot.

Pulling the worn fabric over his head, Roku fashioned a hood, allowing only the tip of his nose to be visible. He clutched the robe near his throat to cinch it closed.

"All right. I'm good for now."

Covered head to toe, Roku appeared and sounded noticeably calmer. Arad wasn't sure if that was a good sign, but he'd sort Roku's mental state once he had pants on again. The shirt in his hand was wrecked with bodily fluid and whatever constituted that amniotic fluid stuff Roku had been floating in. He also didn't want to explain why his trousers were balled on the floor in Daiko and Serene's quarters rather than his own.

Roku followed without instruction as Arad took them to his own room and threw the dirty shirt aside. After wrenching open the one drawer holding his possessions, he pulled out his extra pair of trousers. He ignored the obvious presence of an extra body watching him as he stepped into the garment. Buckling the waist, he finally felt less exposed and a little more like himself.

"This room smells like you. And someone else."

Arad turned, finding Roku staring at the bed. "I had to share this room with the original captain. Accommodations were tight."

The blanket hood hid Roku's face but not his sniffing. "More than shared." An unhappy growl rumbled out of him.

Perfect. He'd spent years being shamed for making necessary choices for his survival, and now he was getting it from a total stranger on his own ship. Once upon a time, he believed himself jaded enough not to take offense over other people's opinions. Apparently not.

Arad turned and purposely spoke over his shoulder to keep from doing something more rude. "One, what I did before you woke up is none of your business. Two, he's dead like the rest of them, so it doesn't matter."

Since he needed to use the laundry anyways, Arad shopped through Torrins's effects for a shirt. He jerked open a second drawer, then pushed aside a series of phase pistols to find one of the captain's old shirts. He swam in it—Torrins had been much larger than Arad—but after spending so long running around starkers, overdoing the coverage wasn't so awful an idea.

"That shirt smells like him."

"He couldn't take it with him, so there's no point in letting it rot. I don't have enough to go around."

A tiger-shaped shadow drifted over Arad and the drawer as Roku moved closer. "Why are there so many weapons in here?"

Arad shrugged. "Torrins smuggled stuff on the ship. The man was practically a pirate. I guess he expected a lot of trouble."

"You're a smuggler?"

Pivoting around, Arad spoke deliberately to make sure Roku understood. "No. The original captain was a smuggler."

"What did he smuggle? Weapons? Narcotics?"

"Apparently DemiShou."

"Why?"

"No one told me." Sighing, Arad closed his eyes, trying to contain his frustration. "Look, I'll tell you what I know, but I think we could both use a meal. Let's get some food and go from there."

Thankfully, Roku didn't press further as they made their way to the galley. Survival was a capricious game, and any level of judgment over how Arad played it annoyed him. Hunger proved a stronger motivation, and both of them dug into their meals in relative silence. Roku's covered mass was almost comical at the small table seated across from Arad. He was on his third noodle bowl and his second protein bar when his eating finally slowed. Who knew when his last solid meal had been?

Arad started calculating food inventories in his head. At three meals a day, years would dwindle to months without some rationing. A new wrinkle in the survival scenario. "At this rate, I'm going to have to get the ship fixed."

"Are we close to port?"

"I don't know."

"Where are we heading?"

An indelicate snort escaped Arad. "You're making an assumption the engines are running."

"We're adrift?" Roku set down his utensils, the remaining food somehow forgotten.

"Yep."

"How did that happen?" Tinged with authority, the question reminded Arad of the officer presiding over the shanty demolition on the docks. It wasn't attractive.

Defenses up, Arad's snark turned on. "It's an old story. Cabin boy gets hired to be the fall guy for smugglers when corporate soldiers come looking for their stolen property. Crew escapes and gets vaporized. To avoid corporate prison or worse, cabin boy does a space fold jump inside a star's gravity well."

Roku's voice rose in shock. "That's crazy. A star's gravity would unbalance the fold. There's no telling what would happen."

"That's what the monitor warning said."

"And you did it anyways?"

Arad stood and dropped his empty bowl into the sink to deal with later. "The warship had already incinerated the crew's shuttle to keep them from escaping. I wasn't about to be next. It was a rough jump, and unfortunately it toasted the external sensors, including navigation."

"What did the crew steal?" Pure offense colored Roku's words, as if he grew up a law-abiding citizen who never had to bend the rules to get by. Arad was curious how much of his past still existed since his personality had survived his cryotube.

"From what I can tell, four highly illegal, freshly cooked DemiShou."

Sitting up tall, Roku stilled for a long moment. "Four? There are others?"

"One of them was already gone before I found you guys, but…" Tilting his head, Arad narrowed his eyes in confusion. "Didn't you notice them in the cargo bay?"

Even under the shade of his hood, Roku's gaze became piercing. "I was distracted by the young man under me."

Warmth flooded Arad's cheeks. "Oh. Yeah."

Roku pushed his bowl forward, signaling the end of his meal. His shoulders swelled and he lowered his head with a deep exhale. "Arad, I'd like to apologize. You've done nothing but help, and I've done so many unforgivable things."

"You just woke up—"

"It doesn't matter."

"Yes. It does." Roku's earnest disbelief was an unfamiliar, if not hard to believe, reaction. People didn't care about slugs.

Shrugging, Arad scoffed. "Roku, you've treated me better than most men I've known."

Roku slammed a fist to the table, making Arad, the bowls, and the utensils jump. "That doesn't make it any better! No one should be allowed to... It's not right. I may be out of sorts, but you deserved...you deserve better than that."

The fractures in Roku's voice carried a sincerity Arad hadn't known in years. He could count the number of times any man he'd ever known had apologized to him and meant it on the fingers of one hand and still have fingers left over afterward. Including his father. It disarmed his aggravation and gave Roku an air of integrity Arad had little experience with.

Leaning backward, Roku attempted to put distance between them. "I'm sorry. I scared you again."

"You surprised me. That's not the same thing." Squinting, Arad scrutinized Roku, trying to understand him. Gallant men usually showed him their seedy side, yet once he was fully coherent, all Roku had done was have high ethical standards and not like the fact that Arad had slept with Torrins. Arad wasn't happy with it either. On top of that, Roku was consumed with regret. In fact, he appeared more disturbed by their introductory sex scene than Arad. The least Arad could do was accept Roku's polite manner and grant him a little peace of mind. "No one's cared about what happens to me in years. Thank you."

With a polite nod, the square of Roku's shoulders relaxed a fraction. It made the blanket shift open, which he immediately pulled closed. "If you don't mind, I'd like to see the other...others like me, Captain."

Hearing the title made Arad grin. "All right. If you're sure you're up for it, let's go."

Chapter Ten

"This maze is ridiculous."

Roku vibrated with a newfound impatience yet allowed Arad to lead them through the crates hiding Torrins's scheme. As they approached the bay's open space, Roku hesitated, hand clutching one of the crate's edges.

"I had nothing to do with it. You look a little edgy. It's okay if you don't want to do this now," Arad said.

The blanket had fallen open enough to see the fear in Roku's wide eyes. "No. I need to do this." He pulled the cloak tight, firmed his shoulders, and soldiered forward.

A hazy film left behind by various fluids from Roku's emergence coated the floor leading to the drain. Arad had slept in many filthy places over the years, but the sight made him cringe. He had a few standards. Aches and new bruises reminded him of the familiar mattress off to the side that he'd wished they'd landed on during the more embarrassing portion of their introduction. He hoped Roku would be too engrossed in the sleeping Demis and the cryotubes to need an explanation.

"Why is there a mattress here?"

And...why would Arad get what he wanted?

"I spend a lot of time watching over you and them."

Inching closer, Roku took a good look at Hachi from top to bottom. "You watched us?"

"Watched over you. What's the point?"

"They're naked." The implicit *we* wasn't lost in that sentence.

Rolling his eyes, Arad laughed. "It's a lot less sexy than it sounds. I brought in a mattress because all the other furniture is bolted down."

Neither said a word as Roku moved between capsules, his fingers barely brushing the surfaces as if he was scared to touch the machines and make it all too solid. The blanket may have hidden his face, but the tension through his arms and back was unmistakable. Shichi held his secrets as well as the mute Hachi. The next tube still sat open like some mechanical egg, and Roku's hands stopped short of contacting the interior.

"What happened to me?"

"I wish I knew. I didn't know you guys were on board until after Torrins and the crew got blown to hell. Best I can tell is you're stolen corporate property. They must have bankrupted a few hospitals putting you together."

"It's illegal to manufacture sentient beings. DemiShou, they're..." Roku cleared his throat. "We're not a commodity."

"Corporate military killed six people to collect you lot without breaking a sweat. I imagine they don't much care."

Apparently content with exploring his own container, Roku moved to the last, empty and dark. "There's one missing."

"Yeah. Go was gone before I found you. From what I pieced together, something happened, and he died. Maybe he had a seizure like you did, and they couldn't save him."

"Maybe they didn't try."

"It's possible, but I'm trying to believe the old crew weren't complete monsters."

"They left you behind to face the corporates."

"I said I'm trying. Didn't say I'd succeeded."

"You succeeded in saving me."

"I couldn't sit and watch you die."

"They would have."

Arad didn't argue that point. The Demis appeared to be little more than a cash crop for Torrins and the crew. A lot of effort had been made to hide them for casual inspection, but it didn't look like they'd spent much time regarding their maintenance, since even the med bed didn't have a DemiShou module installed.

Roku was so enrapt with his methodical examination his hood slipped, leaving his face exposed. He went over each unconscious Demi and their capsules, making sure to read the details on both monitors.

"I see why you keep calling me by number."

"What?"

"Go, Roku, Shichi, Hachi. Five, Six, Seven, Eight."

"Oh. I didn't realize." Awkward moment number 4,289. Language studies had ended when Arad arrived at the workhouse.

The broader truth festered in the pit of Arad's stomach like sour eggs. This group wasn't the only batch of

DemiShou in this project or whatever it was. He could only guess where numbers one through four were. Or if there were more than eight. "Would you rather I call you something else?"

"No. It doesn't bother me when you call me Roku. It's nice to have a name."

Roku didn't share any information he'd gleaned from the monitors and moved to the Demis themselves. While Roku wasn't a blank vegetable, his amnesia might be a sensitive issue. Corrupted Syn users Arad had met got defensive over memory gaps after a binge. He wasn't sure how deep he should probe the issue so soon or how Roku might react. They barely knew each other. Perhaps he'd test it in small doses.

"Do you recognize them?"

Roku huffed softly. "I don't recognize myself."

Arad sighed, understanding Roku's frustration. "I mean, do they seem familiar at all?"

"No. Not even a tiny bit." Disappointment flickered across his feline eyes.

Arad placed a comforting hand on Roku's arm, which softened at the contact. "Maybe they were no one to you. There's nothing saying there's a connection between any of you besides the process."

"How can I be sure? I don't know what the process is."

"I'm not much of an expert on that either."

"You know more than I do. Tell me everything."

Arad hedged. Sharing information was dangerous on the streets when everyone took care of themselves first.

Trust didn't come automatically. Also, how would Roku digest what little he knew? It had only been hours since his awakening, and how stable could he be? Arad had only pressed him carefully as it was. There was no question Arad had no means to restrain the tiger if something popped in his brain and he psychoed out.

Oddly enough, Roku appeared structured and sane enough to handle bad news, even if he was in the worst position of his life.

In the end, Arad had to decide what he would want if their positions were reversed. He would hope someone would help and hopefully save him. Or give him the chance to save himself. Like Sketch had.

"All right. I'll tell you what I know."

Roku stood silent while Arad gathered his details. Deciding which beginning to launch from was difficult. He kicked himself for divulging his degrading position as cabin boy earlier, so he didn't want to expand on those details. There had to be a more relevant—and less damning—event to start from.

"After the crew died, the ship updated me to captain. Since I had access to everything, I started exploring everything I'd been barred from."

"Like the cargo bay."

"Yeah. As the scapegoat, I couldn't be trusted to know you guys were here."

Still examining the cryotubes, Roku nodded. "Pretty standard tactics for smugglers."

"There weren't any data files for DemiShou, so I kept watch. Hachi had a seizure. It passed and he quieted down like nothing happened, so when you had yours after your status switched over to *SYNAPTIC* and you crashed, I aborted the program and got you out."

Roku fingered the edges of Shichi's monitor, careful not to touch any controls. "My status switched over?"

"Yeah. From *BIOLOGICAL*."

"Did I change during that period?"

"Physically. Your animal traits became more and more pronounced." Arad read the remaining active monitors. Hachi and Shichi both were in the *SYNAPTIC* stage of their development. How much longer did they have until they were complete?

"How did the machine do that?"

"Roku, I'm a mechanic who used to live on the streets." Ignorance made Arad's voice rise a notch. "I didn't build this thing, and it didn't come with an instruction manual."

"I'm sorry. I only want to understand."

Arad sighed, dropping down to a more reasonable volume. "Yeah, that's fair. I know how scary it gets when everything you knew is gone. I want to give you answers, but I only know so much. They don't teach this kind of stuff in a workhouse."

With earnest intent, Roku focused that much more on his sleeping brethren. His intense concentration bordered on the theatrics of streetwise psychics, except those hustlers were only trying to fleece funds out of weak-willed pedestrians. Roku was desperate to understand his existence.

Another wave of curiosity buffeted Arad. "Do you remember what it was like? In the tube?"

A slow pause ended with Roku's quiet, haunted words. "Darkness. Silence. Burning through every pore." He glanced over at Arad. "I remember a kind voice in the distance."

"Really? What did it say?"

Roku shook his head. "It was too distant to make out, but it made the fire bearable at times. How long was I in there?"

"I never saw a time-stamp, but it's been a couple weeks since I found you guys."

He didn't ask more, but Roku's scrutiny of the DemiShou intensified, becoming more critical.

"They're strong. You don't make something this powerful without a purpose."

"What's yours?"

"I have no idea. It's like there's claw marks across my brain, leaving bloody scars caked over my memories." Roku brushed his fingers along his temple. "I can tell they're there, but they're buried under these...wounds."

"I wanted to ask before, who you were, but when you couldn't remember your name... You looked so hurt. I figured we can get back to that later."

"Thank you."

Roku processed every detail. Analyzing. Not what one would expect from a zombified tiger. A sharp intellect gleamed from behind the DemiShou's eyes.

"Whatever they did, it didn't scrub your brain completely. You walk, you talk. You know how to do things. You have a personality. If they did, I'd think you'd be more childish and drooling everywhere."

"True. I haven't been lobotomized. Not exactly. All of my knowledge is being kind of fickle, like looking at something out of the corner of your eye. You know it's there, but it slips away every time you try to focus on it."

Another round of silence was filled only by the lyrical notes of the cryotubes. Arad wanted to ask a question but worried about crashing the solemn moment and upsetting Roku. He'd been through so much. However, his curiosity had been scratching at the back of his skull all day, and it needed saying.

"When you woke up, you were kind of...feral. Do you still feel that?"

Roku turned, his gaze meeting Arad's. Guilt spread across his feline face. Arad had asked with a purpose, and Roku caught the underlining intent without specifics. He hadn't wanted to mention how Roku lost control when they met.

"If I think about it, I can tell it's new, something added. Everything is brighter, sharper, more primal, more black and white. I can feel the feral cravings prowling under the surface. At the same time, it feels completely natural, like it was always there, woven into me. And then I see my reflection and know I'll never be myself again. I'm not sure how else to describe it."

"The animal part. Is it dangerous?"

He reached out to Arad, possibly in comfort, but stopped his hand short. "It's not separate from me. It is me. But, no, I'm not dangerous. Not to you."

The admission satisfied Arad more than it should, but Roku hadn't actually hurt him. The circumstances were incredibly embarrassing, and regret stained every inch of

Roku's composure. He was being far more honorable than the sort Arad was accustomed to dealing with. Usually, he didn't trust people like that. Usually.

"All of this makes me wonder who you were before this happened."

Roku's voice became all too distant. "Me too."

Hachi twitched in his tube, his massive muscles flexing, and his horns tapped against the glass in his tight confines before he went still once again. Not a seizure, but the brief event stiffened Roku's shoulders.

"I don't know what I am or what I'm supposed to be. But I know even less about them." Roku pressed the *PAUSE* command on Hachi's panel and did the same to Shichi's.

"What are you doing?"

"Making sure we don't have any more surprises."

Arad grabbed Roku's arm and tugged him around to face him. "I don't want to hurt them."

"Neither do I."

"How do you know this won't?" Releasing his arm, Arad stared into Roku's eyes, demanding him to prove his point. Too many weeks of vigilance had passed to break his promise over a rash decision. Roku's reasoning needed to be solid.

"I'd like to believe whoever did this to us wouldn't have added such a feature if it would risk their profits."

"I guess so..." It made sense. Controlling the DemiShou's awakenings would be impossible without a method to stall the process until the timing was right.

"Until we know more, they should keep."

Arad peered into Hachi's capsule, looking for any sign of distress. The bull slumbered, unaware of the discussion or his incubation being put on hold.

"Are you sure?"

"We've already seen what happened when I woke up unexpectedly. If something went wrong, I don't know if I could protect you from both of them."

Chapter Eleven

Behind the bedroom time panel's cracked surface, an amber four ticked over into a five, signifying yet another lost minute. In the near darkness, Arad counted it seventy-three times, hoping the mindless activity would drift him off to sleep. Make that seventy-four. The day had sapped his every gram of energy, but he tossed and turned as ideas flooded across his waking dreams in bright waves of DemiShou color.

After hitting *PAUSE*, Arad had insisted on staying with the DemiShou, paranoid of a new seizure or episode playing out he wasn't prepared for. He wasn't happy Roku had made the decision without his input but admitted it was a smart move. The DemiShou were an unknown quantity. Roku's comment about being made for a purpose kept repeating. What purpose? Somehow Arad had a hard time believing such powerful males were made to be peaceful entertainers. Plus, how would each of them react to coming out of stasis? Roku had turned out to be infuriatingly honest, but Arad's instincts weren't flagging any outright malice.

In the end, Arad opted for increasing his safety chances. Hachi and Shichi could wait. However, he continued to watch over them. Arad insisted on it. Roku didn't protest. Siting on the mattress, Arad distracted himself with technical manuals on his tablet he barely had the focus to read, and Roku kept quiet company while standing watch. Conversation stayed limited to the other DemiShou's conditions as Arad absorbed the additional changes in his surroundings, and Roku appeared content to think. He made a point to keep his feline traits covered, which sparked Arad's sympathy. No one should be ashamed of appearance traits beyond their control.

Neither man left the other alone, whether for need of company or lack of trust, he couldn't say. They stayed in the cargo bay for the duration, only leaving briefly for food or water breaks, until he and Roku both were too tired to stay upright. Thankfully nothing alarming happened.

"You can have Tank's old room because let's be honest, he's not using it anymore. Take any of the clothes that fit."

Roku wordlessly agreed with a nod, his face hidden beneath the hood. Arad had managed to read up enough during their watch to add Roku into the system to activate the doors, but he stood before the threshold, hesitating to enter.

"It's all yours. Have a good night."

Only turning his head to face Arad, Roku stood still, his eyes sad and silent. It made Arad feel weird. Giving him his own space was a good thing, right? Hating the dead quiet, he left for his own quarters, sensing Roku watching him the whole way. Deep down, a growing well of discomfort sparked as Arad closed his door, glancing over his shoulder to find Roku still standing in the hall.

Now, that discomfort had swollen into a writhing mass of conflict.

Rewinding and replaying out the day, Roku had been polite, attentive, and far more centered than expected given the situation. However, when he first woke, the beast had reared its head and taken what it wanted. He hadn't hurt Arad. Far from it. Given the Syn running through his veins, an argument could be made Arad had encouraged the scene. At some points, he'd certainly urged it on, and he'd definitely enjoyed it. How messed up was that?

It made sense to keep a wall between them at night. Didn't it? Roku was still a stranger, no matter how heartbroken he may have been when Arad had left him behind.

Maybe he wasn't ready to be on his own? He'd stayed nearby all day, not crowding but not leaving Arad alone either.

Arad rubbed his sleepless eyes. With his luck, Roku was still haunting the—

"Oh, shit."

Throwing off the covers, Arad climbed out of bed. He took three long, slow breaths and tapped the door lock. The door wrenched itself open, startling Roku.

His makeshift cloak puddled around him, Roku sat outside the door, looking awkward at being found in the middle of the night. The innate strength in his face was soft like heated wax, melting despite his efforts to stay awake.

Arad hated his intuition as times, but it had saved his life on more than one occasion. "You've been out here all night, haven't you?"

"Sorry. I didn't mean to disturb you." Roku's growl was all sandpapery and coarse. Arad didn't miss how his apology managed to avoid actually answering Arad's question.

"Can't sleep?"

Again, he gave no real answer, only a poor shrug so minimal Arad almost missed it. Weariness slumped Roku's body as he blinked hard to open his lidded eyes.

"Have you even tried?"

Roku's eyes shimmered and he closed his mouth into a thin line. A tiny tremor chased his lips as if uttering the truth was a burden he couldn't bear. So he didn't.

Logic and self-preservation rattled inside Arad, telling him to turn around, go back inside alone, and prevent any misstep. But no matter how he'd lived for so many years, being heartless to someone he'd pledged to help wasn't part of him. "C'mon. You can crash in here."

Roku leaned forward for a moment, then settled even deeper against the wall. "I don't think I should. I don't know if it's safe."

Guilt left a sour aftertaste in Arad's mouth. Despite his obvious fear of isolation, his need to be nearby, Roku echoed all of Arad's concerns. He continued to protect Arad like a decent and honorable person. The very thing Arad swore to do for the DemiShou.

"Roku, I'm going to be really pissed if I have to stand out here all night. Get in already."

Arms crossed over his chest, Arad waited in the doorway until Roku finally stood, sluggish with an invisible weight. The DemiShou dipped his head, refusing to meet Arad's eyes as he entered the bedroom. For good or ill, Arad allowed the door to close behind them.

He stepped past Roku and climbed into bed. In the minimal light, Roku hedged, clutching his blanket tighter as he stared at Arad in a bed large enough to fit them both. It might be a snug fit with his size—Roku dwarfed Torrins—but they'd manage.

"I'll stay right here. This is fine." Voice shaking, Roku turned and curled up on the floor. Back pressed against the bed, he was as close to Arad as possible without sharing the mattress. He wrestled with his blanket and pulled it over his neck and ears. Arad threw his own pillow down to Roku, which after a quick sniff he didn't hesitate to claim.

"Thank you."

Arad stayed silent as he dragged his covers to his chin and pushed Torrins's old pillow into position under his head. If they both found some rest, it would be worth it.

However, he found it impossible to ignore the presence of another man in the room. The gravity of body mass. Additional inhales and exhales. Combined with the extra heartbeat, it made a palpable force holding the power of sleep at bay. Restlessness edged Roku's silhouette no matter how many times the amber numbers turned over.

"Are you okay?" Arad whispered.

"I'm fine."

Every few minutes, Roku shifted. Hard to tell in the dark, but Arad was sure he'd been wiping at his eyes. Gentle sniffling couldn't be smothered by the blanket.

Arad reached over and laid a hand on Roku's back, which immediately stiffened. The flinch nearly startled him, but he managed not to move away, convinced Roku needed the touch more than anything. "Don't worry. It's safe to sleep here. I'll make sure you wake up in the morning."

"You promise?" The quaver in Roku's voice mirrored the shake of his body.

Arad nearly choked. As much as he wanted to comfort Roku, he only had the nerve to offer a few simple words. "I promise."

"O...Okay."

Without moving his hand, Arad resisted the urge to pet the tiger. This time it was his turn to stand watch over a DemiShou. The tension in Roku's shoulder ebbed and he settled, the day's exhaustive pace finally taking its toll. Only when Roku's breathing steadied and he began to purr did Arad finally allow himself to fall asleep.

Without laying judgment for how it had happened, a night's sleep in his own bed was a giant improvement over the cargo bay. When they had showered yesterday, Arad had cringed at the line of purplish marks down his torso and thigh left behind from the floor rivets. He'd ignored the ache and stifled a few groans when he moved the wrong way to spare Roku's guilt. Better to pay no mind than acknowledge it. Much like the dull pressure point on his chest, relentless and insisting, which threatened to nudge him out of the comfy bog of slumber far too soon.

The odd sensation disappeared, so Arad let himself start to sink under. Deep, deep down where sight, sound, and gravity couldn't find him—

Poke.

And it was back, causing him to tense and the nearby bruises to twinge, slowing if not stopping his descent.

"Lemme alone…" Arad pleaded, unsure if he spoke out loud or gurgled in a crappy underwater dream.

Poke.

Each new stab made Arad bob in the mire. A brightness grew, showing him the way up and up. "What's going on?" His voice was less drowned the more words he uttered.

Poke.

He broke the surface, splashing into the real world. And for the record, the real world sucked, with its stale recycled air and humming environmental equipment. Nowhere near so lovely.

Arad risked cracking open a single eye. "Roku?"

Bleary eyed and fur matted about his head and neck, Roku had more in common with a newly woken toddler than a powerful human-tiger hybrid. Hovering with his cloak askew, he filled Arad's sight with a fat, furry finger aimed dead center of Arad's chest.

Poke.

"I'm hungry."

Both eyes wide open, Arad nearly choked in disbelief. "What? You want me to feed you?"

Poke.

"Gah!" Waving wildly, Arad slapped the prodding digit away. "Stop… All right already…"

Arad didn't stop grousing as he swung himself out of bed and shoved his way past the half-conscious DemiShou. The jarring squeal of the drawer opening only fueled Arad's choice to wear one of Torrins's old shirts for no reason other than Roku wouldn't like it.

"You know, when I was a kid, I had an orange tabby named Mr. Twiddles who used to bat my face to wake me up each morning to be fed. Should I start calling you Mr. Twiddles the Second? I'll set up a litter box in the corner."

Even groggy, Roku puffed his chest in offense. "I am *not* a pet."

"No, you're not!" Arad stabbed Roku's granite chest three times with his finger. "Then we won't have a repeat of this tomorrow, will we?"

When Roku refused to respond, he tugged the shirt over his head, punched the door control open, and stomped out into the hall. Unfettered words rolled out of his pursed lips in self-righteous rambling to himself.

"Oh, you're a grumpy kitty now, but we get a cup of java in you, and you're gonna be seriously kissing my butt."

Arad stomped into the galley, slamming doors, snatching supplies, and pushing buttons a little too hard. He couldn't believe he was actually doing this. As soon as the chime went off, Arad filled a cup and shoved it into Roku's hand.

"Drink."

Roku sniffed the brew and obediently took a sip before Arad continued cooking.

After a meal that reminded Arad their food would not last for years at the rate Roku needed, he headed to the bridge, with Roku following close behind and his head dipped sheepishly low. He hadn't apologized out loud but made a special effort to clean up and put away all the dishes. The smug grin on Arad's face was etched in steel.

Sitting in Daiko's station, Arad pulled up the damage control program, specifically the details on the damaged engine. The hours spent reading over the tech manuals were a blessing. Now that he knew what to look for, he spun the holographic simulation and better understood the data scrolling off the side.

Roku peeked over his shoulder as he manipulated the engine image. "If you get the engines fixed, where will we go?"

"I don't know. Other than someplace to get supplies, I haven't thought that far ahead. One thing at a time."

Deflecting the question erased what was left of the smug grin. Being part of an illegal DemiShou project meant he needed to find an outpost or a world outside the corporate umbrella if Roku ever wanted to live off ship again. No small task, that. Their reach, their jurisdiction sprawled into all corners.

Slipping into the nearby seat, Roku stared out the main screen into the vast, unfamiliar beyond. His wistful exhale was tinged in despair. "We're lost, aren't we?"

"Literally? For now. Figuratively? I'm holding out on that verdict."

"How can you be so sure?"

"I've survived lechers, thieves, and addicts for more years than I care to admit without a roof over my head. I refuse to give in. I'm indestructible."

"You lived on the streets?" Once again, Roku calculated the truth with little detail. An annoying skill.

It was almost as fast as Arad's sharp retort. "Is that actually important?"

"No... I guess not."

Roku's subtle wounded tone shamed Arad, but being judged—even in the slightest—always chafed him, and now he doubted whether the judgment existed or not. Arad cursed at himself for relaxing his guard and revealing too much. Too many instances in his past were a little cagey, and with Roku's more conservative streak, he wasn't sure who would be more hurt by divulging it all. Better for him to keep quiet and resume his tech research. Thankfully, Roku didn't press the subject.

"Grrr. Man. This sucks!" Arad slapped the monitor's casing as if it would give him different results.

"What's the matter?"

Slumping into his seat, Arad stared at the ceiling. "I'm not sure what to do next. I can't get in to repair the engines. The section got sealed off when the warship popped us. Assuming I have the parts to do that anyways. The shuttle's destroyed, so I can't use it to get help. The heat shielding held up from what I can tell, but there's a hole in the hull that has to get patched. I don't know if I have any materials that would serve as a heat shield. Plus, I've never done maintenance like this."

"Maintenance like what?"

"The emergency bulkheads are down. From what I've read, the safety protocols won't allow them to be opened until the hole is plugged and atmosphere pressurization is normalized. Which makes sense. Since I can't get into the room in the first place, the only way to fix the hole would be from the outside."

"You mean out there? You would actually consider a spacewalk?"

Arad raised and dropped his hands in exasperation. "The ship won't allow us to land with a hull breach. We're blind with no communications. We may not have a choice."

Roku's one eye threatened to burn him. Crossing his arms, the tiger glanced out into the vacuum and to Arad.

"No. Find another way."

Using only his toe, Arad slowly rotated his seat around until he fully faced Roku. "The last time I checked, this is my ship. I'll do whatever I have to do. With or without your permission."

Unspoken tension followed them throughout the day. Roku had become silent and remote after the possible spacewalk had been brought up. What was Arad supposed to do? He needed the *Ansariland* fully functional, or at least enough to keep them alive. They spent another boring day in the cargo bay listening to DemiShou simmer while Arad combed through the manuals to give him some other choices. If he tried to talk to Roku, he barely responded and gave Arad his back. On purpose. Music piped through the ship made it easier to pretend Roku wasn't deliberately avoiding him in the same room.

The silence continued until it was time to sleep. With barely a word, Roku took his place again at the foot of Arad's bed. As odd as the sleeping arrangements had become, Arad didn't have it in him to say no.

Staying near yet so distant gnawed at Arad. He'd taken responsibility for the DemiShou before Roku emerged. Now, he weighed the strange attachment between them, wondering how healthy it was for a bond to grow out of so little time. Why was it so heavy when stretched so thin?

He focused on Roku's breathing to ease his mind. For his size, the tiger did everything huge. Eat huge, sleep huge. Arad tried to forget what else on Roku was huge and how he wielded it when giving in to his appetites. Better to concentrate on the rise and fall of fur-lined bellows and let it drag him into slumber. Tomorrow would be a better day.

Listening to the soothing rumble, he allowed his own to sync, but before he drifted off, the breathing changed. The rhythm faltered, turning into something grating. A sad moan built, punctuating each exhale until it grew into a pitiful, haunted keening. It tore at Arad with its pain and drew him closer to the edge of the bed.

"Roku? Can you hear me? Are you all right?"

Carefully, Arad reached out and barely brushed his fingers against Roku's shoulder. A chilling scream burst out of him and Arad jumped. Roku spun and scuttled backward away from the bed so fast he slammed into the door with a thud. Dragging his powerful hands through his shallow fur, he shook in terror. Pulse hammering in his chest, Arad told himself to grab one of Torrins's guns for protection, but instead he found himself scrambling off the bed, desperate to help.

Wet, glossy eyes catching the feeble light, Roku threw out an open hand to raise an invisible wall between them. "No! Stay back! I don't want to hurt you!" Each choked word was twined with a dangerous, warning growl.

Arad stood his ground, trying not to make matters worse. "It's okay. You won't hurt me. I know you won't."

A heart-wrenching yowl suffocated the room. Tremors wracked Roku's body as he struggled against the halting sobs.

His first day at the workhouse, Arad had stood alone, surrounded by vagrant boys who hated the world and anyone in it, especially those in nice clothes. Boys who saw him as a target or rival for food. *Don't let them see you cry. Once you start, you'll never stop.* Curled on his bed, he'd been convinced he'd never survive. Then Martin had come along. Bigger and stronger than the rest, he'd sent the other boys scattering, guarding Arad until he learned to fend for himself. That first act of charity had made all the difference.

Roku's hand crumpled into a weak fist and withdrew, maintaining the fleeting distance between them. "Please."

The broken plea tugged at Arad's heart. A tiny voice told Arad to step back, that he was trapped inside with a cornered, distraught beast. He kicked that tiny voice in the balls and told it to go sit and face the wall. He hadn't abandoned Roku yet and wasn't about to start now.

"It's okay. I trust you."

Climbing across Roku's lap, Arad stilled his own fears and wrapped his arms around the tiger's head. Still tangled in his blanket robe, Roku raised his shaking arms but hesitated more than once to return the embrace. He inhaled hard and deep against Arad's neck and shoulder, over the same spot those powerful jaws had held Arad down the night he woke.

Arad didn't let go as the sobbing ebbed into less frightening tears that didn't echo off the room's tight confines.

Eventually, after long minutes passed, Roku spoke in half whimpers. "I think I was dead."

"What?"

"There was a crowd. Everyone was screaming—outraged—and I was trying to calm them down. Keep the peace. But they wouldn't listen. They didn't care. There were too many, and they were so angry."

"They were angry with you?"

"With me. With each other. With everything."

"What happened?"

"It turned into a riot. I tried to protect someone near me, and they beat me down to the ground. I fought back, but I...I couldn't stop them. They swarmed and trampled me. I couldn't see their faces while they kicked and spit on me. It didn't stop until someone picked up a gun. I think it was mine."

Dread filled Arad as he processed the details of Roku's messy tale. "Why would you have a gun?"

Roku shook his head into Arad's shoulder without lifting it. "I...I'm not sure."

"Then what happened?" Arad closed his eyes and hugged Roku tighter against the shuddering inhale wracking the DemiShou, bracing himself for the answer. Grey District had seen its fair share of riots pitting slugs against the establishment in Arad's days. The answer came to Arad before Roku spoke.

"They shot me." Roku sucked in air over and over against Arad's skin, trying to leash himself, teetering on the edge of hyperventilating. "Over and over. My arms. My chest. I felt it chew up my insides. Then they stuck the muzzle in my face. I closed my eyes but still saw it coming as they pulled the trigger." A single sob barked out, and Roku curled his arms around Arad. "My god, they blew my brains out. I watched them kill me. I died."

The pitiful wail vibrated through Arad's shoulder and into his spine, but he didn't let go.

"Shh...Roku. Shh... It was just a nightmare. You're okay." Arad fought to stay strong as Roku's tears tore free, wetting Arad's neck, collar, and chest as hot streaks found the path to his skin. Breaking down was all too tempting, but Roku needed him to stay strong, so he gripped him tighter.

"It was so real. My chest...I still feel it in my chest."

"Dreams aren't real. It didn't mean anything." Arad squeezed harder, convinced he could force Roku's shivering to stop if he applied enough pressure.

"Do you really think so?"

The muffled plea stabbed at Arad. Roku kept his face buried as more agonizing mewls spilled out, more animal than human, underscoring his unique modifications. Fears for Arad's own safety had melted away only to be filled with empathy. He understood how a past shaped a man for better or worse.

"Y...yeah." Arad swallowed down the sympathetic tear, afraid if he let it loose, he'd fall apart. He vowed to maintain his support rather than indulge in co-misery. "You're going to be okay. It was only a dream."

He kept repeating it until he almost convinced himself.

Chapter Twelve

When Arad woke up, he found himself in his bed instead of curled up on the floor where he'd drifted off holding Roku. The DemiShou was already gone, his absence a profound ache after the night before. Dressing quickly despite his newfound mood, Arad headed out hoping to find the wayward tiger. It didn't take long. There were only so many hiding spaces on the *Ansariland*.

Eating alone, Roku paused, food centimeters from his mouth when Arad entered the galley.

"Couldn't sleep?" Arad asked.

Roku barely grunted in response.

Arad gathered a meal for himself in spite of lacking an appetite. He sat across from Roku while they ate without a moment of eye contact between them. Neither spoke of the nightmare or any other pleasantries, silence spoiling any flavor. With Roku's humiliation radiating like poisoned starlight, Arad had the distinct feeling conversation wasn't wanted.

The moment he finished, Roku stood, dumped his bowl on the counter, and headed for the hallway. "Going to the gym."

Arad sighed and pushed his own bowl away. He'd lost interest.

The first night in the workhouse, Arad had had terrible dreams. Lost in mist, abandoned, pleading to be taken back. He could be a better son. The grief the other boys gave him over his cries in the night isolated him even more than being the new arrival. Martin protected him from physical harm, but he wasn't a friend.

Perhaps it was time not to repeat history.

In his room, he collected his tablet and made a trip to Nixta's old quarters, digging through the leftover treasure trove. It took a while to find the item, but once he did, he headed straight to the gym, stopping just inside.

Without a wall dividing the lavatory, Arad had the perfect view of Roku's kilt sliding up and covering his meaty buttocks as he fastened the garment around his waist. Humidity thickened the air, and Roku's darkened fur appeared damp and matted, rough from being toweled off. Arad caught himself staring at the fascinating line patterns crisscrossing his back and tipped his gaze to the floor. He hadn't expected Roku to shower first. Roku had been made uncomfortable enough, so he started to retreat, trying to hide in the background.

"I know you're there," Roku mumbled.

Heat flushed Arad cheeks. "Sorry. I didn't mean to creep up on you."

Deliberately avoiding his reflection in the mirror, Roku grabbed his blanket lying over the sink and set about covering himself. When he pulled the cloth over his head, sadness pinched Arad's chest. Roku may not have known who he was, but he saw his appearance as manufactured rather than natural, and it repulsed him.

"I have something for you."

Roku turned, his gaze tracking the second handheld computer in Arad's outstretched hand.

"This was Nixta's. She was probably the least awful to me, but in truth, she ignored me. This was her personal tablet. I already had Franc's, so I hadn't gone hunting for it until now. Figured you need something to do while I'm doing maintenance or research or babysitting the other Demis."

Gratitude shined in Roku's eyes as he gradually stepped forward and reached for the tablet. When his fingers accidentally brushed Arad's, he jerked back and averted his eyes.

The rejection stung, but Arad refused to show it. He placed the tablet on the sink within Roku's reach. "You can have it. I don't need it. To be honest, I should have pulled it out the day after you woke up."

Rather than wait for a response, Arad turned and left the room. He could only imagine how bored Roku had been the last few days, standing idly by while he read through the manuals. It hadn't occurred to Arad to scrounge up the extra tablet sooner, and he was a little ashamed because of it. They were here for the duration, and Roku had proven far too honorable to ask for things. As he traversed the cargo bay crate maze, Arad amended his promise to help Roku and the other DemiShou to make a better effort. He wasn't on his own anymore.

Stats said Shichi and Hachi were healthy in their paused state, so Arad took his seat on the mattress and started searching for procedures for spacewalking. It would take him some time to figure out the details—assuming the *Ansariland* had the proper equipment—

because even though he was a good mechanic, many unfamiliar systems and technical aspects of the ship required him to sidetrack which schematic he was studying. If he didn't understand a manual's reference, he needed to learn it. Even the horrible boys at the workhouse couldn't hammer his sense of determination out of him.

The reading would take some time, but the distraction was welcome.

He'd read the spacesuit protocols three times before Roku's soft footsteps caught his attention. The big tiger taking a seat on the other end of the mattress caused Arad to gently rock.

Roku's graveled voice, although quiet, was a soothing balm. "Thank you. For the tablet. It was kind of you."

"You're welcome."

Arad wanted to say more but let Roku pace their interaction. The nightmare had unsettled him, like so many things since waking, and it would probably be better to let him talk if he needed it. Or revel in a lack of noise, or even more ideas.

After turning on the tablet, Roku searched through its directory. He opened and closed a few pieces of software until he left a graphics program active on the screen. Trying not to be obvious, Roku pulled the stylus from its holder along the tablet's edge. The slender tool looked ridiculously fragile in his bulky hands, but it didn't stop him from experimenting on the screen, making marks and lines of various thickness and erasing them.

For the next few hours, Arad alternated between reading his tech articles and spying on Roku's efforts. The little strokes quickly advanced into simple line art and, as he grew bolder, into clever drawings. Each random image became brighter and fuller as he tested the tablet's capabilities. Roku's blanket robe slipped as he drew, less concerned with keeping covered as he became absorbed with his new projects.

Standing up, Arad stretched a particularly sharp kink out of his neck. "You ready to get something to eat? Roku?"

Roku startled as he realized Arad wasn't still sitting next to him. "What?"

Arad almost laughed at Roku's stunned expression. "Eat. We've been here for about four hours."

"We have?"

"C'mon. I'm starved, and I could use a break."

Shutting down his handheld, Arad stepped toward the exit and looked over his shoulder. Roku sat, gaze darting between Arad and the tablet clutched in his possessive hands. A faint horror colored his face as if he was torn having to choose between them.

A satisfied chuckle spilled out of Arad. "You can bring that with you."

With a snort and the first smile since waking, Roku stood and followed Arad to the galley with his new tablet in hand.

The nightmare continued to be an unspoken topic while, over the next several days, Arad and Roku slipped into a routine of meals, tablet work, digging through the *Ansariland*'s entertainment hoard because the OS didn't include a chess simulator—thanks again, Torrins—and babysitting DemiShou in between bouts of exercise and sleep. He tried to hide it, but Roku continued to avoid making direct physical contact with Arad. It stung, but Arad put on a brave face and pretended it didn't.

The discussion would wait. Their possession of time made them rich men.

Three hours of research had convinced Arad a space-walk was realistic. Repairing the engine was another matter. Damage reports gave him an idea of which parts needed replacing, but until he dug up the cargo manifest and laid eyes on what he needed, he couldn't be sure if all the effort had been wasted.

Twisting his neck to relieve the tension, he padded into the gym, finding Roku hard at work.

The blanket robe heaped next to his precious tablet nearby, Roku pushed the weight stack to its limit. The capacity had been substantial because of Tank's physical requirements, but Roku's strength made it look easy. His breathing was measured yet strained, more likely from the quantity of repetitions rather than the max kilograms. Roku's chiseled muscles swelled, the striations visible through his fine fur. Once again, the room allowed for an excellent show. It stirred Arad.

Arad raised his hand to say hello but stopped himself. No reason to distract Roku now. He might stop exercising. And that would be bad.

The weights hit the floor with a clang. Roku swung his massive leg over the seat and stood, moving over to the combat dummy mounted on the far wall. The mannequin had seen its fair share of abuse, cracked and weathered yet ready for more battering. Masochist. Rolling his head, then his shoulders, Roku addressed the dummy on bouncing feet. He settled his weight, knees slightly bent, and shifted his stance slightly apart while forming his hands into fists. Ready to strike, the pose screamed police, military, or equivalent authority figure. Arad had seen enough of those goose-stepping jerks "maintaining order" in Grey District to recognize it. Somehow, seeing it in Roku didn't raise Arad's alarms.

Sharp and fast blows rained over the padded leather, the dull slaps singing pleasurable surges up Arad's spine and out through his limbs. Roku's kilt had been split up both sides, allowing his legs additional room to snap out kicks without being hindered. It also gave an indecent glimpse at the curve of Roku's rear when the fabric parted.

The harder Roku worked, the more guttural the grunts and growls. Exertion emphasized the size and power of each heaving muscle in his arms, legs, and back. Few men had ever drawn Arad's fascination enough to fixate over. But watching Roku exert himself... Arad couldn't deny he was staring. He found the whole scene...hypnotic.

Roku paused mid-strike and sniffed. He dropped his combat stance and turned to Arad. "You never struck me as a lurker."

Arad raised his eyes to Roku's face and found using full sentences a touch difficult. "Not usually, but, um, you know..." He rubbed the embarrassment out of his face with a firm hand. "Okay. That was impressive."

"The exercise helps focus me."

"I know it's a stretch, but does it spark any memories?"

"Not so far. But it feels good to push myself, to see how strong I am, test my limits."

"Well, you may not remember your past, but you obviously still have some crazy skills. That was not the workout of a street slug."

"You might be right."

"I know I'm right. Geez, if I tried to do half of that, the dummy would fight back, and I'd end up on my butt."

A soft chuckle graced the beginnings of Roku's smile. "It's good to know I'm here to save you from injury."

Even this short amount of banter lifted Arad's spirits, thawing the current distance between them. Having Roku on board hadn't been planned, but he had found himself missing their growing camaraderie even over what little time they'd known one another. Making Roku smile fed his soul in so many good ways.

"The *Ansariland* can use a man with your kind of skills, my good sir. You want to be head of security? I'm taking applications." The deep timbre of Roku's laughter spurred Arad into a rare fit of his own. It wasn't long before his lungs protested the lack of air, but it was well worth it. "Oh, man, if you were around in Grey District, I'd have traded a piece of ass for that kind of protection."

Roku's humor faded away, and his brow furrowed. "You shouldn't joke about things like that. I'm already ashamed of what happened when we first met. I took something away from you and can barely look at myself, even looking like this. Being intimate with someone should be something special, something that should be shared, to bond over." His nose became ridged in disgust. "It's not something you barter over as payment."

After gathering his blanket and tablet, Roku turned and headed toward the showers.

And as quickly as it began, the banter was gone, leaving Arad stunned as he tried to understand what went wrong. Why did a joke about exchanging sex for funds rub him so raw? If he thought back far enough, virtually every sexual encounter in Arad's past had been a way to gain food, shelter, or some other service. One made do with the opportunities left in their path.

True, it wasn't an ideal option. Selling himself had its downsides. Safety would always be dubious and reliable income fleeting when you didn't embrace the work. Other slugs may have whispered behind his back, but they understood. Arad wished other jobs had come his way, but he'd made some amount of peace with his lot in life. Too many factors worked against him to get out of the life entirely. The only people who had issues, who condemned and threw judgment over the limited choices his life left him, were people with means. People who believed themselves to be above such sleazy prospects while hiring him for the night. People who saw hustling as a gross travesty of law and order.

People like corporate police and other authority figures.

Confusion ignited into outright insult. "Wait a minute. Did you just call me a whore?"

Ear twitching at Arad's angry footsteps, Roku turned in time to take the brunt of Arad's rancor.

"You don't get to judge me." Arad jabbed his finger into Roku's unyielding chest. "Your memory may be in the toilet, but I can take one look at you and know you've never struggled until now."

Roku's eyes may not have been human, but the damnation within the stare was nothing new. Arad had lived under silent disapproval for more years than he cared to admit in Grey District. Clergy, rich, and authorities, they were all alike. Only other slugs had ever respected him completely.

"I wasn't born a slug. My family was stupid wealthy and could trace their lineage to before Earth consolidated countries into conglomerates. But the family money was under some archaic, discriminatory contract that shouldn't have been legal of having male heirs every few generations. And since population laws only allow for one child per family, you can imagine how proud my parents were to have a homo boy who wouldn't marry a female. They were so worried about losing their fortune, they demanded I go in for complete sex reassignment so I'd bear a child because of the subclause forbidding surrogates. I refused. I told them I'm not transgender or third gender, and those surgeries should be reserved for the people who are. They didn't appreciate being told no. As punishment, they sat back as two brutes in black jackets dragged me off screaming to a private workhouse. I begged them not to do it. They didn't even shed a tear."

Arad was ranting, but the airlock was open, and all the oxygen rushed to escape. There was no stopping it. He continued to shove and poke at Roku with every sentence, determined to make him understand. The tiger took it all, wide-eyed and slack-mouthed, without defending himself.

"Workhouses are prisons for the homeless and delinquent. I learned to survive the beatings by the house governors while they forced me to learn the mech trade. I had to earn my keep, and they kept virtually all the money."

"That's illegal," Roku whispered.

Annoyance raised Arad's volume. "Of course it is! And the authorities knew all about it. The company that lost the last work contract to our house had their gestapo kick in the doors. They burned the place to the ground, and everyone scattered like roaches. Out on the streets, I caught pneumonia and nearly died, but I got lucky. Sketch found me lying in the gutter and took me in."

"Who was he?"

"A Syn dealer." Arad narrowed his eyes. "And before you say anything, he treated me better than any police or authority figure I'd ever met. He even helped me find my way back to my family. What a complete waste of time that was."

"They didn't take you in?"

A new swell of rage burned Arad's eyes. "I had to confront them at the door because the concierge wouldn't let me in. Pretended he didn't know me, even when my parents came down with a new son on their arm. He didn't even look like me, the fake bastard, and my parents wouldn't even acknowledge me. When security called the police, they scanned my hand, but my DNA wasn't tagged to any ID anymore. They had me erased from the information grid. And replaced."

Roku was equally shocked and confused. "How did they pass off the new boy as their son?"

"How else? Money and fear of powerful people. I checked the public data, and the family history says he's always been theirs. Me? There isn't a single piece of evidence of who I am anymore."

"That shouldn't be possible."

Arad scoffed. "Then call it magic. I was the son of one of the wealthiest men in the city, and now I'm undocumented. Do you know what that means? The grid doesn't acknowledge me. I'm not eligible for any school or employment programs. I can't apply for housing, and there's nowhere I can go to change that. *I don't exist.*"

"What did you do?" Roku's brow crinkled, his face drooping in sadness, which only added to Arad's frustration.

"The prep school boy with the bright future ended up becoming a criminal, helping deal Syn for a few months until Sketch got arrested."

A long pause stretched out as Arad simmered under Roku's penitent gaze. The DemiShou should have intimidated him, but he held his hands up as if trying to quiet Arad's vicious tirade. For all the good that would do.

"What happened to him?" Roku asked.

Old memories made Arad snarl. Pain and outrage sat front and center of his soul, the toxic bile roughening his words. "The same thing that happens to all slugs the authorities come down on. They vanish. Then you're on the street and doing things you *never* believed yourself capable of. I was terrified of the police but had to steal more often than I wanted, and after what I put up with among the boys in the workhouse, I'd be better off jumping from a tower than joining one of the gangs."

Arad's eyes stung. Roku's face lost its crystal focus. "I was supposed to have friends, dances...first kisses...and all of that was taken away from me. When your only choices are to either go without food for days or let the fat, dirty foreman who likes underage boys be your first or do something stupid enough to disappear like Sketch, your virginity seems less important.

"I've done things and people I wish I hadn't, but I refuse to let the pieces of trash who claimed to be my parents win. And you don't get to make me regret who I've been either. I'm not the spoiled brat anymore, and I won't be him again." Arad sucked in a lungful of ragged air, and a tear streaked down to his jaw. "Ever again."

The past refused to change, and Arad hadn't cried over his shattered life in years. Yet now that he'd dredged it up, confessed his sins to the law-abiding Roku, his anger became muddied with shame until the two emotions fused into one. Roku didn't say a word as more tears fell and Arad's vision blurred into foggy daylight.

Unable to trust himself to say anything further, Arad spun and trod out of the lavatory, thankful when Roku didn't follow.

Chapter Thirteen

"Another empty," Arad groused as he kicked the empty container. It slid across the cargo bay floor, banging into the growing cluster of boxes littering the room. Each time he tossed one aside, Roku's twitchy gaze followed. Arad had finally downloaded Torrins's shipping manifest to his handheld and dragged the tiger along to search the inventory for potential parts to repair the damaged engine.

Most of what he kept finding on the list were vague descriptions with nothing inside the crates. Knowing Torrins, he inflated the documents to give the impression of the *Midas Ascending* being a more professional operation and entice clients for higher-end contracts. Arad glanced over at the sleeping DemiShou pods. The method had worked. Sort of.

"Always scheming for a bigger paycheck, Torrins. Should've skipped this one."

The maze of crates hiding the DemiShou was half-dismantled. Roku pulled another off the stack with barely an effort, and Arad checked it against the list. *Random household supplies*. Arad pressed his thumb to the lock plate, and the lid popped open from his captain's access. He swung the top on its hinges and dug past the packing foam. It only took a few seconds to identify the series of stoppered metal cans and random supplies inside.

"Paints?" Red, white, grey, and black. The colors of the *Ansariland*'s interior. "Typical. We've been living in this rust bucket with the walls peeling, and the fix has been here the whole time. Probably because there wasn't any profit in it. Torrins, I'm glad you're dead."

Speaking to the former captain was marginally better than the weird silence hanging over himself and Roku. His outburst yesterday, while justified, had flayed Arad to the bone and left him more exposed than he was accustomed to. Slashing your past open with a ragged knife took its toll. The pity and condescension dumped on slugs on a daily basis wasn't something he stomached well. Feelings they both must have shared since neither man was talking much beyond what was necessary.

Arad didn't know how or if he was ready to correct that. Instead of facing it, he found a task to distract himself, to stop thinking about unchangeable past events. So far, he'd been successful.

"I guess we'll set this one to the side with the useful stuff."

Arad closed the lid and pushed it across the floor to join its friends along the wall. He turned to decide which crate to tackle next and paused. What was Roku doing?

Quietly reflecting, Roku paced around an empty crate, trailing a finger over the open rim. He stepped over the edge and continued studying the box, standing in the center. Without a word, he dropped to his knees, angling himself for the best fit. Despite his bulk, Roku was determined to squeeze himself inside. Licking his lower lip as he worked, Roku shimmied and shifted his furry muscles lower and lower until only his rounded shoulders and the top half of his head peeked above the crate's rim. He appeared awfully pleased with himself as he wiggled into the confined space.

Arad tilted his head as if it allowed him to see better. This was one of the most astounding things he'd ever witnessed in his life. He covered his mouth with his hand because his mother had always insisted it was impolite to stare with your mouth wide open. A good lesson to follow when he found himself so stunned and amused.

"Are you enjoying yourself?"

Hunched over, Roku froze like a prey animal, eyes wide and unmoving. His nose and mouth stayed hidden within the crate. "Yes…"

The hint of guilt or embarrassment in the careful response was quite charming. Arad sighed with a chuckle, relieved to release some of the present tension. "Now's a good time for a break. Let me know when you're done. I'm still going to need your help."

"Okay."

Without another word, Arad left Roku to explore the allure of the magical trunk. He drifted to the cryotubes and checked on Shichi and Hachi. All health signals still green, they both floated peacefully, unaware of their surroundings or the potential trouble ahead. Arad wished waking and finding a new home for them were an option, but with the current technical problems and limited resources, they were safer where they were. Unless Arad repaired the *Ansariland*… No. He didn't want to think that far ahead. The problems circling them had too many unknown outcomes. Too many ways to go wrong.

Wouldn't it be wonderful if he could be put on pause too?

Now, only the tips of Roku's ears were visible. Arad laughed to himself. Hopefully the goofy lug wouldn't get himself stuck. Arad didn't know if he had a pry bar, and he wasn't about to cut him out of there with a plasma torch.

Since Roku was still busy, Arad slumped down onto the mattress that still lived in the cargo bay. He rolled onto his back to stretch out the kinks and cocked his head to see. Even with all the surrounding chaos, it continued to have the best vantage point. From here he kept an eye on Shichi and Hachi, watched Roku work on turning inside the crate without exiting, and took a mental note of how many more boxes there were to go.

"Are you ready to keep going?" Roku asked.

Arad blinked to find Roku standing over him. So many frustrations were exhausting him he'd actually fallen asleep for a moment and didn't hear him approach. More surprising was that he was comfortable enough to doze off in Roku's presence. He never could in Grey District.

Not willing to think too deeply on it, Arad climbed to his feet. "Yeah. Let's do this."

Back on track, they worked their way through the remaining inventory. Hours passed as they inspected and reorganized the containers until they had checked every crate in the cargo bay. The crate maze segregating the DemiShou had been reduced to blocks lining the outer walls. They found the series of water and air recycler modules Arad had been hunting for last week. Two containers held more food packets, which he guessed might extend their stores for another few months. Other boxes, if they had anything inside them, were filled with a myriad of other useless items. What they didn't find were the spare engine parts Arad needed that were specifically listed on the manifest. More of Torrins's bogus entries.

He hazarded if it wasn't too huge, he could weld a piece of deck plating over the breach, but without those engine parts, there was no way to repair the *Ansariland*. Once again, the captain had managed to screw Arad. At first literally, then figuratively from every moment after he'd been incinerated in space.

"I can't believe this! You're as worthless dead as you were alive, Torrins!" In utter frustration, Arad lashed out at the nearest container, sending it tumbling and catching his hand on the edge of the lock plate. "Ow!" He made an instant fist and clutched it to his chest.

Roku rushed to Arad's side. "Are you all right?"

Blood seeped between his fingers as he tried to hide it from Roku's probing stare. "I'm fine."

"No, you're not." Roku took Arad's arm in a firm yet gentle hold. "Come with me. Now."

Arad jerked his arm free. "Bugger off. I can take care of myself just fine."

"You're bleeding."

"It's a scratch."

With a growl, Roku grabbed Arad by the waist and hiked him over his shoulder.

"Sonofabitch! Put me down!"

Between Roku's determined pace, his unyielding hold, and being upside down at a dangerous height, shaking himself lose was a bad idea. He did, however, vocalize his unhappiness with each stomach-jolting step. A line of blood droplets marked a dotted path from the cargo bay to the infirmary. Thankfully, there wasn't anyone else to see, but it didn't make the experience any less humiliating. After the pneumonia scare, Arad's health had become a matter of pride. He'd managed to avoid major illnesses and injuries for years by being smart. No random idiot would tell him what to do and how to survive. Sketch had been the last survivor tutor he'd had, and look where it had gotten him.

At least Arad managed not to scream when Roku spun him around and deposited him into the exam chair. Fuming, Arad blew his hair out of his eyes and scowled with every ounce of energy he had while Roku went after the first aid box.

"It's not that bad." Arad's defiance faltered when he caught a wayward streak of blood threatening to drip off his elbow with his free hand. Wiping it up left a smear up his forearm and a puddle cupped in his palm. Maybe it actually was that bad.

Ignoring Arad's comment, Roku tore open the box and scavenged what medical supplies he needed. He lowered the tray hinged to the wall next to Arad and dropped half the kit's contents on it.

"At least the supplies here are sufficient. I won't have to toss you in the med bed." Roku pried open Arad's hand and pressed a sterile pad to sop up the wound.

"Ow. That stings."

"Hold your hand open."

With a lack of squeamishness Arad didn't share, Roku prodded and examined the cut, probably to look for any debris, but his bedside manner begged for improvement. Arad turned his head. The sharp twinges from Roku's unusual rough handling made him nauseous.

"You keep poking that hard, I'm gonna puke."

"If you do, I'll definitely throw you in the med bed."

"Wonder what that's like. I've never been in one before." Even when Arad still had his parents' favor, he'd never been ill enough to require automated healthcare.

Roku side-eyed the med bed and gave a caustic snort. "I noticed the other day it doesn't have any DemiShou parameters, so let's hope nothing horrible happens to me."

"Oh, well, you know the Demi module is on order. Probably lost in shipping."

"Your sarcasm is refreshing." Roku was unimpressed as he squeezed the cut closed and applied a wound sealer.

Arad hissed at the sting but insisted on keeping his composure. "Did you want me to sugarcoat it?"

"Why start now? It doesn't change the fact that the DemiShou on board, myself included, were only a commodity to be sold. I don't even understand why you care so much."

"Maybe because I know what it's like to be used for someone else's profit and have no choice in how to exist."

Closing his eyes, Roku paused. His shoulders swelled, and he let out a gradual, cleansing breath. It did little to ease the tension in his body. "I'm sorry. Your being injured has me on edge."

"I don't see why. It's hardly life-threatening."

"I can smell the blood. It distresses me."

"Yeah, well, too bad. I know how to do this myself. It's not the first time I've ever gotten cut. I don't need you manhandling me over this kind of thing like some defenseless child. I haven't been that in a long time."

"I know. I didn't say my reaction was rational."

Roku finished the wound sealing and cleaned Arad's hand. Far more carefully than before, he tested the cut for seepage. Satisfied Arad was no longer bleeding, Roku cleaned the area and applied a new bandage, wrapping Arad's hand.

Tender care was so foreign to Arad he wasn't sure how to react. In his world, men tended to take what they wanted, and selfishness ruled amongst the slugs. But Roku wasn't a slug, and his skilled triage lacked the dispassionate treatment available from a Grey District doctor or medical kiosk. The dissimilarity defused Arad's anger and made him sit still while Roku worked.

Without stopping, Roku cleared his throat. "I want to apologize for what I said before, implying your past was a reflection on you. You didn't deserve that."

Arad shook his head. "I know you didn't mean to judge me—"

"Yes, I did, and I'm ashamed to admit it. My past is missing, but I must be hardwired to be a little inflexible in my moral views."

"A little?" Head tilted and brow raised, Arad caught Roku's eye.

"Perhaps more than a little."

"And now?"

"They're flexing." Roku averted his gaze to Arad's damaged hand.

The angry slash in his palm appeared more superficial than not. Roku prompted him to open and close his fingers. They moved fine with only the burning pull of knitting flesh making him want to stop. Fortunately, there didn't appear to be any nerve damage. Arad didn't want to spend time in the med bed.

Since they'd entered the infirmary, Roku had tended to him without initiating eye contact. As if he was only allowed either to touch or look, not both. Still keeping a distance, but he lacked detachment.

"You've gone out of your way lately to avoid touching me."

Roku paused without looking at him. "It's for your safety."

"You're touching me now."

"You're injured."

"You're taking care of me."

Roku tested the bandage and released Arad's hand. "It's a distraction."

"You wouldn't hurt me."

"You don't know that."

"Not on purpose."

A sad laugh lacking any humor tumbled out of Roku. "Ah, but there's the point. Not on purpose." Roku lowered his voice as if terrified someone else might hear his confession. "I have these urges. I remember how we met. How it felt. How you smelled. The things I did that I shouldn't have, acting solely on some kind of instinct. Sometimes I want to give in...touch you...hold you down. Stomp my morality into the floor and make you do things. I'm afraid if I give in, take what I want, I might lose control and be more animal than man because I won't want to stop. I crave it." A heady shudder raced through Roku's neck and shoulders. "Some days I think I should be locked up on the other side of the ship where I can't see or smell you, but I can't bring myself to do that."

Was it suddenly warmer in the infirmary? Arad didn't understand why his mouth was so dry. "I don't think the ship is big enough to do that."

"Please. Don't joke about this. I'm serious. I...I need to be near you. It will have to be enough."

Arad covered Roku's hand with his. "Roku, it's okay. You don't have to live like this—"

"*Stop it!*" Roku snatched his hand back. "Yes, I do. I can't trust myself. I can't."

Eyes glossy and hands shaking, Roku gathered up the used supplies, throwing the soiled items in the dispenser. Both in the same room, yet so far apart. The chasm grew. Now that he'd admitted things, Roku would walk out, and it would all be different. Different as in worse, and the realization panicked him.

"What about your human half? What does it think?"

"There isn't a human side and an animal side sitting on my shoulders like spirits of consciousness whispering in my ears. If I've learned nothing else since I woke, there's only me."

"I'm sorry. I didn't mean anything by that."

Nodding, Roku collected the remaining med supplies and put them into the kit, slamming it shut harder than required. Arad sat cradling his wrapped hand as Roku stopped in the doorway, clutching the jamb.

"If there really were two sides to me, Arad, I doubt the human side would stop me."

Chapter Fourteen

Arad had no idea how to process his day with Roku. Most attracted strangers found it easier to get along the more time they spent together, didn't they? For Arad and Roku, each passing day tangled their lives into something far more complicated. Given the growing connection between them, it shouldn't have been so easy to drive them apart. A curious situation for two people so fond of one another.

So fond of one another? What a glaring understatement.

Pulling to free the cover's tension, Arad turned over to better see Roku in the dark. Watching Roku sleep had become a habit he should consider breaking. It had started as a response to an unknown person on board, but now it had become something else. Curled on the floor, Roku snored, soothing in its gentle rumble. The proof of normalcy in what was anything but.

At first, Arad had dismissed his attraction as a byproduct of caring for the DemiShou clan. Then from the awkward circumstances of their first encounter, which still aroused him even without the Syn. After that, he passed it off as admiring the physique of a well-constructed male. Purring voice, godlike muscles, and, yes, an unfairly ample endowment added up to appreciating Roku's more primal aspects.

Roku's torso swelled and shrank with his breathing in a smooth motion. No sign of agitation. No sign of new nightmares. Only the same one every few days or so. It wasn't like the automatic knowledge of first aid, martial arts, or general information. The sharp fragments of his buried memories piercing the surface made Arad ache. They barely had enough details to craft an unsupported rumor, and if what he suspected was true, it chilled worse than an unprotected spacewalk. Roku mostly knew peace when he slept. Mostly.

Yeah...it was all about animal attraction. Sure it was.

Arad relaxed, finally feeling like he might drift off, but cursed silently over the need to pee. It was always something, wasn't it? Getting out of bed required a careful dance around the tiger blocking the floor. Arad suspected that was deliberate on Roku's part. His position created a barrier between Arad and the door. Not that they had to worry about intruders, but the intent was appreciated.

Bracing his hands on the mattress, he reached out with his foot, arching his leg over the sleeping tiger. He gently poked with his toe, making sure he'd found the floor and not a body. Roku hadn't slept consistently enough to wake him. Once Arad's foot was firmly planted on the floor, he began the inexorable gymnast routine to climb over Roku without actually touching him.

Please don't wake up. Why he was hovering over Roku might be hard to explain. Clearing his leg trailing behind him almost blew the whole deal when he slipped and nearly kicked Roku in the head. He didn't, and Roku continued to sleep.

Once free to move, Arad tiptoed to the door. He cringed at the noise of the door opening and peeked over his shoulder to find Roku exactly in the same state. Neither of them liked to sleep with the hatch open. Roku and Arad shared similar issues about shelter and security, but while Arad's stemmed from living on the streets, Roku couldn't explain why.

Barefoot, Arad made his way to the lav as quietly as possible. The automatic lights were reduced to the minimum because he hated how Torrins enjoyed letting them blind everyone in the middle of the night. Arad relieved himself and took a quick drink from the sink. He was pretty sure he'd crash now.

As he stepped out into the hallway, a figure crouched in the shadows. He jumped, clutching his chest, the scream trapped in his throat.

"Roku! Son of a bitch! You about startled me to death!" Arad stage-whispered, for whose benefit he didn't know.

Not moving or speaking, Roku sat on the floor waiting, face in his bent knees.

"Roku?"

The tiger snuffled into his knees. Dead asleep.

Arad shook his head as his pulse settled. "My hero from the terrors in the night."

He may have been mocking the DemiShou, but Arad found Roku's attachment strangely endearing. Roku was tortured by his animal instincts. Frightened by their intensity, he didn't trust himself to stop if he gave in to his baser urges. He wanted Arad. The taste he'd had when waking hadn't curbed it, and Arad didn't know how to handle it. He wanted to believe Roku had enough self-control, but he had also been seriously groggy when he woke. If he had been more aware, would he have been less animalistic? Or more?

Neither could be sure, and Roku refused to risk it. So, he made do with being near Arad, although Arad caught the big tiger sniffing him, or at him, from time to time. Did his scent settle Roku's nerves? During the rare times they weren't in the same room for any length of time, Roku would be agitated until he set eyes on Arad, then insist on staying close for safety. Arad suspected his protection would extend past their being sequestered on board. Something more than casual companionship had spawned in their time together.

If only Arad knew what to do with that.

Nobody ever lasted in his world, so long-term relationships were basically the stuff of fiction. Sex had always been a tool. A pleasurable tool, but a tool nonetheless. Perhaps not the most seemly of skills, but it had its advantages. Learning to seduce a man became an easy thing to learn, and knowing how to use it to extract a trade came soon after. Arad had never known a man he wanted to bed down without getting a prize in return until Roku. Only problem was he didn't know how. It had always been part of a transaction. Trading services in that way made Roku uncomfortable, so Arad would have to teach himself how not to be a whore.

Assuming, of course, Roku ever gave him the opportunity.

With a sigh, Arad tapped Roku's shoulder, trying not to startle him. "Roku. Get up, you overgrown stray. Let's go to bed."

It took three tries to get a response, and it was limited. With a garbled murmur, Roku nodded as he rose without really opening his eyes. Arad headed to the bedroom, Roku's incoherent mumbling trailing behind him. He peeked back more than once to be sure the tiger didn't fall and break his face open during the short trek.

Leaving the bedroom door open, Arad got into bed and arranged the covers to keep himself cool in the warmer atmospherics while keeping watch to make sure Roku survived the return trip.

Shuffling his feet, Roku crossed the room with all the grace of a brain-dead tweaker, stripped off his kilt, and crawled in bed. He rolled on his side and pressed his gloriously naked self—thick muscles, cock and all—against Arad. A lullaby of snoring immediately resumed.

Arad froze, unwilling to breathe out loud.

Rigid with indecision, he stared at the ceiling, praying his heartbeat—which thundered for a completely new reason—wouldn't wake Roku.

Endless profanities spun through Arad's brain, brought on by each point of contact with Roku's bare body. Truly the universe hated him. It must, considering after granting him the *Ansariland,* as well as giving him the chance to save himself and free him from Torrins, it would gift him an attractive male—fully human or not—who had enough issues to prevent them from being physically intimate in spite of tumbling them together the day they met. Cruel and unusual punishment.

If Arad had said all that out loud, he'd be accused of babbling like a damned fool.

He definitely felt like one.

Roku shifted, throwing one brawny arm across Arad's chest and pulling him closer. The fine coating of fur had all the qualities of delicate silk. A strange contrast to all the power coiled in Roku's frame. Arad gave off a heady shiver as Roku's nose brushed above his temple. A deep inhale rustled his hair. Then a second, deeper still. The timbre of Roku's snores changed, blending seamlessly into a purr.

Barely audible murmurs escaped Roku. "Arad...smell so..." The furry, muscled arm flexed tighter, and the third intense sniff was accompanied by a happy rumble. Arad found himself pulled closer into Roku's unconscious embrace.

Cruel and unusual punishment.

Oh, man, Roku was so, so naked. The crappy hallway lighting coming through the open door caught his kilt on the floor. Despite the dense shadows, enough showed to keep himself from blinking. Whether in shock or hoping to see more? Better not to own up to the question. Rather he should ignore the situation and pretend Roku hadn't sleepwalked into his bed.

The gentle nudge at Arad's thigh—which clearly wasn't Roku's finger—ruined all pretense. Roku rolled his hips in his sleep, and it lurched and gradually crawled its way upward in a lazy arc. It swelled and warmed as it grew like a live creature on a mission, insistent on finding its way up the leg of Arad's loose shorts.

Cruel and unusual punishment.

Could skin burn skin? Because that question seemed awfully important under the circumstances. How many times had he asked himself that in the last minute?

Roku grunted and shifted his hips, causing the veiny length to snake up Arad's thigh. And, yes, he felt every vein and velvety ridge. The upstroke edged the gaping fabric out of the way, giving the DemiShou unrestricted access to his hip after a series of strokes. With his arm pinned at his side to the mattress, the weight grew past his wrist, the heavy sac firming with every pivot of Roku's body. If he reached for it, he'd have a handful of hot pipe— Holy crap! Was it bigger than before?

"Roku? Roku, are you awake?" Arad whispered, trying not to startle the tiger.

The only response Arad got in return was heavier breathing in his hair and stronger purring.

A slick spot formed as Roku's skin rolled back. The plump head started juicing, leaving its slippery trail, enticing Roku to press himself even firmer against Arad's hip. The entire greasy length was trapped between them in a rhythm of tender rutting. Resisting the urge to push against the motion took a great deal of Arad's fraying concentration. Before long, the nutty scent reached him, and his own traitorous dick responded in kind, doing its best to undo his efforts to be good.

A flash of familiarity caught Arad's memories. Davis would behave similarly when he wanted another round rather than let Arad sleep. The main difference was how Davis didn't care what Arad wanted while he rode out his Syn high—he was paying, after all—and Roku wasn't actively aware of anything he was doing. He was too upstanding an individual to be faking sleep. A rare find in Arad's world.

The other difference was he didn't find Roku's attentions the least bit repulsive. Much the opposite.

Closing his eyes, Arad said a silent prayer into the night.

Please let me get through this without doing something stupid we'll both regret.

Fair and life were two words with little connection in Arad's experience. Trading sex had become a way of survival for Arad, but he couldn't remember the last time anyone had shown an interest in him without an ulterior motive. Davis and Torrins wouldn't have been able to say that. When was the last time someone had wanted him for him rather than the service he provided? And when was the last time Arad had been able to say the same?

Roku wanted him. Arad knew that. But he also understood Roku's misgivings on the whole subject. If he woke right now, found himself in Arad's bed, humping his way to a sticky end, he'd probably never forgive himself. He'd yet to come to terms with their first questionable encounter and all its dubious levels of consent. Arad was more pragmatic. Neither had been in their right head at the time. It happened. Hustling carried enough risk he wasn't about to spend hours, days, weeks overthinking sex he'd enjoyed where no one had been hurt.

But Roku was at war with his own values, and Arad refused to make matters worse for him.

Cruel and unusual punishment.

Purring became rougher as Roku's moan turned into frustrated mewling as if what he desperately needed to live lay out of reach in spite of his unconscious efforts. The tone speared Arad's chest and accelerated his already quickened pulse. Could lust be so painful it drove a man to cry? What if it was more than lust?

"Arad...touch me...please..." Roku may have mumbled, but his groggy plea possessed too much gravity to be simply born out of a dream.

Something inside Arad broke free. A craving for pure contact untarnished by the subtext of transaction. A substantial thing they both wanted, whether either one was willing to admit it out loud, and a thing he wouldn't go without.

A man only had so much strength. He'd sort out his repentance later.

Inside Roku's tight embrace, Arad managed to twist himself until he faced the mumbling, slumbering DemiShou. Another heavy inhale across his scalp ignited a fierce shiver over Arad's skin. He knew what he wanted—what Roku wanted—yet he found himself hesitating. The line he dared to cross skimmed so close to the near non-existent boundaries of consent a hustler dealt with.

Roku took in another ragged sample of his scent, coupled with a second whine bordering on begging. The shift in position had left the tiger's hot member rutting along Arad's stomach. If he didn't participate, Roku was going to get his regardless. Arad preferred not being a spectator. He reached for Roku's cock, stopping short of touching. Was this the right thing to do? Another thrust against his body made him test the question. He took a handful of hot flesh and gave the thick stalk a tentative squeeze. The thankful growl he received in return made his doubts flee the room.

No going back now.

With barely enough light to see by, Arad mapped out Roku's chest by rubbing his face against the furred slabs of muscle. The faintest hint of soap and musk clung to the crevasse between the firm and lightly yielding swells. Better than any other he'd had the fortune to indulge in over the years.

Little by little, he shimmied his way lower, sniffing and kissing the thick ridges along the way. The fur spanning Roku's abdomen thinned to nothing once he reached the beast between Roku's legs. Awestruck, Arad shuddered at its impressive length and girth, but it wasn't anything he couldn't manage. It was a thing of pride, and the weight of it in his hand bestowed upon him a lustful reverence.

What would the religious street barkers in Grey District say if they saw him now?

Anything other than "you lucky bastard," and he'd call them lying bitches. Every last one of them. He might do it anyways if he ever found himself planetside again.

All mental side trips vanished as he gave the beefy stalk a lazy yet purposeful squeeze, bringing up a fresh drop of dew from the gaping slit, which glistened in the meager light reflecting about. Too thick to run, the glossy bead beckoned, and Arad wasn't fool enough to ignore its call.

Arad flattened his tongue and drew a wide, wet trail up the veined shaft to the bulbous head, taking the honey-eyed sample coating the flesh. Salty and savory, the flavor was subtly different from any other man he'd known. A DemiShou trait, perhaps? It taunted him, demanding a second taste. A new warmth spread through him centered on his lips and mouth, driving him for more. He placed a kiss to the weeping apple, drilling his tongue into the well as he stroked the length to encourage a stronger flow.

A finer liquor never tasted so sweet.

Arad dared to look up at Roku over the hilled land-scape of his muscled torso. There wasn't much, but there was enough light to glint in the tiger's eyes. Eyes that were open. Watching. Caught, Arad froze, unsure how Roku would react.

Reaching out, Roku palmed the back of Arad's head. He gave a silent signal, a quiet nod, and Arad relaxed his jaw and body, ready and willing. With a slow pivot of his hips, Roku sank his cock deeper and deeper until the base met Arad's lips. Roku held him there, grinding his full sac against Arad's chin, groaning in approval when Arad choked around his meat but didn't resist the intrusion like a good boy.

The whole time Arad's eyes hadn't left Roku's, and the DemiShou appeared pleased without saying a single word. Indulging was easier at times when you didn't have to voice your desires out loud.

Roku backed his hips away, sliding his dick out of Arad's throat, allowing him to take a wicked breath through his nose because his mouth was still full. He wasn't about to release the swollen glans. Oh, no. He was keeping hold of that for the time being.

Now that the pretense was over, Arad went to work. With one hand massaging Roku's balls, he used the other to help stroke and feed himself. The increasing groans spilling out of Roku encouraged him to do more. He may not have preferred the profession he'd fallen into for sur-vival, but it didn't mean Arad hadn't learned the required skills to the best of his ability.

Roku shook with the effort of holding back, regardless of how his hips pushed forward in restrained increments. He must have been dying to bury himself and stay there, but he was a decent man, even in near-mindless ecstasy. Between the noise, the tremors, and the way Roku's cockhead flared, the end was only moments away.

With a stifled roar, Roku stiffened, and the first of several gushes painted Arad's tongue and filled his mouth. He swallowed it all, not willing to waste the delicious nectar beckoning to him like Syn. Roku twitched and yowled with each heavy spurt.

Without releasing Roku's softening member, Arad dug into his own shorts and attacked his own aching need with a desperate urgency. Using both hands, he came with blinding speed. Semen pooled quickly in his cupped hand, threatening to overflow. His labored gasps made Roku's penis fall free, leaving a residual arc along his cheek.

"Get up here," Roku growled.

Suddenly everything became all too real, and Arad hedged. "I should go close the door."

"Get up here, Arad."

"Okay."

Arad scooted into Roku's line of vision as ordered. The tiger took Arad's wrist and brought the messy hand upward while Arad struggled to keep it from spilling. His feline tongue snaked out and licked through the puddle. He cleaned every trace of fluid from Arad's palm, including the wayward streaks seeping from between his fingers. It was a little too soon for a new erection, but Arad saw the potential.

Once finished, Roku gave Arad back his hand and pulled him close. "Now go to sleep."

"Okay."

And Arad did.

Wakefulness dragged Arad to the surface with a firm pull he resisted at all odds. He hadn't slept so well in ages. His efforts ultimately failed, and he opened his eyes to find a handsome tiger watching over him.

Arad croaked, his voice thick with sleep, which hopefully hid his nervousness. "Hi."

"Good morning."

"Is it a good morning?" For Arad, that was the real question. Their first encounter could be blamed on a number of factors, making it no better than waking next to a stranger after a party, but this... This stepped across the consent boundaries Roku had continued to hide behind. How would he react now?

"I think it is."

Relief flooded Arad's chest, leaving him grinning. "Good. Because I don't regret last night one bit."

The eyes sparkling as part of Roku's content expression spoke when he didn't. No blatant evasion. Nothing kept them from lying together and basking in each other's presence without guilt rising to ruin the moment.

Only a sheet covered them, and with an arched brow, Roku lifted the edge, peeking underneath. "Explain a little something to me. We seem a little mismatched here. How did I end up the one naked in your bed?"

"Oh, that was all you." Arad raised a hand to swear the truth. "I tried to be good and keep my hands to myself—"

"Excellent job, I see."

"—but you started humping me in your sleep."

"I did not."

"The crusty cock snot all over my hip and stomach says otherwise. Doesn't matter though. You can only tease a man so far before he retaliates."

Roku gasped in mock offense. "You took advantage of me."

"The big, bad tiger could have stopped me when he woke up."

"But then you wouldn't have finished."

Arad's mouth fell open, too stunned to speak. Not only had Roku made a joke inside his oh-so-earnest comment, but he'd made an entirely inappropriate joke at that. Once Arad wrapped his head around the idea, he burst out laughing, and Roku joined him.

Roku reached out and pulled Arad into his arms as they calmed. He inhaled deep and strong along Arad's temple before his voice sobered.

"I still worry I might hurt you."

Arad pulled back and looked into Roku's eyes. "You've been more human to me than most people I've ever known. I'm not worried you're gonna maul me." Roku didn't look especially convinced. "Look, let's not overthink this. I know we've been kind of thrown together, but I'd like to believe we can figure this out from here. Wherever it goes. We don't own each other, and I don't expect anything from you."

He didn't resist as Arad shifted out of his arms. "I know, but sometimes I get an urge to hide you away and keep you safe."

"We're the only ones here."

"It doesn't mean I don't want to protect you." Roku raised a hand and brushed his knuckles along Arad's cheek.

"Roku, I've been on my own for a long time. You'll learn to get over that." Capturing Roku's hand, he drew it to his chest. "Right now, all I'm asking is that you don't pretend last night didn't happen."

"I won't. I promise."

"And in case I seriously mess this up, in my defense, I'd like to say that no guy in his right mind's ever stuck around before."

"I don't remember if anyone has for me either."

"Blind leading the blind." Releasing his hand, Arad slapped Roku's chest and started to climb out of bed. "Come on. I've worked up an appetite."

Not totally ogling Roku as he dressed took some doing, but somehow Arad managed.

Scratching his waist, Arad spotted the dried remnants on his skin. "I should probably clean up before we eat."

Roku sidled alongside him and sniffed along Arad's neck, clearly sampling inside the collar of his shirt. "Not yet. I like how you smell right now. Your scent is sharper somehow. It reminds me of last night. You can shower later."

"You marked me."

"I was asleep."

"Whatever. Don't think I'm going to stop showering just because it turns you on." Unlike many slugs, Arad had always prided himself on his need for habitual cleanliness.

They padded to the mess hall, walking close enough to bump along each other through the hallway. For a change, Roku prepped their meals. Seeing him trade the unspoken roles they'd fallen into helped alleviate a tiny fluttering of worry.

Roku continued to have his concerns, but he appeared to be setting them aside enough to get to know Arad properly. They weren't gone, of course. No one had that kind of luck. There were still sheer walls to climb and Roku's lack of memory and history to contend with, but the here and now held a much broader scope of possibilities between them. Possibilities Arad wasn't ready to give up. Not anytime soon.

When the cooker chimed, Roku juggled the piping hot bowls of food with a comical series of yowls, nearly dropping both while trying to get them to the table without scorching himself. He skidded one over with a quick poke, and Arad stabbed his utensil in it to keep the bowl from flying off the edge.

Roku shook his hand and blew on his singed fingers. "I've been noticing something. I know we found another case of rations, but we both know that won't last forever."

"Yep." Arad paused, staring into his bowl. Utensil in hand, he'd stopped short of stirring his food, feeling the cozy bubble pop under the weight of reality. He'd been dreading and avoiding this topic.

"And we don't have the parts to fix the engine, right?"

"Yep."

"Do we have a backup plan?"

Thankfully, Roku said *we*. It was good that whatever came next, he expected them to take that next step together. However, it didn't make the answer Arad had been concocting over the last few days any less awkward. Arad's sigh pushed curls of steam from his bowl across the table.

"Yep...but I've got a feeling you're not gonna like it."

Chapter Fifteen

"I still don't understand why you have to go out there."

Arad barely kept his frustration under control. "The reboot didn't work. The problem is something mechanical, and the access is out there."

Two days. For two days they had continued the circular argument, tempers flaring and ebbing. Flaring and ebbing. Two nights Roku had slept on the floor, stalling whatever had begun between them. Standing in front of the airlock, Arad considered pushing Roku outside. Instead, he made final checks on one of the spacesuits stashed in a storage locker for in-transit repair work. Readouts said the seals were intact and the oxygen cells at full capacity. Nice to know Torrins kept them charged. Almost as if he expected to send someone out to fix things. Now if only the suit were designed for someone his size.

It reminded him of when he'd gotten caught dressing in one of his father's bespoke tuxedoes as a child. The sleeves and legs bunched around his shorter limbs. Only the gloves and boots cinched tight around his ankles and wrists kept them from sliding off completely. The helmet rattled around on his shoulders, and he had to keep repositioning it to see properly through the faceplate. Hopefully the spacesuit would fare better than his father's formalwear had.

"The sensors shouldn't be this fragile. The whole grid is out, which doesn't make any sense."

Without a way to enter the room to fix the engines, Arad had scoured the logs and ship specs for another option. Damage reports centered the malfunction on one sensor relay node, which shouldn't have been enough to knock out the entire system, but it was, and it left the *Ansariland* drifting blind with no way to see, navigate, or communicate outside of the ship's confines. Logs narrowed the disruption to the haphazard space fold that had stranded them, pinpointing the issue to the access panels outside the ship.

In outer space. The big, fat nothing of existence.

"And if you need to know why I have to do this, it's because you can't fit into a suit."

Tank had barely fit into one of the generic-sized suits, and he was a huge man. *One size fits all, my ass.* Roku didn't have the slightest chance of getting it past his giant thighs, let alone his chest and shoulders. That plan also assumed he had the tech knowledge to do the repair work, which he didn't. That left the job falling to one person.

Terrified didn't even begin to describe Arad's state of mind. He was about to do something unbelievably dangerous he'd only learned out of an instruction manual. The trauma of living in Grey District left most people at various levels of practiced wariness, but the edginess growing under his skin was brand new. It made him barely aware of the skittering discomfort growing between him and Roku, and that bothered him more than he wanted to admit. No man had ever affected him enough to leave him off-center. The discontent only reinforced the need to repair the sensor array and hopefully end the discussion with angry voices.

Arad raised his hand, showing the monitor panel woven into the suit's forearm. "I uploaded all the schematics. I can do this. While you've been painting on your handheld, I've been studying the instructions and mechanical specs. It's what I do."

"You should be looking for safer alternatives. Another option has to be out there."

"I already have. For weeks now. Frankly, I'm out of ideas, and I need to do something. You, on the other hand, could start trusting that I'm not some idiot kid who can't handle himself."

"Trust has nothing to do with this." Crossing his arms over his swollen chest, Roku somehow took offense, which only pissed Arad off more.

"What does it have to do with, Roku? I've gotten through a lot of garbage in my day. It may have been a shitty life, but I managed to survive fine before you hatched. So either you trust me to do this, or you don't."

"Have you ever done anything like this before?"

Arad made a quick inventory of the tools slung to his belt. "No, I haven't."

"How can you be sure you know what you're doing?"

"One hundred percent? I'm not. I stopped being an overconfident little snot when I got thrown into the workhouse. Anyone who ever thinks they know everything is stupid, and it eventually bites them in the ass. That's not me. I'm doing everything I can to make this as safe as I can. I'm not planning on dying. Not yet."

"I could stop you."

Arad glared. "I wouldn't advise it. I'd never forgive you for it. Plus, you can't stay awake forever."

The crease between Roku's eyes deepened as his shoulders dropped and he uncrossed his arms. "I still don't like this."

Arad wished Roku's objections were rooted in his artist's eye balking over the suit's ridiculous fit. It wasn't, but now was hardly the time to discuss his recent protective streak rearing its head. A job needed to be done.

"Me either. But we need to be able to call for help or we're both screwed."

Arguing was fruitless, and Arad took advantage of the pause. After stepping into the airlock, he closed the hatch behind him. Sounds inside the suit rang hollow, making the increased rhythm of his heartbeat echo as the air cycled out. Readouts on his forearm said the seals were holding. From his waist, he extended the umbilical cable and inserted the plug end into the security socket next to the outer door.

He chanced a peek and found Roku's worried face pressed tight in the hatch's tiny window. The DemiShou was as scared as Arad but didn't have the good sense not to let that overwhelm the truth: This needed to be done, or their chance of long-term survival was nil. They hadn't had enough time together to shorten their futures with irrational fear. If the streets of Grey District couldn't crush Arad's spirit, one spacewalk wouldn't do it either. Right?

With a small wave, he pressed the control, and the hull opened to the nothingness of space and unfamiliar stars.

Arad reminded himself to breathe.

The first thing before him was the darkness. Wherever the *Ansariland* had reappeared after his desperate jump to avoid being incinerated lacked a star close enough to give off more than a smattering of light. The stars in the distance were useless, random pixels of illumination. Cast in near-absolute shadow, the ship's hull was defined solely by a minimal number of landing lights and transponder beacons.

The lack of gravity was next. He held tight to the open hatch, noticing how every little move left him buoyant. Equal and opposite reactions wanted to send him drifting, his weight non-existent.

"Just gotta be careful. Real careful."

With his free hand, Arad tapped the side of his helmet. An oblong spotlight revealed the ship's surface, ridges and niches barely visible without the severe shadows highlighting them. He reached out and found a handhold. Not much of one, but the weightlessness required less. He'd never have the strength to climb the side of a mountain, but out here in the nothing, things were different.

It was no less unnerving, however.

Arad pulled himself out of the airlock and painfully, gradually crawled over the ship. Each new grip was careful and methodical because his body swayed when he moved too quickly. The last thing he needed was to fling himself into the vacuum.

"Roku, can you hear me?"

Nothing.

"Roku?"

His sigh fogged the faceplate, which the suit's automatic system immediately evaporated. At least something worked as intended. He'd suspected communications would be out once he left the airlock, and the specs noted no audio hardline in the umbilical. He was on his own out here.

"Dammit, Torrins. I know somehow this is your fault. No, wait. I know this is your fault. If you hadn't been such a scheming jerk, none of this would have happened."

Arad checked his oxygen levels. Ninety-nine percent. Not bad for five minutes out.

"Let's be careful, Arad. We're not dying out here after all we've done so far."

He needed to stop talking out loud. The suit smothered every word, making it clear how inhospitable the environment outside was. Or lack of environment. Or lack of anything. Nothing around him for light years and all he thought about was how this dead noise must be like being buried alive under kilometers of dirt. No one can hear you. The random speculation only fed the continuous agitation. Under it all grew the urge to scramble inside, cling to Roku, and rub himself raw into his silky coat while he screwed Arad stupid.

That idea wasn't the problem. It was the urgency he found disturbing. Arad didn't count on anyone for longer than necessary because people couldn't be trusted, yet here he was, fighting a craving beyond their obvious connection. The separation grated his nerves, but he had to set it aside. Better to focus on the task at hand rather than decipher his weird thirst for tiger.

Hand over hand, he worked his way across. The pace stayed achingly slow, partially from keeping the visor positioned properly to see. The gloves dulled his sense of touch as well due to the ill-fitting garment, but what else could he do but push on? He was afraid to look and see how close he was to the open airlock hatch because he might turn around.

Was it possible to be claustrophobic in a sea of nothing?

"Did you hear something?" Arad rapped his knuckles on the plating. "No, of course you didn't, because the only thing to hear is your pulse as your heart tries to kick through your rib cage." Hysterical laughter surfaced, trapped by the suit's confines, but he stuffed it down, refusing to let it escape.

No, no, no. Calm down. Now's not the time to hyperventilate.

Sweat dampened his clothing, causing the clammy layer to bind and gather with each movement. *Is it getting hot in here?* A fine dusting of frost glistened off the hull under the headlamp's glare. *Probably not.*

He'd memorized the ship's problem area through the schematics, but recognizing it in real time proved harder than expected. The vantage point of inching along the hull at this ant-sized scale made keeping track of his location a chore. From the outside, the *Ansariland* made some of the mech ships that used to land in Grey District's ports appear wimpy in comparison.

A quick glance left Arad's oxygen cells at ninety-five percent. "I'm not suffocating yet."

Occasionally he'd turn his head, trying to sight the hull breach over the engine room, but that sector was much farther away than he was traveling. However, when his headlamp swept across the spot he'd been hunting for, he didn't have to guess to know he'd found it. Scorch marks blackened the edges of one of the bent hull plates. The panel was wrenched half-open, hanging on by one welded side. Sparks flashed and arced between the exposed circuit boards underneath.

Fingertips wedged into shallow niches, he swung a tight circle around the opening. The jump must have been hard enough to warp the plating and pull the boards out of position. He recognized them from the files as part of the sensor array. Not seated properly in the connection slot, the circuit flared, most likely shorting out the entire system as it tried to reconcile the error and reboot the system.

In spite of the carbon scoring the area, the best option would be to complete the connection so the rest of the system could compensate for one weak zone. The array was designed to deal with partial outages, not one node causing a cascade failure.

The real question was, how to accomplish it? A flat edge rimmed the protruding board that might give a surface for leverage, but how would he safely lever it back into place with the tools he had? Plus, the live sparking might cook him through the handle. He needed to do something fast and sudden, but he didn't even have a hammer, because why would he have needed that?

An idea came to mind. It wasn't the greatest idea, but he only wanted to waste oxygen resources going back for more tools if he had no other choice. Better that than letting Roku further question his ability.

"Oh, Roku, if you could read my mind, you'd be really pissed right now. I wouldn't blame you though." A new rush of sweaty heat filled the suit as he shifted closer to the faulty circuit. "Man, I hope this thing's well insulated." *Don't get electrocuted. Don't get electrocuted.*

Arad raised his knee high, then stomped the panel with all his strength. It bottomed into the slot, ending the sparks. The weightless recoil shoved him backward, sending him floating away from the *Ansariland* and into space.

"Oh, shit."

Chapter Sixteen

No rushing wind signaled the speed of flying into the distance of outer space, only the sight of the *Ansariland*'s hull shrinking through Arad's visor. Horror spiked in short, rapid gasps, freezing his voice until Arad remembered the umbilical connecting him to the ship. He could use it to drag himself to the airlock, and everything would be fine. The lazy cable spun in his vision as it snaked between him and the ship. It drew taut and gave a quick jerk and...

Detached from his suit.

.

.

.

.

.

Time turned sluggish as the reality set in. The cable bumped between his flailing hands clad in clumsy gloves, and the umbilical fell out of reach. Arad could only stare, panicked and helpless as his lifeline teased his safety, gradually floating away. The minuscule distance was no less daunting than a canyon and, given enough time, would become one. The tension during the disconnect had slowed him, but he was still drifting out into the vast wasteland.

.

.

.

.

.

The screaming only stopped when Arad's throat went hoarse.

.

.

.

.

.

Oxygen levels 56 percent.

.

.

.

.

.

How long had he been out here? The hysterical edge had leveled into numb clarity through pure exhaustion. The giggling fit abated, having replaced the last round of sobs. Able to think again, he pieced through his dilemma.

Somehow the cable hadn't been engaged properly, whether by user error or faulty design. He scrounged his memories over all the instructions. He'd been so careful, hadn't he? Followed every step and received all the green lights. Did he screw this up, or would it have happened no matter what? Did it matter? Either way, he was going to die for it.

After all he'd been through, where was the fairness in that?

Ousted by his parents. Surviving the workhouse. Pneumonia. Escaping the raid on Sketch's apartment. Learning how to hustle on the streets of Grey District and managing not to wind up in a trash compactor in some serial murderer's attempt to hide the body.

Torrins and his crew—no matter how less than ideal—had been a gamble for real future opportunity. No one had believed his stint on board the *Midas Ascending* would be permanent. The change of scenery and Torrins's bed were simply a means to an end. He'd intended to eventually walk off the ship with money in hand and actual references to use toward new employment. Legitimate employment. Once it became the *Ansariland*, the idea of staying on forever wasn't so bad. The ship was his, banged up and all, to make use of. Being grateful for acquiring the ship was hardly charitable based on how it had happened, but he wasn't about to thank Torrins any time soon, the scheming prick.

Certainly not with the time he had left.

Checking the display only reinforced Arad's understanding. Once the oxygen cells were dead, so was he.

The worst part? There was no way to say goodbye to Roku. He imagined how devastated Roku would be when Arad didn't return. Or once he'd realized there was a problem. He had to know something was wrong after so long. Had he seen Arad's stupid amateur maneuver that had led to this, powerless to do anything? Imagining Roku's horror made Arad want to start crying again, but his eyes were dry and his cheeks caked with salt. There was no way to let him know for sure. Communications wouldn't be restored without a fresh restart, even if settling the circuit board corrected the fault. While he'd been able to grant Roku access to roam the ship, Roku hadn't been added to the crew roster and given a rank. Arad hadn't researched how to do that yet. They had been distracted with other things and he hadn't seen the urgency, so the operating system wouldn't update the tiger with command controls once he'd left the ship. No engine to travel. No communications or sensors. Eventually the food would run out, and Roku would be left alone with no way to reach out for help after Arad was gone.

Arad's mistake had killed them both.

Guilty tears didn't come but still forced dry, painful sobs out of him. "I'm so, so sorry, Roku."

The craving for Roku clawed at his soul, never having quieted despite the amazingly poor timing. His despair and resignation had done nothing to smother it, and the only cure sat so far, far away on the *Ansariland*. He would give anything to curl up in those sheltering arms, if only for one more day. So much they'd barely touched on. So much to still explore. Arad would never wake up to find the purring giant in his bed again, and the loss tore at the raw space under his ribs.

His eyes burned knowing they'd never even kissed.

How many days had passed with him standing watch over the sleeping DemiShou before Roku woke? He'd promised himself to care for the outcasts, the people like himself. Who knew a promise had a shelf life?

"I should have listened to you, but what else could I do?"

He'd been so sure about the repair. Roku's objections had wounded his ego and spurred Arad to prove him wrong. Obstacle after obstacle had grown in his path through his whole life, and he'd managed to leap over each one. Yes, he'd tripped here and there, but he'd honestly believed despite his worries, this would be yet one more step forward. A difficult step, but forward nonetheless. Like all the rest. Perhaps pride was his sin rather than lust?

Thankfully, he'd never have to reveal this to the crazy preacher shouting scripture at all the heathens in Grey District. She'd never have shut up about it.

A raspy peal of laughter echoed inside the suit. Better to laugh than start crying again.

Why was the edge of madness such a real thing?

Arad shifted the helmet's sloppy fit to see better. The *Ansariland* was much, much smaller in the distance. He hoped whatever station Roku haunted right now, he had no viewport to see Arad as he gradually disappeared in the airless void. Given the lack of light, it was doubtful either of them could have kept an eye on him.

Oxygen levels 35 percent.

This was taking an awfully long time. At least the oxygen cells worked correctly. Hopefully death by asphyxiation wouldn't hurt too much, but somehow he doubted it.

No. He was not giving up. Not now. Not after all he'd been through. Roku needed him, and he wasn't ready to give him up. Not yet.

But the real question: How would he fix this?

A deep breath forced his brain into a shaky order through sheer will. Arad needed to cancel his momentum and generate new thrust. How? What did he have to do anything of the sort? Releasing air through a small hole in the suit might push him in the right direction, but he had no way to seal it again, and who knows if he had enough oxygen to last until he reached the *Ansariland*?

Think, Arad, think.

How did this happen? It all started from stomping the circuit board. The physical force rebounded and uncontrollably pushed him off. Equal and opposite reaction. He chuckled without humor. Maybe his science classes weren't a waste after all.

He needed to come up with an option to reverse the process, and he needed it now.

What he wouldn't give for a can of compressed air or other propellant. The tools anchored to his belt were more mechanical in nature, intended for use in a vacuum. None of them had a power source useable for propulsion.

Oxygen levels 33 percent.

A solution needed to appear soon, or his chances of making it inside were slimming into nothing.

Arad wracked his mind in frustration. Whether it was his desperation or the constant yearning for Roku—which shouldn't be building while he scrounged for ideas—he couldn't find a solution. There wasn't an option to get himself home. Rage swept over him because crying hadn't given him sufficient release. Snarling, he snatched a wrench off his belt, wishing for something, anything, to smash. Right now, he'd crush the circuit board if he had a chance.

The circuit board.

Physical action had provided the first thrust that had launched him into the dark. Could another undo it? Only one way to find out.

Carefully, Arad kicked and twisted, causing him to turn around until the *Ansariland* faced his back. He hated doing this to perfectly good tools, but they were going to be lost out here anyways, so…

With all his might, Arad heaved the wrench out into the abyss.

Hopefully the force would cancel his current speed and send him back the way he came. Arad allowed himself to spin around while holding his breath to see if he'd done it correctly. He squinted to be sure, but the ship grew in his visor. Barely. He was drifting toward the *Ansariland*.

Unfortunately, he'd burned too much oxygen getting to this point, and he wasn't moving fast enough. But there were more tools on his belt, and he was determined to get home. Every time the *Ansariland* was behind him as he spun, Arad hurled a tool for thrust, checking his trajectory between each to speed up the trek until his belt sat empty.

Oxygen levels 29 percent.

Reaching the end of the tether had slowed him initially but not stopped him. Now, he had to hope to cover the distance with the air he had left. Arad prayed he'd built up enough momentum to make up the lost time. Agonizing minutes passed as he continued in a lazy spin, afraid to ruin his speed by trying to halt it. Watching the *Ansariland* come and go in his vision helped pass the time. Keeping his eyes off the wrist monitor's time-stamp proved difficult.

Achingly slow, the ship grew as he closed in, almost giddy at his decent aim, considering how poorly he'd managed the rest. The area's feeble light tricked him into thinking he was flying at a more reasonable rate, but slamming into the hull erased that mirage. With a mad scream, Arad scrabbled to get a grip on the nearby exhaust port's rim, barely preventing himself from bouncing back into the dark. His side ached from the impact, and the bruising would be spectacular, but he would worry about that once he was inside once again.

"You can do this."

He'd landed on the ship's underbelly. A quick scan caught a faint reflection. The umbilical waved in his headlamp. Too far off to reach, but seeing it marked his goal. Following it to the airlock was a possibility.

WARNING — Oxygen levels 9 percent.

"Stop looking at the damn screen already!"

This would be close. He had farther to travel, and he could only hold his breath for so long. Without wasting another moment, Arad crawled across the hull. The pace was somewhat reckless, and controlling his breathing took effort. *Don't waste the air.* There was a good chance the oxygen cell would expire faster near the end of its life. Losing the game through hyperventilating would be a poor way to go.

He skimmed along the surface, the cable in his sights. A beacon of hope in a hopeless night.

Working as fast as he dared, he pushed along, grabbing the edges between panels and ports, trying not to count the minutes he was losing. Images of Roku flickered behind his eyes, the main fuel for keeping him moving and not giving in. There was still a chance, even if the target appeared so far away.

When the lamp swept over the open airlock, he nearly shouted in success. Almost there, but he needed to get inside before he passed out. The timer threatened to zero out if he lost focus now.

WARNING — Oxygen levels 2 percent.

Climbing into the airlock, he disconnected the umbilical and tossed the useless piece of shit outside. He punched the control and waited for the hatch to close. The moment it sealed, he spun and activated the airlock cycle, praying not to make a mistake with the fat-fingered gloves.

WARNING — Oxygen levels 1 percent.

He couldn't speak. He couldn't breathe. Only wait for the atmosphere to level out and the inner lock to release. His eyes filled and he ground his teeth.

Oh, please don't let this be the time I don't survive my life.

WARNING — Oxygen cell depleted.

The indicator light went green, and Arad punched the button. The door ground open, and he lurched inside.

Fog coated the visor as the air inside the suit grew dank faster than Arad expected. His lungs seized as he scratched at the helmet, searching for the seal releases. The gloves' poor fit required him to have a surer hand, and with the rising panic, he did not. Darkness crept into his sight. Colors separated and turned grey. Suffocating in his suit after barely making it inside would be an unfair way to die.

Many things in Arad's life were unfair.

Chest burning, he fell over but curiously didn't hit the floor. His hands were slapped away from the helmet, and the vacuum seal broken open, letting in a fresh burst of atmosphere.

Recycled air had never tasted so sweet. He inhaled like it would be the last breaths he'd ever have. Color and light restored themselves in concert with hard, wheezing gasps. His vision settled, and Roku came into focus, holding Arad with one arm and slinging the helmet aside with the other.

Roku's brow furrowed in concern, and matted fur drew dingy lines from his wide eyes to his jawline. The sleek hair coating his arms and shoulders stood up in patches, a mark of disquiet.

"Arad. Arad, can you hear me?"

"Yeah...I'm okay." The suit confines became unbearable the moment Arad couldn't find the next seal clasp. The outfit had nearly been his burial shroud. It needed to come off. He scratched at the seams with an increasing apprehension, but his fingers inside these stupid gloves refused to grasp the release. The lack of success made his breathing race and his pulse surge. Tears filled his eyes. "Get...get me out. I need to get out of this."

Without a word, Roku flipped the catches Arad had missed and opened the suit. Arad scrambled to free himself even as Roku peeled away the reinforced fabric. Only once his feet hit the deck did Arad calm somewhat, keeping one hand firmly on Roku's arm, unwilling to break another lifeline.

Acrid sweat and other indignities wafted from the suit, reminding Arad of the hours spent at its mercy, and he kicked the suit aside. The scent revolted him. He could only imagine what Roku's heightened sense of smell picked up from it. The stink permeated his clothing and skin. He wanted to remove it, to wash away the memories.

"I...I need a shower."

Arad wiped at his eyes and snuffling nose as he headed for the lavatory, his grip on Roku's wrist. The tiger allowed himself to be dragged, not protesting or resisting for a second. The lights turned on automatically when Arad entered the room and strode to the shower. Catching his haggard reflection in the mirror, he nearly burst into tears. He tore at his clothing, unable to figure out how to remove the tacky, clinging garments.

"I...I can't get them off." Arad's vision blurred as he came unraveled.

Roku's enormous hands covered Arad's. "Shh... Let me help you."

Arad sniffled and nodded as he let Roku's hands trail down the hem of his shirt and peel the fabric upward. It tangled for a moment around his head, and a spike of panic howled out of him. Once the shirt cleared his face, Roku palmed the back of Arad's neck and held him close, rubbing his cheek and jaw along Arad's. It soothed Arad, bringing the first signs of calm under his rib cage.

Once Roku had completely stripped Arad down, the sensation of choking finally let go. Unlike his grip on Roku's arm. He only gave up the contact long enough to lose his shirt and claimed it again. Now undressed, he found himself unwilling to give it up, so he leaned forward into Roku's chest and made the touch swallow him.

Roku reached in and started the shower. "Are you ready to bathe?"

Arad simply nodded into Roku's chest, comforted by the muscular arm holding him close, but made no move to enter the stall. An endless minute passed before Roku reached down and unfastened his kilt. The heavy weave brushed Arad's shins and feet as it fell to the floor.

Still holding Arad against him, Roku led them into the steamy shower, protecting Arad's face from the spray. The two of them inside was a tight fit—especially given Roku's size—but it didn't trigger Arad's fears. He simply stood, letting Roku rub the soaking warmth into his bones. Not even a soft moan left his lips when Roku collected some body wash and tenderly soaped his hair, taking his time to do a thorough job. Once complete, he rinsed Arad's head clean and worked his way down, bit by bit, cleaning every centimeter of Arad's weary frame down to his feet.

Neither Arad's nor Roku's body responded to the intimate touches, even when Roku washed his privates and backside. Not even when they were pressed together under the water to prevent Arad from puddling to the floor. An act he was certainly capable of at that point. No, Arad simply luxuriated in Roku's ministrations, letting them overwhelm the lingering horror and bringing him ever so gradually into the real world.

Roku cleaned himself briefly without losing hold of Arad, who was in no condition to help. He shut down the shower and edged Arad out into the lavatory. The disposable towels scuffed his bare skin, but the deliberate care of Roku's efforts drowned out any discomfort.

Roku grabbed a few more towels and rubbed himself dry as best he could with an arm around Arad's shoulders. His fur resisted some of his efforts. Leaving their clothes in a heap on the floor, he curled his free arm under Arad's knees and lifted him off the floor. Wet footfalls echoed off the hull as he carried Arad into the hallway.

Nuzzling Arad's temple, Roku took long telling inhales that tickled Arad's hair. "Let's get you dressed and in bed. I think we both need some rest."

Arad curled his arm around Roku's neck and snuggled in deep. He couldn't agree more.

Chapter Seventeen

Fitful sleep chased Arad through the night. Roku's purposeful inhales against his skin kept him from finding it, yet he wouldn't give up the sensation for all the funds in Grey District. The tiger dozed, but his distress was clear, visible along the ragged edges of his usually smooth fur.

Arad hadn't said a word about the state of the *Ansariland* when Roku had escorted—or rather carried—him from the shower. No comment about the weight bench that had been flung against the wall or the broken exercise machine. Silence over the gouged metal showing through the hallway paint scoured with an overlapping quilt of claw marks. Arad didn't ask, and Roku didn't share.

Carefully, Arad shifted to see Roku better, trying not to wake him, but found him watching, eyes heavy and lidded.

"I thought I'd lost you." Roku's thick whisper dripped with fatigue in spite of their nap. Anguish spilled across his damp eyes. His whole face sat in half shadow as if under harsh antique neon, and Arad put together the fragile pieces of Roku's continuous despair.

"Oh, man, you saw me out there, didn't you?"

Deep knife lines marred Roku's brow as he averted his eyes. "I watched you out every viewport I could find as soon as you stepped out of the airlock. I was scared something would go wrong. Then you were floating away, and there was nothing I could do."

"I'm sorry. I should have listened. You were right. I probably shouldn't have been out there."

"I don't want to be right. I don't care if I am. You did what you needed to do. I'm glad you made it back." With a deep exhale, Roku nuzzled the side of Arad's face and neck. "In your absence, I may have done some damage to the ship."

"Define some."

Eyes narrowing, a tiny frown painted Roku's mouth. "You already know, don't you?"

A tiny shrug punctuated Arad's grin. "I think it's pretty superficial. You can fix the bench press and repaint the walls later."

"Is that an order, Captain?"

"Yes. I believe that is."

Even through the fear, the near-death experience, and the caretaking during his meltdown, Arad still rode his messed-up cravings for Roku. What kind of man wanted to get laid when his life was in danger? A mentally deficient man, that's who. The cinders never extinguished, continuing to smolder even greater now, especially given their current proximity. And hearing about how affected Roku had been made Arad weirdly happy. Oxygen deprivation may have damaged his already dubious morals.

He put it out of his mind for now, but the damn itch proved persistent...and continuous.

Roku rolled onto his back, taking Arad with him. Lying on top of Tiger Mountain's peaks of muscle made for a lumpy mattress, but Arad wasn't about to climb down anytime soon. He settled his head on the expanse of chest as Roku breathed and examined the unnatural pattern of stripes. Roku studied the ceiling as he rummaged around in his own head. "The only part I don't understand is, how did it happen? You studied the procedure for days. You were being so careful."

"I thought I was. Everything was going smooth until I found the open bulkhead."

"Was that damage in the sector you were looking for?"

"Yeah. A panel got ripped open either from that cruiser shooting us or the fold. A bunch of circuit boards for the sensor grid got exposed. One of them had gotten dislodged—maybe during the jump—and was out of its socket."

"Is that why the sensors won't restart?"

Chin perched below Roku's collar, Arad nodded. "Most likely. Probably shorting the system. The way it was sparking, it was too dangerous to handle, so I stomped it into place. But I misjudged the zero gravity and bounced off the ship. The cable disconnected—"

Roku closed his eyes and covered Arad's mouth with his hand. "Stop. Please. I'm not ready to hear any more details. Not yet. I have enough nightmares to deal with."

Arad nodded and let the conversation fade. No attempt was made by either of them to leave the bed, and something about that felt right. Luxuriating in another's company without worrying about where the next meal would come from or where he'd sleep the following night. An indulgence Arad hadn't experienced in far too many years.

Men in Arad's past had been allies, enemies, or customers. No lovers to be seen. Torrins and Davis didn't count. Contact with both men was a transaction, not a relationship. It was sad to think how much time had passed as a slug.

That was strange. He'd referred to himself as a slug less and less recently. His self-worth had been an absent friend for so long he almost didn't recognize it when it showed its face. Who could blame him, considering the scars and bruises it wore? Being an up-and-coming socialite one day and tossed into a workhouse with only the clothing on his back the next had battered it into submission. Too much in the beginning, not enough after the fact.

But then Roku entered his life in the outrageous, unconventional way he did. Being sex mauled should have brought Arad even lower, but seeing Roku's genuine regret for something out of his control endeared him to Arad. Watching Roku struggle to contain himself, showing his honorable nature in spite of the lack of memories, only added to his esteem.

While not perfect, Roku had proved himself many times over, and the *Ansariland* would have been an extremely lonely place without him. Instead, it had turned into a home. A home Arad was willing to fight for to preserve and protect the family inside. Even if it was a small family, it meant more to him than the biological ingrates who had turned their backs on him before.

The peace he swam in surrounded by the half man, half tiger was sublime. He'd ignore the ship repairs to have every day be like this. It was almost a shame they still needed to fix things.

"You said you put the board back in place?"

Roku's question startled Arad out of his pleasurable musings, and it took him a significant pause to rally an answer. "Yeah, I think so."

"Are the sensors working now?"

Arad pushed himself upward on one arm to stare into Roku's eyes, blinking in wide-eyed confusion. In all the chaos, he'd ignored the most obvious result of the outer space drama.

"Um... You know what? I don't know."

Without waiting another moment, Arad threw back the cover and bounced out of bed. He headed out into the hallway, not waiting for Roku to follow. A new energy suffused his body, igniting a spark in the gloom. The mishaps during the spacewalk were shoved out from under the microscope and into a glaring spotlight.

Bare feet slapped the metal floor with increasing speed the closer Arad came to the bridge. His heart thumped with the rising tension. Now with the question out in the air, could he bear the answer? No path inside the ship took long, but getting to the front of the *Ansariland* and the command controls appeared endless. Anxiety extended the corridors into a trek through dry desert.

Too bad he never broke into Tank's liquor stash. A dose of courage sounded like a good idea.

Many days over the last few months had been spent on the bridge, yet he crossed the threshold with wary steps. A life full of near misses and near escapes could only be pushed so far. The ship was his, but he found himself praying to it, begging for it to grant him this small privilege.

Arad slid into the navigator's seat. Tremors unsteadied his hands even as he tapped at the monitor. Finding the path through the menus was easy for a change. After the jump, he'd ran this program so many times. Each time hoping the system would resolve its error and allow the restart. Clean out the glitch. Refresh and become operational. And every time it had failed.

INITIALIZE SENSOR GRID – Y/N?

Step one complete. Now if only it would continue.

Arad licked his lips and swallowed, hands hovering over the control. The chance of the system being fixed was so remote, but in all likelihood, the initial problem hadn't appeared to be a complicated one. However, luck was fickle, and he'd danced on its razor's edge for longer than most.

"No time like the present." Holding his breath, he pressed an index finger to the screen.

SENSOR GRID INITIALIZATION IN PROGRESS

Step two complete. Two more to go.

For once, Roku's natural feline stealthiness didn't hide his entrance to the bridge. "Any news so far?"

"Too early to tell."

Roku settled close, peering over Arad's shoulder. His firm chest pressed against Arad's shoulder blade. "How long should this take?"

"I don't know. It hasn't worked since the *Ansariland* became mine."

"What will we do if it doesn't work?"

Exhaling, Arad shuddered. "I'm not sure."

Doubt spiraled Arad, closing in after so many failed attempts. Lasting solutions had been out of his grasp for so long. Why would this be any different? If Roku hadn't been anchoring him, he'd have walked out, unable to bear another loss.

An electronic chime finally broke the wait.

*** SENSOR GRID ACTIVE ***

Step three. Arad stifled a gasp to hide any premature excitement. The next prompt did not help.

*** INITIALIZE SUBSYSTEMS – Y/N? ***

Without another word, Arad chose *yes*. According to every schematic he'd laid his hands on, communications was integrated with the sensors in a way where disabling one had shut down the other, without a user-friendly method to untangle them. Since the jump, the *Ansariland* had drifted blind, making Arad want to strangle the idiot engineer responsible for the design flaws. Probably someone who had never set foot inside a spacecraft or held a wrench in their lives.

Admittedly, being adrift with no prying eyes had been a godsend at first, but once Roku woke, everything changed. The stakes were new, and the survival game needed new strategy.

COMMUNICATIONS SUBSYSTEM ACTIVE

Step four.

Roku leaned closer, pushing Arad off the seat. "Is it working?"

After so many failures, it shouldn't be active. Arad swiped the windows to fill the screen, allowing the data to flicker through intermittent static. "It's a little sketchy, and there's still gaps in the sensor range—"

A gentle, happy chuckle floated out of Roku. "But it's working."

"Not completely—"

"We can see what's out there again, right?"

"Yeah, but it's hardly perfect—"

Sincere reverence and wonder coated Roku's voice. "But you did it."

The honest compliment made Arad wince. "I guess." Despite all his plans, he'd spent years skating by on sheer dumb luck and sly maneuvers. It drove this success into unfamiliar territory. A loser from Grey District didn't deserve this kind of praise. Not for plugging in a loose circuit board.

"Arad, stop!" Roku grabbed Arad by the shoulders and gave him a shake. "You went outside and risked your life for us. Before this, we were floating blind with no long-term hope of survival. We have a chance now. A *real* chance. You did it!"

Eyes alight, and grinning, Roku shifted his hands down to Arad's waist and tossed him in the air, smacking Arad into the ceiling with a dull thud of skull on metal.

"Ow!"

Smile flashing into shock, Roku gathered Arad close, stroking his head with panicked but delicate caresses. "Oh, I'm so sorry. I'm so sorry."

"That's gonna leave a mark." Covering the throbbing point with one hand, Arad didn't fight Roku's attentions. The more contact, the less he paid attention to the ache. "I'll be okay. It's just my head."

"I didn't mean to do that. I swear."

"I believe you. For the future, I don't think the ceiling's high enough for that kind of celebration."

Arad laughed, and the concern filling Roku's expression became warm and giving. While he had stopped checking Arad for injuries, he had yet to lower Arad's feet to the floor. "You're amazing…"

Arad's brain stalled trying to remember the last time anyone had said such sweet words to him without expecting anything in return. Slugs weren't accustomed to kindness. Promises from men like Davis were the most they could hope for. Until today.

The sight of Roku's earnest smile made Arad's eyes mist. Maybe shards of splintered bone shredding his grey matter had added to his brain damage. There had to be an explanation. Something in Roku's rapt focus drew Arad in, made the nightmares and memory loss seem unimportant, overlaying all their trials and suffering with a feeling he hadn't known in ages. Hope. Palpable and savory between them, they shared it, and it sang of the potential future. The sensation flooded Arad as he reached out and cradled Roku's head between his palms.

Roku's raspy whisper thickened. "Arad, what...what are you doing?"

"Shh...now's not the time for talking." Leaning forward, Arad covered Roku's lips with his own.

Roku froze but warmed with little coaxing. The kiss was different—Roku's lips weren't human anymore, yet they found a rhythm of mouths and teasing licks to one another easily enough. Need sang inside Arad. Despite all his experience, it was a clumsy act he rarely allowed in his years hustling. Too intimate. Too personal. And now they'd shared the first taste together with equal hunger and equal consent, he only wanted one thing.

More.

They separated, and Roku fixed his lidded gaze to Arad's. "We shouldn't be doing this. I might hurt you."

"When you woke up, out of your mind, you managed not to hurt me."

"But—"

Arad silenced Roku by whispering fingertips over his mouth. "You didn't then. You won't now. I don't expect anything in return. I only want you. Stop making me wait for what we both need."

For a tense moment, Roku searched Arad's gaze as if waiting for a sign he might change his mind. It never came. With a brief nod, he lurched forward and claimed Arad's mouth for his own. No tentative nibbles. Permission given, he devoured Arad with full abandon. He didn't even back off as he lifted Arad and stumbled out of the bridge. As long as he didn't slam them into the wall while he rushed them through the halls, Arad didn't care where they went.

The world spun and they fell. Again, Arad did not care as long as Roku held him close. Familiar sights and sounds of the bedroom surrounded them. They bounced on the unmade bed, with Roku covering Arad with his body.

Taking strong inhales, Roku rubbed his face and chin along Arad's neck and shoulder. "Your scent makes me so... It makes me want you so much. I'm sorry I made you wait for me."

"Don't be sorry. I think we both had to wrap our heads around it all. We're here now."

Roku's sniffing caught in Arad's collar, and he suddenly sat up. Arad stayed confused only until Roku grabbed his shirt and yanked it over his head. It was still floating in the air when Roku attacked Arad's shorts and divested him of them just as quick. Arad's head continued to spin when Roku jumped backward long enough to unfasten his kilt and toss it aside. His ample member mesmerized Arad as it bobbed in concert with his racing heartbeat. Without warning, Roku pounced, rubbing his entire silky, fur-laden body over Arad's.

Less than a minute passed before Roku froze, pressing his forehead into Arad's chest. "I'm sorry."

"For what?"

"I'm rushing this, and I shouldn't, but your scent... It makes me want things."

Gripping Roku's jaw with both hands, Arad raised his head and forced the tiger to look him in the eye. "Roku, c'mon. We've spent *weeks* doing foreplay. I think it's okay for you to nail me now."

Arad reached for the bedside drawer, but his hand came up short due to Roku's weight pinning him to the bed. Taking the cue, the tiger grasped the handle and jerked it open. Peering inside, he paused.

"There's a lot of items in here you've never talked about before."

"What do you mean... Oh, no."

Roku started poking around in the drawer. "This is...incriminating."

"Can we get back on task here?"

"Why do you have handcuffs in here?"

Heat flushed through every part of Arad's body. "Shut up and grab the slick already."

Roku chuckled and pulled back, treasure in hand. He went to work unstoppering the bottle with a quick flip of his thumb. It may have been a little while since anyone had been inside him, but Arad hadn't forgotten how to re-lax, how to fall into the stretch as Roku worked one, then two big slippery fingers down to the last knuckle. Desper-ation, experience, and impatience sped the process through three fingers.

"For no memories, you've got this prep work down." Arad almost protested when Roku took back his fingers.

Licking his lips, Roku upended the bottle again. "Some things are pure instinct."

Slathering a coat of gel on his length, Roku aimed for Arad's needy hole. Arad raised his knees and shifted his hips, noting how eager he was, something he didn't re-member being in years of encounters in Grey District.

Arad gasped as Roku rubbed the fat head in slow cir-cles at his twitching opening, teasing, dipping it slightly inside. Roku knelt transfixed, watching the dirty display, until Arad bore down and drew him in. The wet length breached him, and Roku inched forward, leisurely feeding him the entire beast.

When Arad had every inch, he exhaled hard. "Whoa. That's a lot of dick."

"Am I hurting you?"

Arad clamped down and forced a pleasurable grunt out of Roku. "Don't even think of stopping. I'm not some blushing virgin you're deflowering."

A lecherous grin curled the edge of Roku's mouth. "No, you are not, my captain."

Roku curled his torso, abdominals rippling as he pulled back, dragging that delicious piece of meat nearly out before sliding in at the same luxurious pace. And repeat. And repeat. At his size, there wasn't any place for his dick to go that didn't rub Arad's internal gland into an overstimulated nerve within minutes.

The craving intensified with each passing second as if it were a living thing close to getting what it wanted. It drove Arad to wrap his legs around Roku's hips, pulling at him with every stroke to force the tiger to bottom out.

Drive him harder. Give me everything. Make him spill.

Roku's words twisted within a growl. "I want to ruin you for anyone else."

"Stop bragging and do it already."

With that challenge, Roku rode Arad hard. Each thrust should have been paired with a noisy slapping of flesh, only to be softened by Roku's rapidly dampening fur. Pleasure shocks ripped through Arad with each plunge, making him cry out uncontrollably. He'd never ached so badly before. He didn't dare touch himself. Instead he held on to Roku's neck and lost himself in the chaos.

With a feral roar, Roku buried his entire length and came, holding himself in place as the deep, flooding pulses left their mark, claimed their territory. The warmth spread inside Arad, triggering an unexpected wave of carnal bliss. It surged through him, the greatest high he'd ever known, and his cock erupted between them.

Breaths heaving, Roku rolled to his side without letting go, holding Arad down so they didn't disconnect. The nagging craving quieted, and contentment bubbled all the way through to Arad's fingers and toes. He hoped the next time would be as sweet at this. Every time.

Chapter Eighteen

"Do you trust me?" Arad held Roku's hand in a tight grip, gazing into his eyes. Sitting in the tiger's lap, he had a magnificent view. A constellation of reflections dotted the brilliant amber, enhancing their already inescapable allure.

Arad wore only a shirt like the day they'd met, his bare buttocks brushing Roku's thighs. Neither man had bothered with much clothing over the last several days because tearing them off so frequently had become tedious and simply another impediment. Roku's glorious muscles were on full display, the fine fur coat glimmering over each ridge and swell. He may not have had the use of his hands, but his impressive pole rose and bumped its way between Arad's cheeks as if it knew its own path.

"With my life." Roku tugged at the restraints holding both his wrists to the armrests of the captain's chair. "Even like this. Tell me again why this is necessary?"

Arad shrugged and planted a kiss on the tip of Roku's nose. "You asked me why there were handcuffs in the drawer. Don't ask if you don't want the answer. Besides, you're the one who's worried about losing control. You'd think you'd be thanking me."

"I could break out of these. You know that."

Leaning forward, Arad rubbed himself all over Roku's firm muscles while whispering in his ear. "You've never been forced to do anything you didn't want to. And I know you like being right where I have you right now."

A lusty shudder coursed through Roku's body, dropping his voice an octave. "You are correct about that, Captain Ansari."

The handcuffs wouldn't hold if put to the test, but having Roku willing to play the game emboldened Arad. In Grey District, few of his customers were interested in power exchanges. At least, not where Arad had the advantage. Most simply wanted to get to the action and move on. But on those rare occasions, the role-play returned some of Arad's dignity and made the whole experience less unsavory.

Leaning, he deliberately ground Roku's solid cock between his buttocks, riding the length until the foreskin drew back, allowing sweat and fresh sap to slick the way. Roku purred as he rolled his hips underneath Arad.

Reaching for the side table, Arad ignored the bottle of lubricant and chose the metal flask instead. He unscrewed the top and poured a generous helping of clear-ish liquid into the short glass next to it. Scalding vapors preceded Tank's homemade hooch, singeing his nostrils as he took a healthy mouthful. The liquor could likely degrease an engine, but that wasn't what he planned to use it for. Palming both sides of Roku's head, Arad pressed his lips over Roku's, urging his mouth open. When Roku complied, Arad kissed him hard, sharing the drink between them.

Roku licked at Arad's tongue as if trying to taste more than what was there. "That's some strong booze."

"Tank made it himself. Liquor prices kept going up, and he was a cheap jerk."

"I wonder if we should be drinking a dead man's stash."

Arad poured a second drink. "Tank didn't speak up for me when Torrins decided to leave me behind on the ship to die. I didn't wish him dead, but I'm sure not going to read his eulogy. Or any of the rest of those dicks for that matter. The hooch is the least he owes me."

"Then I'd hate to think his sacrifice went to waste."

With a sly grin, Arad shared the next shot the same way, but this time took even longer. He squeezed Roku's chest, thrilling at how the muscles barely gave way, so firm and strong. So his. A gentle pinch of both hardened nipples made the tiger arch into Arad's grind. His shirt had risen enough to allow his bare cock to scrub along Roku's abdominals while his balls stroked the shaft running under him.

The craving for Roku had come back with a vengeance. Since the first time, they'd been after one another so often the sensation had been sated, but never extinguished. Arad raised up on his knees and reached behind him, taking Roku's penis and touching it against his opening.

"What do you want?" Arad asked, only allowing the slippery, spongy head to kiss the ring.

Roku curled his torso, trying to embed himself. "You know what I want."

Each time he pushed, Arad rose barely out of reach. A teasing game of chase not intended for children. Arad gripped the length with a firm pressure and ran his thumb over the slit.

"I want to hear you say it."

Roku ground his teeth, his jaw set. For all his new-found animal instincts, the DemiShou still had some of his conservative nature to shed. They'd had sex in most areas of the ship. Oh, he wanted Arad in vague, lusty terms, but when it came to verbalizing it, the specifics left him mute. Shame and risk of rejection were old habits many men never learned to break, but Roku had the ability to do better.

"Come on, big guy. Tell me what you need. Exactly what you need, and I'll give it to you."

Shoulders tense and eyes narrowing, Roku struggled to voice it. "I...I need...to be inside you."

Arad beamed. "All you had to do was say so."

All the tension left Roku in one yowl as Arad grabbed the slick and greased him generously. Days of practice gave Arad the skill to take the girthy organ in one plunge. Muscles responding to the familiar stretch quickly, Arad prepared to give Roku a hard ride when he paused.

"What's that?" Arad leaned his head to reach out with his hearing but ignored Roku's pained disbelief.

"You're asking now?"

"I heard something. Where's it coming from?"

Roku's brow furrowed in frustration and curiosity. "Seriously? You're killing me."

"Hush. No one's ever died from an unused hard-on."

Arad wanted to ignore it, but the incessant chime was distracting. It wasn't coming from the captain's chair or attached console. Trying not to disengage, Arad twisted, scanning the bridge. A flashing icon on the communications console caught his attention.

"Holy shit. I think we're getting a hail."

Roku tensed under Arad, and not in a carnal way. His eager erection flagged and slid from its welcome home to slump between his thighs, the moment lost. In full force, the craving stupidly urged Arad to finish what he'd started and answer the comm afterward. Thankfully he had enough sense not to listen to the newfound demands of his sex drive. Possible salvation had all the hallmarks of a cold shower.

Before doing anything else, he climbed down from Roku's lap and unlocked the cuffs using the key on the console. Fun time was over. Roku strode to Franc's old station with a determined step, where sensors struggled to pull basic information from the incoming call. He tapped the screen, trying to clean up the scrambled transponder data the way Arad had coached him recently on ship systems. They couldn't have sex all the time.

"It's too small for a cruiser and too large for a warship. Possibly freighter class. How'd they find us?"

Arad shouldered himself between Roku and the console, forcing the tiger back and brushing his big hand aside to make his own adjustments. "I put out an automated distress beacon days ago once the array was fixed. Communications are still a little spotty, and I wasn't sure how far it was transmitting."

"Better than you realized."

"Or we're more remote than we thought." A series of numbers settled long enough to read. "They're within ten thousand kilometers."

"How many are on board? Do they have weapons?"

The tactical question unnerved Arad. No matter how appropriate, Roku's shift into authoritative, military-esque point of view brought a perspective Arad hadn't considered. The new arrivals had as much chance of being dangerous as beneficial.

"No way to tell. The sensors aren't working that well."

Torrins had always bragged about how the *Midas Ascending*'s shielding could keep out corporate-level scanners. In its current condition, hopefully the DemiShou in the cargo bay were safely hidden.

"We need to get dressed," Roku said.

Frowning, Arad passed his gaze between Roku's fabulous nudity and the monitor's signal, being briefly reminded of what they were up to only a minute ago. How long would the hail last? "I don't want to waste time hunting for our clothes. Wherever they are."

"Sit in the chair and keep your bottom hidden."

"Yeah, yeah, as if I'm gonna flash our potential savior unless it's the only method of payment they're interested in." Roku gave a soft growl. "I'm kidding. Seriously, calm down. That's not happening." A sobering yet obvious idea came to Arad. "You realize this might mean we're not stranded anymore. What happens next?"

Endless possible scenarios skittered through Arad's imagination, sharpening his anxiety. He'd only just found Roku and didn't want to give him up, but there were dangers lying in wait. Some corporate stooge was still out there trying to collect him, and businessmen rarely gave up when large sums of money were involved. Making Roku and the rest of the DemiShou must have cost a fortune.

"I'm not going anywhere without you." Roku hugged him tightly, as if afraid he'd vanish if he let go.

Arad hugged him as fiercely because he understood. As unconventional as their lives may have been—adrift and at risk of eventual starvation—the *Ansariland* had been their world, and strangers were about to breach their private borders for good or bad. The recycled air tasted like change, but the harsh flavor gave up no answers.

Although paranoia was no reason to pass up a potential lifeline. Their lives had an expiration date given the current scenario. The *Ansariland*, no matter how freeing, was a death trap if things stayed the same.

Leaning inside the crushing embrace, Arad stared upward into Roku's eyes. "I have to answer this before they give up and move on."

"I know." Roku's sigh vented his concern. "I'm nervous."

"You and me both."

"I'm going to step aside, out of view, while you answer. We don't need to scare them off before we know if they can help."

Arad hated the self-loathing undertone he was hearing. "Roku, you're hardly a monster."

A faint crease of disbelief marred Roku's brow. "Maybe not, but you know I'm right. We need their aid, but if I'm going to keep us both safe, I'd like to know more details about them first. They might not be willing to help a DemiShou."

"All right. But I'm not lying about you if they ask. I'm not ashamed of you."

Bending forward, Roku pressed his lips hard to Arad's. Nothing sexual was shared, only an affirmation to one another. An unspoken promise that Arad answered with equal intensity.

Cradling Arad's head in his huge hands, Roku stroked Arad's cheek with his thumb. "Be careful. We don't know who they are or if they can be trusted."

"I'm a slug. I can count on the fingers of one hand how many people I trust, and I still have a lot left over." Holding up a single index finger, Arad poked Roku in the chest. The DemiShou stood tall, almost preening. "Now go get that big dick out of sight."

Roku stepped out of range as Arad took his seat. He shifted and tugged at his shirt hem, making sure his bare ass was well hidden. Clearing his throat, he reached for the communications control with a hesitant hand and made the connection.

"This is Captain Ansari of the *Ansariland*."

Seconds passed. Then minutes. Arad pressed the button and repeated the call out.

More seconds passed.

Without warning, the main screen came to life, flickering and static-ridden. Slightly off-center, a handsome man with kind features filled the monitor, grey peppered throughout his simple, unpretentious hairstyle. Fine lines creased his eyes as an easy smile graced his face.

"You have no idea how good it is to see there's some-one alive on board. Salvaging a dead ship gets a little creepy. Not a fan." The man breathed out in relief between digital squalls distorting his image. "Greetings, Captain. I'm Captain Hodge of the *Nightingale*. It was a bit of a mess, but we came across your distress call. What can we do to help?"

"I wasn't sure anyone would get the message this far out. The ship had a bad fold jump, and the main engine's having a few issues. I don't suppose you have a mechanic on board?" Arad did his best not to act desperate despite the ship's obvious problems. Be gracious, but don't give away the details. No one was going to find out about the DemiShou. The *Ansariland* needed aid, but he couldn't know if Captain Hodge would exploit the situation. In Arad's past, most men did.

"Sure do. The *Nightingale*'s a cargo vessel specializing in medical tech transport. We wear a fair number of hats on this crew to keep up. How long you been out here?"

"A number of weeks now. I only got the sensors and communications online this week."

Hodge grimaced. "Ouch."

"Not so bad, really. It made for a nice vacation, but it's time we got moving along."

"Fair enough. I bet we can probably spare some sup-plies to get you on your way again. Where are you headed?"

Arad shrugged with a grin, not wanting to give any-thing away. "Nowhere in particular. Once I can read the navigation again, I'll plot a course somewhere sunny."

Hodge's easy chuckle soothed some of Arad's rough edges. It wasn't forced. He read no agenda under the surface. Only polite and personable. A rare quality of men in Arad's orbit, save Roku. Hodge sat close to the screen, only his head and chest visible, like in a private chat, defusing what might otherwise be read as a captain's pompous authority. First Commander Bard could have taken a few lessons from him.

There wasn't much to see behind Hodge. Low lights with enough monitor glow reminded Arad of the bridge. A young woman's impatient voice came from off-screen. Apparently, he wasn't alone.

"How soon is he coming?"

Brow cocked in disbelief, Hodge slowly turned his head. "I don't know that he is. We've barely started talking."

She huffed as her voice pitched into a whine. "Hurry up."

"Do you mind?"

Without warning, a ginormous head with shocking pink hair pushed between Hodge and the screen.

"Are you coming over?"

"Yosei! What the hell?"

She narrowed her eyes through her tech goggles as the lenses spun and focused on an unknown number of details. That kind of eyewear had any number of scanning capabilities. Her face filled the screen so closely Arad was looking up her nose. "The screen's all crappy. Don't you know how to tune your own comm?"

Leaning in his chair to create some distance, Arad almost forgot he wasn't wearing pants and stayed seated.

Even so, he muttered a response. "Um...the sensor array is kinda busted."

Hodge attempted to corral her out of the way, but she squirmed out of his hold and shoved him aside with a hand in his face. Clearly, he held back, trying not to hurt the smaller woman, but she was relentless to hold court with the screen. Slapping his hands away, she nearly pushed him out of his chair.

"Agh! Would you sit down so I can talk to the man?"

While they wrestled, Yosei continued her barrage of questions as if she weren't vying for dominance with her captain in front of a total stranger. "Why is there carbon scoring on your hull? Were you in a fight? There's a rupture near the main engine. Was it pirates? Why did they leave you alive?"

Horrified by the spectacle, Arad stayed quiet. Slugs wrestling for a blanket in winter were less ruthless.

"I'm in the middle of a conversation here..." Speaking through gritted teeth, Hodge struggled to keep his seat from being hijacked by the hyperactive woman. Yosei may have been petite in comparison to the captain, but she thrashed like a stray cat over a puddle. Hodge had his hands full.

"How many crew do you have? Your ship's shielded. That's not normal. Are you guys crooks?"

"Yosei, get off!"

Yosei crammed both her hands into Hodge's face, trying to stay in possession of the screen. "Why are you stranded? Are you on quarantine? Do we need to sterilize the ship?"

With a frustrated yell, Hodge stood. They spun in the monitor as he wrapped his arms around the flailing crew-person and manhandled her out of view.

"Sit down and let me bloody well finish!"

Hair askew and wide-eyed, Hodge returned to his seat, appearing positively frazzled. He spun in his seat and pointed—obviously at her—silently promising retribution.

"Don't look at me like that." While not currently visible through the comm, Yosei's pout was practically audible.

Skin flushed a dusky scarlet, a touch of mania thrummed through Hodge as he faced Arad once again. The effort to regain his composure—and a certain amount of his dignity—was almost comical. Almost. Since laughing might not be in his best interest, Arad kept his mouth shut about how chunks of Hodge's hair stuck out sideways.

"Sorry about that. Yosei is my resident tech genius and she means well"—tilting his head, he shouted over his shoulder—"*but she lacks boundaries.*" Hodge paused, glancing her way, body tensed, preparing for a fresh interruption. When it didn't happen, he relaxed and continued. "Back to where we left off, if you'd like, I'd be willing to give you a hand."

"If it's no trouble," Arad said, appearing as nonchalant as possible.

"No trouble at all. I don't like the idea of leaving anyone floating out here."

Arad nodded. "I appreciate that. Let me chat with my crew, and I'll get back with you over the details."

"Sounds good. *Nightingale* out."

The monitor winked out, and Roku emerged from the shadows.

Arad's shoulders deflated as he blew out the awkward frisson from the conversation. He smothered a peal of uncomfortable laughter with a hand over his mouth. "That was unexpected. Oh, man, what have we gotten ourselves into?"

"We can't send them away, but for now, I think it's safe."

"I think you're right, although it's not as if we have much of a choice." Standing, Arad collected the handcuffs and lube from the captain's station and cupped Roku's ample manhood as he walked past. "Let's finish what we started, and then we can get ready to meet the crazy neighbors."

Chapter Nineteen

The cargo door slammed shut with Arad's hand on the access pad. Green text switched to red.

LOCKED — *Rank Access Enabled**

The *Ansariland* would only allow a captain or above to open the door and grant access to the supplies and sleeping DemiShou inside. Since the system wouldn't see anyone from the *Nightingale* as important enough, the others would stay hidden, stay safe. When it was still the *Midas Ascending*, Serene's attitude and the various restrictions had been based on him being the cabin boy. Repeating the process made him feel a bit hypocritical, but he'd promised to protect Shichi and Hachi, and he refused to break his word. The *Nightingale*'s crew didn't need to know about them to repair the ship.

"You remembered to close out the history and sensor logs?" Roku asked.

With a finger swipe, Arad blanked the screen. "Yep. With a little luck, it'll keep our cover story. Let's get going. They're waiting."

Arad turned and headed for the airlock with Roku in tow. The argument over leaving Roku behind to prevent any problems with the new crew was quashed as fast as it appeared. Roku would never be Arad's dirty secret.

Outer space didn't greet them when they opened the airlock. A claustrophobic tunnel extended from the *Nightingale*'s hull to dock the two ships together, allowing access between them. Arad pressed the control on the far side to signal their arrival. He hoped they wouldn't have to wait long. The airlock wasn't exactly Arad's favorite place these days. He hadn't set foot in there since the spacewalk. It was the portal to *outside* after all.

A beep accompanied the start of underlying mechanicals. Seals parted and air blew through the tunnel as the outer hull hatch motored into the wall. The interior door sat wide open with a full view of the *Nightingale*'s cargo hold and their crew.

The space was larger yet less open than the *Ansariland*'s, with rows of shelves and metal boxes eating up the available real estate. Strangely, Arad found himself thankful not to see a series of containers filled with sleeping DemiShou.

Leaning against a stack of crates, Hodge sipped from a steaming metal cup, hands safe from the heat by a pair of thin insulated gloves. Everything about the man screamed sensible relaxation. Standing by his side, Yosei would likely challenge that in her pink hair, jumpsuit, and clunky boots. Her spiky hair barely the height of Hodge's shoulder, the pixie-sized tech had a face that was practically filled by her eyes and smile as Roku stepped through the doorway. Hodge placed a hand on her shoulder before she launched herself at them. Yosei vibrated with excitement, the impending question avalanche barely restrained. When she settled, he placed his cup on the crate and walked over to shake Arad's hand.

"Welcome aboard, Arad."

"Thanks. This is Roku, my first mate."

Without the slightest hesitation, Hodge reached around Arad and gave Roku a hearty handshake. "Good to meet you. Sorry it couldn't be under better circumstances, but I'm glad we can show you a little hospitality."

Hodge's lack of shock or surprise at Roku caught Arad off guard. It shouldn't have, but unfair hostility was often directed at the DemiShou. One look at the remaining crew answered where Hodge's comfort came from as he led them to the others present.

"This is Vosh. He handles security on the *Nightingale*."

Bigger than Roku, the brown bear DemiShou filled his snug overalls. Big feet solidly planted, he stood with his burly, bare arms crossed over his swollen, furry chest. If his size wasn't domineering enough, his tone as he narrowed his eyes at them amplified the effect.

"You're really the only two on board a ship that size?"

Vosh's sudden scrutiny unnerved Arad, but he refused to let it show. "Um, yes. It's a long story."

Head shaven with full dark brows, the bearded man standing next to Vosh came forward, clasping Arad's hand with a hearty pump. His eager smile was dazzling against his dusky skin.

"Ignore him. Vosh's suspicious of everyone. It's part of his job. I'm Pakko, the mechanical engineer. I'm glad to meet you. I do everything Yosei can't 'cause she's tiny."

"Hey!" Yosei whined.

Pakko's overly friendly greeting must have concerned Roku because he stepped up close to Arad's back and placed a hand on his shoulder. *Marking his territory?* Vosh leaned forward at the display and gave a few indelicate sniffs in their direction. Bending over to speak in Pakko's ear nearly folded the bear in half.

"They're mated. No baby bear for you on this trip."

Pakko's smile curled into a frown. "Dammit!" The engineer stomped off in a childish pout over into the corner. Sighing, Vosh followed him, rubbing his shoulders in sympathy.

"Sorry, babe."

"I really wanted a cub."

Vosh slid his hands over Pakko's chest, enveloping him in a smothering hug. "Maybe we can do a group thing next time."

Yosei's face twisted in comical disgust. "You guys are so gross."

Rolling his eyes, Hodge nudged them all away from the bear and his boy. "Sorry about that. Pakko grew up on a small colony where polyamory was standard. He doesn't take monogamy well."

"We don't share." Roku had yet to let go of Arad's shoulder.

Hodge chuckled. "That's obvious."

Arad scanned the carbo bay. "Is this everyone?"

"One more. Bryce, our doctor. She's working in the infirmary right now."

A woman's voice drifted down from the ceiling, echoing between the crate stacks. "I may not be in the room, but the channel is open, gentlemen. I can hear every word you say, so don't start talking about me. Welcome,

Captain Ansari. Welcome, Roku. If you're planning on spending any amount of time on the *Nightingale*, I expect both of you to stop by my office for a quick medical scan. I don't like sick people on my ship."

Arad couldn't remember the last time he'd been seen by a live doctor rather than the medical kiosks littering the streets of Grey District. "I'm not sure how long repairs will take. Any idea?"

Hodge gave a minimal shrug. "We'll have to figure that out. It might help if you told us what happened. How'd you guys get stranded in the first place?"

"We got fired on by pirates. They didn't waste a lot of time explaining. Shot the main engine, and then the captain and crew abandoned ship. Pirates blew them out of space."

The moment Arad began explaining, he became everyone's focal point. Hodge stood quietly with a hand on Yosei, possibly the only thing keeping the pink-haired girl from exploding with a barrage of questions. Even Pakko had stopped pouting and returned to the group with Vosh as his faithful shadow. Security being the bear DemiShou's job description, he wasted no time testing Arad's tale.

"The crew left you two behind?"

Arad scoffed. "I didn't say they were upstanding citizens."

"How'd you get away?" Less pessimistic than his Demi partner, Pakko sounded a tad awestruck.

"Emergency space jump. It trashed the sensor array and knocked out communications and navigation. We'd been drifting since until I figured out how to fix it."

Doubt and a touch of accusation tinged Vosh's voice. "So you're captain now? That's quite the promotion."

"When the crew died, the ship automatically upgraded my rank. I didn't know it would happen, but now the ship's legally mine. I'd be stupid not to use it to my full advantage."

"Why you and not him?" Pakko pointed a thumb at Roku and ducked his head, looking chagrined. "No offense."

"I don't think I was important enough to give a rank in the system." Displeasure made Roku's growl more prominent, whether aimed at Pakko or Torrins and his dead crew.

"So they treated you like a slave?"

"Maybe not even that much."

Roku played his role better than Arad expected. He'd agreed to let Arad take the lead and speak only when necessary so Arad wouldn't have to speak for him, which would raise eyebrows. They needed the *Nightingale*'s aid, and with Roku's honorable streak, the story might not hold if pressed too hard. Lying, even indirectly, chafed him. A cop or military officer in his previous life maybe, but a spy? Nope.

Vosh brought the questioning back to Arad. "What was your job?"

"I was barely a mechanic. They gave me the crap jobs."

"If the crew were so awful, why would you join in the first place?"

Arad sighed. He didn't need to fake this part. "No money, no food, no options, no choice."

Stories fed to strangers went down smoother when peppered liberally with bits of truth. Learning to sweet-talk colony authorities was one of the first things Sketch taught Arad. No one had the right to know everything. Knowledge was ammunition filling the guns of corporate-run law enforcement.

When he was younger, Arad had considered himself a good person. He valued honesty and integrity in spite of his wealthy family's failings. But living on the street quickly taught him the virtues of lying, cheating, and sometimes stealing to keep from starving. They weren't skills he prided himself on, yet he understood their necessity. Survive first. Over the years, the guilt had lessened to where he barely felt it these days.

Either way, the answer satisfied Vosh enough he backed off and left the floor for anyone else.

"I can help you optimize the ship systems." Yosei's comment, while off topic, was oddly polite and reserved.

Based on their original on-screen conversation, her restraint impressed Arad. He'd been prepared for a verbal ambush by the eccentric tech, but clearly she'd somehow managed to leash her enthusiasm to a more manageable level.

Well, marginally manageable. Tapping her clunky boots in a rapid patter, she ground her teeth and fidgeted with her hands held behind her back. If she didn't release the pressure valve on her curiosity soon, her skull would burst and spray them all in techie blood.

"Thank you. I'd appreciate that." With a sigh, Arad took pity on her. He urged her on with a wave of his hand. "Go on. Ask already before you stroke out."

Without warning, Yosei exploded, words practically running together in quick-fire succession, not bothering to breathe between sentences. "You said communications and navigation were down. I checked the specs on your ship. You're flying in a repurposed XS-B278A corporate cargo carrier, theta class, designed to house up to six crew, including the captain. The AR-657 sensor array has a history of cascade failure caused by short circuit due to traumatic events. I assume you attempted to reboot the system and failed. Finding the error would be easy enough, but how did you correct the anomaly and re-establish connectivity?"

Her intensity nearly dazed Arad. "Um...I did a spacewalk."

"So you manually realigned faulty hardware and reset the parameters."

"Uh, yeah."

"Slick. Space folds aren't usually so violent to a vessel of that size, so I'm guessing you were jumping in the gravity well of a star or planet, doing a panic jump to keep from getting blasted to atoms?"

"Uh, yeah."

Listening to Yosei's evaluations threw Arad off-kilter. He'd spent weeks learning the *Ansariland*'s specs, and Yosei's knowledge appeared to eclipse his in spite of the few short hours they'd been aware of each other's existence. His tech skills were good. Better than he let Torrins know, but Yosei...she was in a class all her own. The urge to bow down and pledge his unworthiness to the master grew strong.

Hodge burst in before Arad embarrassed himself in front of everyone. "Okay, okay. Enough of the inquisition.

How about we give you boys the tour, and tomorrow we start figuring out what essential repairs you need?"

Bryce's forceful yet sultry voice reappeared through the speakers, causing everyone present to search the ceiling. "I didn't close the channel, gentlemen. If you're planning on walking through the ship, you need to make a stop in the infirmary first."

"And here I thought I was the captain."

"My contract has medical authority privileges that supersede you."

A bark of laughter exploded out of Arad. "I think I'll stay out of this battle." Chuckling, he gave Roku a playful swat. "You heard the lady. Let's get a checkup."

"I don't know how we'll be able to pay you for helping us. Roku and I are pretty much broke. We didn't actually get paid before the crew got ashed." Arad kept pace with Hodge's casual steps. He'd ordered his crew members to go away so he could escort Arad and Roku in peace. It's what Arad would have done.

Hodge brushed off his concerns with a wave. "Don't worry about it. When I die, it'll look nice on my good deeds list."

Compared to the *Ansariland*, the *Nightingale*'s brighter interior was sleeker and more polished. No peeling paint on the wall plating from lack of maintenance. High-contrast graphics clearly marked one section from another. The crew wouldn't need this level of identification, so the ship must have hosted guests often enough to make the effort worthwhile. *Intriguing.* The *Nightingale* was nice, but it was no cruise ship.

Arad found the differences welcoming, but the *Ansariland* was his home in spite of how he'd acquired it. Something he'd given up as possible a long time ago. He'd take his dodgy clunker with its sordid history any day.

Although, Arad still needed to make the most of Hodge's hospitality. "Lively crew you have."

"Ha! More like a motley crew, but they have their uses. Vosh and Pakko know their jobs, and they're harmless as long as you stay out of their bed."

"That will not be a problem." Roku chiming in behind them was not unexpected.

Hodge snickered. Arad rolled his eyes.

Since setting foot on board, Roku had displayed an increased level of possessiveness. Given his memory loss, Arad wondered if it was a common trait among DemiShou. It may have been a touch embarrassing in front of Hodge and the crew, but he added it to the layers building between them, reinforcing their growing connection. Vosh had used the term *mated*. A deliberate choice of word that left Arad with more niggling questions he didn't have time to dig into. Why not simply say *together*? Or *shacked up*? Or something equally obvious? Perhaps later he'd have the opportunity to ask Vosh to fill in some gaps in his understanding of DemiShou. All of the *Nightingale*'s crew might have useful knowledge to share.

Arad decided he might as well start with the most obvious. "Yosei's a character. What's her story?"

Hodge tapped a control, opening a hatch he left open behind them as they passed through. "Yosei's our newest acquisition. I found her on a colony station looking for work about five months ago. Brilliant as hell, but not a lick of common sense. A group of crooks found her tech status and tried to hire her. You know how she bombarded you with statistics and questions until she scoped you out?"

"Yeah. That's an eerie talent."

"She did that with them and deciphered their entire smuggling operation in public. If there weren't so many witnesses, they probably would have killed her. It didn't occur to her she was doing something dangerous. So I hired her before something messed up happened to her. Keep her out of trouble." Hodge huffed and shook his head. "All intellect, no street sense. Reminds me of my daughter."

"We didn't meet her, so I'm guessing she's not on board."

Hodge's chipper mood dimmed a tad. "No. She passed away several years ago."

"Oh. I'm sorry."

Sadness tinted Hodge's grey eyes, yet his pleasant veneer failed to falter. Arad understood, having seen that look on other's faces who survived in Grey District. Grief existed in his past. He respected how it shaped him but refused to allow it to own him.

"Nothing to be sorry about. Lost Jonna and her mother after a transport accident. The available auto-medical was fried, and the local med kiosk wasn't equipped to handle trauma. They were gone before emergency services finally arrived. It's why I focus mainly on shipping medical tech. Street-level med equipment is traded down from the nicer facilities, so keeping the improved models flowing helps everyone at some level."

"Explains why the kiosks in my neighborhood always looked nicer than the actual neighborhood. Sounds like they might have been hand-me-downs." Arad took in the immaculate hallway. "You figured out how to work it into a profit all right."

With a smirk and a shrug, Hodge took a right turn. "If you want to do well in this universe, you gotta understand your niche market."

So far, Arad found every member of the *Nightingale* intriguing, especially Hodge. The man's natural charisma drew him in without the flash and glam of a captain like Torrins. That magnetism was what made Arad hesitate to follow. Too many schemers and charlatans had played their games with him. Some more successfully than others. But each success added a brick to his wall of skepticism. A barrier that kept him safe when nothing else did. Once completed, only Roku had ever been truly allowed through. Some, like Davis, believed they had, but they'd been wrong.

Roku gently cupped his shoulder, as if sensing Arad's indecision. They needed the help the *Nightingale* could bring, and no real alarms had gone off as he scrutinized the people and their odd interactions. Caution was fine—appropriate even—but it shouldn't govern his every step forward until he swam in paranoia. Because that was where he was heading in the presence of strangers. Old habits were hard to break.

Patting Roku's hand, he took a step, then another, until they were following once again. Thankfully, Hodge had ignored the interruption and didn't say anything as he waited patiently for them to catch up. Perhaps he understood how overwhelming all this new interaction could be.

Polite conversation continued. Nothing too deep, but it bred a familiarity that took off some of the rough edges of Arad's distrust. Roku's presence bolstered his inner strength, and he found himself enjoying the new company as their pace slowed. Emblazoned in emergency red over the upcoming doorway was the universal medical icon. They'd arrived at the infirmary.

"Time to meet Bryce." With a smile, Hodge stood with an outstretched hand, coaxing them through. "Don't touch anything," he whispered as they crossed the threshold.

If Arad had been impressed with the *Nightingale*'s general upkeep, it was nothing compared to the infirmary.

Translucent plasti-steel walls of antiseptic white glowed from within, generating an omnidirectional light source. Pristine medical equipment filled every corner. Arad tried to calculate the astronomical cost of this set-up and came up short. A med bed—much nicer than the *Ansariland*'s—filled one wall, while a workstation surrounded by a forest of monitors lined the opposite. Most screens contained medical data, active with various biometrics. Arad raised an eyebrow at the others, centering on Yosei and the crew in various places on the ship.

Hodge shrugged. "Bryce spends most of her time in here."

Head shaved to her dark umber scalp, the statuesque doctor wore a form-fitting bio-suit that reminded Arad of corporate scientists flooding the streets of Grey District during a hazmat incident. Bryce's lack of eyebrows minimized her expressions, making her difficult to read. Even her polite smile was reserved.

"It's simpler to do my work from here and interact through communications." Bryce raised a hand when Arad made to step further into the room. "Please stay inside the yellow line while I run a decontamination sweep."

Arad looked down. The three of them stood inside a yellow box engraved into the floor that extended from the entrance. Hodge made no move to cross the line, so Arad followed his lead.

A short lyrical chime rang as Bryce tapped at one monitor with her gloved hands. "I'm not about to allow some strange germ to ravage the ship. I still say we need to install these at every entrance."

Without crossing the line, Hodge leaned forward. "I already told you I'm not spending that kind of money when every guest ends up here anyways."

"Your pandemic protocols are appalling."

"But I have you, so it all evens out."

Warmth passed over Arad's skin with a gentle tingle that passed as quickly as it came. Bryce nodded and waved them inside. Hodge wasted no time introducing them.

"This is Captain Ansari and his first mate, Roku. Gentlemen, this is our doctor, Bryce."

Without offering her hand, she greeted Arad with a pleasant nod. "Thank you for indulging me." She focused on Roku, her curiosity obvious. "Interesting. Your stripe pattern is unique. I've never known about a splicing that didn't generate a natural pattern. I'd think it was a custom design. You can step aside. I won't need to do a deep bioscan on Roku."

"Why do you say that?" Arad asked.

"DemiShou were designed to be disease-immune and can't be carriers." Edgy inside a doctor's office, Arad leaned against the nearest station. Bryce's gaze fixed itself to where Arad's hand rested on the countertop. "You, on the other hand, are a potential breeding ground of plague. Don't worry. I'm disconnected from the corporate medical database. You'll have complete privacy."

"I'm all for privacy, but is that a good idea? I don't want to void any of my supply contracts." Hodge's concerns didn't surprise Arad. It was his business, after all.

"I think it's for the best. Captain Ansari appears uncomfortable enough. No need to make matters worse." Without touching him, Bryce directed Arad to stand near a different workstation.

Arad did his best to hide his offense. Wealthy people had always seen slugs as less than or inherently unhealthy, so it wasn't a new experience. "Thank you. You have a good bedside manner. I bet you'd make yourself filthy rich as a private physician."

"I could. But planetside, there are too many people in too small a space. I don't trust the biofilters to keep up. And they do nothing when people leave their greasy residues behind." Reaching into one of her suit's many pockets, Bryce withdrew a small device and ran its ultraviolet light over the counter where Arad's hand had been.

Hodge snickered. "She means fingerprints."

"Residue DNA is residue DNA. I'm better off on board the *Nightingale*."

After retrieving a new item from storage, Bryce passed the scanner over his body, checking the reading on the nearby panel. Once complete, her shoulders relaxed as she exhaled.

"You're in excellent health."

"That's good to hear. I'm impressed with your infirmary. Most hospitals aren't this slick." Arad walked the room's perimeter and casually touched a device he didn't recognize. He moved on, dragging a finger along the counter surfaces until he found another random item to pick up. Bryce followed a polite distance behind, trying to be discreet about using the handheld to sanitize each spot of contact. Petty? Yes, but even though she wasn't broadcasting any findings to the universe, she'd taken one look at him and implied he might be contagious. Arad pretended not to notice Hodge's snicker. "I'm guessing since you have Vosh on board, you're prepped to treat DemiShou?"

"Of course."

"Our med bed doesn't have any parameters for Demis. Any info you can share would be appreciated. If something happened to Roku, I'd like to be prepared."

"I'll have Yosei check to see if the protocols from ours are compatible with your equipment. We might be able to upgrade you."

"That's very kind of you, Doctor. I have the impression you seem to know a great deal about DemiShou biology. Am I correct?" Roku's rumbling voice drew Bryce's complete attention.

"Better than most. DemiShou are not monsters or second-class citizens. I was sick a lot as a child. DemiShou resistance to illness would have been a blessing. At one point, I was even in line to receive DemiShou genetic splicing before the program was banned."

"I think you would have made a fine DemiShou."

Contrasted against her skin, Bryce's smile was vivid. "Thank you. That's flattering. Would you like a screening?"

"No, thank you. My health is not in question."

"All right. But while you're on board, I expect you to contact me if you need anything. Both of you. The channels are always open."

Roku dipped his head in agreement. "Of course."

Hodge stepped to Roku's side and clapped his shoulder. "I'm hoping you boys will stay with us long enough to share a meal tonight. We can use that to figure out what you need to get running again. Don't worry. We know how to feed a Demi."

Arad wrung his hands together. The best meals were always made by someone else. Grey District may have been poor, but some street vendors had the most amazing chow. Plus, sharing a meal with Hodge and the crew brought him one step closer to fixing his ship.

"That sounds like a great idea."

Chapter Twenty

"Bryce isn't eating with us?" The spicy aroma made Arad's stomach growl as he took a conservative scoop of noodles from the serving bowl. The *Nightingale* either had a much better food selection or a proper cook. Maybe both.

"Don't take it personal. She prefers her own space," Hodge said. Seated next to him, Yosei poured water into cups from a plastic pitcher.

Bryce's voice hovered out of the ceiling. "But I do like to join the conversation."

"Bryce joins in from the sick bay because we won't let her irradiate our food and turn it glow-in-the-dark under her decontamination protocols after it's been properly cooked by our up-to-date food prep system." Sarcasm dripped from Yosei's words but not from her cups as she passed them around the table to Roku, Arad, and the rest of the crew.

"And thanks to those protocols, I've never had meningitis, Solarian flu, or botulism."

"Neither have any of us—"

Pakko raised his hand. "I got botulism from a sketchy vendor on Narnian 5."

"Okay. Minus Pakko, the rest of us are clean. Which I must say seems highly unlikely given all of our histories, but if it keeps you from going psycho and murdering us all in our sleep, you do your thing."

A soft chorus of chuckling circled the group, which included Bryce. Contagious insanity didn't exist, but witnessing this version threatened to shake Arad's beliefs.

"You get used to it." Hodge reached over and slid the main dish closer to Arad. "Here, have a little more. We have plenty. You're not on the streets. You don't have to ration it."

"Why do you say that?" Arad stiffened in his seat.

"Nothing I haven't seen, or lived, before. No shame in survival."

Arad hesitated but, in the end, took another full ladle, grateful the noodles were spicy. It would make it easier to explain the heat in his face and neck. He'd been reducing his meal size, little by little, for the last two weeks to compensate for Roku's needs. In Grey District, free meals were hard to come by for those with nothing, so stretching food was an unfortunate skill he didn't like to broadcast.

Before he'd been cast out, Arad's family had grown increasingly distant, too obsessed with financial matters to cultivate their personal relationships. The *Nightingale* crew bantered amongst themselves with a familiarity Arad had never known yet longed for the same. The differences in how they all interacted only heightened his sense of otherness while it warred with his need to belong. Yet this ragtag lot of misfits enjoyed each other's company and radiated closeness. Even Yosei, as the newest acquisition, appeared to enjoy the bond, smiling and joking with them all. *Is this what family is?*

As if sensing his unease, Roku reached over and placed his hand on Arad's thigh. The warm pressure centered Arad at once, reminding him, *Nightingale* or not, he wasn't alone anymore.

Conversation continued to flow as they ate, and Arad became more and more like part of the group as the meal went on. Casual chat eventually shifted to the *Ansariland*, and Yosei rambled off her newfound knowledge of the ship's schematics as they planned their repair schedule.

"From what I've seen, the hull breach isn't massive and doesn't intersect any major internal systems. It's mostly a panel rupture, so we should be able to patch it and restore access to the engines. After that, we should be able to restart the core and get them running."

Hodge nodded. "Sounds good. We have a stretch before our next appointment. Do we have enough time?"

"I'll have time to upgrade a few systems as well. Some of the OS protocols are over three versions behind the current model. I have to deal with that so the ship doesn't explode."

Alarmed, Arad spun to Hodge, who promptly shook his head.

"No ship ever explodes from old software. That's a myth you techs use to force updates. Pakko, can you suit up early tomorrow and seal that hole?"

"I suppose I could be persuaded to help out our handsome neighbors." Pakko leaned over and peered under the table. "I like your clothing choices. Kilts rock."

Roku's wardrobe was still comprised of what few items of Tank's old wardrobe were modifiable to use. His black T-shirt had been slashed open at the neck and down the sides to give him breathing room. The kilt only reached mid-thigh and, like the others, had to be split near to the hip to avoid indecent exposure.

"I don't own much. Hopefully if we get the engines functional, we can visit a station market, and I can get something less revealing."

"Do you see me complaining?"

Arad agreed with Pakko, but he wasn't about to encourage him. While he didn't want to think of Roku with anyone else, the tiger was too even tempered to be baited so easily. Even after the scene in the cargo bay, Pakko wouldn't be completely put off. Apparently, if the scowl that vanished as fast as it appeared was any indication, Vosh took issue with Pakko's flirting. Understandable, given their obvious relationship. Pakko's hardwiring went right to polyamory, and Vosh...not as much. He'd been sizing them up since they'd arrived—a normal routine for security staff—even as he slurped down the last of his food. At first Arad had assumed it was simply a case of being cautious, but now he wasn't so sure.

With a sly grin, Vosh turned his attention on Roku. "You look pretty sturdy, Roku. How much you bench?"

Roku shrugged. "I'm not sure."

"I've heard some felines are quick but not as strong as some Demis, but tigers can be both."

"I haven't spent much time figuring it out. The *Ansariland*'s equipment is designed for human strength, not DemiShou."

Vosh cocked a scheming brow. "I can think of a few ways to test it."

"Oh, here we go..." Hodge rolled his eyes with a laugh.

"What are you suggesting?" Roku asked.

"A little sparring action in the gym. You and me." Vosh's idea would seem innocent enough to a casual observer, but Hodge's reaction confirmed Arad's suspicion. Every con he'd ever seen and performed had happened much the same way. Start a line of suggestions. Lead the mark where you want him to go. Then go for the prize, using their ego against them if necessary.

Arad placed a hand on Roku's wrist as he sized up Vosh's motivation. Usually, matches like this were often stacked in the challenger's favor. At least if any money was involved. No one had started throwing out odds, so the reasoning had to be different. Vosh either believed he would win or wanted to size up Roku's potential threat. Granted, he might only be trying to impress Pakko's wayward eye back to his partner.

Vosh picked up his cup and took a sip with a cocky shrug. "Unless you think you can't handle it."

Bullies always annoyed Arad. Because of his size, he'd had his fill. He didn't want to cause problems that might affect their willingness to help, but he didn't want to be perceived as an easy target either.

"Roku..." Arad gave Roku's wrist a squeeze. "Kick his ass."

Cheers erupted around the table.

"Hot damn! We have ourselves some live entertainment!" Hodge hooted as he and everyone else scooted their chairs from the table in anticipation. The sudden enthusiasm was infectious enough even Roku seemed eager. "Follow me, boys. I'll show you the way to the gym."

The *Nightingale*'s gymnasium fostered a seed of jealousy in Arad. Sleek and well-equipped with more square footage than the *Ansariland*'s, it was a beautiful thing. A padded sparring ring sat dead center with everything surrounding it, including the crew as spectators.

Vosh entered from the adjacent locker room wearing only a snug pair of black shorts. Less defined than Roku, he still packed an impressive furry physique. Meaty and powerful, the man was big everywhere, as shown by those clinging shorts. They weren't exactly discreet and were a bit of a distraction. At least they were until Roku stepped into Arad's view and oh-so slowly stripped out of his shirt, keeping his sultry gaze on Arad the whole time. Dragging the fabric upward, he flicked a thumb over his nipple and flexed his chest for Arad's benefit. He tossed the shirt aside, and his whole torso rippled. Rippled! Now which DemiShou had the cocky smile?

Why were all DemiShou such physically impressive specimens? It was enough to give a guy a complex.

After shaking out his monstrous limbs, Vosh made a show out of cracking his knuckles. "House rules. Non-lethal and nothing below the belt. Hodge referees from the outside and declares a winner. Tap out to forfeit. You ready for this, pussycat?"

Roku's feet shifted, stabilizing his stance. "You talk too much."

Second thoughts pricked at Arad. The longer they danced, the more he figured Vosh's game was about establishing top dog—or top Demi. Whatever. Did Vosh even know what he'd set in motion? Roku became more at ease the longer they faced off on the mat. Without appearing overconfident, he bounced and stretched, like he had before he'd beaten the hell out of the combat dummy. His memories may have been in shambles, but he had ingrained skills at his disposal.

At Hodge's signal, both opponents circled the mat, assessing, gauging strength, while the spectators urged them on.

Vosh moved first, taking an exploratory swipe at Roku, who slapped it away with frightening ease. The second swing ended the same. Roku danced, caution assessment clear in his eyes. Huffing, Vosh tried another punch, only to have Roku block it aside and land one of his own on Vosh's open side. The next few minutes were more of the same while Vosh's swings became less playful. Using his mass to his advantage, he cornered Roku, picked him up, and body-slammed him to the mat. Vosh jumped to his feet and gave a taunting kick to Roku's shoulder as he stepped away. Staying outside, Hodge kept an eye on the action but said nothing.

Arad wasn't sure if he should be worried or not.

Chest heaving, Roku sidestepped in a wary arc. "You said this was supposed to be friendly sparring?"

"I'm still being friendly. Aren't you? Gotta give the boys a show." Breathing hard, Vosh's mouth curled into a fiendish grin. Roku crouched and sprung forward, raining a flurry of blows to Vosh's torso that sent him stumbling backward.

For a brief moment, Vosh appeared stunned, but the expression turned furious. With a roar, he rushed Roku and tackled him to the mat. They rolled and tussled, huge bodies slamming together. Legs entwined as they grunted and struggled, each sneaking blows in the clutch. Roku's kilt rose perilously up his thighs as body parts rubbed against body parts. Backs arched and grappling for control, this was more like a few of Arad's old Grey District hustling encounters than a sparring match.

Eyes locked on the fight, Pakko shifted closer to Arad, voice subdued into an awestruck whisper. "Holy shit, this is so hot. How much would it cost to get them to do this naked?"

"Shut up." Arad didn't want to admit that had already crossed his mind. *Is it getting hot in here?* Slug fights in Grey District were never this...exciting.

Punching disappeared as they wrestled. Writhing on the floor, neither conceded. Roku's ability to strike negated in close proximity, Vosh used his bulk to his advantage. His speed may not have been a match to Roku's, but his sheer mass cast a doubt on the tiger's ability to win as he covered Roku's body with his own, grinding his hips against him.

Roku resisted, and Vosh worked to keep him pinned, both Demis wearing half grins with their effort. They were enjoying every second of the bout, and Arad found his feelings mixed. If Roku lost, it would leave the *Nightingale* crew seeing himself and Roku as weaker, potential targets. They needed to be seen as equals or more. Of course, his concerns about the delicate power balance were being overridden by the purely carnal sideshow. At least he acknowledged being aroused and unhappy at the same time was a tad hypocritical. He'd chastise himself for it later. He didn't want to miss any of the action.

Refusing to quit, Roku thrashed and found himself on his back with Vosh straddling his torso. With his weight tipped forward, he had the leverage to pin Roku's wrists up and out of the way.

Vosh humped Roku's chest a few times with a confident chuckle. "My boy needs a reminder of who's boss around here."

With a defiant growl, Roku lurched off the mat, dislodging Vosh enough to curl a leg forward and hook it around Vosh's neck. Every muscle in Roku's body swelled, and he pitched them over with a roar. The move rolled Vosh onto his chest with Roku sitting on his upper back, one leg wrapped around Vosh's throat.

Roku's words hissed with exertion. "You're done. Tap out."

Vosh growled and thrashed to get free, so Roku flexed his leg, coaxing a choke out of the bear. There was no escape. Roku reached out and smacked Vosh's buttock...hard. The crack echoing through the room made Arad squeeze his own bottom in reflex. Vosh inhaled sharply and froze.

"I *said* tap out."

After receiving another stinging slap across the ass, Vosh did.

"Winner! The mighty Roku!" Hodge shouted, fist raised. Cheers erupted all around.

The combatants disentangled, and Roku patted Vosh's shoulder. "Good match. Let's do it again some time." Vosh nodded and offered his hand for Roku to shake, which he did.

"Baby! Are you okay?" Pakko swooped in to cater to his fallen comrade, massaging, kissing, and clutching the mounds of Vosh's flesh in a suspiciously pornographic way. Arad asked himself if they'd make it to their quarters, but his grey matter stalled as Roku—body tight with exertion—collected his shirt and came his way, gaze fixed on Arad.

Eyes gleaming, Roku effortlessly hefted Arad over his shoulder. "Time to collect my winnings."

"Put me down!"

Roku clamped a big hand on Arad's ass. "Quiet."

The dominance in his voice caused a surge to Arad's groin, and *quiet* became Arad's new favorite word. He shut his mouth and pretended there weren't so many witnesses.

Rolling her eyes, Yosei crossed her arms over her chest. "All of you guys are so gross."

With his free hand, Roku shook Hodge's hand. "Thank you for your hospitality. We're heading to our ship for the night. We'll coordinate repairs first thing in the morning."

With a crooked grin, Hodge side-eyed Arad's vulnerable position. "First thing?"

"Hmm... Perhaps later than that." Roku patted Arad's behind. "I'll make sure the captain contacts you."

Arad didn't say a word as Roku turned and walked away, carrying Arad like a sack of produce. He didn't even respond to Hodge's laughter echoing after them down the hall.

Chapter Twenty-One

With Arad slung over his shoulder, Roku closed the *Ansariland*'s hatch and continued down the hall until he reached the lavatory. Arad followed Roku's order like a good boy and kept his mouth shut as he was lifted and sat on the nearest sink's edge. Roku stepped back and tossed his unworn shirt aside. A mischievous glint in his eye, he reached for his kilt, keeping his smoldering gaze fixed on Arad. With a lick of his lips, he unfastened the garment, consciously flexing groups of muscles—chest, abdominals, hips, and thighs as the garment slid to the floor—all for Arad's benefit.

Well charged from the match, Roku sauntered close, his words laced in smug confidence. "I can smell how much you enjoyed watching me fight. Should I be exerting myself for you more often?" Roku stepped between Arad's seated legs, nudging them apart.

If Roku smelled Arad's arousal, he was getting a nose full. Even so, Arad had never considered himself easy. He'd always made a cocky man work for it.

"Maybe it was the fight. I wasn't the only one there, you know."

Roku chuffed as he leaned in close, inhaling along Arad's shoulder and neck. "Yes, I'm aware. Everyone was watching. Bryce too. I heard her cheering over the speakers."

"Yes, well, make sure no one talks you into getting naked over there for any reason. Bryce has a little more than professional love going on for DemiShou, and she has screens turned on the entire ship."

"You noticed that too?"

Oh, Arad noticed, all right. He nearly bit his tongue keeping quiet because he couldn't risk alienating the *Nightingale* when they were so close to getting repairs in order.

Roku's hands skimmed under Arad's shirt. Dragging his fingertips against the heated flesh, he lifted the garment up and off Arad's body. Heat radiating from Roku fought off any chill. "Once repairs begin, make sure she doesn't get access to any of our communications net. I don't care what she does over there, but I'd like us to have some amount of privacy on the *Ansariland*. I don't want anyone seeing you undressed but me."

His ability to be official and commanding while being oh-so sexy impressed Arad, but he wasn't about to cede all control. "As long as you promise to keep your kilt on around Vosh and Pakko. I think they'd be more than happy to get you going all sweaty, naked dom on the two of them. Especially after that match."

Roku's hands stilled. "I would never touch them like that. Not for real."

Using a single finger, Arad prodded Roku's granite chest. "You spanked Vosh."

"He had been humping my chest. I needed something to make him face that he'd lost. It was domination. Not sex. That is something strictly, and only, for you."

"Make sure they don't confuse the two." Arad lowered his head so he didn't have to see anything in Roku's eyes. Something about the idea of Roku with Vosh and Pakko—or anyone for that matter—left an uneasy fluttering in his chest.

With a nudge to Arad's chin, Roku placed a gentle kiss on his lips. "I will be happy to remind them of the difference."

Arad stared into Roku's eyes, searching for any hint of deceit. When he found nothing but unerring loyalty and more, he kicked himself for doubting him. Even if only for a few moments. The fluttering turned into a smolder, and Arad returned Roku's sentiment. The longer they kissed, the gentler Roku became, but no less in charge. The fear of losing control had been fading lately, being replaced by a welcome confidence to take command. Authority used to repel Arad. Men with it weren't to be trusted. They used and abused the people under them all the time. But Roku's gradual emergence brought a comfort and warmth he hadn't expected to find.

Roku pulled Arad close, pressing his hardening meat into Arad's groin, but made no effort to remove Arad's shorts even as he continued to trace firm lines over Arad's skin. Arad used the opportunity to touch Roku, never tiring of the unyielding physique highlighted in silky fur. Roku's natural musk piqued, spicy from exertion, and he took it all in. Nothing was rushed between them, and the cockiness from earlier became a relaxed foreplay. Rather than speeding the pace, it reduced to a crawl but refused to halt, if the pair of hard organs crushed between them was any evidence. The craving had returned, and it simmered, waiting to be pushed into a full boil once again.

Arad shuddered as Roku pulled back, giving him a bit of breathing space but without losing contact. "So you think we're good to let them help us?"

"I don't see how we have a choice, but Hodge appears genuine, and Yosei seems to be excited to play with anything as long as it's tech. She was enjoying the match but was the only one who didn't smell aroused to some extent. Hodge was the least affected but still hyped up from the fight."

"Most guys like to watch a fight. It tends to blur the lines of homo and hetero in the heat of the moment. Nothing new there."

Urging Roku to one side, Arad hopped down from the sink. The cushionless edge digging into his behind threatened to end the moment before it properly began if he stayed put. One hand on Roku for balance, he stretched his legs to ward off the discomfort. A reminder the sink was a crappy sex perch no matter what the porn vids showed.

Arad hadn't stopped touching Roku but made no move to disconnect. "All right. I'll follow your lead, but remember we don't know any of them enough to trust them too far. Once the ship's fixed, we're moving on. Hachi and Shichi still need somewhere safe to go."

"Agreed. Be cautious, but don't create an issue. We need them."

"For now."

"Yes. For now."

What the hell was he doing? Arad had the hottest male he'd ever laid eyes on wanting and waiting for sex, and here they were discussing the strategy of repair scheduling with the *Nightingale*. Discussing strangers they weren't planning on sleeping with for any reason. It was an important talk, but did it have to be right now? They were both ready to go. What was wrong with them?

With a quick movement, Arad unbuckled his shorts and bared himself to his ankles. After stepping out of the pile, he removed his footwear and headed for the shower. "Enough about them. Are you planning on taking advantage of your winnings yet, or am I going to have to wash my own back?"

Roku didn't hide the slap of eager footsteps on the deck following Arad.

Even as a child, Arad had understood the impact of labels. For good or ill, they defined a person, distinguished their place in the status hierarchy. *Corporate* flew free above the towers. *Slugs* crawled in the dirt. *Authority* served as gatekeepers between them and all the other stages from top to bottom. Rarely did anyone climb higher, find a way out of their placement. Slip and fall out of the sky and land in the dirt...that was far more common.

Recent conversation had dredged up little trails of doubt over where he stood with Roku. He shouldn't have cared. On the streets, nothing was permanent. What changed?

As DemiShou, Roku was little more than a second-class citizen sitting on the lower social ladder rungs. Prejudice would limit how high he climbed, but Arad was convinced he'd been part of the authority in some capacity.

That authority was in full force as he held Arad's chest and hands spread against the shower wall while he buried his snout and tongue between Arad's quivering buttocks.

It started out simply enough. Sharing the warm spray, they lathered one another, lingering over sensitive areas the longer they dragged out the bathing phase. He'd followed lazy rivulets of foam trailing around the crevasses of slick-furred muscle, down the torso, running off the tip of Roku's gradually swelling member. By the time it reached full size, the foreskin had rolled back and a tiny bead of dew shined at the slit.

Arad had dipped his head and licked the drop clean. Warmth spread through his tongue. The taste ramped the craving to new heights, and he pumped Roku's shaft, determined to draw more to the surface. The tiger could only be teased so long before he spun Arad and took command.

Without breaking his feast, Roku reached into the shower niche and snatched the bottle of sex oil. It only made sense to keep some handy since the tiger loved to pounce in the water, and it hadn't taken much searching through the other bedrooms to find more than one bottle existed on board. Roku stood tall, his broad shoulders sheltering Arad from the water as he stuffed slippery fingers into Arad's opening, prepping him for more.

And it was so much more. The girth of Roku's cock at his back door was almost too much, but he had been beyond caring for a while now. Roku lifted him off his feet, and Arad had no choice but to enjoy the long slide until the entire length impaled him.

"Are you all right?" Roku held still, his voice a mask of restrained lust.

Overwhelmed, Arad nodded with a barely coherent grunt of assent.

Roku's arms tightened around him, and he clamped his jaws over Arad's neck and shoulder. Held in place with his feet off the floor, Arad submitted as Roku slid out and in again. Every nerve inside Arad flared into full brightness as Roku picked up speed and took what he wanted, what they both needed.

Arad shouldn't have been able to feel Roku's release. Yes, he flexed, heaved, and thrusted deep, but not the actual flood that burned and chilled Arad's insides in delicious ways, sending tendrils of ecstasy through his blood like the headiest whiskey. It charged through his spine and groin and tore a screaming orgasm out of him, leaving a pattern of sticky trails on the wall. The shower washed them away as the craving subsided.

Roku carefully disengaged and held Arad close as he rinsed them both off, taking care with Arad's more tender areas. He turned off the water and led them out, grabbing a towel and gently drying Arad before dealing with his own wet state.

Now that the itch had been scratched, Arad's wayward thoughts came alive once more. "Vosh called us mated. Is that something special for DemiShou?"

Roku stopped scrubbing his fur and gave Arad a pointed stare. "I wouldn't know."

"Sorry. Memories. I forget sometimes. The way Vosh talked, I guess mating's a bigger deal than just fooling around."

"I don't see us as fooling around. I can't." A hard crease marred Roku's brow and he averted his eyes. "The longer we've been together, the more I've hated being apart from you. Even being in different rooms when it's only us here on the ship."

Arad flushed. "Yeah, I saw. Kinda hard to miss."

"I want to protect you at all times."

"I...I don't need protection." Pulse quickening, Arad nearly stammered.

Both men paused, only the drip in the shower providing noise. Roku finally spoke, his breath shuddering. "I don't know what I'd do if you made me give you up."

Big, strong, and so vulnerable. The fear he recognized in Roku's eyes stabbed Arad with a depth he'd believed himself immune to after being wounded on so many levels in the past. It startled Arad because the same worry resided inside himself. Permanent wasn't typical on the street, but they weren't technically on the street anymore. Didn't that change the rules of social standing?

Before he said something stupid, Arad flung himself forward and wrapped his arms around the wet tiger, squeezing as hard as possible, trying to say more than he could out loud. Roku hugged him, and it made Arad's chest flutter.

Arad buried his face in Roku's chest because it was too hard to look him in the eye, and he was not about to cry. "No. I wouldn't do that to you...to me...to us." Arad scrunched his face and forced it out. "Can you make me a promise?"

"Anything. Just ask."

But that was the problem. Asking. It should have been easy and straightforward rather than halting and risky. Other people managed it every day, yet here he was, struggling to unclench his teeth enough to speak. His parents and the men in black had a lot to answer for.

A tear rolled down Arad's cheek as he barked out the words. "If I promise to keep you forever, would you do the same for me?"

Roku rubbed his cheek and jaw along the top of Arad's head. "I've already made that promise."

"When?"

"Since the first night I woke up in your bed." Leaning back, Roku wiped away Arad's errant tear with his thumb.

Arad's shaky exhale was filled with relief. "Me too."

They stayed locked in their embrace until Roku dried and Arad's doubts lifted. Forever was a long time, and a thing he'd never guessed he could count on. Life in Grey District would never have allowed the pipe dream. Yet here in outer space, perhaps a man could apply a new label over the old one he'd been saddled with. He'd be more than a slug for the first time in so, so long. It gave him new meaning and maybe even a step higher on the ladder.

For once, a label freed a man rather than restrained him.

"I like the word *mated*."

"Are you sure you know what you're doing?" Arad asked.

The viewing window was larger than on the *Ansariland*. He, Roku, Vosh, and Yosei watched Pakko settle the helmet on his spacesuit and check the seals with a practiced hand inside the *Nightingale*'s secondary airlock rather than the main since it was occupied tethering the two ships together. A toolset and a spare piece of deck plating sat at his feet with a loose cable connecting them to his belt.

"Yeah. I do all the outer ship fixes. I've spacewalked a thousand times. I'm good. But it's nice to know you care." With the door closed, Pakko's gruff voice came through the ship's comm as he performed his final checks.

Roku's crossed arms flexed in sharp relief. "I don't like anyone going out there. Arad had to go out of the ship to fix communications. I almost lost him."

Arad placed a hand on Roku's arm, feeling the tension leashed under his skin. "This is different. I'd never done it before and got myself in trouble. Pakko looks like he knows what he's doing."

"That I do." Pakko banged on the door and waved at them all. "Okay, let's cycle the airlock so I can get this done."

Vosh double-checked the readings from the nearby panel. "All systems are optimal, babe. See you in a little while. We'll be watching."

"I'll get that hole welded shut and be back in time for lunch." Pakko saluted and picked up his tools.

"Works for me."

With a series of touches, Vosh cycled the airlock. As the air safely vented, the artificial gravity lowered, causing the plating and attached cable to float in a lazy drift with the lightest tug.

"Do you plan on monitoring his status from here?" Roku asked.

Vosh tapped the panel, which switched to a series of health statistics that reminded Arad of the screens on the DemiShou cryotubes and Bryce's equipment. Medical displays appeared to be consistent regardless of the device.

Vosh's gaze fixated on Pakko. "Yes."

"Do you mind if I watch with you? In case Arad ever needs to go out again. I was…unprepared last time."

He pondered Roku's request for a moment and answered with a wordless nod.

The airlock finished and the outer hatch opened. A ring of lights marking the door helped the darkness seem less intimidating. Pakko latched on his security cable, waved to them all, and climbed outside.

A solemn hush fell over the group, causing Yosei's voice to startle the men. "Okay, watching med stats will bore me to tears, and I can be more useful in other places. So if you don't mind, I'll take Arad to the *Ansariland*, and we can check the damage control reports. From there, I can calibrate the wonky systems and link to Pakko's compad and direct him to the breach. Easy-peasy. It'll only be me and Arad."

Her breakneck jabbering caught everyone off guard, and Roku simply stared, eyes wide. The tiny pink-haired woman wrapped her arms around one of Arad's like schoolgirls did with their besties.

"Don't worry, Roku. If he gets fresh, I'll tase him." Yosei's smile was all teeth.

Roku snorted. "Go on."

Yosei dragged Arad away from the group with a jarring command. "C'mon! Time's a-wastin'!"

Arad called out over his shoulder, letting her take the lead. "I'll check in once we make some progress." His sight lingered on Roku as she pulled him away. Hopefully learning more about the spacewalk process would distract him enough to calm the impending separation anxiety. What else could he do? The work needed to be done.

Yosei's pace made him work not to stumble while being careful not to resist her tugging at his arm. He didn't want to accidentally jerk her backward and trip her. Arad wasn't the biggest guy around, but next to Yosei, he felt huge and clumsy. It made him grasp Roku's obsession with treating him carefully. Strangely enough, her arms were thin but amazingly strong. The girl was a dichotomy. He was probably worrying for nothing.

Before long, they reached the tunnel connecting the two ships.

"Sorry for asking permission like that. After he cavemanned you at the sparring match, I figured it was the smart play. Getting mauled by the big kitty is your job. No, I don't want a single detail of what happened. Gross. Forget I said that. Are you sure you're really the captain?"

Arad laughed. "Yes, I'm the captain. But some things Roku makes his mission. He has a bit of an overprotective streak."

"A bit? I've seen corporate-level starcraft hyperspatial induction coils that were smaller than his hovering."

"That was way above my tech level, so I'll have to take your word for it."

While she wasn't attached like a leech to his arm anymore, Yosei still led the way, always one step ahead of Arad. A variety of tech tools were latched to her jumpsuit, some peeking out of the various pockets. How did the sheer volume not weigh down her waifish frame? Her boots clomped through the hallways as she walked with an obvious knowledge of the bridge's location. Well, she had announced she'd uploaded the ship's model specs.

"You're pretty new to being captain, right? The OS promoted you when the crew got zapped. You said you were a low-level tech. How did you learn the ship systems? Did you already know them?"

Arad shook his head. "I've had a lot of time to read."

"Wow. You did good in such a short time. Starships are complicated, and your model is a fussy girl. I'm impressed you were able to fix the communications array well enough to send out a distress call. If there hadn't been a hull breach, I bet you'd have fixed the engines too. Once we get your ship running, you're going to have to land—or at least dock—to replenish supplies. You haven't flown your ship yet, have you?"

"Um, not yet."

Yosei's energy was so different than the bleak resignation to hard life of Grey District's people. Positive and refreshing, it made for a delightful, if unnerving, change of pace. It was difficult not to divulge everything in her presence. An innocence permeated her every move and word, and he understood Hodge's interest in protecting her from a more jaded world. She was disarmingly personable.

Yosei lowered her voice as if they shared a special secret. "You're a smart dude. I think you're a lot better at this than you admit, but I still think I can teach you some stuff."

"You're insanely brilliant. I certainly hope so."

The color of Yosei's cheeks deepened as she restrained her smile. "By the time we're done, you'll know how to fly this ship better than Hodge. But don't tell him I said that."

"I won't. Promise."

They entered the bridge, and Yosei wasted no time taking Daiko's old chair. The screens came alive under her masterful fingertips, pulling up the ship's diagram, specifically outside. A signal noted the location of a lone life form inching its way along the hull.

Arad leaned over for a closer look. "Is that Pakko?"

"Yep." Yosei tapped the icon representing him and opened a channel. "Pakko, you hear me?"

"I'm here." Distortions affected the speaker quality, but Pakko could be understood.

"Good. Arad and I are on the *Ansariland* bridge and have eyes on you."

"Don't let me fall off. There's a whole lot of nothing out here."

"I'll do my best, but if you do, I'm telling Vosh it's all your fault." Without looking, Yosei pointed at Franc's old seat. "Sit."

Arad did as he was told. The first steps were underway. Anticipation flavored the air, but smart men did not scrub against the grain of good tidings.

Yosei reached over and activated Arad's monitors, drawing the navigational controls to the front like a seasoned professional. "It's going to take Pakko some time to get to the breach, so we might as well use it wisely and get your Starship Piloting 101 course under your belt. Buckle up, we're taking the crash course."

Nodding, Arad readied himself to be a human sponge. As the whirlwind lesson began, he debated reaching for the seat belt.

"Pakko, the hull breach should be twenty-five meters ahead, forty-six degrees from your current position."

Still outside the ship, Pakko replied with a voice layered with static. "Got it, Yosei."

Multi-tasking was her mojo. For the past half hour, she'd kept passing occasional instructions to Pakko while teaching Arad various piloting sequences on the *Ansariland* without losing her ever-constant speech tempo. However, the constant audio distortion continued to prompt face scrunching.

"Your communications and sensors are working, but they're still wonky."

Arad sighed, happy for the break. "Tell me something I don't know. So is there anything else I need to know about the autopilot?"

"Only that everyone uses it to dock and land and then pretend they did it by hand."

A snicker escaped Arad. "Does Hodge do that?"

Despite her appearance, Yosei's innocent features turned positively conspiratorial. "He's one of the worst offenders. But starship captains and pilots spend a lot of time patting each other's butts, so you might as well learn to be part of the crowd now."

Happy banter and more instructions filled the bridge as Yosei had Arad repeat what she'd already gone over. They'd been adrift for so long the details of what to do next had gotten lost. Assuming the repairs had ever been managed, Arad was only a starship captain in name. He knew next to nothing when it came to running his ship. Reading manuals and trials by fire could only be successful for so long.

The tide turned in tiny increments, flowing with him rather than leaving him swimming against the current for a change, but he didn't expect life to treat him like a wealthy elite. That time was over. He would take what he could get and appreciate it for as long as it lasted.

"Pakko, you still out there?

"Yeah, what's up?"

"I wanted to say I appreciate you making this effort to help us out," Arad said.

"Aw, it's no big deal."

"Seriously, it is. I don't know many people who'd go this far for anyone else. I just wanted to say thanks."

"I know how you can thank me." Even unseen, Pakko's sleazy grin filled the room.

"Now, that's more like what I expected out of you. It's a flattering offer. It really is. But your bear can bend you over and thank you instead."

Yosei shuddered and gagged. "Ew. Stop talking about copulation in front of me. Why can't you guys settle for fully clothed hugs and hot chocolate?"

Arad and Pakko both erupted in laughter, yet neither bothered to answer. That question was better left alone. It didn't take much detective work to know they each approached sex from different directions. Pakko was all about recreation, and for Arad it had been more of a transactional activity rather than strictly for pleasure. Often after encounters with most of his customers, he appreciated a lack of human contact for a while, and he rarely allowed anyone another visit for a length of time. At least long enough to forget the shame involved. Then Roku came and changed it all. He wanted Roku near before, during, and even afterward. Learning how to exist in a sexual relationship without commerce was a beautiful thing. But he recalled enough days in the past where he'd wished to do without it altogether, so he understood how sex wasn't the goal for everyone. If Yosei preferred platonic relations, she was welcome to it.

"Hey, Yosei. Are you sure there's no major systems under the breach? I don't want to get blown up out here. Can you give me a more precise location?" Pakko asked.

"I have the specs and my scans from the *Nightingale*, but the sensors here are messy. Hold on." With one hand flying over the monitor attempting to tweak the feed with little effect, Yosei shoved her com-pad in Arad's face without looking. "Touch a thumb to it. Minor permissions only, so I can sync the pad. If there's a power line I'm not seeing, Vosh'll have to trade up at the next station."

The static didn't dampen Pakko's squawk. "I heard that!"

"Chill. There's only a minor chance of that actually happening. Infinitesimal. Sort of. Arad? Permissions?"

Arad hesitated. "Oh. Right."

He understood her request, but giving away any level of authority on the ship made him think twice. With everything she and the rest were doing for them, Arad told himself it was a small concession, necessary to move forward. Praying he wouldn't regret it, he pressed his thumb to the screen, and the pad chimed. Yosei made more adjustments, and the static-filled communications feed became a clean stream, free of audible debris.

Yosei drew up a hologram of the *Nightingale* and hailed them. "Vosh, our boy is starting the patch job, and my locator beacon is keeping good track of him on the map. Anything I need to be worried about?"

"No. His health stats are all good." Well-focused, Vosh likely hadn't taken his eyes off the screen. "Let me know when he's on his way back."

"Will do." Yosei dropped the line, her grin brightening in satisfaction. "Now that sounded much prettier. After we get Pakko sorted, we have to get this array calibrated. You can chat fine, but otherwise, once the engines are fixed, you'll crash into an asteroid because you won't see it coming. Your jump shook this up worse than I thought. Static city. What a mess. I'm totally demoting you to deck swabber if I find more of this. Pakko, five meters and counting. On your left."

"I see it." Without the pervious noise garbage, Pakko's voice was pure enough to hear his breathing.

Arad perked up. "Are you sure?"

"Yeah. The hull's scorched, but the hole's not too big. Blast didn't punch through. Looks like it found a weak spot and popped. Just a fist-sized blowout."

"It's seriously that small?"

The description surprised Arad. First Commander Bard may have erased the shuttle and crew, but it was almost like he wasn't trying to incinerate the ship. A warning shot to get them to surrender? Perhaps.

"Looks like they got lucky and hit it in just the right area to disable the engine. Explosive decompression probably didn't do it any favors either."

Arad didn't offer any insight. There were enough potential questions lurking. "So you can seal it?"

"Don't see why not. I'll have to soften the edges with my torch so I can flatten it and weld the panel across. You guys can check to see if it's airtight, and then we can reinforce it from inside. Won't take long."

The relief came in a rush. Luck hadn't exactly been a familiar friend. An occasional visitor at best. "Sounds like you'll have it fixed faster than it took to find."

"Too right. Get this set, and we'll tackle the engine."

Arad leaned in his chair and allowed himself to hope a little bit. The *Ansariland* was on its way to being whole once more. His dreams of living free with Roku—money in their pockets and food in their bellies—grew brighter and more tangible. Years of toil and hunger became history rather than a daily struggle. A story to look on in their old ages.

Yes, he deserved it. The universe owed him that much.

Chapter Twenty-Two

Memories disguised as dreams were a special kind of hell.

Arad wasn't awake, yet the truth woven through the scenes kept him hoping for an alternate ending even though he knew this story better than anyone because it was his. Unimportant parts played at high speed. He screamed inside as the highlights slowed down, showing off their gritty detail.

The men in black jackets intercepted him on the way to his chess lesson. They grabbed his arm and dislodged his personal game set from his hand. The box fell and burst open on the sidewalk. Bishops and rooks bounced into the gutter. Pawns tumbled down the sewer grate. No one stopped them. No one helped.

Flash forward to the workhouse. The invasive examination—stripped and probed like a criminal—being catalogued like property. Crying in bed after the beating for making a costly mistake on his first job. The panicked flight the day the workhouse burned.

Flash forward. Sketch asked him if he wanted to see them again, and like a wishful child, Arad said yes because, deep down, he knew the madness was a misunderstanding. Once he apologized to his parents, he would do whatever absurd plan they asked. They would be a family once again. He'd learned his lesson.

Rain soaked him to the bone in the dream, but in reality the dingy sky had been clear. He argued with the concierge, the man he'd flirted with days before his induction to the workhouse. Now he refused Arad entry, using his appearance to pretend he was a vagrant. A stranger. Bystanders gathered as everything escalated until, finally, the doors opened and his parents stepped onto the sidewalk, glowing with a heavenly aura. Untouchable by peasants.

The dream rain didn't touch them or the willowy boy accompanying them. Skin too dark, features too slender, he had no resemblance to Arad or the family. None whatsoever. How did they believe this impostor could stand in his place?

"Mom! Dad! What's going on? I'll do whatever you ask."

His father stayed silent. His replacement sneered. His mother studied him, her dark eyes dilated with whatever recent pharmaceutical was at her disposal. "We have no idea who this boy is."

The concierge's fingers bit into Arad's arm. "Time to go, son."

Arad dug in his heels, refusing to be moved. "Let go! You know who I am!" He spun his stare on his parents. "How can you do this to me?"

The rain streaking his face tasted surprisingly salty while his family remained unaffected by the fictitious weather and his pleas. Security arrived in quick time to the concierge's call. Uniformed men attempted to remove him from the premises, but Arad demanded to be scanned to prove his identity. Surprisingly, they agreed.

Undocumented.

"You're no one," said nobody but the voices in his head.

Greedy to a fault, his family had erased the impediment to their fortune. His parents denied everything, leaving him the choice to walk away or be arrested. Betrayal flayed him to the bone, but he dredged up enough sense to leave. Enough stories were passed around the workhouse about what happened to incarcerated slugs. And, as of that day, it was what he was: a street-dwelling slug. No one of importance. He didn't exist.

Arad looked over his shoulder, and his parents didn't even watch him walk away.

Hopefully Sketch would forgive him for being so colossally stupid. How much lower could he go knowing a drug dealer was his sole lifeline?

That hadn't been intended to be a challenge to the universe.

The downhill slalom came next, but the story rewound and played itself again, over and over.

Nightmares were supposed to end once a person opened their eyes.

Arad counted the ceiling rivets, barely visible in the dark. Roku slept soundly for a change, and he found himself envying the tiger's missing memories. His fingers twitched, and he ached to curl into a mass of DemiShou muscle and fur but couldn't bring himself to disturb Roku. At least one of them deserved a quiet night.

Carefully, he edged himself off the bed and shuffled out the door, thankful it wasn't closed, because the mechanical tech hidden in the *Ansariland*'s walls had never been quiet. His bare footsteps in the hall were silent.

On the bridge, starlight shined off the *Nightingale*'s hull as it drifted in tandem, docking moors in place. He stared at the sister ship, looking for evidence of activity, signs of something sinister because no one gave charity. Even the preachers in Grey District spouted gloom and doom to scare people into filling their tithes, few willing to aid the desperate and homeless. Weren't the clergy supposed to be the caretakers of the underprivileged? Even his parents fell short, so what could he expect out of random travelers?

With a growl, he scrubbed his hands through his hair and over his face. He hated how hard trust came to him, but it had been broken out of his splintered soul, and now only Roku had earned the honor of holding the remaining shards. In its place sat layers of suspicion that had kept him alive long after Sketch disappeared and left him on his own.

Listening to be sure Roku hadn't woken, he pulled the bridge computer out of sleep with a few deft taps to the screen. Weeks of free time with ship manuals gave him the command logs open only to the *Ansariland*'s captain, however he gained the rank. He pressed his thumb to the screen and typed in the encrypted password. The thumbprint alone couldn't get anyone into this data.

Dates, times, and systems were displayed in a neat graph for easy reading. There was Yosei's access to the sensor grid after Arad had no choice but to give it up. Her pad's ID signature stayed isolated to the bridge. No other log-ins detected, hers or any other. She hadn't attempted to abuse the privilege he'd granted her and apparently hadn't shared it either.

The *Nightingale*'s crew had given him nothing but kindness, but it didn't smother his traces of lingering doubt. The lack of faith weighed heavy on his shoulders, but no one in Grey District lived long without expecting the worst, even in good situations.

Since sleep was lost, Arad spent the rest of the night watching the logs.

Familiar heartbeat chimes echoed off the cargo bay's walls. Shirt hem bunched in his hand, Arad wiped a barely-there layer of dust off the cryotube. Hachi slumbered, big bull face pressed against the plexiglass, floating unaware of Arad's care in the early hour. And it was indeed early.

Disturbing anyone present wasn't possible, yet Arad insisted on whispering to be respectful of the sleeping DemiShou. "I'm sorry I've been a little busy lately, but we haven't forgotten you guys."

Ventilation noise didn't overpower the capsule's soothing hum. Weeks of listening had made it a constant in Arad's newfound life. Hearing it again sanded the dream's burrs and rough edges into something within reach, sleek like the cryotubes' surfaces. The soft whirring gave him purpose and streamlined his nerves, unlike the barrage of approaching footfalls echoing into the bay.

Still naked from bed, Roku burst into the room, exhaling in relief as he locked eyes with Arad. "There you are. I woke up and you were gone."

Arad shrugged. "Couldn't sleep."

Without losing step, Roku swept Arad into his arms, rubbing his cheek and jaw along Arad's. Gradually, his breathing settled into something less harried. His panicked edge made it impossible to enjoy his lack of clothing.

"I dreamt Hodge and his crew had stolen you. Then I woke and you weren't in bed. I almost grabbed some of Torrins's weapons and stormed the *Nightingale*."

Arad shuddered. Roku's hand-to-hand skills were impressive enough, and arming the man had all the ingredients for a recipe of widespread carnage. He'd never seen a weapon in his hands, but if it came to him as naturally as martial arts, a rampage would likely be bloody and unforgiving. Not something for the faint of heart. Arad had never been a violent man, even when pressed by the sort who truly deserved it. "That would have been bad. Really bad."

"Extremely. I would likely be outnumbered and outgunned. I have the feeling that other than Yosei, the crew are ex-military or some other authority."

"Makes sense. Bryce was definitely military. DemiShou conversion wasn't open to civilians, so she'd have to be if she'd been on the list and got passed up."

Roku growled. "I know they said the repairs would take a few days, but the longer this goes on, the less I like it."

"I'm sorry I worried you. I should've known better." Arad squeezed Roku tight, hoping to ease both of their souls. The last few days with Yosei and the gang had gone well, and wanting it to end made him feel guilty. Survival on the streets had left him poorly equipped to function in groups for extended periods.

"It's not that I don't like the crew, but all these extra people walking through our ship has me agitated."

Arad caught the *our* in Roku's comment, which made him smile inside, even as the tiger wanted to defend his territory. More of his animal nature peeked through, which didn't bother Arad in the least. No matter how kind the *Nightingale* crew were, they would always hold a certain title of intruder to Roku. Strangely comforting since Arad wasn't part of that crowd.

"It shouldn't be much longer, then we'll be on our way. I like them, but I'm not joining them either. We're better off on our own."

Leaning back, Roku palmed Arad's cheek. "The *Ansariland* is my home."

"*Our* home. *Our* ship." Arad smiled as any persistent doubts were quashed. "They can visit on holidays."

"Maybe."

"They can send us holiday vid messages."

"I find that option acceptable."

Separating, they clasped hands as they circled the cryotubes, both men assessing the DemiShou. They examined the monitors and casings, looking for any flaw or degrading seams. All connections were solid, and the health telemetry appeared unchanged from before the *Nightingale* had arrived.

Arad wiped dust from Shichi's window. "You know, before you hatched, I used to spend all day in here watching over you guys while I read tech manuals because I had the idea that if something went wrong, I'd be able to help."

"You saved me."

"I got lucky. I didn't have a clue what I was doing. I'm not sure I did the CPR thing right either."

Roku squeezed Arad's hand in support. "Yet here I am, alive and well."

Arad paused, sighing as he reflected. "I feel like I'm neglecting them lately. Like I'm doing something else instead of watching over them."

"Staying out of sight is in their best interests. The *Nightingale* has been good to us, but the fewer people who know of their existence, the better. We don't need to pass out knowledge that can be used against us."

They stood unmoving, side by side, as they continued to stand watch over their charges. One tube had been Roku's, and seeing them now with him by Arad's side brought back all kinds of images, reminding him of how far they'd come and how far they still had to go. A solemn air passed over them, quelling any concerns Arad had of Roku's state of undress. He made an effort not to look at the mattress still lying nearby or where Roku had originally awoken in an incoherent and horny daze and ravaged a Syn-high Arad.

Nope. He wasn't thinking of that at all.

Roku stepped forward and checked the health status readouts, exactly as Arad had done earlier. "I think we should stay away from this area for a while. I don't want any chance of the others thinking there's anything valuable enough in the cargo bay to pique their curiosity. In case they might be scanning us."

With the sensors functioning properly, Arad had been checking for that all night. So far, no trackable signs. If he wasn't going to sleep, he'd channel the paranoid man who had survived alone in Grey District. Being blindsided by events on this ship was a thing he had no interest in repeating. Enough surprises colored his time on board from the *Midas Ascending* to its current identity.

"Do you have any ideas on what to do after this is done?" Arad asked.

"I'm not sure. All I know is the sooner we complete repairs and are on our way, the better." Roku tugged at his hand, ushering them toward the exit.

Arad sighed. "Do you think we'll ever save them?"

Pausing, Roku turned and cupped Arad's cheek with one hand, ensuring his complete attention. "If there's one thing I don't doubt in this universe, it's your willpower to succeed. You'll find them a new home. But, first, let's see if we can get this ship to right so we have a way to get them there."

Roku's confidence and the warmth of his palm cut through Arad's mood and brought a smile to his face.

"I like the way you think."

Chapter Twenty-Three

Several scans to test the integrity of Pakko's patch on the hull were performed before Arad overrode the emergency protocols to re-establish the atmosphere and drop the bulkhead separating them from the engine room.

Balling up a fist, Pakko gave Arad a friendly tap on the shoulder. "Told ya the weld would hold."

"I've already seen people blown out into space. I'm not looking forward to a repeat." Arad shuddered.

"I hear that."

The rupture hadn't been large, but ragged lines in the metal webbed where the air had violently escaped after the shot. The breach was sealed, but Pakko planned to weld additional layers from the inside as insurance. With images of the *Midas Ascending* crew's deaths in his mind, the extra work couldn't happen too soon.

Arad, Pakko, and Yosei—the techs between the two ships—assessed the damage. Anything not nailed down had been scattered when the air voided. Some container doors barely hung on their hinges. A lot of debris was either too large to fit through the breach or the atmosphere emptied before it could be blown out. The result: The entire engine room was a wreck.

"Ya know, those pirates were awful precise. They hit you just hard enough to keep you from running. Seems a bit above the wage scale for those types." Pakko's new suspicious nature had to be from Vosh feeding him more conspiracies. If only the bear's theories weren't so accurate. Protecting the existence of the remaining designer DemiShou continued to be Arad and Roku's first priority over the *Ansariland*'s restoration.

Thankfully, Yosei appeared to be immune to Vosh's stories. "Not if they wanted to salvage the ship. The *Ansariland*'s not new, but it has some valuable modifications. It could be sold for a decent price to the right people."

"Pirates didn't waste much time explaining themselves," Arad groused. This line of questions needed to end before the story details revealed something he wanted to stay hidden.

Clearly, Pakko hadn't been briefed. "Why didn't they tag the jump drive? That would have made more sense."

"The jump drive's shielded. It doesn't show up on any scan we've made. They wouldn't have known it was charged, and then bam! Gone. Beautiful tech, and so not standard equipment." Hands on her hips, Yosei let out an awestruck snicker. "This is totally a smuggler's ship."

"Not anymore it's not." Arad had never been more sure of anything.

Once the ship could travel again, Arad had already been scheming on how to support themselves. The *Nightingale* was giving them a handout, but the help would be for a limited time. He had every intention of running a legitimate business. A starship needed funding, and delivering cargo wasn't the worst option. They'd choose their hauls and maybe even transport a person or two for a fee. They had the extra space. Living off planet would help keep Roku's profile out of the public as well. They'd do everything the *Midas Ascending* had done without the smuggling and DemiShou trafficking. He would not be the next version of Torrins.

Arad walked away from the others to view the powered down engine up close. A lot of hours had been spent doing maintenance on this beauty. It was a shame to see it in such condition. The ship deserved better. A pity it took the deaths of the crew to give him access to the schematics to understand the nuances of the engine specs.

He ducked under a fuel line whose seals had been spared from First Commander Bard's attack. It was a precision strike. The engine lacked the expected kind of damage and carbon scoring if they'd tried to strike the engine directly. Otherwise, half the room would have been missing, and he'd be staring into the vacuum from here. Whether he'd admit it or not, Pakko was right about the shot only intending to cripple the ship. No matter what threat Bard had made, he'd known exactly how to do the job with minimal destruction.

"I narrowed the problem down to the flow regulator." Anything Arad did to steer the conversation to repairs would be a good thing.

"And you would be one hundred percent right. I'm still impressed you figured that out before we fixed your sketchy sensors. Nice work." Yosei squinted at her pad as she zoomed in on the scan image. "I'm seeing all sorts of internal fractures. Explosive decompression must have junked its alignment and cracked it. If you try to reinstall this and fire it up, this baby's probably gonna explode."

Arad's breath caught. "Is it repairable?"

Pakko took a peek at Yosei's findings and frowned. "'Fraid not, but I think we got a spare we can fix up."

"We don't have any money for that." Enthusiasm seeped out of Arad.

"It's the old one we upgraded last season. It's got plenty of life in it still." Moving closer to the engine, Pakko examined the damaged regulator, oblivious to Arad's distress.

"If it's in such great shape, why did you replace it?"

Pakko peered over his shoulder to give Yosei a dirty look. "Because someone convinced Hodge getting a newer model was a brilliant idea."

Yosei sniffed. "It was brilliant. The fuel consumption is one hundred and fifty-seven percent more efficient. Having up-to-date equipment is in everyone's interest. You're only mad you didn't think of it first."

"Anyways, Hodge said to do what we needed to get you fixed as long as it doesn't gimp us. The part's growing dust. I'm using it." Pakko grabbed at Yosei's pad to look over the graphics. Her mouth gaped and her eyes went wild in silent offense as if he'd laid an inappropriate hand on her. Considering her relationship with her tech, he probably had. She snatched it out of his reach and clutched it to her chest.

Arad groaned. "I'm not sure."

"No charge. Honest. And I'm gonna do it anyways, so you'd better get over yourself. I like new projects."

"Sorry. I'm not used to people being generous without expecting favors." Only the clergy ever gave charity in

Grey District, and even that had its cost. It was how Arad found himself hustling rather than being in debt to abusive zealots. Floating in space may have been a far cry from Grey District, but he didn't like owing Hodge and his crew more than he already did.

"Yeah, well, you quashed that idea already, and now I have to do it to be a nice guy." Pakko sighed, talking at the ceiling to himself as much as anyone else. "I know it's not happening, but the four-way oil wrestling match would've been epic."

Arad didn't say a word. Some ideas were better ignored than acknowledged.

Making gagging noises, Yosei continued her work. "Anyway... It'll need some modifying, but we can do that. We'll have to synthesize a few minor parts to reconfigure it for the *Ansariland*'s specifications and recalibrate the operating system to recognize the new part, but it's doable."

Hopeful relief sprouted in Arad's chest, threatening to bloom. "How long will that take?"

"A few days."

"That's all?"

"At most."

A few days more was a small price to pay to get his life started up again. Maybe his suspicious nature read the scene wrong for a change. Arad sure hoped so.

Yosei's demands were regular and insistent. "Thumb scan so I can sync up the calibrations."

Arad retreated to get her com-pad out of his face, giving the device a dubious stare. "Again? You already did this."

Yosei gave Arad a horrified look. "I don't save keys. That's like reading someone's diary or opening their data drive and finding their private intimate vids. Ick."

The last two days dragged waiting for the *Nightingale*'s fabricator to modify the spare flow regulator. He'd checked the *Ansariland*'s logs as often as possible—day and night—but found no evidence of outside access. Yosei may have been hyper and obsessed about her work, but she'd been honest throughout. A new experience for Arad.

What wasn't new for him was the workshop space he, Roku, Pakko, Vosh, and Yosei were crammed into. Filled with random parts, circuits, and assorted tool kits, it reminded him of the workhouse and every tech job he'd ever had, for however long they'd lasted. That may have been a stretch of sad days in his life, but without it he wouldn't have had the skills to get him and Roku to this point.

Arad pressed his thumb to the pad, watching the screen change and the initialization process begin.

"Awesome. Once this loads up, the regulator's good to install." Yosei appeared more excited than Arad at their progress. He'd made a point to hide his reactions.

Casual chatter between the techs continued as they discussed the details of the repair's final stages. Vosh shifted closer to Pakko, listening in but staying quiet, maybe a bit out of his depth with all the shop talk. Even Arad became lost at times when Yosei got going. Roku perused the active equipment lining the workspace. A flickering light caught his eye on one device, and he reached for it.

Yosei spun and slapped his hand an inch away from contact. "That's a good way to lose a finger."

Stunned by her boldness, Roku cradled his hand to his chest. "Because of you or the device?"

"Both. I'm heating up the torch so we can do the final welds. Haven't you ever seen one of these before?"

To prevent Roku from revealing his damaged recall, Arad spoke up. "Cats like sparkly things."

A rumble of kind laughter rose through the group. Roku gave Arad an appreciative grin, clearly thankful for deflecting the question. His memory loss was a private matter between them and didn't need to be shared whether the *Nightingale* crew would be sympathetic or not. Explanations would come next and put the existence of Hachi and Shichi at risk.

Addressing them all, Roku changed the subject. "We can't thank you enough. I'm not sure if we could have repaired the ship without your help."

Pakko chimed in. "Don't knock your boy's skills. He's good at this."

Chest out and proud, Roku pressed close to Arad, spreading his hand along Arad's lower back. "Yes, he is. He accomplished amazing things with little to work with. If we'd had the parts he needed from the start, I have no doubt we wouldn't have required any assistance."

Brow furrowing, Arad shook his head. "I didn't do anything special."

"You're far more clever than you give yourself credit for. We wouldn't have gotten this far without you."

"Roku? Does Arad always turn that shade of red?" Vosh asked.

With a lusty rumble, Roku stroked Arad's jaw and neckline. "Only under the right circumstances."

"Okay. Enough. You've been spending too much time chatting with Vosh. Where's Hodge at? I have a thanks or two to pass his way."

Still chuckling, Pakko pointed a thumb over his shoulder, down the hallway. "His office most likely. Next to the bridge."

"Got it. Be back in a few, Roku." With a quick pat on Roku's chest, Arad headed out, only too happy to end the conversation centered on him.

"Take your time."

Creating some distance from the group helped cool the awkwardness heating Arad's face and chest. He'd spent too many years as a slug to feel comfortable with compliments whether deserved or not. In his experience, praise was a vehicle of trade: something given while expecting something in return. No one ever talked kindly to slugs, but he wasn't a slug now, and he needed to accept that. If he didn't know Roku's drive for honesty, he'd accuse him of trying to get in his pants. It would take time to believe flattery existed without shady intentions. With Roku's help, he might actually make it.

Some of Arad's unease came from his innate distrust of Hodge and the crew. History had jaded Arad, so his responses weren't unexpected, yet the *Nightingale* hadn't proven any of his suspicions to be true. Class distinctions were hard to ignore. Arad had begun in the elite sector and ended as a slug. Hodge and his crew were not slugs, and the implied stations were a thing Arad had difficulty with. He had expected them to treat him poorly. The realizations shamed him, an uncomfortable sensation he should have shed long ago.

Hodge and the crew had defied his every expectation. In less than a week, he'd found himself connecting with the ragtag group, thinking of them as friends. He wouldn't go so far as calling them family—that was not something he offered easily—but he cared what happened to them and where both of their futures would take them.

All these conflicted feelings made Arad want to search Hodge out and thank him personally because he wasn't sure he could bring himself to say the words with an audience.

They'd spent enough time on the *Nightingale* over the last few days, and combined with Hodge's initial tour when they'd first come on board, he found the trail to Hodge's office. He hoped. The pristine walls were virtually identical through most corridors. The last thing he wanted was to ask for help. He made a wrong turn once or twice but finally recognized icons marking the route leading to the bridge.

Ultimately, Arad found his way by following Hodge's annoyed voice drifting through the halls.

"About time you answered my call."

Arad stopped short of the door, not wanting to walk in on Hodge's conversation. Given his tone, the captain might not appreciate the interruption.

"You're hardly my main business associate. I have priorities, Hodge." The second man's voice was sharp with a vicious edge like most wealthy, privileged men Arad had ever known. His family dripped in such connections born from old money and uncalloused hands. The unknown man's tone chilled Arad, raising an urge to cower, halting him before he turned and left. What business did Hodge have with a person like this?

Hodge was not intimidated by the snotty man in the least. "Maybe you'd be less of a dick and move me up the ladder if I told you I found the *Midas Ascending*."

Chapter Twenty-Four

Hiding from authorities at a moment's notice was second nature to Arad. Scrunching down low, he kept out of the doorway with a view of Hodge's back. He positioned himself to prevent any shadow from casting into the room and to stay out of the monitor's view.

"It's about time. Everyone in the chain of this deal comes with an expiration date. Including you, Hodge. Where's Torrins?" Slim and bespectacled, the snotty man oozed the arrogance of privilege. The kind Arad recognized from his past life. Snotty Man made demands, clearly ranking higher than the *Nightingale*'s captain.

"Dead. According to the kid—"

"What kid?"

"Arad. The new captain. Torrins and the crew got themselves killed, and the ship auto-promoted him. Says he was a tech, but the ship houses six, and he makes seven. I'm thinking he was Torrins's boy. Fits the man's type."

Snotty Man frowned. "Charming. The whole crew dead?"

Hodge leaned forward in his chair, closing in on the screen. "Kid says pirates attacked. Shot the engine and blew the shuttle out of space when the crew tried to ditch him behind as the last man standing. Kid did a messy fold jump to escape. They landed on the other side of the sector from the meeting coordinates. Took us forever to find them because he changed the ship's name and messed up the transponder codes. Funny thing though: The shot that hobbled them was seriously precise, and Pakko's scan picked up a military energy residue. That's in conflict with all the intelligence I have about the pirates operating in this sector. Pirates would have nuked the ship by accident trying to steal the bounty."

"And your point?"

"So...military. One of yours?"

Frowning worse than before, Snotty Man paused. "No. ApexCorp did not sanction any military intervention. They wanted this handled with some discretion. We have a rival company after our product. We believe they want to enter the market by reverse-engineering their own DemiShou version since the process is proprietary and locked down. You need to collect the product and deliver. These sales are already months behind schedule. The clients are becoming impatient, and we run the risk of being exposed. If we default, I don't think I have to explain how—or rather who and whose crew—the company will see as loose ends to retire while protecting its interests. None of the executives responsible will risk a formal inquiry or a prison sentence. Do you understand?"

Hodge's shoulders rose and fell with the slow inhale and exhale. A tiny shiver revealed how much the snotty man annoyed him. "Yes. I do. You need to get a grip on yourself. The *Midas Ascending* has been lost for weeks.

Under the circumstances, it's a miracle they fixed their communications. The only reason we came across their distress call instead of someone else is because we were looking for it. We can handle this."

A pounding filled Arad's ears. The panicked rise of his heartbeat. *Stay small. Stay small. Don't be seen.* He wanted to run, but his need to understand the danger he was in overtook his baser survival instincts. The same instinct that told him this conversation was critical. Once he had enough information, he'd take it to Roku, and they could plan.

Don't get caught.

"I'm glad to hear it. You're sure the product is still on board?"

Hodge nodded. "Bryce identified Roku's designer markings. Not natural. Clearly special order."

Hard lines dug trenches through Snotty Man's brow as his eyes narrowed. "Bryce is your medic, correct?"

"Yes."

"The same medic who's an agoraphobic germaphobe?"

"Why do you ask..." Hodge's wary responses dragged out further with each question.

"So she would likely have had to see these designer markings ordered by the client in the med bay. First-hand, perhaps?"

"Yes..."

"Are you doing your damnedest not to tell me one of the products is awake?"

Hodge sighed, rubbing his temples. "I wasn't hiding it, but yeah, Roku's one of the Demis. And you're gonna love this...he's imprinted on the kid."

Everything about Snotty Man chilled Arad, from his disdainful timbre to his controlled, yet venomous temper. He wished he had an explanation for why Hodge was doing business with such a man, but the more he heard, the faster his trust eroded.

"I am most certainly not loving this. Please tell me you're joking. Are you sure?"

"Ninety-nine point nine nine percent. Vosh smelled the scent markers. Said they're mated. Hey, don't blame me. He was already awake when we found them."

Snarling, he thrust a finger at Hodge through the screen. "I needed an extra set of hands to pass the product through to make it harder to trace. *You* vouched for Torrins, so I can most certainly hold you responsible for this fiasco." Pinching the bridge of his nose, Snotty Man took a deep breath and blew it out again. He struggled for control as his frustrations swelled. "It's a complication, but we've dealt with complications before. In retrospect, given the lost time, all of them should have matured. Either something went wrong or the process stalled. Have you secured the rest of the product?"

"Not yet. We're repairing the ship, so it doesn't need to be towed, and I can strip it down or sell it after. Bryce confirmed the cryotubes are in the cargo hold."

"Confirmed? You haven't examined them in person?" Snotty Man's eyes widened in disbelief.

"Not yet. Bryce stole permissions off Yosei's tablet and accessed their security feed. It's a specialty of hers."

"The more I hear, the less confident I become in your ability. Why haven't you simply commandeered their vessel?"

"Look, I'm just in this for the money. If I shove in and take over, there's going to be fighting—serious fighting—and it's gonna be ugly. I don't want anyone getting hurt."

The half snort, half laugh lacked any true humor. "That's very humanitarian of you, Hodge, but with the amount of money involved here, that might not be possible."

A long pause in the conversation followed. Arad worried his heartbeat might give him away as its incessant pounding grew more deafening, but neither Hodge nor his overprivileged companion gave him notice. Eventually, Snotty broke the silent impasse. "You called him Roku."

Hodge shrugged, not turning away from the screen. "That's the name he gave us."

Snotty Man's tapping away off-screen ended as he focused on text reflecting in his glasses. "So it's the tiger that's awake?"

"Yep. He doesn't talk a lot, so I don't have any intelligence on him. Where do you find him and the rest of these guys?"

"Never mind. I've said more than I should as it is." The text scrolling over his lenses vanished.

"A little late for that now. I'm in the thick of things, and if you expect me to follow through, I need a little quid pro quo here. After all these years, I've never screwed you over. It's about time you trusted me better."

Snotty Man paused and exhaled sharply through his slender nostrils. "Fine. This is a privileged conversation and completely off the record."

"When isn't it?"

"You asked how we find the subjects. Well, military contracts don't end post-mortem."

Hodge's back stiffened. "He's military?"

"Specialized military police to be precise. Well trained."

The news didn't surprise Arad. He'd seen Roku train enough to know he wasn't an ordinary citizen before his revision.

"What happened to him?"

"He was part of a squad assigned to quell a food riot. He found his scruples and disobeyed orders. When he refused to fire upon the rioters, they didn't treat him as a savior. They swarmed him, beat him, and shot him to death with his own weapon. He made an ideal candidate."

"What were the rest of his squad doing while this happened?"

Even through the screen, Snotty Man managed to look down his nose at Hodge. "Doing what they were told."

Arad shuddered, praying it wasn't audible. Roku's nightmares were splinters of his past memories working their way up through the skin. He'd hoped they were nothing but dreams, but somehow, Arad didn't have that kind of luck. He hated being right sometimes. Just like his original reasons to distrust the *Nightingale* and its crew.

Hodge crossed his arms over his chest, the line of his torso projecting his displeasure. "So you collected him off the field. An MP back then, what is he now?"

"The client ordered a companion slash bodyguard."

"Is that what all of them are?"

Snotty gave Hodge a minimal, unaffected shrug. "More or less. There are variations."

"How do you guys even know how to do this? It's no secret DemiShou manufacturing is classified at the military level. Technically, you're not supposed to have access to the technology."

"We headhunted one of the original team members when the military locked it down. For a substantial raise, he was more than willing to continue his work."

"How can you keep this quiet?"

"ApexCorp will zealously protect its interests and erase anyone who reveals any part of the project that might connect to them. A lot of effort has been made to scatter the knowledge. No one person knows the entire process."

"You seem to be privy to quite a bit."

Snotty Man adjusted the fit of his glasses. "Legal division needs to be in the know."

"That only leaves me with more questions."

"You don't need the answers."

Hodge leaned forward, hands on the armrests like he was about to leap up and throttle the man through the monitor. "This is happening on my ship and putting me and my crew at risk. I'd say I need to know as much as possible. You owe me this much."

Snotty Man chewed on his thin lips as he pondered.

"You're right. You've been employed by me for a long time. I think it's important to impress upon you how involved you are now. No authority in the universe will give you amnesty for DemiShou trafficking. There's no walking away from this."

"I'm aware of that. Keep my mouth shut and everyone benefits. What about the clients? Wealthy people who can afford this kind of thing are publicly known and connected. They can't be wiped away so easily."

"Their relationship with their product ensures their loyalty."

"What's that supposed to mean?"

"Once a product imprints on its purchaser, there's a biological trigger. Their bodily fluids adapt to become a low-level variant of Syn that's keyed to the particular individual."

The clinical efficiency of his words reminded Arad of every seedy aristocrat he'd ever known when they spoke of delicate matters. And in those moments, one only paid attention with morbid fascination. Most likely the reason they learned the skill in the first place.

Hodge raised an open hand. "Wait a second. Are you saying they get addicted to sex with the DemiShou?"

"It facilitates attachment to their product and provides a need to keep them close."

"That's fucking twisted."

"It's a security protocol."

Chest tightening, Arad's stomach plummeted. His mind wrapped itself around this new information and connected it to Hodge's comment about Roku *imprinting* on him. The prospect horrified him. He didn't have to worry about his breathing alerting the two men. It had stopped outright.

"What if something happens to the client?" Hodge asked.

"If the client dies, the products are programmed to ultimately search out a new mate."

Hodge's voice rose in disbelief. "After raging out and slaughtering everyone within reach beforehand? Roku is attached to Arad enough I could see that happening."

"The legal team is prepared for the possible eventuality."

Slumping in his chair, Hodge scrubbed a hand over his face. "So, I can't risk anything permanent happening to the kid. Roku might imprint on one of my crew, and we'd still end up with the same problem."

"At least not until we can deliver the product to the client."

"That's cold."

Snotty Man's eyes narrowed with a laser-like focus. "Correction: That's business."

Arad had enough. His heart couldn't take listening to another word, and it wasn't safe to stay squatting in the shadows for a moment longer.

Silently, Arad scuttled back the way he came, down the hallway with all the quick stealth learned from years of avoiding authorities. Such as ducking out unseen during a raid on an unlicensed workhouse or avoiding being beaten and arrested during a food riot. A violent food riot. Like the kind Roku had originally been killed in.

He imagined the entire horrible scene. Roku trying to keep the peace. Wild, starving people overwhelming him because he was too honorable to defend himself. His murder. ApexCorp invoking their post-mortem clauses.

Arad did everything he could not to vomit.

Arad found an alcove and slumped into the niche, overwhelmed by the truth. The cool metal wall warmed as he rolled his forehead against it, struggling to ease the clench in his chest. He may have guessed parts of Roku's past, but others crushed the air from his lungs. Impossibilities made real.

Hodge's and the ApexCorp lawyer's words were unforgettable.

"...you're gonna love this...he's imprinted on the kid."

He'd written off the encounter with Roku when he'd cracked open the cryotube as animal instinct coming forward while semi-conscious. Now, if what they'd said was correct, Roku was programmed to mate the first person he laid eyes on? Did that mean it didn't matter who was there when Roku's eyes opened? Would he have chosen Arad if given a proper chance? Did he actually care?

"Once a product imprints on its purchaser, there's a biological trigger. Their bodily fluids adapt to become a low-level variant of Syn that's keyed to the particular individual."

"Are you saying they get addicted to sex with the DemiShou?"

Arad's eyes burned. As if he didn't already feel hideous after hearing about the imprinting, now he had to swallow this too. The sex cravings had grown over the last few weeks little by little, but he hadn't delved too deep into

their origins. He'd believed it was some emotional connection to Roku because in the past, all he'd ever known
was faking attraction for payment. What did he know
about the real thing? Were his feelings no more than Syn
addiction? Without it, would Arad have continued to want
Roku?

With the back of his hand, he scrubbed the moisture
building along his eyes. *Suck it up, mister. You have work
to do.* He'd have his meltdown once they were safe. Which
right now, they were not.

The ship and Roku were all Arad had in this universe.
However they'd come together, he wasn't ready to toss it
all aside until he talked to Roku and figured out what to
do next. He'd promised to care for him and the rest of the
DemiShou sleeping in the cargo bay. The task had become
infinitely more complicated because the secret, which apparently wasn't a secret, was out.

*"So I can't risk anything permanent happening to
the kid."*

Roku was still a valuable commodity to Hodge and
the *Nightingale* crew, and they needed Arad for now.
Even if it was only to save themselves, the selfish pricks.
It wasn't much, but it was the only advantage he had, and
it gave him time to plan a few moves ahead. Working the
pawns across the board to make a queen would be astro-
nomically difficult.

Arad had survived a dysfunctional family, corrupt
workhouses, and the streets of Grey District. There was no
way he would simply lie down and be erased by a group of
greedy corporate backstabbers.

Once he and Roku were on the *Ansariland*, they'd
play along and stall until the engines were repaired. He'd

figure out how to escape. He'd done it before. He'd do it again. Roku could help with the tactical end of defending them while they found their way to a new home.

Conflicted laughter simmered at the surface. According to Hodge and the scummy lawyer, his and Roku's relationship was a result of manufacturing rather than two men sharing and coming together on their own. He was sure it had been real though, but what did he know of such things? Roku was a science project, and Arad was a damaged slug.

No. He refused to keep believing that.

Roku had revered him, been oh-so careful with him. Even after their sleazy introduction, they got to know each other. Roku resisted for weeks, showing Arad an honorable spirit he'd never seen before. When he'd finally given in, he treated Arad with careful enthusiasm, meeting Arad's needs before his own. When had he ever known that in his life?

Too much science and too many doubts smothered his brain. Arad questioned every aspect of their bonding—mating—but he wasn't about to leave Roku behind. Abandonment was his parents' slimy tool used to end their relationship, not Arad's. If he and Roku broke, it would be because they both chose to.

In the meantime, he'd gather himself and pretend the world was good. Like hustling. Putting on the happy mask was no different than faking it for clients. Bragging about how great it was instead of running for the nearest medical kiosk. Smiling and making nice instead of wanting to find the nearest object and bludgeon a man to death. Not a new experience at all.

Minutes passed. *Breathe in. One, two, three. Breathe out. One, two, three.* Repeat.

He could do this. For the first time in his life, it was *their* lives depending on him.

Bryce's sultry voice interrupted his racing mind. "Hello, Arad. Are you feeling all right?"

Arad rose to his feet, brushing himself off. "Yes. I'm fine. I tripped is all. Thank you for asking."

"I'm glad to hear it. Be sure to let me know if you need any medical treatment of any kind."

Looking up and around at the ceiling—not knowing exactly where she was—Arad gave Bryce the smile he saved for shitty clients. "Of course."

"Thank you. I appreciate your willingness. On a separate topic, as a guest it's considered highly impolite to eavesdrop on your hosts. I'm afraid Hodge's call was intended to be private. I believe we have a problem."

An enraged roar ripped through the hall, sending a sharp chill through Arad's spine.

"Roku..."

Arad's rapid footfalls drowned out his panicked heartbeat as he sprinted, reversing his route. He wasn't sure what he'd do in a situation Roku couldn't handle, but there was no way he'd let him face this nonsense alone. The rage in Roku's roar had triggered something inside. There were problems and issues to contend with between them. However, that would be later. Now, he needed to help his mate.

Mate.

Bryce's annoyingly soothing voice kept pace with him through the corridors. "You're too late, Arad. You can't help him."

"Shut up, voyeur bitch!"

She huffed in feigned aggrievance. "That was rude."

Arad ignored her, recognizing a distraction. Slugs in Grey District understood the technique. Lived it even. Babble talk at the shop owner so they don't see someone else lift the food packets off the shelf. Not a glamorous skill, but a necessary one to prevent starvation at times.

Feet flying, Arad had nearly reached the workshop door when it slid open. Roku and Vosh burst out in a tangle of snarling fury, punching and grappling with no hesitation. Arad screeched to a halt, keeping a safe distance. This was no friendly sparring. Both DemiShou were out for blood. What happened?

Yosei slipped out and backed farther down the hall, making sure to stay well out of the melee. She watched closely, her expression giving away nothing on who she was rooting for. Almost as if she expected this fight to happen.

Rows of red lines appeared over Vosh from Roku's claws, fine droplets of blood spattering them both and the walls. It didn't slow Vosh. In fact, he gained ground as they fought, which made no sense. Roku had clearly dominated the bear during their match. Arad had been there. No way had Vosh thrown the fight. Roku appeared to be off, his reactions sluggish compared to his norm. Had they done something to him?

With his full weight, Vosh slammed Roku into the wall, winding him. He snatched a sleek metal loop hanging from his belt and clamped it around Roku's neck. He leaped backward out of reach, stuffing a hand in his pocket and drawing a small item. He pressed the surface, aiming it at Roku.

Sparks flared, the scent of singed fur drifting to Arad's nose. Roku howled, scratching at the collar in agony, thrashing as he dropped to the floor. He continued to spasm, gripping the metal ring. It should have bent to his superior strength, but the restraint appeared designed for DemiShou. The *Nightingale* crew were prepared to contain a Demi. Not surprising, since they were trafficking them in the first place. How could Vosh do this to one of his kind?

Arad had no intention to waste time asking. Eyes on Vosh, he dove at the bear, targeting the remote in his hand.

As he passed the workshop doorway, Pakko jumped out and tackled him hard. Outweighed by several pounds, Arad took the painful brunt of them hitting the deck.

Pakko wrapped an arm around Arad's head, muffling his mouth as he wrestled him down. "Stand down, Roku, or we'll be forced to hurt him."

Roku stopped resisting but followed Pakko with a murderous gleam over Arad's shoulder. Breathing rough and bleeding, Vosh stayed out of reach. Yosei's gaze flitted over each combatant, the *Nightingale* tech unusually silent.

No. Arad may not have been able to fight free from the thick arms lashed around him—he tried with everything he had—but he wasn't giving up. No. Not like this. Panic flooded his brain, feeding his desperation. Arad bit down and drew blood.

"*Sonofabitch!*" Pakko screamed, releasing Arad's head enough to speak.

"Roku! Get up and beat his ass!"

Roku's deafening roar startled everyone present. Coiled muscled sprang, and he leaped, claws extended, at Pakko.

He didn't make it. The collar flared, making Roku twist and land alongside them. His eyes rolled back as he fought the device's hold, this time too strong for Roku to resist. Tiny wisps of acrid smoke spun out from under the metal even as Roku seized on the floor, almost close enough to touch.

Tears filled Arad's eyes as he shrieked. "Roku! Stop it! You're killing him!"

Jaw set tight, Vosh stood with his thumb pressed firmly on the remote, still aimed at Roku. Disdain radiated from him in a palpable wave.

"*Stop it!*" Arad screamed.

Bryce's voice came over the speakers. "Vosh, that's enough. We don't want to risk damaging the merchandise."

He wasn't listening. The collar continued its assault, and Roku jerked and convulsed. Clearly unconscious, his body was defenseless to the constant shock level.

Hodge finally appeared, stepping over them to stand in front of Vosh. "Vosh, stand down! That's an order!" His voice rose to the cadence of a military professional. "If you don't comply, I will airlock your furry ass faster than you can say court martial. I will not say it again. Stand down!"

Vosh's gaze spun to Hodge, the command finally breaking through his fixation. With a frustrated snort, he flicked his thumb and the collar went quiet. So did Roku.

The world froze until Arad was sure Roku was breathing. Shallow, but breathing.

"Please. Don't hurt him." Whispering, Arad slumped in Pakko's hold, all the fight within him fleeing.

He didn't resist as Hodge ordered Vosh around, and the big bear pulled more items out of the workshop and secured Roku's arms behind him with a set of manacles fearsome enough to be DemiShou-grade.

Bryce's order filled the hall. "Vosh, I expect you in medical at once so I can tend your wounds."

Huffing sharply through his nose, Vosh barely nodded. "As soon as we have everyone secured."

Hodge kneeled in front of Arad. "You play nice, you might get out of this in one piece. Pakko, take him to the brig."

Arad made no effort against them as Pakko pulled him to his feet. Hodge escorted them as they dragged Arad down the hall. His legs refused to make him move.

Yosei continued to watch. Saying nothing. Doing nothing.

Chapter Twenty-Five

Avoiding the police, dodging workhouse raids and shan-tyville sweeps, Arad had never seen the inside of a precinct cell. Occasionally, there were narrow escapes, but he'd somehow managed to stay a free man. Others hadn't been so fortunate. He used to worry about Sketch's fate. Now all he thought about was Roku. A fine layer of dust coated the *Nightingale*'s jail from apparent disuse. Other than that, it was as well maintained as the rest of the ship.

It didn't improve the experience.

Four beds lined the walls with a commode mounted in the far corner. A small viewing window perched high in the massive solitary door, yet he'd given up seeing anything on the other side hours ago. It didn't matter. His short future held no good tidings.

A shadow passed over the window moments before the door slid open. Vosh dragged Roku's limp body inside, dumping him on the floor. Roku didn't react, even with the manacles holding his arms behind him. Arad schooled his worry. They needed Roku to get paid.

Hodge entered with Yosei following silently. He ordered his crew members out, and they shut the door, leaving him inside.

"He's a little doped. Bryce needed him compliant while she made sure there wasn't any lasting damage from the collar."

Arad crawled over to Roku and placed his sleeping head in his lap. The fur around the shock collar was shorter than the rest and blackened into fine clumps. "Oh, well, that's mighty humanitarian of you. I'll be sure to sign you up for an award. That's sarcasm, by the way, since we both know I'm not making it out of here."

Hodge grunted. "Your time on the street's made you paranoid. We'll drop you off at a distant station after the transaction's complete."

"Don't placate me. I know I'm alive until I'm not useful anymore. Somewhere around the point where Roku needs to be presented to his new owner. I'm surprised you didn't off me and keep Roku drugged until you get there." Arad petted Roku's forehead, praying his touch might hold back any nightmares.

"It was suggested. I said no."

"Gee, thanks. I'm in your debt. Tell Vosh he's a dick."

Shifting in a sideways arc, Hodge sat on the corner of the bed closest to the door. "It's been said. The least I could do is give you both a little last quality time together."

"Before you sell my ship and traffic Roku. So much for transporting medical tech."

"It's a side business."

Arad snorted without mirth. "That some side hustle, selling men into slavery."

"He's not a man anymore."

"Nope, he's better than that. And even then, it's not his fault. He was military, like you and all your crew at one point. I always thought you guys had a fraternity code. You know, spanking initiations and leave no man behind kinds of things. Every soldier I ever met had an unshakable, if not overblown, morality about him and the military as a whole. What happened?"

Hodge leaned back and sighed. "The universe got complicated."

"It gets complicated for everyone. Try being homeless for over a decade."

"I bet you've done a shady thing or two in your time."

Arad shrugged, careful not to disturb Roku. "True. Survival can be a messy game. Even then, I never chose to let someone die to save myself. But I was never in the military, so what do I know? Acceptable losses and all that garbage."

A twinge of guilt lit up Arad's insides. Saving the DemiShou had been a great motivator to move forward, to do something with his shattered life. He'd already been planning the next steps once the ship could travel under its own power again. Now his goals would be piled up with all his life's losses. Many he'd accepted over the years as part of being a slug. This loss, failing to find a safe space for Roku and the others...

It gutted him worse than watching his family disown him before his own eyes.

"I like you, kid. I wish there was another way."

Arad huffed. "There never is when someone's looking to get filthy rich. I can see your dilemma."

"It goes deeper than money."

"That's the price for getting in with corporation schemes. But don't worry, I'm happy to pay the bill for you." Arad gave Hodge an unimpressed stare. "That was sarcasm too."

"You know, when you're pissed, you can get a little condescending."

"That means I talk down to people."

Needling Hodge may not have been the smartest move, but Arad didn't see a downside to venting his frustration. The situation seemed hopeless. His days were counting down while the tiger under his hands was going to lose his life in a totally different way.

Arad refused to shed a tear in front of Hodge. "I know your employer only sees him—and the rest of them—as a product to manufacture and sell, but he's so much more."

"He only likes you because he fucked you." Hodge's snark was uncharacteristic. Getting under the man's skin was satisfying.

"Maybe. You said you like me and you're definitely screwing me too. Which one's better? At least he didn't have a choice. Not at first."

Hodge stood with a sudden jerk, discomfort staining his stance. "This has been a lovely chat, but there's plenty to do over the next few days."

"I bet."

Hodge turned with a casual salute and headed for the door. He pounded the door twice with his fist, and it opened. Yosei obediently stood in the doorway, hand on the lock control. Their eyes met, and a new wave of disdain filled Arad's wounded heart. Hodge's perfect surrogate child.

Twisting the knife was a great idea. "Would your dead wife and daughter be proud of you if they could see you now?"

Hodge paused. Yosei's eyes widened a fraction, her otherwise blank gaze tracking Hodge as his hands fisted and his posture sharpened into jagged edges.

"Get comfortable. You might be here for a while."

The lights dimmed as the door slid closed.

Arad sat on the hard floor petting Roku's head, praying for no more nightmares beyond the one they were living in. A prickling numbness grew in his left leg, but he ignored it to keep from disturbing his unconscious partner. The shallow yet steady rise and fall of Roku's chest was the only thing holding Arad's growing anxiety at bay as he felt around for injuries. A small, curious circle of scorched fur similar to ones lining the shock collar marred Roku's back, the only new evidence he found. At least an hour passed before the tiger stirred.

Roku tried to move his arms, but the shackles impeded him. Every muscle from shoulder to forearm flexed, and he thrashed and growled, forcing Arad to climb out from under him. A difficult feat with one near-dead leg.

"Stop. Roku, stop." Grimacing through pins and needles, Arad gripped Roku's head and spoke firmly, trying not to startle him more than necessary. "Roku, wake up. Don't struggle so hard. You're handcuffed, and they're too sturdy. Hodge was prepared for DemiShou. You'll only hurt yourself."

Roku rolled to his knees, stretching his head to look at his arms behind him as much as the collar allowed. His nostrils flared as he tugged, testing the metal restraints. With a final yowl and jerk, he gave in, accepting the situation. Eyes and body coiled tight, he looked ready to murder until his lethal gaze crossed Arad. Concern softened his expression, even in the cell's minimal light.

"Are you injured?" Roku's voice was filled with gravel.

"No. Are you all right?"

Ears twitching, Roku scanned the room, taking in every detail. "I'll be fine. Where are we?"

"The *Nightingale* jail. Brig. Whatever."

"They imprisoned us?"

Images of Roku seizing under the collar's power hadn't stopped haunting him. He didn't know whether to nod or shrug, so he did both as he averted his eyes. "I surrendered. I was afraid Vosh was going to tase you to death. I didn't have a choice." Inhaled air hissed through his gritted teeth. "I'm sorry."

Roku crawled forward, rubbing his snout gently along Arad's neck and head. "Don't apologize. I'm no use to either of us as a corpse."

Leaning forward, Arad gripped Roku's head and neck, relishing the fur between his fingers but making sure to avoid the damned metal around Roku's neck. He'd held together so well during Hodge's visit, thrown all the viciousness in the captain's face, but it hid the cracks in his soul. The ones marking every bit of misery in his life. He clung to Roku for all he was worth because it was all he had.

"After I left the workshop, what happened to you? Do you remember?"

"Bryce messaged over the comm, and they shocked me from behind. Most likely Pakko."

The circular burn on Roku's back. If Arad had the chance, he'd airlock Pakko and Vosh both without a moment's regret. Arad leaned, staring into Roku's eyes. "Vosh shouldn't have been able to take you otherwise. Bryce's message was probably a signal. She sees and hears all."

Roku nodded. His cautious nature understanding what was said and unsaid. With them in the brig, Bryce was most likely spying on their every move. Common knowledge, however, was a safe topic between them.

"It was a coward's move, but effective. I misjudged the situation."

"How?"

"You were gone longer than I expected. I was getting anxious and let my guard down."

Arad sighed, hesitating to continue. "I stumbled across Hodge taking a call from a lawyer from ApexCorp."

"ApexCorp? Who are they?"

The name was familiar, but Arad hadn't walked on that side of life in a long enough time to know for sure. Street slugs didn't interact with business types. "Some multi-planet corporation doing illegal things. Or at least a corrupt division."

"Hodge is intelligent but isn't bred well enough to run in those circles. What business would he have with them?"

"Someone has to do the dirty work. The *Nightingale* is a step in a high-end custom DemiShou trafficking ring. Special order for wealthy clients."

"And I'm one of the special orders," Roku snarled derisively.

Arad frowned. "It looks like Torrins and the original crew were bringing you and the others to Hodge, who delivers them to the customers. Only I took the weird fold jump and landed in the wrong place. They've been looking for you guys ever since."

"What else did you overhear? I need to know everything."

Distaste creased Arad's brow. He wished he'd never overheard Hodge and the snotty man. "They talked about you. Who you were from before. They didn't use your name, but they said you were special forces military. You were killed in a food riot because you wouldn't shoot innocent people. Your contract gave them power to use you for the...program."

"Like some of my nightmares."

"Or memories seeping through. It's like all of you were reclaims from military post-mortem clauses. Some loophole that gives them authority."

Roku nodded sadly. "That confirms what I'd already guessed. Did they say more about what happened to me?"

Arad hedged. Rolling back, he sat on the floor, creating some space between them. The days of simple existence they shared when they had no access to the truth had a certain charm to them. Roku deserved the knowledge, but it might harm him, and Arad had vowed to protect the DemiShou, hadn't he?

Roku's eyes pleaded, reading Arad's indecision. It might hurt Roku to know more, but wouldn't it be cruel to withhold the information from the man missing his life and memories? He wasn't a child to coddle and shield.

With a shudder, Arad took a shaky breath. "The lawyer said you're designed to seek a mate when you wake up. To bond you to your buyer. But it appears there's a problem. You're already imprinted on me."

"I don't see that as a problem. What does that mean for you?"

Arad wrapped his arms around himself as if it might prevent him from shrinking into something insignificant. "I think you know. They only need me to keep you in line. If I'm gone, you'll eventually imprint on another dude."

Even with his arms securely behind his back, Roku's upper body straightened and swelled as his growl returned. "Never."

"It'll happen whether you want it or not." Without moving his arms, Arad scrubbed his face on his sleeve to smother a sniffle. He wasn't going to cry. He wasn't. "I have an expiration date."

Cast out and replaced by a greedy family, surviving workhouse disasters, pneumonia, and predatory ship captains, and this was how Arad's story would end. Discarded like rubbish after falling into a clandestine program he wasn't high enough on the social hierarchy to know about.

"I won't let them touch you."

Even with Roku bound and shackled, his chivalry had no obstacle, branding him as Arad's personal shining knight. Only in this fairy tale, the villains would win because they had the money and resources, not because good would triumph.

"You may not have a choice."

"There's always a choice." The determination of Roku's earnestness was boundless. Too bad it wouldn't matter.

A sad, sarcastic laugh completely devoid of humor spilled out of Arad. "Not really. Neither of us got a choice in this."

"What's that supposed to mean?"

Arad cursed himself internally and waved it off. "Never mind. It doesn't matter."

"No. You brought it up. That means it's important. Arad, tell me."

Hopelessness hadn't feasted on his heart so powerfully since he had stood before his parents and an impostor had taken his place. Its gaping maw made his head ache under the weight of his shortened survival. He didn't want to say a word, but the growing misery threatened to explode. Maybe letting out a little bit would ease the pressure and his conscience since he wouldn't be able to fulfill his promise to Roku, Shichi, and Hachi in the end.

"He said that once you...imprint on someone, your body changes somehow. Bodily fluids become like Syn that only affects that person."

"I don't understand."

Arad crushed his eyes closed to hold off the first tears. He swore he wouldn't cry, but all this...it was too much. Too much anger at his parents, Sketch, corporate schemes, Torrins. Hodge and the entire *Nightingale* crew had slipped in under his well-constructed defenses. It was all too much. Survival had been the only skill he counted on, and now it was taken from him, and the razored edges it left behind blinded him in anger. When his eyes snapped open, he no longer cared if Bryce still listened. Shrill rage tore at his throat as he rolled forward and pounded his weak, human fists on Roku's chest.

"It means I get addicted to sex with you. Like when I was high on Syn the day you woke up. I've seen what happens when people get corrupted on that stuff. It's not pretty. If it's anything like Syn on the streets, it starts out small, but the more you have, the more you crave, until it's all you live for. You and I are linked whether we want it or not. Everything about us together has been manufactured." Arad's breath stuttered. "None of it's real."

Unable to keep watching the sight of Roku blurring in front of him, he dropped his ineffectual arms and faced the floor.

Air gusted through Roku's nose in hostile rushes until his broad chest became a bellows strong enough to stoke a smelting plant. A dangerous growl built in his throat. Arad ducked as Roku's furious roar echoed off the walls, and he questioned his safety when Roku knocked him to the floor with a rough shoulder and straddled him, pinning him to the floor. Hunched over and teeth barred, Roku roared, blowing back Arad's hair, mere inches from his face.

"You don't get to say that! It's not true!" Fury and sadness twisted Roku's features in a way Arad had never seen, peeling away his usual reserve. Roku's shins held down Arad's forearms, leaving him no way to defend himself if Roku lost complete control.

"Roku..."

Roku's eyes shimmered in the poor light, wet and glossy. "I know I imprinted on you! I know I couldn't walk away from you from the first day we met! I may be a monster, but there's enough man in me to hold back. I never took from you what I wanted, what I really wanted. I never forced you into anything because I worried I might hurt you. I caged my animal instincts, and you still treated me like a decent human being. You treated me like I mattered. You took care of me. You cared for me. Made the best of this horrible situation, and now it's so much more than imprinting.

"And you wanted it too. I saw how you looked at me, and I smelled how aroused you would be around me every day, but I said nothing because I didn't have it in me to say no once I'd tasted you again. So I didn't. You say I changed and now you're addicted. That sex with me addicted you."

Arad nodded, unwilling to say it again.

"You said you used to deal Syn. Does it absorb through skin?"

A spark of confusion loosened Arad's lips. "N...no."

"Why would this be any different? Sex diseases don't transmit through the skin, do they? If not, you were never exposed to anything addictive until the night I sleepwalked and wound up in your bed. And I didn't imprint until after our first time together. The day I woke up. It happened then, only I didn't know what it was. So the changes in my body wouldn't have happened before the first time. You wanted me and cared about me before anything serious happened between us. This addiction...that happened after. Did you ever feel like that for anyone else before? For Torrins?"

"No, I didn't."

"You have to know that this thing between us is real, more than biological programming and sex addiction."

"Roku...even now. Trapped like this. I'm scared, and I crave you even now."

Arad wanted more than anything to believe everything Roku said, make it real. But underneath the worries and fear, the craving—the need—still lingered. The one he'd noticed weeks ago. The one Roku had sated time and again on the *Ansariland*. It had been running under his skin since Hodge dumped Roku in the cell with him. It ran with him now, making him want inappropriate things, feeding him a dose of shame with every perverse impulse he stuffed down.

"I don't care. As wrong as this moment is, I would let you have me if you asked. Because you asked me. Because I would do anything for you. I will always take care of your needs." Roku turned his head away and whispered. "This craving...is it only for me?"

"Yes."

He turned, brow furrowed. "Do you feel it toward anyone else on this damned ship?"

"No. Never."

Roku leaned forward and caressed Arad's head with his own. It was the most glorious sensation ever. "I don't care how it happened. There's more here than lust between us, isn't there? You've spent so long surrounded by people who've used you for one reason or another, you can't see when you've found the real thing. Admit it."

Tears flowing freely, Arad's mouth opened and closed, the word fighting to be thrust into the world. "Yes."

"Tell me what you want. If I never touched you again, would you still want me? Because if you ask me, I will. I love you enough to make that sacrifice."

"You do?"

Roku stared into Arad's eyes. "Yes."

"But they want to erase me and sell you."

"They can try. But until the day I die, you are my *mate*, remember?"

Roku shifted, releasing Arad, who threw his arms around the tiger's neck, squeezing tight.

"Yes. My mate. I forgot for a moment. I'm sorry." Arad buried his face in Roku's fur to hide the tears that continued to come.

"There's nothing to forgive. As long as I have you, we will survive."

"But—"

"I will kick in each of their skulls if they try to harm you. Now come here."

Roku stood and rolled into one of the beds, scooting until his back and arms pressed against the wall.

"There's not enough room in there for both of us."

"There will be if we squeeze in close to one another."

Arad hesitated as the craving spiked. "But what about..."

"No sex. I want to feel you against me so I know you're all right. I need to smell you, hear your heartbeat. Your anxiety leaves a sharp acid taste in my throat."

With a nod, Arad climbed in. "You can tell how I'm feeling?"

"I always know how you're feeling. Now, rest while I keep watch. No one will come near you. I won't allow it."

The space was tight, but the familiar warmth of Roku's body helped chase the craziness away, or at least put it under his heel for now. Their troubles were far from over, but he needed to forget them, even if for a few hours. Their limited chances for survival demanded it.

Chapter Twenty-Six

Hours later, the lights returned to full brightness, bathing the cell in an artificial glow. Still pressed into Roku's warmth, Arad woke from his troubled sleep, shielding his eyes from the glare. Roku continued to stand guard, his sharp gaze fixated on the door. Something passed in front of the window. The lock chimed, and the door hissed open.

Pakko edged in, a tray in each hand, a careful eye on Arad and Roku. He set the trays on the bed opposite, keeping his distance.

Arad climbed out of bed, reading Pakko's tension. Roku didn't move. The trays were loaded with food, one carrying DemiShou-sized portions. The rations were normal enough, undoctored at first glance and smell. "I'm surprised you'd bother to feed us."

Pakko flinched at the remark. "We're not monsters."

"Says you. You have to keep Roku healthy." Arad waved a hand at the food trays. "Why waste good food on me? Is this my last meal?"

"It's not going to be like that."

Arad scoffed. "Keep telling yourself that. If you doubt it, talk to your employer."

"Hodge would never—"

"I'm not talking about Hodge."

A tiny flinch and Pakko's face darkened in disquiet. He'd yet to stop twitching, and his discomfort grew. Every reaction revealed Pakko understood Arad's fate, and his denial was fracturing.

"ApexCorp owned the transport vessel Hodge's family died in. They settled the wrongful death charges with him for the *Nightingale*. He leveraged work from them in the process because he'd lost everything in the accident," Pakko blurted out.

Arad crossed his arms over his chest and made a show of rolling his eyes at Pakko. His clients often tried to clear their consciences by spilling their secrets since he had no power to share them, and the more he appeared to disbelieve, the more they said to prove him wrong. Remorse made men predictable, and Pakko was not unique.

"It costs a lot to keep a ship like this running. They sucked him in. Now it's too late to walk away. Sometimes I think they conned him to recoup their losses from the accident settlement."

Arad almost laughed. "So Hodge is the victim. Got it. Vosh, now, I can't believe he's involved. Selling his own people into slavery."

"Vosh never wanted to be DemiShou. His commanding officer ordered him up as part of the last batch processed. He doesn't see himself as Demi."

Arad cocked his head and snorted. "But he does seem to have a problem when he's beaten by one."

Pakko's brow furrowed. "That's not what happened."

"I guess you and I were watching different matches. I'm screwed because he's a self-hating Demi who enjoyed being dominated a little too much."

"That's not fair."

"No. It's not fair, is it?"

Roku stayed silent as Arad continued to dig verbal needles under Pakko's fingernails. He'd been called too clever for his own good by more than one person in Grey District. The dodgy preacher had taught him that with the right prodding, any guilty person would confess for a chance at absolution. He hadn't needed to be so cruel about it in the past.

Well, no one ever accused Arad of being unadaptable.

"So what's your excuse for selling out your friends? Because I find it hard to think you've been faking it these past few days."

Lines creased Pakko's face, twisting his beard into an unappealing frown. "I wasn't... You don't understand."

"Enlighten me."

"It wasn't supposed to be like this. We were only supposed to pick up and transport product. None of them were supposed to be awake."

It was possible Arad had never thought less of another human being, and he poured every ounce of derision into his words. "And now you have to see them as living, breathing people."

"We know too much. It doesn't matter what we want. Corporations like ApexCorp won't let us breach contract. We're fucked."

"No, you just have to feel bad and watch the deposit fill your bank accounts. We're the ones everything is actually happening to."

Brow tight, Pakko shook his head. "It's not gonna be that bad—"

"Stop pretending you don't know what's going to happen!" Arad snarled, his voice booming in the confined space. "Stop pretending they aren't going to break my connection to Roku! Stop pretending the company won't murder me to do it!"

"They...they won't do that..."

"Yes, they will, and make someone filthy rich in the process, even if it's not you! Stop pretending you're okay with all of this!"

"I...I..." Scrubbing a hand over his face, Pakko ducked his head and turned away, guilt radiating from him in toxic waves. "I...I'm sorry."

Arms still shackled, Roku pounced off the bed. Landing behind Pakko, he snapped his leg out, sweeping Pakko's feet out from under him. Pakko had barely hit the deck before Roku placed a brutal kick to his midsection and vaulted for the door, which had stayed open since Pakko entered.

"Follow me," Roku growled over his shoulder.

Roku lunged for the exit, only to jerk backward as his collar sparked to life. He collapsed to the floor, grunting as he landed on his bound arms and rolled over. Arad flew to his side, ignoring Pakko's pained moans in the corner.

"Roku, are you all right?" Arad ghosted his hands over Roku's body, afraid to touch him and get caught in the shock powerful enough to subdue the tiger. He breathed a sigh of relief as Roku nodded, gasping air between his teeth. No fresh scent of burned fur. The charge had been short compared to Vosh's earlier treatment. Something, or rather someone, in the hall caught Arad's attention.

Back against the wall, Yosei sat stoically in the corridor, com-pad in hand. Her usual frantic mirth was subdued.

"Sorry, dude. The sensor grid's configured across the doorway. I was hoping you wouldn't test it, but he'll get zapped if he tries to cross the threshold. You'd better get comfortable." She tapped her pad's screen. "Vosh, looks like you're gonna have to come down here and get Pakko. I told you what would happen if you sent him in alone. You owe me twenty credits."

Less than a minute later, Vosh held up the collar's remote as he entered the open cell, brandishing it like some ancient ward against evil. Arad placed a hand on Roku's shoulder. The muscles underneath were wound and tense, ready for action. A warning yowl made Arad shiver. Roku had rolled to a crouch, poised on a hair trigger to take another shot at Vosh, restrained or not.

"Don't. Please," Arad whispered. The tension remained, but Roku eased a bit. Now was not the time.

One eye on them, Vosh crouched down to check on Pakko.

"You oughta zap him." Whiny and dazed, yet coherent, Pakko would be fine. Arad had seen worse over the years.

Vosh poked and prodded for injuries. "Shut up. You should've waited for me to be ready. Any of us would've done the same."

"You bet against me."

With gentle care, Vosh lifted Pakko easily, cradling him in his arms like a child. "I bet you wouldn't be dumb enough to go in alone."

"Nope. I'm dumb enough, for sure." Pakko didn't raise his head, falling asleep on Vosh's shoulder.

Arad wanted to puke watching Vosh treat Pakko like something precious while imprisoning and selling other people without seeming to care. It was tempting to sic Roku on them all. With his skills, he could probably beat Vosh with his arms tied behind his back.

Apparently, his fantasies broadcast over his face because Vosh gave him the nastiest sneer as he settled Pakko. "Stay right fucking there."

"Don't worry. Roku's stuck in here. I'm not leaving him behind." Arad had yet to stop touching Roku, silently asking him to hold back and to ground himself. Perhaps the imprint included something psychic because Roku didn't move, only staring daggers at Vosh.

"I don't want any more trouble out of you, slug."

Arad removed his hand from Roku. He stepped forward, head cocked, reading Vosh's audacity and outright stupidity. "I may be a slug, but where I come from, you wouldn't rank any higher as a Demi. We'd both be on the job lines, no matter who you're sleeping with."

"I'm not DemiShou."

A laugh filled with outrage and disbelief erupted out of Arad. "Why? Because you were drafted? Roku didn't ask for it. ApexCorp waited for him to be gunned down and used some messed-up legal loophole to put him through the program. He sure wasn't a volunteer. It doesn't make him any less a DemiShou, and he shouldn't have to suffer for it because you don't like your own reflection."

Vosh hedged, glancing between Pakko and Arad as if he might dump the one to maul the other. The old adage about not poking bears came to mind. He suspected the man in Vosh's arms was the only reason he was still standing, so Arad eased his hostility.

"I get it, Vosh. Corporations like ApexCorp keep a stranglehold on their employees. Do the job, get paid, everything turns out fine, right?"

"You don't quit from these places. They retire you." Vosh passed a wistful gaze over Pakko. "And everyone you know or love."

Honestly, Arad tired of hearing how the entire crew had elevated self-preservation into a reasonable excuse for acting like dicks. He understood how blackmail turned good men bad, but seriously...they all needed to grow spines. Or at least eat a healthy dose of reality.

"What happens when one of ApexCorp's customers decides they want a bear slave? Or they realize there's more profit in using DemiShou already on the payroll rather than making new ones if you fit the description? Do you think you saying 'I'm not a Demi' will matter to them? If they'll put you down for not doing a job, don't think for a second they'll protect you over increasing their sales bonuses."

Vosh glared at Arad but kept his mouth shut as he strode out carrying Pakko. Yosei stood in the hall, gave Arad a small smirk and nod, and then closed and locked the cell door.

"I guess he didn't like the truth," Roku said.

With everyone else gone, Arad breathed a little more normally. "No, I don't think he did."

Taking digs at the crew was Arad's only weapon. Each attack, however, returned less and less satisfaction as time passed. He couldn't rely on them leaving him and Roku alone for what he had left. The deadline, whenever it might be, was looming. Roku was hobbled and, despite his skills, was at too much of a disadvantage to fight against this group.

Arad needed to even his odds.

Spinning, he assessed the cell in closer detail. Everything was welded to the wall or bolted down. Except the food trays. Arad snatched one of the hard plastic cups, dumped it out, and laid it on the floor.

"What are you doing?" Roku asked.

Since Bryce might be watching, he didn't answer. He stomped the cup until it broke into several shards. One of the sharper ones might be sufficient. Impatient, he spun and grabbed Roku by the collar, dragging him close. Roku didn't resist. Arad didn't miss his implicit trust. He counted on it.

He searched over the collar's surface, looking for access seams. They were tight, but on close inspection, they were there. Two matching lines, each in front and back, had to be the hinge and locks. What he wanted was a different port. The locks didn't matter unless the device's power could be severed. After finding a subtle panel along the side, he slid the shard's point inside the groove, looking for a little give.

"I'm a tech. A good tech. I can do this."

Barely slender enough, the shard lifted the panel a hair, giving him a chance to get under it. He worked the edge until he found the catch. The panel released, and he carefully swung it out of the way, showing the hardware inside.

Sparks shot out of the collar. Arad screamed as the violent quake ripped through his whole body, and the shock slammed him against the wall.

"Arad. Can you hear me?"

Phosphorescent fireflies danced as the dark and blurry world came into view. All Arad saw was the ceiling and a distressed DemiShou hovering over him.

"Arad. Are you all right?"

His whole body twitched and ached, like every muscle had contracted and refused to release. Both hands were numb, but life seeped into them, replaced by a hot sensation at his fingertips, bright red from instant burns. By sheer luck, he'd taken a shock intended to take down a strong DemiShou and lived. And yes, it hurt, much like the endless depths of concern in Roku's eyes.

Arad coughed to ease his tight chest. "Yeah. Only my pride's wounded."

Roku didn't appear convinced.

The collar still sat fixed around Roku's neck. Arad reached up for it, but Roku jerked backward. "Don't. I think it's still active. I can feel an electric hum through the device." The access panel sat slightly ajar, but pinprick lights inside told him Roku was probably right. If the collar contained tampering countermeasures, the shackles might have the same features. The *Nightingale* crew were well prepared.

"I'm sorry, Roku."

"About what?"

"I thought I could free you, and we'd have a chance to escape."

"You have nothing to be sorry for. No part of this is your fault."

Kicking his doubts would take a lot of work. Arad had spent years having been told being a slug was his own fault, a lack of effort on his part. He knew better, but self-loathing was a harsh companion. The best strategy was to replay Roku's faith in him over and over because the man had never lied to him before and probably never would.

Arad grunted at the effort to stand, his flesh scraped as raw as his soul, leaving behind aching waves of exhaustion. The energy required to fuel his anger lacked the potency to draw a real reaction out of Arad. A cold numbness seeped into him, drowning anything short of apathy. There wasn't much else to be done.

Sleeping away the daylight until his time came held a fair amount of appeal. He scanned the cell's attached beds, debating on the most comfortable, and came across the trays of uneaten food. Arad sighed, knowing he couldn't rest yet.

"Come on. If I've learned nothing else over the years, you don't waste good food." Because some days you didn't know where the next meal would come from.

He sat on the bed and arranged the trays for ease. Neither of them had eaten since they'd been captured. Thankfully, they provided one tray with a larger than human amount. Roku would need his strength for whatever came next. Arad motioned Roku over, and the tiger kneeled in front of him. Both of his arms were stuck in an awkward position from being fastened behind him. It had to ache after so much time, yet he didn't complain, didn't say more.

The *Nightingale* crew had wisely not given them any utensils to use against them. Growing up, Arad had been taught knives and guns were the providence of criminals and the insecure. Hand weapons left him uncomfortable, even in defense, but this situation left him with the urge to shank one or more of his captors.

Arad broke off a piece of the ration bar and fed it to Roku, mindful not to touch the collar. He wasn't about to make him eat like a pet, face first in his dish. Roku accepted graciously, one piece at a time, taking care not to harm Arad's stinging fingers. He took drinks from the cup held by shaky hands without complaint other than insisting Arad eat too, whether he had an appetite or not.

He'd never done this before, shared this special intimacy with another man. None of his clients in Grey District had made the time or had the interest for such roleplay except maybe Davis, but he'd been too busy spending their transactions under the influence of Syn to be creative.

Under other circumstances, this would have been fun. A lover's game for both to enjoy, but Hodge and his seedy gang had ruined it for what few hours, days, weeks they had left.

Once both trays sat empty, Arad stood to place them near the exit, out of their way. Without a word or a shout, he swung the metal trays against the door. Over and over, he slammed metal against metal until both trays were a mangled, useless mess, ignoring how the edges dug into his hands. They dropped to the floor with a dull clang. Arad tipped his head upward and shined his middle finger to the ceiling as he pointed to the wad of ruined, cheap steel.

"This is trash. I am not. Learn the difference, you pieces of shit!"

Hopefully the entire crew were watching, not only Bryce.

With slow resignation, Arad walked back and slumped into a seat against the wall opposite the door. His body felt marginally better, but he was still wrecked. Roku took a spot next to him, leaning in close, offering comfort while Arad quietly seethed. Before this was said and done, someone was going to die. Yes, by all accounts Arad was the most likely suspect, but he wasn't convinced it needed to be a solitary experience.

He wasn't sure how much time passed. Minutes stretched easily into hours and vice versa with nothing to occupy him other than his rage and fears. Roku's ears twitched, and his sudden movement startled Arad. He rose to his feet with a feral growl, shifting to a position between Arad and the door as the cell opened with the *Nightingale* crew standing in the hall. Hodge, Vosh, Pakko, Yosei, and even Bryce. None of whom made him feel at ease. Roku's warning grew in volume even as his legs tensed and his feet braced.

Hodge raised both hands, palms out and empty. "We didn't come here to fight. We need to talk."

Chapter Twenty-Seven

Every muscle in Arad's body continued to ache, so he kept his seat, arms resting on his knees and head propped up against the wall. He refused to show Hodge and the crew any more weakness. The buffer Roku provided between them bolstered his confidence and a bit of snark all at once.

"It's your house. Don't wait on my account. But you might want to keep your distance. Roku's been looking mighty murderous these days."

Hodge crossed the threshold, hands still open as if making a point to appear non-threatening. "How're you feeling? That was a nasty jolt you took. Those devices don't take well to being messed with."

Ignoring the strain, Arad shrugged. "Don't worry about me. I'm fabulous. Thanks for rushing in with the medical attention."

"Thought about it, but the last guy who came in here got the shit kicked out of him."

"So I hear." Leaning way over for a better view around the wall of Roku, Arad raised his voice for everyone's benefit. "How you holding up there, Pakko?"

Vosh growled. Yosei covered her mouth, smothering a snort. Bryce stood silent, ever watching. Pakko gave Arad the finger. Straightening up, Arad laughed in that low, mean-spirited way the corrupt police back home used to before stealing a vendor's money and kicking over their fruit carts.

Looking around the room, Hodge's gaze landed on the twisted wad of metal at his feet.

"You can have your tray back," Arad said.

Hodge grunted. "I misread you. You didn't strike me as this aggressive."

Usually, Arad's sense of survival tactics didn't include this much viciousness—normally, he'd vote against it at every opportunity—but he'd lost the will to be charitable. He wasn't going quietly anymore. He deserved better.

"What can I say? The *Nightingale*'s hospitality brings out the best in me."

Blowing out a lungful, Hodge dropped his head, deliberately avoiding looking Arad and Roku in the eyes. His mouth opened and closed several times, whatever words he had stalling under an expression and body language Arad only linked to...shame?

Vosh's eyes narrowed in suspicion. "Why are the rest of us here?"

Arad wondered that too. If they hadn't come as a group, what did Hodge have to say that required an audience? It took an effort to appear nonchalant when his curiosity was so well primed. Thankfully, Hodge found the strength to speak.

"The *Ansariland*'s engines are initializing. She'll be ready within a few hours."

Roku's voice held an unending tone of menace. "Congratulations. That should make for quite a payday."

Hodge raised his head. "I expect you two to be on that ship."

"Come again?" Arad asked.

The weight balanced over Roku's feet lost a hint of that ready-to-strike agitation. Keeping the shock off Arad's face was easy. He didn't trust Hodge enough to believe this wasn't a ploy to get them to behave. Surprise, however, found itself painted on the face and posture of every *Nightingale* crew member, as well as a fair amount of confusion.

Not surprising was Vosh breaking the silence as he stepped forward into the doorway. "You're letting them go?" His ursine shoulders swelled, but Hodge appeared unaffected by the display.

"Yes."

"What about the money? We could use that."

Hodge's face darkened. "I know, and if I knew a way to cut them loose and get paid, I would."

Pakko snorted. "Good luck with that."

"Hey. None of us are angels, and we've all done a lot of shady crap lately, but no one's ever died because of it."

"That you know of," Vosh growled.

A ragged sigh deflated Hodge. "Maybe. But I know it now, and I can't live with that. You still wake up screaming from the shit you did on your last tour behind enemy lines, so I'm not sure you can either."

Right there, Hodge's veneer cracked, the first signs of truth seeping through. The chances Arad and Roku would walk out of this cell were growing, but not guaranteed. Too much had happened to simply take him at his word, and Arad frankly was still pissed off. Pressing a knife into Hodge's guilty wounds came to Arad without a second thought.

"A lot harder to sell the product when you meet it face to face?"

Hodge winced. "A little something like that. I'd like to think that someday when I meet my wife and daughter on the other side, they'll be able to look me in the eye."

A sobering idea. It had been years since Arad had entertained the idea of facing his family again after they cast him out. Hodge's family were dead rather than he being dead to them, as in Arad's case. Arad understood the wish but questioned whether Hodge would actually end up with his lost family in heaven.

Before he said something counterproductive, Arad changed the subject. "Forgive me if I'm feeling a bit skeptical, but what's the plan here?"

"Once you're on board and ready to leave, we'll send you the command keycodes to unlock Roku's restraints. You go on your way, and we never cross paths again."

"So far I like the plan. Why don't you let him free now?"

Hodge's gaze shifted squarely on Roku. "I don't want you killing us all in our sleep."

While his stance may have retreated from pouncing, Roku managed to keep his presence commanding and unforgettable despite the shackles. His throaty chuckle chilled. "The idea has merit."

Everyone's reactions were at various levels of visibility, but all of them were unsettled, even Vosh.

"What about the other DemiShou?" Arad asked. He wasn't leaving without them, but they weren't in a position to fight to force the crew's hands given the current situation.

"Take them with you. I'm canceling the deal."

Vosh's jaw nearly hit the floor. "Are you kidding? ApexCorp won't let us breach contract."

"The contract is illegal, even by their own standards. Besides, I've gathered enough evidence to make them keep their distance."

"They have lots of contacts. We'll be looking over our shoulders in every port."

Hodge turned his full attention on Vosh, standing inches away. "If you want to stay on this ship, it's not up for debate."

Vosh face twisted into a fearsome snarl. "You can't do this."

"Stop being an asshole," Hodge barked. "The only reason you don't like Roku is because you had a dick-measuring contest in the ring and came up short. There is always someone out there bigger and badder than you. Have a little honor about losing in a fair fight. You should be better than that. It's why I hired you in the first place, because I can trust you to watch my six."

Vosh flinched at Hodge's assessment. The core of his animosity toward Roku was prime toxic alpha male crap. The type not easily bred out of thousands of generations no matter how hard some might have tried. Arad had seen it far too many times, the men whose entire egos were built on being stronger than the rest around them. A waste of time when a man with a bigger gun comes along.

"I did some digging and snatched a copy of Apex-Corp's customer list. The people on it..." Gritting his teeth, Hodge shook his head. "There's no way we'll walk away from this once this deal is done. Contract terms or not, the law will override them all. We'll be accessories to murder, and they have the clout to pin that on us. Don't think they won't."

Arad wasn't impressed but kept his mouth shut. Guilt might have spurred Hodge's change of heart, but the rationale for bringing the rest in line was all about saving their collective butts. Pointing that out at this stage wouldn't do him any favors. He needed to sit and let this play out, praying it ended with he and Roku safely on board the *Ansariland*. It was the only option he had.

"What'll we do?" Pakko asked.

Hodge gave them all a resigned huff. "What we should have done from the start. Not do the job. We have our own contacts. We can barter our safety with the information I have. There's more than the list archived. A lot more. If they leave us be, we stay quiet and go about our business in another sector if need be."

"You'd better be right—ow!" Vosh turned to Pakko. "Did you just pinch me?"

Pakko stared back in absolute disbelief. "What? No."

Frustration and impatience turned up Hodge's volume. "Dammit, Pakko. Can you keep it in your pants for five minutes? This is important!"

Looking positively affronted, Pakko clamped his mouth tight, crossed his arms over his chest, and faced away.

Vosh and Hodge locked eyes. A long, tense minute dragged out as the consummate leader held his ground under the stare of the ego-driven DemiShou. A hint of challenge tainted the air, which no one interrupted.

Eventually, Vosh exhaled, his shoulders relaxing. "Do you think we can do this?"

Clapping a hand on Vosh's arm, Hodge nodded. "We'll figure it out. I won't let us all down."

"I never liked working for ApexCorp anyways." Vosh wavered on his feet.

Hodge's eyes narrowed. "Are you feeling all right?"

"Not really. Something's wrong..."

Vosh stumbled two steps forward and collapsed hard, taking Hodge with him to the floor. Panic flashed across Pakko's face as Vosh groaned, only to have any noises turn to forced grunts as his eyes rolled back in his head and his entire body seized.

Pakko dove to his knees. "Vosh!" Over and over, he reached out, hands coming up short, as if afraid to touch Vosh and make matters worse.

Swearing, Hodge tried to pry himself out from under the massive bear as the fits increased.

Something wrong hovered in the room, thickening the air enough Arad couldn't bring himself to take advantage and run out the door.

Roku took a careful step backward, crowding Arad as he growled. "Something smells wrong."

Vosh's arm flailed out and caught Hodge in the face. "Shit! Bryce! Help us here!"

The doctor came into the room, pulling a hypodermic gun from her pocket. Calmly, she stepped over Vosh, keeping a careful eye on his convulsions. Frothing at the mouth, the bear was drowning.

Hodge gave up trying to free himself, his cries becoming more harried. "Dammit, Bryce! Do something!"

"I am," she said in her insufferably stoic tone, holding the device over Vosh as his movements slowed. "I'm waiting for him to die."

"What?"

Bryce reached down near Vosh and picked up an object: the dropped control to Roku's collar. She raised it and pressed the button. Sparks brightened the room for a good thirty seconds. Roku's deafening roar faded, and he fell, slamming into the bed's edge and slumping over Arad. Breathing shallow and unmoving, his solid weight held Arad down.

"Bryce! What the fuck are you doing?" Hodge shouted.

Pakko lunged at her, and she snapped a knee into his face, sending him sprawling. The audible crunch had been sharp over the noise.

Bryce side-eyed Hodge while scanning the cell. "ApexCorp was afraid you'd bail on the project. So they made me a counter-offer."

"You bitch!"

"I'm afraid your commission has been revoked." Over her shoulder, she called out into the hallway. "Knight takes bishop."

Arad's attempt to climb out from under Roku stalled as a man-shaped section of the corridor...moved. It shifted—walked—forward and shoved Yosei with a yelp into the room next to Pakko. The figure's surface rippled like a million miniature sequins rolling and shivering, changing color until each individual dot returned to a range of solid tones, leaving a muscular, scaled DemiShou standing before them all. Arad barely found the courage to whisper his name into the chaos.

"Shichi."

With uncaring eyes, the lizard DemiShou strode across Vosh's twitching body, grabbed Hodge by the hair with one hand, and raked his claws across Hodge's throat with the other. Blood splashed the walls, ending Hodge's frantic struggles with a wet choke. Yosei clasped both hands over her mouth and shrieked at full volume, scuttling deeper into the corner. Pakko did the same, his voice lost in horror.

Shichi released Hodge and turned his steely attention on Pakko. Bryce laid a gentle hand on Shichi's shoulder, stroking him tenderly. "No. We need the techs. For now."

A faint rush of air escaped Vosh, and he stopped moving. Bryce kneeled, pressed a finger to his neck, and scanned the data displaying on her small wrist monitor. "A touch slower than I expected but still effective."

Arad hissed and shook Roku, whose dead weight pinned him down. "Roku, wake up. Wake up!"

Standing up, Bryce ignored Arad, letting her hand drift up Shichi's chest and neck, across his hairless skull. The multicolored scales shimmered in shades of dangerous reds and orange, bleeding into less heated shades of yellow and green as he leaned into the touch, sniffing along her wrist and forearm, all without losing sight of everyone else. His body relaxed, but the remnants of

Hodge's throat dripping off his claws made the threat clear.

He would kill anyone in the room if Bryce asked.

"ApexCorp suspected Hodge would breach their trust and were kind enough to give me Shichi's verbal command codes so I could secure the ship. He was designed to be a private mercenary to his client."

"I can't believe you're touching him." Arad was stunned. The amount of contact she'd had with Shichi flew in the face of everything he'd seen and understood about her. And judging by the dumbstruck reaction from the others, his assessment was held by everyone left standing.

"DemiShou don't spread random disease like standard humans. They're superior in every way."

"You woke him?"

She shrugged. "His processing was complete. Shichi only needed someone to give him direction, isn't that right, darling? Binding him to me wasn't a hardship."

"How did you get in my cargo bay?"

Bryce nudged at Hodge's pale corpse with the toe of her boot, satisfied with the lack of reaction. "I copied your command access off Yosei's pad days ago."

Arad gasped as Shichi gravitated toward Bryce, following her every motion. "He's imprinted on you."

Bryce's sly smile chilled Arad as she leered over Shichi's naked body, pausing at the thick organ swaying between his legs. "Like I said, it wasn't a hardship."

What was that noise? That pounding, growing louder by the second, reverberating through Arad's chest and head, suffocating his reason? No one's heartbeat should drum so strong. It made his lungs move in quick, choppy spurts.

In all the messed-up situations he'd ever been in, Arad hadn't known a spiraling terror so deep it drowned his ability to decipher a way out. He was so screwed. They were so screwed. Blinking back tears, Arad shook Roku again. He didn't respond.

They might actually die here. Today. He thought they'd have more time.

"Ship, identify the *Nightingale*'s commanding officer," Bryce said to the ceiling.

A synthetic male voice replied, "Protocols following the cessation of Captain Hodge's life signs have auto-promoted Dr. Bryce Southerland to rank of captain."

Pocketing the hypodermic gun in her lab coat, Bryce looked absolutely pleased with herself. "Perfect. Now, Hodge was correct about one thing. We need to talk. You and I need to have a serious conversation about the future of the DemiShou." She nodded in Arad's direction to Shichi. "Bring him."

Without hesitation, Shichi stalked his way. Arad shouted and shoved at Roku in a last-ditch effort to wake him, but he didn't react, barely making a sound when Shichi tossed the tiger's unconscious body aside. One look into Shichi's cold stare and panic flooded Arad.

Run, run, run!

He scrambled to escape, to get out of reach in this tiny, tiny space. Diving onto one bed, he scramble-crawled to get around the killer Demi, only to scream out in pain as Shichi's bloody hand caught a fistful of his hair.

Arad grabbed at Shichi's wrist, trying to prevent his scalp from being torn off in chunks as he was hauled outside.

"*Let go of me! Roku! Wake up! Roku!*"

He kicked at his captors to no effect, being kept out of Bryce's reach as she locked the cell door with everyone else inside. He never stopped fighting for all the good it did as they pulled him down the hallway and away from Roku.

Nothing short of a plasma torch could release him from Shichi's steel grip, yet Arad cursed and thrashed until they crossed the border of the infirmary. When no one stopped inside the lines for decontamination, Arad freaked. His feet flailed out recklessly, kicking over a tray of instruments. Only when Shichi slammed him onto a bed hard enough to force the wind out of his lungs did he stop yelling.

"Be quiet or I'll have Shichi remove your tongue. You don't need it to keep Roku's imprinting instinct in check." Bryce tapped at the bed's controls near his right hand, and restraints spun out, lashing him down at the ankles, thighs, waist, chest, arms, and wrists in the space of a second.

Anger and fear braided into a tight coil, making it difficult for Arad to find his breath as Shichi stepped aside to give Bryce room to maneuver. She wove around the pristine space, picking up the scattered medical devices he'd knocked to the floor.

"Where's number five?" Bryce asked without looking.

Arad had never been so furious and frightened in equal measure. The dread was gaining new traction, but confusion blunted his racing brain cells enough to answer. "Number five? What are you talking about?"

Pausing, she sighed softly, filled with quiet aggravation. "Number five...the wolf DemiShou."

"I don't know what you mean."

Bryce set down her instruments and stepped closer, forcing herself to speak gently as one would to a child. "Hachi, eight. Shichi, seven. Roku, six. Go, five. They're numbers, not names."

That's right. Roku had told Arad as much, but in the excitement, he'd almost forgotten. "Go was a wolf?"

"Good. You can understand me. Where is he?"

"I have no idea."

Bryce's jaw drew tight, and a fleeting hint of mania danced in her dark eyes. "Don't take me for a fool. I've seen the unsecured logs. Even if your promotion to captain was a fluke due to those morons' deaths, you were still part of the crew before Torrins picked up this custom group for delivery. Time-stamps prove it. The wolf is the only product unaccounted for."

"I never laid eyes on him. When I found them, his cryotube was already empty."

Arad's breathing came in quick, unhealthy puffs, and his pulse rate had yet to slow, but it didn't stop his memories from sharpening into focus. The day it all began, he'd walked onto the bridge and interrupted the conversation between Torrins, Franc, and Daiko.

"Are you sure they're still going to be there? We've already lost Go."

Go, the wolf, had likely died, possibly the way Roku almost had had he not been present. Torrins had sent Arad into the maintenance shafts for hours before, probably to give them a chance to dump the body without him knowing because he wasn't part of the crew and they needed to keep their secrets. There wasn't any other reason for them to have parked so close to that star. Destroying evidence.

Not knowing whether the truth would be good or bad, Arad held it to himself as potential leverage. Bryce's subtle unhappiness resulted in impatient movements that led her back to her workstation, ignoring Arad for now.

Arad had every reason to worry since Bryce could have asked all of this without resorting to killing Vosh and Hodge. The sight of each of them going down and her clinical regard for homicide was something he'd never forget. He tried to rein in his nerves because repeating the scene in his head roiled his stomach and the brace around his neck restricted him enough to be a problem. The last thing he needed was to drown in vomit.

Arad scanned the infirmary as much as his restraints allowed, hoping for the tiniest bit of information to add to his story about Go. Something he could use. When he craned his head to the right, Shichi stepped into his sightline. Unobstructed by murky cryofluids, Arad saw the details he'd previously missed.

Practically carved in stone, Shichi's body appeared layered in a fine, pebbled texture that hyper-defined each sculpted muscle. The chiseled effect's severity made him look larger and more dangerous than Roku. Every color shimmered over his skin, courtesy of the flexible scales vying for attention, although the dominant sheen currently cast shades of green and blue. From what he'd guessed, it might be anything Shichi wanted. Miniature rainbows rippled down every inch from the top of Shichi's hairless skull to his powerful chest and abs, leading to the proof swinging between his reptile thighs that DemiShou designers were all a bunch of pervs.

"Can we put some pants on him? I've seen enough bare penis for one day." A humorless laugh escaped that nearly triggered Arad to cry. Settling himself would be harder than usual because his life sat more precariously now than it did earlier inside the cell.

Bryce gave a sultry chuckle and raked her dark gaze over Shichi's naked body. "Why would I do that? He's perfect the way he is."

Shichi kept inching closer to her as she moved around, the imprinting obvious to anyone with a brain. His otherwise cold gaze followed her every move. Roku admitted he'd struggled in the beginning to keep his hands to himself until Arad had been ready, but their introduction had been complicated with medical emergency, Syn, and Roku's half-conscious instincts. Bryce may have otherwise been insufferably collected, but it didn't look like she was being coy regarding his needs. The last thing Arad wanted was to watch her get mounted by the lizard Demi, so he turned his head to search out the other side of the room before anything went pornographic.

Searching the room did more to draw his fears in line than rummaging through his memories. It wasn't extinguished but rather drawn into a constant flow he could tune out. Somewhat.

Every major area of the *Nightingale* showed live through the monitors lining the wall. One of them must have been the brig, but it sat outside his field of vision. There were so many screens. The desk on the far wall, while still tidy, held a few personal items, including a checkered game board hosting a well in-progress chess match. Even from the awkward vantage point, he saw it clear enough. Half the pieces were already captured on both sides. White held the advantage. A castling would be required to prevent checkmate.

It explained her *knight takes bishop* reference. Interesting that she ranked Hodge as the bishop and not the king. Did she see herself as the queen? It didn't take much to guess she viewed Arad as a lowly, sacrificial pawn.

"That's a chessboard. An antique game of strategy from the Old World that never lost its elegance. I don't expect someone of your status to understand, so I won't waste time going into detail."

Someone of Arad's status? Arad had been weaned on chess well before his parents had enrolled him into a private elementary school. If not for his family's greed, he would still be living a life of privilege Bryce could only hope to beg for. What kind of classist stooge would he have grown up to be then? She would be seen as beneath him, less than in every way, and the irony wasn't lost on him. A scheming murderer believed herself to be better in wealth, breeding, and intellect than a young, penniless man who lived on the streets even though he once sat at a much different dinner table.

If that didn't prove constructs of social standing were a farce, nothing would.

A shame that it took a psychopath to hammer into him how being a slug was a worthless word to describe a man's circumstances, not a rank or true value of person. If he hadn't been strapped to an operating table, he might have cheered.

Closing his eyes, Arad inhaled deep through his nose, swallowing against a new rise of panic. *Don't cry. Don't cry. Don't cry.* A line of hot salt seeped out, trailing to his temple and soaking the hairline. Opening his eyes to find Bryce standing over him did nothing to cage his reactions.

The doctor examined him up and down, the faintest sneer curling her lips. "You're such a filthy human being."

Arad's voice trembled as he babbled. "In all fairness, I haven't had the chance to bathe recently, and when you go unconscious, you tend to piss yourself. Not my fault. If our places were reversed, you'd be a filthy human too."

"Well...not for long." When it appeared, he wanted to slap Bryce's smug grin off her face. With a pipe wrench.

Creepy smile aside, her comment tripped a relay in his head. The significance spun wild and clear, a beacon in his hysterics. He gasped as the reason coalesced into something solid.

"Is that what they promised you? To turn you into DemiShou?"

"Aren't you the clever one. But yes. With my revised contract, once I deliver the four of them, that is my main compensation, as well as a stipend."

"Why would you do that?"

She titled her head rather than laughing at him out-right. "Why wouldn't I? After all, they are the superior species."

"Is that what you told Vosh?"

"Vosh was a necessary sacrifice. He wanted to be human rather than be better. You don't leave a dangerous bear at your back that risks biting you at any opportunity. He had to go."

"What did you do to him?"

Bryce pulled the hypodermic gun from her pocket. "A type of genetically engineered venom. It's unique to Shichi's design, but he was kind enough to provide an ample amount. I needed something potent enough to take down the strongest DemiShou on board."

"Roku is stronger than Vosh. You saw."

Cocking her delicate brow, Bryce shook her head with a sigh. "Roku is a product. Not an adversary."

"What about Hodge?"

"He was in the way."

The fact Bryce was so willing to answer Arad's questions didn't give him any sense of security. Only the certifiably insane or stupid confessed—or bragged—every detail of their crimes when they were already ahead. And Bryce was not stupid. But maybe, just maybe, if he kept her talking, rambling on about all her machinations, he might manage to piece together some sort of plan to save himself and Roku. He hadn't given up on his promises. Hopefully he'd drag something useful out of her, some tiny, useful tidbit, but his ability to stay focused frayed with each passing second he continued to be exposed to her ruthless lack of empathy. He'd met enough heartless executives growing up, but Bryce made them all look like whining toddlers. The danger was cresting, and it was all he could do to not start screaming.

"So you had Shichi kill him. How did he do that thing? Appear out of the hallway the way he did?"

"A custom camouflaging skill his client requested for clandestine mercenary work. A biological version of high-end military skin suits. Designs were initially extrapolated from Earth chameleons. Shichi's is infinitely more advanced."

"I've never seen that before."

Bryce scoffed. "Of course not. Police officers don't require that kind of sophistication to control the unwashed masses."

"What happens when Shichi's client wants him back?"

"They'll change my scent in processing, which will break his imprint. Shichi will be free and reintroduced to the correct buyer. A shame that won't be your future when Roku is acclimated with a new master. I imagine you'll be another nameless slug piled at the top of the incinerator heap."

Angry tears welled in Arad's eyes. "Once ApexCorp turns you, I hope they sell you to a zoo."

A stoic mask came over Bryce's face, washing away any last hints of emotion. She opened a small drawer and drew out a pair of surgical gloves. With slow, deliberate expertise, she pulled them on without looking, covering both hands and her coat's form-fitting sleeves to mid-forearm. She raised a hand, stretching out each finger in a wave, before she balled it into a fist and struck Arad in the face, breaking his nose.

Crying out in blinding pain, Arad coughed and sputtered, spitting all over himself in reflex so he wouldn't choke on the sudden pool of blood rushing down his throat. Searing agony flared through his nose and cheeks, tearing loose the dam blocking his tears.

"That was for calling me *voyeur bitch*."

Bryce gestured to Shichi, and her obedient servant rolled over to her a surgical cart lined with various medical instruments, many of which were mundane enough for Arad to recognize despite his bleary eyes. She selected a slender scalpel from the grouping, the glow from several screens glinting off the blade. "Now, I need all four DemiShou to fulfill my contract, and you're going to help me. I'm going to ask you about the wolf's location. If I don't like the answer, I'm afraid there will be consequences."

Rapid breaths sped into erratic gasps as Arad thrashed against the bed's restraints to no effect. His stuttering voice went shrill as he fixated on the knife's near-invisible edge.

"P...Please. Don't do this. I don't know where he is."

Bryce's inexpressive face didn't move a fraction, but an unmistakable storm glinted from behind her eyes. "I don't believe you."

He jerked again, trying to flee as she brought the scalpel closer to his arm. Inside his head, Arad screamed.

Roku, I'm so sorry.

Chapter Twenty-Eight

First there was darkness.

Then the darkness ended with cold shards of reality.

Chemical fire spread through Arad's over-sensitive flesh, forcing his eyes open and into the glaring lights. His back tried to arch as his body seized but failed due to the unyielding bar across his chest. His ribs ached. His heart pumped at an unhealthy pace. He couldn't scream with his teeth clenched so tight as he resisted the burn, barely able to hiss frantic air between them. For an all too brief moment, he'd forgotten where he was. The doctor's voice pulled him fully out of the dark his mind yearned to hide inside.

"A little stimulant to keep you awake. We don't want you missing anything important."

Tears ran in scorching rivers over his cheeks at the sight of Bryce as the awareness returned. He was still strapped to her operating table.

"Please… Stop," Arad rasped, his voice having gone dry and raw some time ago.

Nightmares were only supposed to haunt you while you slept. The light was supposed to free you, but he'd found safety in the darkness. Everything was backward.

Shichi hovered nearby, sniffing at Bryce while she organized her tools. How long could she wait before the cravings caught hold of her and she'd need a new fix for the addiction his body created? The feeble hope died as fast as it flared. Days might pass before it overwhelmed her, and she wasn't resisting it the way Arad had at first.

He made a silent prayer to the Saints of Seven Sins that Bryce wasn't creative enough to dose him with Syn as part of her procedure. Corrupted addicts tended to fetishize their experiences. If Arad had to risk a permanent connection—and it could likely happen—between uncontrollable lust and physical suffering, it might kill him.

How appropriate.

Bryce had started simply enough. A razor-thin cut here and there, only to be sealed closed before much blood was lost. Eventually she bored, and the cuts went far below the surface into the meat after slicing away his shirt for better access. The skin was fused shut, but the bruising showed the internal bleeding in darkening patches. Now, Arad's right arm was a useless appendage. Those restraints had been lifted for the most recent series of punishments, and the latticework of deep muscle lacerations throbbed far too much to risk moving.

Seeing the twisted, swollen fingers on his right hand made his empty stomach churn. At least three had been broken by Shichi. Ever the faithful servant, he'd done as he was told. No regret. No remorse. Arad had howled through each snap, one finger at a time. When Bryce had become disinterested, she'd sent in her minion to keep Arad from becoming used to her tactics.

His right eye was partially swollen shut from repeated blows from Shichi's fist, but he'd seen enough to recognize hell. Despite being held down, he shifted his weight in an agitated attempt to create some smidgen of comfort, only to have his damp clothing saturated with sweat, blood, and other fluids refuse to peel away from his clammy skin.

The whole time he'd lain there, between every abuse, Bryce repeated some variation of the same question.

"What happened to the wolf DemiShou? Where is Go?"

Every time, Arad only had one version of the answer.

"I don't know. I never saw him."

The doctor never liked that answer.

After the first hour or so, Arad was convinced she believed him. He'd screamed through it all, confessing everything about Torrins, Roku, and the other DemiShou. It didn't stop her switching from elegant sadism to Shichi's brutality, no doubt as payback for not knowing what she wanted to hear or because deep down she was that sick. Arad had lost track of how long this went on before he'd passed out and Bryce had woken him.

With a ragged inhale, Arad steeled himself, promising to be strong in spite of the terror hooked solidly into his tattered flesh. If these were his last moments, he would bear them with what little dignity he could muster. Which wasn't much, considering how hard he trembled from either the cold or the trauma or both.

Bryce selected the familiar scalpel, its razor edge long stained red. "I have three of the four DemiShou in my possession. I believe you when you say you don't know where the wolf is."

"Then you'll let me go?"

"I'm afraid not. You may have gone from cabin boy to captain in a bizarre set of circumstances, but you were present the entire time the DemiShou were housed on your vessel. I'm convinced there's some tiny bit of information, some random bit of pillow talk hidden in your memories that will give me a lead to follow." Bryce sighed. "Our results have been less than stellar so far. We may need to apply more drastic measures to dredge them up."

Arad braced his spine, knowing things would only get worse from here because Torrins had his secrets and took them to his grave. Even when the man drank—which wasn't often—he was too much of a control freak to babble. He offered nothing worthy of gossip to the man who shared his bed. The arrangement with Arad didn't come with confidences.

Bryce may not have shown the satisfaction on her face, but it radiated from every line in her body. She was eager, looking forward to the next step in interrogation, but allowed the quiet to ratchet the tension higher. The only audible noise was Arad's short, rapid breaths until the ship's AI broke the stillness.

"Captain Southerland, the *Nightingale* is being hailed."

Mouth pursing at the interruption, Bryce replied to the ceiling, "Forward it to my location."

A gentle static pop heralded the communiqué opening through the hidden speakers, the only precursor to an unwelcome yet familiar voice.

"*Nightingale*, this is First Commander Hyland Bard, *Alpha One Flagship*. Respond at once."

Arad gasped, a new layer of dread spiking into the chaos. Bryce's gaze flitted to his face, clearly noticing the tension he failed to hide.

"This is Captain Southerland of the *Nightingale*. What can I do for you, First Commander?"

"You're not the captain. Where's Hodge?"

"There's been a change of venue. I'm a busy woman, Commander. I assume there's a reason for your call."

"My vessel is en route. I've been seconded to Apex-Corp to retrieve stolen property. Prepare to be boarded." Bard's arrogance came through in full force, the bearing of a man whose rank allowed no amount of insubordination. Since losing the *Midas Ascending*, his impatience had grown alongside his attitude, and Arad feared a clash with Bryce, because who would survive in the aftermath?

"If this is regarding what I believe it is, I'm currently under contract with ApexCorp to retrieve the property."

"Your contract has been revised."

Annoyance tinged Bryce's tone. "I was not notified—"

"I am not discussing the details of confidential documents outside of an encrypted command channel. Contact me when you've done so."

The communication's abrupt cut-off left a still silence in the air.

"Ship, reroute a command channel to the infirmary."

The synthetic voice was polite yet devoid of emotion. "I'm sorry, Captain. Command channel locations are fixed on the bridge or day cabin. Rerouting is not possible."

Bryce set the scalpel down on the tray hard enough to make the other instruments jump and clatter, losing their methodical alignment.

Arad would love nothing more than to leave Bryce to Bard's tender love and care, but having him on board would lead to a different type of disaster. "Don't trust him. Bard is the pirate that crippled the *Ansariland* to get to the Demis. Once he has them, he won't need you anymore. He'll cleanse the ship like he did Torrins and the crew."

The narrowing of her eyes was nearly imperceptible. "Why are you telling me this? Do you honestly think it will protect you from more questioning?"

Arad's pained laugh lacked any shred of humor. "I'm dead whatever happens. I just want to save Roku."

Meeting his gaze, Bryce pondered Arad without the slightest arch of her brow. Focusing on her cold stare kept him from paying attention to her bloodstained hands. He winced as she pulled off her surgical gloves with an aggressive snap.

"It's fortunate I still have need of you to keep Roku in line. Don't go away. I'll be back soon to continue our conversation."

Bryce turned and walked with purpose to the exit, gesturing for Shichi to follow. The door swished shut, and Arad waited for a few seconds to be sure he was alone before he allowed himself to exhale.

"Can't wait."

He wanted to cheer. He wanted to melt down into ugly tears, but he had to press this tiny opportunity because it was all he had. Convinced he was incapacitated, Bryce had never reshackled his right arm, and the table's controls were right off the edge of the bed and within reach.

It might have only been an arm's length away, but given his current condition, it might as well have been mounted on his destroyed shanty in Grey District. Lifting his arm jammed hot pokers into his flesh, but he told himself the pain was fake. He could endure it a little longer. Sweat burst across his skin as he reached over the bed's edge, fingering the panel's edge. *The pain is fake. The pain is fake.*

He'd been paying attention when she'd released his arm to experiment. The small panel next to the large one had what he needed. The controls didn't seem to be overly complicated, but he had to find the right spot on the panel and do it with his thumb since his broken fingers weren't capable of doing the job.

A baritone buzz mocked him with an incorrect choice.

The restraining bar across his chest and tender ribs prevented a deep inhale and exhale. As best he could, Arad relaxed for a moment before trying again. *Maybe the other corner of the pad.*

Another buzz.

"Oh, come on..." Arad's eyes welled in frustration. There were no guarantees on how long Bryce and Shichi would be occupied. First Commander Bard's arrival provided an opportunity but could hardly be called a blessing. It bought Arad time, but he imagined far too many ways the man's presence would doom them all. If ApexCorp tapped him, escaping was the only option. Again. Groaning at the effort, Arad stretched his thumb down to another edge of the panel.

Please, please don't make this worse.

Arad crushed his eyes tight, yet wet salt still leaked. He swore if this worked, he would find the street preacher who used to shout brimstone scripture in his face and join his congregation.

With a bright chirp, the entire series of restraints retracted into the table with a gentle whirr.

Choked laughter and tears of relief spilled out of him. "Oh, man, I'm going to need so much therapy after this."

The release lightened his soul, but he only indulged for a moment. Danger lingered, and he was damaged goods at best. Rolling out of the bed squeezed more awful noises out of him, and when his feet found the floor, he had to rest a moment before he bore his full weight on them. His bare torso chilled in the recycled air, and so many points and lines on his body protested. The effort left him light-headed. He'd never been so fragile before.

Even so, he'd never join the Saints of Seven Sins in Grey District. That church was filled with a bunch of certifiable kooks.

He took a brief moment to breathe. Too weak to run, he'd need a weapon if they found him. The tray of used instruments sat within reach, but he couldn't bring himself to touch the scalpel or the wad of bloodstained gloves. He pocketed the scissors Bryce had used to cut away his shirt and picked up a pair of clean medical-grade pliers made of heavy surgical steel because she hadn't yet found a use for them. He wished he had the energy to rummage through cabinets and shelves. Bryce had a fully stocked infirmary, which meant drugs and other items with multiple uses, but he wasn't about to waste valuable time trying to translate them. Not now, when if they came back and cornered him in the room, he'd never survive.

Now that he had his opportunity, Arad had places to be. However, nowhere on the *Nightingale* was safe or out of her sight. To give himself a fleeting chance, he would need to put out her eyes.

Wielding the pliers in his shaky hand, he battered each and every monitor, splintering the fragile screens into masses of static. Nothing hurt so much and felt so good at the same time.

"Pawn blinds queen, you bitch."

Leaning against the counter, Arad stalled to ease his panting, his stamina too thready for strenuous action. Saying he was held together with adhesive and string wasn't too far-fetched. He needed a chance to recover. Maybe he'd get lucky and have the chance later.

Arad turned, his vision landing on Bryce's chessboard. He shuffled over, taking a closer look at the game's layout. He hadn't played in ages, and this psychotic quack had one in progress. Ignoring the pain, he reached over and rearranged the pieces in a wave of pure pettiness. It made him feel slightly better.

Enough resting. He had work to do.

Arad staggered out of the infirmary, bouncing off the doorjamb crossing the threshold. Cradling his right arm, he closed and locked the door before cracking the control panel as deftly as he had Bryce's bank of viewscreens. Ignoring the tearing fire in each step, he trudged down the hall in the direction of the brig. Weariness flooded each step, but he let the goal give him strength.

"I'm coming for you, Roku."

Chapter Twenty-Nine

\

Catching his breath, Arad shoved himself off the wall, leaving a dirty red blotch in his wake. He wasn't bleeding, but the pervasive sweat from pushing himself so hard kept the blood smears tacky on his chilling skin. The trek to the brig had been longer than he recalled, but he risked sabotaging a few more doors on the way. He'd only been gone a few minutes at most, but he hoped if Bryce found him missing, it might buy precious seconds. Any spare amount he gathered would be worth it.

Carbon-copy doors lined the corridor, but the one with the bright *engaged* lock display stood out from the rest.

Multiple people had entered the brig before, and it didn't open from the inside, so he bargained Hodge had never coded the lock for specific crew members. He counted on Bryce's ego and a lack of opportunity that access wasn't restricted from this side. He'd cross his fingers on that bet, but a bunch of them were broken.

Light-headedness made his head swim. Dehydration and blood loss. He pressed his forehead to the wall to keep himself steady. Pinning his wrecked hand to his bare stomach with his good arm, Arad leaned in and knuckled the control. How much penance would a heathen do for making an endless list of prayers in one day? The door swished open, and he prepared for the imminent wave of shock as he moved in front of the doorway where everyone could see.

Roku struggled to say his name. "Arad…"

"Fucking hell! What happened? Did Bryce do this to you?" Pakko's voice quivered in horror while Yosei gasped aloud. Arad grimaced. He'd avoided his reflection the whole trip back for good reason. Roadkill had always unsettled him. No need for a visual comparison. Everyone's reactions said enough.

"I don't want to talk about it." Arad stumbled forward into Roku's space, burying his face into the tiger's chest in case he started sobbing. The silk-covered muscle mass lacked the power to erase the terrible images in his head or the aching pain woven through his body, but it did a great deal to begin softening its sharpest peaks.

"Arad, your face…your fingers… I can smell the blood." Roku's words devolved into a yowl dipped in distress and frustrated rage. His shoulders bunched as he resisted the manacles holding his arms. Unable to free himself, he was forced to do no more than curl his bulk around Arad.

It would be enough. "I'll be okay. Honest."

The replying growl didn't leave Roku convinced. "You're shivering. Pakko, your coat, and get him some water."

Without a word, Pakko stripped off his light jacket and draped it over Arad's shoulders with a delicate touch before snatching one of the remaining cups and racing for the sink.

"Where's Bryce and Shichi?"

"Distracted on the bridge, but I don't know for how much longer." A tap at his shoulder made Arad drag his face out of Roku's fur, and he gratefully accepted the drink from Pakko with his functional hand. "Are you guys okay?"

Hodge and Vosh had been shifted to the side and under a bed, with one mattress pulled out of the frame and used in place of a non-existent sheet to cover the bodies. The surface of a second mattress had been stripped apart and, judging by the condition of the walls and floor, had been used to scrub down the evidence of murder. Eyes wide and wet, Yosei gripped her tablet like a security blanket.

While Arad drank with greedy swallows, Roku didn't stop nuzzling his head and neck. "Pakko insisted we couldn't leave Hodge and Vosh the way they were. I helped him as best I could. He washed the floor and walls to ease Yosei's panic."

Feeling Roku against his skin grounded Arad, yet the metal security collar bumping along his face and neck continued to remind him of why those massive arms weren't part of his comfort. Turning his head, he found Yosei staring. Her haunted eyes stayed locked onto the bruising and swelling that left Arad feeling deformed.

"Yosei, I need you to unlock Roku's collar and cuffs," Arad said.

A dim spark of recognition lit her eyes and she nodded. "Right. Right. Gimme a second." She tapped at her tablet with timid fingers. "This shouldn't be so hard." Sniffling, Yosei paused and wiped her face. "I've been trying to delete her dirty spyware out of my pad so I can access Hodge's server. I can't believe she hasn't seen me pawing through her code."

"She's been a little preoccupied with me."

Yosei winced. "Sorry."

"Why do you need Hodge's server?"

Chewing her lip, Yosei worked, her efforts gaining confidence with each passing second. "So I can make a copy of all his data and find the codes to do this."

Roku's collar and manacles disengaged with a sharp mechanical huff. They fell to the floor, making a loud racket. Suddenly free, Roku's arms hung at his side as he stretched and groaned, trying to undo the strain of being bound for so long. Without warning, he slapped Yosei's tablet aside and pinned her to wall with one hand on her collar.

His growl frightened Arad. "You betrayed us!"

"Oh, wow. You're really strong." Yosei paled and her eyes glossed with unshed tears. "I'm so sorry. It wasn't supposed to happen like this. I had no idea Bryce was this crazy. No one was supposed to get hurt."

"A little late for that now."

Arad tuned in to her last sentence. "Why did you say no one was supposed to get hurt? Are you working for someone?"

She stalled for a moment but finally blurted out, "I work for PlanetGenCo."

"You gotta be fucking kidding me." Pakko was not happy.

Arad, however, was confused. "Who are they?"

"PlanetGenCo are the original designers of the DemiShou matrix. Ow, ow, you're squeezing me..." Yosei rose up to her toes when Roku lifted and started talking faster. "They found out Dr. Chakijane had been recruited to make new DemiShou, but they couldn't track down a list of buyers, so they planted me on the *Nightingale* knowing Hodge's survivor's guilt wouldn't let him resist helping out a young, innocent tech girl."

"Nice profiling." Pakko was disgusted.

"It was the easiest in to the trafficking scheme. My whole goal was to find the client list and get out. The *Midas Ascending*...I mean, the *Ansariland* going adrift turned it all sideways."

"You've been spying on us this whole time?"

Fear didn't dampen Yosei's resolve as she snarled at Pakko. "You were selling people!"

Pakko flinched, his face scrunching up in embarrassment. "We didn't get that far."

"Be quiet, Pakko." Without moving his eyes, Roku returned his attention to Yosei. "You helped them capture us. Chain me like an animal."

Yosei lowered her trembling voice. "I didn't want to. Please believe me, but Bryce watches everything. I had to play along and wait until the *Ansariland* was fully functional before we could get out of here. When Hodge changed his mind, I thought it was over and I'd stow away on your ship and finish my job. I had no idea Bryce was so crazy. That she would..." She inhaled sharply through her nose, as if forcing herself not to cry. "I prepped the way out. No one knows the jump drive is charged and coordinates are already programmed. It's shielded. Remember you totally have a smuggler's ship? We can bounce out of here now that I have all the data Hodge stole from Apex-Corp, and no one will be able to chase us."

"Where do you think you're taking us?" Roku gave her a shake.

Yosei clenched her eyes shut. "Moreau. PlanetGenCo's private colony for humans and DemiShou. It's a safe space outside any corporate jurisdiction."

"They want to study us?"

Her eyes shot open, wide in disbelief. "N...No. They don't want anyone to profit off their designs by creating a black market for DemiShou slaves. They didn't care when the military classified the process, because it was their idea. They had plenty of other contracts to keep them happy. Geez, ease up. You're choking me."

Sidling close, Arad placed a hand on Roku's arm, feeling the unsteady tremors under the surface. Not as poor as Arad, but he was far from peak strength. He squeezed Roku's triceps to make himself known. Sorting out their conflicted positions surrounding the *Nightingale* crew members would have to wait. Time wasn't trustworthy.

"Roku, it doesn't matter how we got here or where we're going. We've got to get to the *Ansariland*. First Commander Bard is coming."

Roku snapped his head around in Arad's direction. "Bard? The officer who killed your crew?" He dropped Yosei and shook out his tired limbs. "We're leaving now. Yosei, make no mistake, if I even think you'll turn on us, I'll maul you faster than you can blink."

Wide-eyed, Yosei gulped. "Duly noted."

Not missing a beat, Roku took the jacket from Arad's shoulders and helped him put his arms in the sleeves and zip up the front. It didn't fit—Pakko was more than a few sizes larger than Arad—but covering the bloody results of Bryce's handiwork did a lot for humanizing Arad's sense of self.

"Come." Roku led them into the hallway, only to have Pakko dig in his heels at the threshold.

"Wait! We're not going to leave them—Vosh—behind, are we?"

Arad's heart broke at Pakko's lost expression, torn between survival and grief over what once was. He wanted to give him the time to process, to lay his captain and lover to rest, but their lives were at risk and none of them were at their best.

Fingers poking out of the oversized sleeve, Arad cupped Pakko's shoulder. "Pakko. Pakko, look at me. We don't have a choice. We have to get off this ship now or we're dead too. Save yourself now and mourn them later."

Pakko nodded. His shoulders bunched as he stifled a sob. The tears still ran down his cheeks.

The group started down the hall, and Roku picked Arad up in his arms.

"I can take care of myself." Arad rested his weary head along Roku's neck.

"I know you can," Roku said.

Arad wanted to run. Instead, he lay cradled in Roku's arms as the group hurried through the hall. Roku had to keep shifting his weight, something he wouldn't have had to do if he hadn't been manacled for so long. He hated being a burden, but Arad was running on fuel vapors and if he wasn't being carried, they might as well have left him behind with what remained of Hodge and Vosh.

They rushed through the halls with a speed on the brink of reckless. Everyone was on high alert.

The electrified shackles were gone, but an ozone tang hung sharp and bitter in the air. Arad didn't have to ask to know they all tasted it. A dangerous spark was coming, waiting to burst into flames.

No one greeted them when they entered the cargo hold and rushed to the airlock. Layers of their rushed steps reverberated over the metal surfaces. Lights were minimized, leaving darkness and shadow lurking around every corner and between the stacks of crates. The cargo hold was not a safe place to be. Granted, given their condition and the threats hovering over them, nowhere on the *Nightingale* was safe.

Yosei tapped the airlock control, and the door refused to open. "It's not recognizing me. My access has been revoked."

Reaching over her shoulder, Pakko tapped twice and punched the panel. "Mine's toast too."

"Where's the manual override?" Arad asked.

"Behind this panel. I don't have many tools on me." Yosei pulled a meager pair of microwrenches from one of her leg pouches.

"You'll have to make do. But be quick."

After dropping to her knees, Yosei attacked the side panel, digging at the hidden bolts. At least six were visible, needing to be pulled, and her wrenches were manual, not power driven. The first one hit the floor with a high-pitched clang, and she went after the next.

Roku kept turning in a circle, trying to shield Arad with his body. "We have to hurry. Something smells wrong."

"Look out!" Pakko jumped in front of Roku and Arad as the nearby shadow shifted, colors rippling and changing. Shichi's strike came up short, claws raking crimson lines across Pakko's shoulder and chest rather than Arad's face and neck.

Rolling Arad to the floor behind him, Roku shouldered Shichi away from the group. He landed on his feet a few meters away where he shifted in an arc while Roku turned and faced him, standing his ground as they squared off, growling and hissing at each other.

"Clearing your ship access was the first thing I did while caring for our young Mr. Ansari." Bryce stepped out from between a stack of crates and stopped next to Shichi, stroking his head.

Yosei's voice quivered. She was trying to be brave but didn't stop working. "Don't you mean committing murder and mutiny? Last I heard, that's a capital offense." Another bolt hit the floor.

"I knew you'd be trouble when Hodge brought you on. You played his grief, and I was the only one who saw through your game. You made him decide to breach contract and put us all at risk."

Arad shifted next to Pakko, trying to urge him to crawl closer to the door. "No one made you pull the trigger."

"Someone had to."

A tremor shook the *Nightingale*. The lights strobed and an alarm klaxon went off. Bryce's normally expressionless face bloomed with surprise.

The ship's AI broke in. "Captain Southerland, a tractor beam has locked on to the ship. You're being hailed by First Commander Bard."

The comms came to life without Bryce's approval, and Bard's voice filled the room. "Your time's up, Southerland."

"I'm completing my contract." Bryce began to shout, her calm veneer peeling at the edges. Her distress drew Shichi's attention.

"It's been withdrawn. Prepare both ships for boarding."

Bryce peaked into full volume. "You can't do that! I need that contract!"

Roku pounced, slamming Shichi backward and snapping out a kick to the side. It caught Bryce in the chest and sent her careening into the wall. She crumpled to the floor, barely moving.

Chameleon scales rolling into oranges and reds collided with Roku's golden fur. The pair rolled and landed on their feet, snarling and trading blows. They tore into each other in staccato freeze-frames and bursts of movement under the strobing lights.

Arad said another prayer to a power he didn't believe in for Roku's safety while he kneeled next to Pakko, who lay on the floor, hand pressed to his chest.

"Pakko, are you okay?"

"Shit, that hurt." Rusty patches soaked Pakko's T-shirt. The angry red slashes marring his chest bled but didn't appear life-threatening. At last Arad hoped not.

Another bolt bounced on the deck. How many had that been? He'd lost track during the insanity. "My hand's mangled. Can you help Yosei with the override?"

"Yeah, yeah. I'm on it." His body bearing too many wounds, Arad lacked the strength to do more than guide Pakko to his feet using his one good hand. They were in a hurry. He'd caught Bard's mention of *both* ships. The arrogant bastard intended to confiscate the *Ansariland* as well. They needed off the *Nightingale*.

Escalating animal noises drew Arad back to the fight. Half martial arts, half savagery, it was terrifying to watch. Shichi jabbed an elbow into Roku's shoulder and raked him with his claws, drawing blood, adding to the growing number of cuts already there. Roku was not winning. For every blow he landed, Shichi landed three.

Arad's heart rate rose over the alarm. Dread tangled its slimy tentacles into his head and chest.

Another strike to Roku's arm.

What can I do?

Two more to Roku's stomach and thigh.

I can't watch him die like this.

Roku kept glancing at them, always knowing where the soft, soft humans were, herding the fight away from them. It left him distracted, and it was going to get him killed. Shichi was fresh, not burdened with being cuffed for days and shocked into submission. He was focused. Driven. And the only thing Arad had ever seen to draw his attention was...

Knowing time worked against them, Arad shuffled over to Bryce, half-conscious and moaning. He hesitated, unsure if he had the nerve.

Roku took another claw mark to the chest.

Pulling the medical scissors from his pocket, Arad stood behind Bryce, then stabbed her in the shoulder. Shichi's head spun at her pained cry, and his entire body coiled in threat. One look at Arad and every scale flushed into the bloodiest shades of red. All his rancor, all his vengeful intentions, all for Arad.

Roku struck.

Those claws that had once scarred the metal walls when Arad lost his spacewalk tether found the unguarded patch of Shichi's neck and ripped it open.

Eyes agog, Shichi futilely clutched his neck, life spilling between his fingers in sanguine rivers as his scales greyed. His body trembled, and before his knees buckled, he lurched forward and sank his fangs into Roku's shoulder. The agonizing roar echoed off the walls. Roku's arm flared out straight, his hands quaking and flexing in spasm. He pried Shichi's limp body off, leaving Roku strangely shaking. Growling uncontrollably, he placed each powerful hand inside Shichi's upper and lower jaw and tore them apart with a primal cry.

Turning his head, Arad struggled not to vomit. Partly because he'd never scrub the gory image out of his head, and partly because he'd failed to save Shichi like he'd promised. Bryce had exploited his programming and given them no choice, but it didn't patch the deep, guilty hole festering in his stomach. Someday, he'd parse the conflicting emotions regarding the DemiShou who'd helped beat and torture him for information he didn't have. For now, he needed to check on Yosei and Pakko's progress. The side panel had been tossed aside, and the pair of techs were pulling the hydraulic release. Air gasped through the door as the seals parted and the hatch opened.

"Got it!" Yosei shouted.

Arad risked a look to find Roku wavering on his feet. The ship quaked again, and he dropped to one knee but didn't rise.

"That felt like a tractor quake." Yosei was worried.

Pakko's jaw slackened. "How crazy is this Bard guy?"

"Very. Why?" Like every other sanctioned authority Arad had ever known, if Bard treated this as a battle, the only acceptable outcome would be to win at any cost.

"If he ramps up the tractor beam power high enough, he could crack the hull and call it an accident."

Arad blanched. "Help me get Roku. I think he's been poisoned."

"Like Vosh?" Pakko sounded so small and distant.

Arad tried to stuff the conclusion he'd already come to down deep because they weren't safe yet, but tears fell without his permission. "Maybe. I don't know. Help me, please."

A soul-wrenching wail rose over the alarm. Filled with wary tension, Arad stared as Bryce rose, allowing her emotionless façade to shred itself in tatters. She screamed as she stumbled to Shichi's lifeless body and slumped to her knees. Curling over, she cradled him and sobbed in giant, hideous gulps as his arms didn't return her embrace. Arad should have felt some kind of regret, some tiny bit of sympathy because he would be no better if Roku were on the floor, but Bryce had willingly broken that part of him on the operating table without the slightest remorse, and he'd lost the will to care when monsters grieved.

Besides, he had his own emergency to deal with.

"What do we do about Bryce?" Pakko asked.

"Nothing. She wanted the *Nightingale* so badly, she can keep it."

Down on one knee, Roku swayed facing the floor as blood seeped from a variety of slashes. Arad gently lifted his head, trying to see the man inside, who was vanishing. His tiger eyes were dull and unfocused, and a thin line of bloody drool hanging from his sagging jaw shivered with each rapid exhale.

"Roku, we can't lift you. If you go down, we'll never get you out of here. I won't leave you behind." He shook Roku by the burned fur ringing his neck. "Look at me. You have to stand up. We have to go *home*." Muddy awareness grew in Roku's eyes, and he gave a lazy nod. He nearly toppled as he struggled to his feet with a grunt, but Pakko and Arad both dove under his arms to steady him. Yosei held the door open as it kept trying to automatically close while they shuffled to the airlock, the walk of the critically wounded.

Yosei led the sad group, dashing in front then behind to open and lock doors through the temporary passage connecting the two ships. Blaring alarms greeted them on the *Ansariland* deck. Arad's head pounded from the noise and Roku was faltering, so he directed the group to their bedroom, the closest place big enough on board Roku might comfortably fit. It took all three to roll Roku into bed without dropping him, and it nearly happened anyways.

"This is your bedroom?" Yosei reached over and picked at a chunk of peeling wall paint. "You guys need a maid."

"Not the time," Arad hissed.

Snapping to attention, Yosei licked her lips nervously. Sweat glossed her pale skin. "Sorry. A little nervous. I'll run down to sick bay and get some supplies. I can help him, but you need to get us out of here."

Arad fixed his gaze on Roku. Fragile and bleeding, he'd closed his eyes the moment he'd hit the bed and hadn't reopened them. Did they expect him to walk away? "I can't leave him."

With a sniffling inhale, Yosei carefully took a handful of Arad's borrowed jacket and pulled him closer. Her voice cracked like a whip, even if her face didn't share the confidence. "Captain Ansari, your access is the only one of us in the system. You are the only one who can save us all. Get to the bridge."

The command splashed cold water over Arad's narrowing focus. Getting this far defied the odds, and not following through after Roku sacrificed himself to remove Shichi's threat would be a disservice. He placed a kiss on Roku's feverish brow and headed out. Pakko immediately followed, helping him maintain pace despite his own injuries, because his ravaged body was still a road map of pain and weakness.

He did his best to tune out the alarms as they entered the bridge. Both men froze, awestruck at the ship off the *Ansariland*'s bow.

The original encounter with the flagship hadn't prepared Arad for the vessel's sheer size. Monstrous in scale, it dwarfed the viewport, blocking out any visible bit of outer space. The hull's details grew as it closed in, a mass of tech and metal and shining pinpricks swelling into full searchlights. Caught in an invisible pull, the *Ansariland* drifted toward a colossal landing port. A gaping maw large enough to easily house the tethered starships.

Arad shook himself back into the real world. "C'mon. We can't let that beast run us over."

Pakko helped him slump into the helmsman's chair, and Arad groaned in relief. He was functioning on pure fear and adrenaline, and the supply was burning his meager reserves. Everything ached. After a few good breaths, he started thumbing through the controls with his one good hand as Pakko took the seat next to him.

"We're being hailed by the flagship." Layers of trauma tainted Pakko's voice. They needed to find someplace safe soon. He'd walked such a fine edge since they'd broken out of the cell and left Vosh's body behind, it was a miracle Pakko hadn't combusted by now. Arad wouldn't blame him if he did.

"Put it through. I need to stall." Arad didn't look over as he tried not to scream. He struggled to remember the sequence to open the right control group. How many times had he been through the ship schematics? Broken fingers masquerading as fat sausages throbbed, fracturing his concentration, and his intact hand barely moved faster than an addled grandparent. The murky vision out of his swollen eye wasn't making matters easier.

Pakko's hand flew over the communications screen, showing his familiarity after repairing the *Ansariland*. Probably to make sure they had a competent second crew to man the ship once they'd taken over before Hodge had aborted the plan. Arad shoved his resentment down. Deep down. Because he had enough to deal with as First Commander Bard's imperious face appeared on the monitor.

"You can't hide forever by changing the ship's name, *Midas Ascending*. Or by running between vessels like vermin."

"No one's hiding. That requires real effort. I've barely thought of you since the last time we crossed paths." Arad barely spared Bard a glance. The pressure to find what he needed, on top of all the injuries, was dragging his efforts. However, he had to keep Bard talking to stay on task. There were too many reasons to obsess over the tiger who might be dying— No. He wasn't thinking of that.

"You've seen better days. Perhaps you should surrender before you drop dead in your seat."

Arad wanted to shine his middle finger at Bard, but he needed that hand. "Oh, Bardsy. I didn't know you cared."

A shaky gasp came out of Pakko. "They have weapons locked on us."

Bard scoffed. "Of course we do. You're the head of a dangerous criminal organization. We're expected to take reasonable precautions for our safety as we prepare for your arrest."

"Really? Is that what you're going with?" Arad couldn't even laugh. The idea anyone would believe the *Ansariland* was a threat to *Alpha Flagship One* was absurd.

"Formal charges will be read to you after your vessels are confiscated."

"Making up the charges as you go along, I see. I'm sure you'll have something conveniently drawn up once you need it." Arad shook his head at Bard's audacity even as he worked to steady his hand. Bard was like all the rest.

From the poorest street cop to corporate military, authority figures craved control. It was a Grey District specialty. As long as they had the upper hand, you could ramble any stream of nonsense at them because in the end, you were beneath them. Why else would Bard waste energy taunting perps other than to jerk himself off?

"You were simply lucky we underestimated you last time. A ship your size shouldn't have space folding capabilities. Most likely an unlicensed modification. Further proof of your criminal activities."

"Like you need a justification." *Come on. Where is that sub-file?*

"We won't be fooled again. If we see the first signs of fold engine charging, I won't waste ammunition crippling your engine. You will be treated as fugitives, and there will be a repeat accident of your shuttle and the previous crew. All resistance will be treated as acts of hostility."

"This sounds familiar. Pretty sure I've heard this before." If his face weren't so hot and stressed, Arad would have rolled his eyes. He'd considered ending Bard's sanctimonious gloating from the beginning, but he had better chances of not being turned into scorching debris if he let the narcissist drone on.

"I'm not going to cry if ApexCorp doesn't have a living product to sell or not. I won't be humiliated a second time. Enjoy your last minutes of freedom." Communications blinked out, but Arad didn't care. He'd already found the menu, shining and gorgeous in bright holographics.

SPACE FOLD ENGINE AT FULL POWER

COORDINATES LOCKED

INITIATE?

YES ***NO***

"I guess the shielding's as good as Yosei says it is." Arad wanted to smile, but anxious threads sewed his body together. The bridge vibrated under another tractor quake, and his ribs crooned a song of thorns as he braced against it.

"What are you waiting for? They don't know we're good to go." Pakko's fraying sanity leaked from every pore.

"The fold isn't instant. I'm not going to get us shot before we jump." The shivers racing over Arad's dirty skin had nothing to do with his wounds. He hoped. It had to work. They'd been through too much to fail on his promise to save Roku now. Another blasphemous prayer rolled through his panicked brain. They were starting to pile up, weighing him down.

"So what are you going to do?"

Gritting his teeth to focus past the disquiet, Arad stared out the cockpit. If he didn't stop hyperventilating, he'd pass out. The landing bay filled his compromised vision, looming ever closer. Slowly, far too slowly, its edge threw a shadow over the bow and gradually swallowed the ship.

"Their weapons can't aim at us once we're inside, can they?" He reached over and pressed *yes*.

WARNING — PROXIMITY ALERT

Engaging space fold will cause significant structural damage to nearby vessel.

Safety protocol engaged — Engine paused

Command Override Required.

"Are you kidding me? Can't you do what I ask the first time around?" Tapping the onscreen menu, he used his thumbprint to call up his captain's privileges. Bold red letters centered in the monitor gave Arad a glimmer of hope.

SAFETY OVERRIDE?

YES ***NO***

Pakko's eyes were more white than color as he clutched his chair's armrests. "Holy fuck, you're insane."

"No. Just too tired to put up with all these pricks." Arad tapped the inner communications array. "Yosei! Hold on tight! This is going to hurt."

He punched the control and braced himself as the universe brightened and twisted itself inside out. Exploding lights and violent quaking from every direction overwhelmed his senses. The *Ansariland* cried out, protesting in alarms and shrieks of metal, while every wound and sealed slice of Arad's flesh screamed out in horrible synchronicity. An eternity of mere seconds passed before he hit his limit.

As Arad's consciousness faded to black, he hoped in his zeal to escape he hadn't killed them all.

Chapter Thirty

"If I still had a torque wrench, I'd have you bless it, you lucky bastard. Can't believe you're alive. I was gonna slap you to try and wake you up, but your face is still all fucked up."

Of course Arad was alive. The dead wouldn't hurt this much. "Thanks, Pakko. I think."

A mangy pit fighter once told Arad the more times you got knocked out, the more brain damage you'd end up with. Man, he hoped that guy was wrong.

A seam in the metal floor dug into his back. No worse than what he'd suffered earlier, but he couldn't recall why he was waking up on the deck. The violent jump must have thrown him from his seat. Great. Hopefully it didn't make his injuries any worse. Pakko helped him roll over enough to get his feet underneath him. It wasn't pretty. Exhaustion and unhealed wounds dragged a cry out of him with every movement. He was forced to lean on Pakko as he wobbled, sucking air in stuttering wheezes.

"I need to get to Roku."

"We will, but you can barely stand. A minute or two isn't going to make a difference."

Pakko was probably right, and he hated it. Minimal lighting cast the bridge in harsh shadow, but it didn't hide Pakko's swollen eyes and sallow skin. The claws marks on his chest were ragged and messy, but he managed not to show it. He didn't strain when he moved or appear ready to collapse. Perhaps the initial meltdown had blown through and given him a chance to vent. Arad hoped so. It might be selfish, but he wanted someone else to share the burden for a while. His own spirit was stretched thin and translucent. It wouldn't hold up to much more stress.

"How are we doing? Is my ship busted?" Arad asked as Pakko eased him into his chair. It felt a million times better than standing.

"We're running on emergency power while all the systems reboot. I don't think there's any damage we can't handle, but damn, that was lucky. That fold was suicidal."

"Did it work?"

"Yeah. I guess you could say that." Pakko turned to face forward, and Arad followed his line of sight.

Arad stalled in mid-inhale. "Oh."

Out of the main viewscreen, a new set of stars blinked in and out, competing with a dancing wave of debris. Lazy and weightless in the endless night, chunks of metal and parts of a flagship landing bay pirouetted in front of the bow, ripped away by the fold jump's bubble. Some pieces sparked, refusing to die off like the rest.

The eerie display might have been called beautiful if it weren't for the soldiers' floating bodies. Frost glistened off dead skin, faces almost visible in the inconsistent light. Some were intact. Some still clutched their weapons as if they could ward off their untimely deaths. In his haste to escape, the idea of people being caught in the fold hadn't occurred to him. Words like *explosive decompression*, *suffocating*, and *freezing vacuum* came to mind. Bile bubbled and rose in Arad's stomach, offering him a taste of guilt.

Arad tipped his head downward. He'd seen enough bloodshed and cruelty, as well its aftermath, since he'd stepped on board this ship. He didn't need to see more. Pakko placed a hand on Arad's shoulder, taking care to be gentle with his support.

"What do you think Bard would have done with us?"

Arad's snort lacked even a smidgen of humor. "Either take us to prison and dump us in a deep, dark hole or put us in front of a firing squad and dump us in a deep, dark hole."

"Then I can't feel so bad about this." Pakko may have been unrepentant, but he still spoke in hushed tones. He reached over and activated a panel. Large shutters slid down the viewports, hiding the destruction from sight.

Arad squashed the minor offense over Pakko knowing where the control was in favor of a major sense of gratitude. "Thank you."

People had died from his choices, his actions. Internal accusations ran rampant in Arad's mind. Where did the micro-thin boundaries between self-defense and murder lie? No one would accuse him of being a righteous man. He'd committed crimes out of necessity in the past, but nothing had ever led to someone's death. That he knew of.

Echoes of familiarity pricked at his memories. Hodge and Vosh had argued as much before they died.

Pakko might compartmentalize his survival, probably because of his dodgy history, but Arad would have to live with the guilt of killing people who meant him harm. Absolving yourself when saving your life and others was better in fiction than in reality.

However, Bard and his soldiers were not the only ones who'd held a gun to Arad's head.

"What about the *Nightingale*?" Arad asked.

"What *Nightingale*?" Pakko queued up a security feed—from the shockingly still-functioning sensor array—aimed at the temporary tunnel between the ships. Or that was between the ships. Still attached to the *Ansariland*, the tunnel swayed in the non-existent wind, while remnants of the *Nightingale*'s docking wall topped the shaft. A technological flower in the vacuum of space. Anything, or anyone, in the docking bay would have been lost when the atmosphere voided or torn apart by the gravimetric forces the fold employed.

Either way, the *Nightingale* was ready for salvage in another sector far, far away.

"I think we're finally in the clear," Pakko said.

"I think you're right." The relief brought by that statement edged out the regret. A beginning at least. Many days, weeks, and months would likely pass before he'd talk openly about the whole mess.

"When everything was hitting the fan... I know you were freaked out, but I can't believe how you handled Bard. I've never seen anyone talk out of their ass so easily."

"Where I'm from, people like me who wind up in jail tend to disappear forever. Lying to corrupt cops pretty much lands in the zone of mandatory survival skills."

"Just saying it was pretty smooth." Pakko's voice trembled, probably as much as Arad's. His attempt at humor did a poor job of covering his grief, alive and thriving, barely under the surface. Arad sympathized enough to set aside his distrust for Pakko's hand in their current situation. He didn't have the energy or interest in pulling that thread. Too much unraveling had already been done.

They sat in silence, drawing strength as the seconds and minutes passed without any new disaster striking. Relief lightened Arad's shoulders as the overhead lighting brightened and additional consoles came to life. Perhaps the ship wouldn't crack open and suck them out after all.

"It's so nice to see systems coming online." Yosei entered the bridge, carrying the white med kit in hand, her pink hair even more disheveled than when they'd scrambled on board. "A little more warning before you bash us around like that. We made the jump?"

"Yeah. We made it." Pakko gave her a shaky smile, but he genuinely looked happy to see her.

Yosei's eyes narrowed at the lack of view. "The shutters are closed. How close to Bard's ship were we?"

"Inside."

"Ew."

Arad didn't have it in him to talk about the war zone outside. Not yet. "How's Roku?"

"Sleeping. There's no antivenom in your med kit, but I was able to hit him with a broad-spectrum antibiotic. All we can do is let him rest. I think he's strong enough to get through it. His pulse is weak but steady, so I think he's managing."

Arad's eyes burned at the news in a good way for once. "How do you know what to do?"

"Human-DemiShou first aid was part of my job requirements. Honestly, I'm way better with tech."

"I'll take what I can get. Thank you."

Yosei closed in on Pakko, grimacing at the mangled remains of his clothing. "C'mon. Let's go to the lav and get you cleaned and bandaged. Oh, so gross. We're gonna have to soak that shirt off you. Hope I don't barf."

"We can dig up some spare clothes. There's plenty left over. I'm going to check on Roku." Arad climbed out of the chair, pausing to test his stability.

Pakko reached out a hand. "Do you want some help?"

"No, thanks. Go take care of yourself. I'll be fine." Tired of feeling weak, he waved them off, well aware of their watchful gazes as he made careful steps down the hall.

He tried not to hurry. The chances of landing on his face were high, so he took a cautious stride to let him take in the scenery. The *Ansariland* made not have been sleek and stylish like the *Nightingale*, but its bones were solid and had sheltered him for months, been his home. His home. When was the last time he had said that about anything? Anywhere? The ship was his. No one else had a legitimate claim on it, and he drew comfort from the fact. A comfort that sprouted confidence in his future. A future including the wounded tiger lying in bed before him. In the bed they shared.

Arad's feet scuffing the bedroom floor as he entered didn't cause a reaction in Roku, and it struck a note of worry in his heart. Sneaking up on Roku hadn't ever been possible. Hearing too keen, he was ever alert, ever listening. However, the rise and fall of Roku's chest pushed back Arad's concerns, even if it didn't close the door on them. The sight of him kept it open.

Bandage pads were applied to so many places on his body, and Yosei had used an insane amount of medical strapping to hold them in place. As in five times what was necessary. Holy crap, she practically mummified him. Well, she did say she was better with tech. Warning Pakko drifted into his head, but Arad let it drift right out. Pakko was on his own.

It hurt to see Roku so broken. His protector. His mate.

Strangely, Roku's condition hadn't diminished his power, his breath-stealing presence, even if it left him defenseless. And like when he'd first found the DemiShou in the cryotube, weightless in amniotic fluid, Arad swore to be by his side no matter what.

Roku would survive. With all they'd endured, the universe owed them that much.

"We made it, Roku. You have to get better and come back to me."

He envied Roku's deep, quiet peace. How his untroubled brow remained unmoving even as Arad leaned over and placed a kiss upon it. Cuts and slashes couldn't find him sleeping. What a lovely sentiment.

Taking care for his own sake and Roku's, Arad crawled into bed, nestling himself against fur and muscle and heat. It may have only been a few days, but being in his own bed brought about enough safety he allowed himself to drift off.

A hard yank in Arad's hair dragged him out of sleep and bed, upright against a body he didn't recognize.

His yell froze at the snarling voice in his ear, horribly familiar and branded into his memories. The source of nightmares for the rest of his days.

"Not one sound. Not a move. Or I'll kill the tiger," Bryce whispered, holding that damned hypodermic gun pressed into Roku's arm. "You'll both be dead long before anyone will find you."

Newfound panic ripped Arad into full awareness in an instant. *She's on the ship. She's on the ship. She's on the ship.* It did not, however, focus him past the fear swelling in his chest, robbing him of breath.

Bryce's unsteady chuckle was tinged with madness. "Shichi's bite may have been weakened since I milked him, but I guarantee there's more than enough of his venom in this hypo to finish the job. You think you've ruined everything, but I still have moves to play. ApexCorp canceled my contract, but with enough money, anyone can be bought. It's the one universal truth even they can agree on. Profit from the bull should improve my bargaining position. You can make sure everything else falls into place."

"What makes you think I'd help you?"

"Because if you do, you'll get your fondest dream. Deep down we both know what you've always wanted. Don't you remember what you told me? All you've ever wanted was to save Roku."

Arad wanted to scream. He couldn't stop shaking out of shame and rage. On her operating table, he'd divulged so much. Every wish, every moment of life before and after the *Ansariland* with each cut of her scalpel. All in some vain attempt to appease her sadistic urges. She had violated him in so many ways, and now she wielded it as leverage.

He didn't want it to work.

Bryce dropped her grip to his collar. "Unlike you, I don't enjoy wasting the lives of DemiShou. Having Roku on my side will make things easier. I'll like having a bodyguard while I negotiate the bull's price."

"Roku won't help you."

"When you're gone, he'll imprint on me, and I'll take good care of him."

Snarling, Arad spun and took a swing at her, but she countered it and, with one punch, drove him to the floor against the bed. More pain racked his already compromised body. Arad was no fighter. He'd spent years avoiding conflict to avoid the attention of the authorities, and she was trained military, even if only as a medic.

Arad wheezed, feeling every searing pull at his ribs. "You're a monster."

Bryce stood over him, well within reach of Roku. Bloodstains tainted her normally pristine lab coat—clearly Shichi's or she would have probably left it behind—and she was mad enough to ignore the stab wound in her shoulder. Perspiration dotted her dark skin in sporadic highlights. She shifted her weight back and forth like a stalking predator, waiting for her moment as she blocked the only exit.

"Human beings are monsters. I intend to be much more. I can still transcend. To do that, I'll need the ship, but I don't need the crew. I promise I'll make it quick. It will be humane. I promise. Yosei and Pakko won't even feel it.

"If you want me to keep my promise, you're not going to scream or warn them. If you do, I will tie you down and make you watch as I dissect them. I will cut out their eyes, peel off their skin, and remove their organs. They will be awake through the entire procedure. Don't think I won't. You know how much we enjoyed our time together, and theirs will be even more glorious."

All teeth, Bryce had yet to stop smiling like a demented clown. On the *Nightingale*, she was disturbed, but now, she was unhinged.

"If you make me do this, I'll be forced to do the same to Roku. It would be a waste of a fine specimen, but I will. Don't worry, I'll save you for last so you won't miss even one beautiful moment. You'll know you've failed before you die, and it will be your fault."

Angry tears streaked down Arad's cheeks. Roku hadn't so much as twitched, oblivious to the danger. Arad gritted his teeth so he didn't accidentally cry out. Pakko and Yosei wouldn't be prepared. Not for this. There was no reason not to believe Bryce's threats. She would kill them all.

"Who's first? I'll even let you choose. Yosei or Pakko? I don't have a preference."

Mind racing, Arad spun his trembling gaze around the room. Think fast. Ideas. There had to be something, anything to use—

The butt of her gun across Arad's jaw snapped his head to the side. Copper filled his mouth, pain lancing from his teeth up through his cheek, but he shut his mouth tight to keep from screaming.

Bending at the waist, she leaned in close as if he hadn't heard her the first time. "I'm waiting for an answer. Which one?"

Blinking the spots out of his vision, he glared at the medical device she used as a weapon, and it all became clear.

Pawn takes queen.

Bryce was right about one thing. All Arad wanted was to save Roku. Even before he'd woken in the cargo bay, Arad had wondered how far it went, how much his promise would sacrifice for the DemiShou's safety. Roku had risked his life, become the wall between them and Shichi when it mattered. He'd suffered the consequences of being noble. Could Arad say he'd do the same?

Yes. Yes, he would.

All those lessons on staying safe—don't fight, avoid the cops, don't make yourself a target. He airlocked them in an instant. She knew his weaknesses? Well, he knew hers too.

Blood still pooled in his mouth.

Arad spat in her eyes.

Crimson splashed across her cheeks and nose, some in her mouth. Shrieking, Bryce reared in revulsion, wiping at her face like she'd been doused in toxic waste. After rolling to his feet, he shouldered her aside with all his weight, leaped across Roku, and wrenched open a rusty drawer with all his feeble strength. His hand was inside when there was a pinch in his back, a sudden hiss, and a sickly heat that spread from the mark.

Hypodermic gun in hand, Bryce's clown grin melted away as Arad raised one of Torrins's pistols—the kind he kept primed and loaded at all times in every bedroom drawer—and pulled the trigger over and over, punching gory holes in her face and chest until the weapon ran dry, and a few more times for good measure.

The world dulled and lost its sharpness. The venom had worked its damage in a short time on Vosh. In Arad's weaker human frame, he imagined it happening much faster. Burning oil sped through his veins, shredding control of his weary flesh. First, the pistol slipped from his numbing fingers. Then his legs bent without his permission, and he slumped to the floor. *Dammit, Torrins. Your criminal habits served a purpose after all.* The floor cooled his cheek as he watched Bryce, half sprawled into the hall. Her body refused to breathe. Not even so much as a twitch to be found.

I saved you, Roku. I kept my promise.

The world's edges fogged even as the heat grew into an inferno. Inhales and exhales took on an odd echo, louder than they should be. Everything was condensed, as if trapped inside a metal can. When he strained, he made out the rumble of footfalls and incoming voices, even if he couldn't tell them apart.

"Arad? Roku?"

"Holy fuck! What happened? Is that Bryce?"

"Not anymore. Is that the hypo gun she used on Vosh?"

"Oh, no, no, no, no, no…"

"C'mon, hurry! Help me get him to sick bay!"

"No, no, no, no, no…"

"Pakko! I can't lift him myself!"

"Okay, okay…"

Arad rose into the air and flew, the overhead lights zooming over him. The burning had overwhelmed all his injuries. He didn't feel his broken fingers or the ache of his swollen eye. Fire was in him, around him, filled his being, and it continued to grow.

"Into the med bed!"

He stopped flying, and the world closed in with mechanical hiss and click.

It's like I'm in a coffin.

"Is it working?"

Laser lights scanned over him in all directions. Automatic arms and tendrils danced in and out of his hazy vision, poking and prodding as little more than mild pressure. They couldn't compete with the fire.

"It's mapping out his injuries. Oh, my—what did that germophobic skank do to him? Come on… What? It can't identify the toxin in his system. It's says it's DemiShou in origin."

"Aren't there DemiShou profiles in the database?"

Uh-oh.

"What do you mean, *file not found*? Who has a med bed that isn't completely updated?"

That would be Torrins.

"Oh no, no, no, no, no…"

"Stay with me, Arad."

They're so sad. They actually care what happens.

So much movement, so many medical noises Arad didn't understand. A jarring alarm caught his attention and drew it to a digital drum.

Is that my heartbeat? Why is it so slow?

"Do something!"

"I can't! The bed can't keep up with the toxin. We're losing him."

I wish Roku were here.

Loud banging made everything rock. "No no no no no! Dammit, Arad, fight! Stay awake! We need you!"

It's so hot in here, I think I'll take a nap.

The drumbeat rhythm slowed and flattened into a sharp whine and faded into nothing. The room darkened.

Oh, wait...one last thing. Tell Roku I love...

Chapter Thirty-One

Dulcet tunes and operatic vocals sang of how to survive heartache and lost love.

The control panel cracked under Roku's fist, and the audio stream abruptly ended. Lies were meant to be silenced. No one ever survived losing their love.

Fingerprints smudged the over-touched holographic image of Arad Yosei had imported from the *Ansariland*'s security files. Somewhere during the midpoint of repairs after finding the *Nightingale*, Arad had grinned watching Roku paint on his tablet as they lounged alone in their bedroom after retiring for the night. Arad had been happy then.

Roku let out a shuddering exhale. He'd promised himself he wouldn't shed any more tears, but some days keeping his word was a wasted effort.

The sketching tablet lay on the floor, gathering a fine layer of dust. He couldn't bring himself to paint new images, and paging through the old sketches had ruined him for days. Memories cut far too deep. Some day they might bring back a tide of fondness, but for now they only drowned him. To stay afloat, Roku required assistance.

Unfortunately, nothing could be done for Arad.

He'd been dead well before the ship approached the colony of Moreau. Yosei was brokering clearance when Roku had woken. Alarmed by the blood still lingering on the scrubbed floor, he'd followed his mate's scent to find him still in the med bed, pale and lifeless. Gone. Forever. Roku had clawed the bed in grief, refusing to let them near, protecting Arad even though he was beyond further harm. The medical staff had to sedate him—

No. He wasn't taking that road today.

Six excruciating weeks had passed—wait, make that seven—and he'd been on that path every day, sometimes more than once a day. If he didn't find a new route soon, he would fade into nothing.

Only Roku didn't know how.

He kissed the image and carefully placed the frame on the nightstand so he said good night to Arad every night and woke up to him every morning. From the way his body ached all the time to the pull of tangled clothing he'd been wearing for the past three days, climbing out of bed was a trial. He wasn't rested, because he hadn't properly slept in six—make that seven—weeks. Last night he'd spent hours patting the side of the bed where Arad should have been and never would be.

An unpleasant amount of light spilled into the small studio quarters as the shutters pivoted open, revealing the colony of Moreau's elaborate architecture. Pristine spires of every height imaginable dotted the landscape interconnected with walkways allowing easy travel between them. Sleek transports floated between buildings in designated airways, making no sound to disrupt the serenity.

Roku wished he enjoyed it.

The morning was the usual exercise in forced routine. Having forgotten to set the program again, he had to start the beverage dispenser to make coffee, needing the caffeine jolt before he chewed down a flavorless ration bar formulated for his specific dietary requirements after his doctors and therapist noted the first signs of weight loss. Eating was easier than receiving lectures.

Stripping off his shirt, he crossed the room to the lavatory. It took less than a dozen steps since his quarters resembled more of a hotel room than an apartment. Everything—bedroom, virtually unused kitchenette, and sitting area—existed in one cube-shaped space with doors for a closet and restroom flanking the bed along one wall. It was enough square footage to pace a circle in.

He did what needed to be done, following a routine of hygiene ingrained in him by a lifelong past scorched out of his brain. Showering required more inertia than present, so he opted to splash hot water on the foulest body parts. A haunted creature spied back at him in the mirror. The medical staff had done marvelous work undoing the damage wrought by Shichi and Bryce. Not a scar showed, not a mark on his flesh. The epitome of physical health. Except where what should be sleek, his fur was full of dull and matted patches.

"What are you doing to yourself?" he asked the reflection. Arad would never have allowed him to stay so shabby.

Arad never gave up, no matter how slim the odds, ever the master of surviving anything thrown his way. He'd taken spacewalks and endured torture only to save them all. Tenacity was his gift. Sullying his memory was akin to sacrilege. The least Roku could do was honor his mate by learning the lesson.

To do so, he would have to leave the apartment. A good idea, if only to keep the therapist from knocking on his door. But before he left, there was one thing he had to do.

He retrieved the medical dispenser from the shelf and checked the readout. Only four days left. He would have to comm Dr. Windsor to refill the prescription. She'd make him endure another round of conversations about his physical and mental health and being excluded from details of the investigation into ApexCorp's affairs. However, the meds were critical, and he would persevere. Staring into his own reflection for courage, he touched the device to his shoulder and pressed the button, feeling the warm tingle feed under his skin.

"I promise, Arad. No other mate. I will love you, and only you, forever."

The drug would suppress the stupid biological trigger he couldn't escape. He'd already imprinted once. There wouldn't be a second time. It wasn't safe to set him loose in Moreau without it. Grief had held it off in the beginning, but Dr. Windsor's tests showed it would eventually re-emerge—and most likely without warning. So the formula was tailored for him exclusively. Apparently, only the black market DemiShou had this problem, and each had to be dealt with individually. Roku hated the association of being considered illicit property, even if he was now a free man.

Leaving the lav, he circled the bed and opened the closet. He used to look forward to having a proper wardrobe after the limited selection he'd once been saddled with. At least everything in here fit properly. Grabbing the first items he laid eyes on, Roku dressed. He needed to go out.

Kilts were no longer part of his life outside the *Ansariland*, so he walked the street to the recreation center dressed in a shirt, boots, and pants. DemiShou of every breed and species walked in equal numbers with humans, everyone coexisting without fear or suspicion. He understood the prejudice, even if no specific memory was attached to it. Moreau was designed for his kind. A paradise of sorts. Most politely nodded as he passed, likely curious at the new arrival who rarely came out in daylight, but they never interrupted him, as if they scented the pain and loss staining his soul.

The architecture continued to be unfazed by his pain. Sleek and efficient in shades of white and grey, the entire colony appeared to be more about clean aesthetics and practicality than making any kind of artistic statement in spite of the impressive network of building structures. It succeeded in function, untouched by the lives of its inhabitants.

The neutral environment allowed Roku to stride to the center without finding something fascinating to focus on, because these days, nothing held his interest for long. Only a few minutes passed before he arrived, the building almost camouflaged in its surroundings of plastic, metal, and concrete. Thankfully, well-designed directional signage hung on every corner and facade. It was difficult to get lost here, and Roku had tried on more than one occasion.

Frosted into opaque panels, the handleless door sat cleanly mounted into the outer wall. Roku tapped the adjacent monitor as prompted. A perfunctory beep accompanied the change in displayed text.

Seo Eijiro

Classification: DemiShou Tiger

ID: A621-S35FC

****Access Granted****

Every time he read the name, he had to look twice. Dr. Windsor had shared some information regarding ApexCorp when records of the project's sealed "donor list" had surfaced and Roku's identity had been verified.

Seo Eijiro of EarthAsian descent. Military employee of ApexCorp killed in action during a food riot on Halcyon V. Without memories of his past, the name lacked connection and the attached photo was of a stranger. A man who didn't exist anymore. Hardly an endearing way to view oneself.

Apparently, he was Seo Eijiro, but in the end, he didn't know who that man was.

"Excuse me."

Startled out of his fog, Roku turned and found a young woman waiting to enter.

Averting his eyes as if it hid his embarrassment, he stepped to one side. "I'm sorry."

"Nothing to worry about," she said as she tapped the panel for access and entered without a worry. Without the specters lording over his every second of every day. She went inside and moved on with her life.

Straightening his spine, Roku took her example and stepped through the open door.

Human and DemiShou both made up the fair number of facility users, although there was some segregation based on DemiShou power levels for safety. Rows of strength machines and exercise areas dotted the floor plan. Roku ignored them all, heading for the section in the corner fitted with martial arts training equipment. The sparring circle made his eyes burn with too many memories of the *Nightingale*, so he gave it his back in favor of the striking dummies.

He chose one mounted center along the wall, focused on the grey mannequin's lack of features. It stood in for anyone he'd ever met or any person he'd ever forgotten before his rebirth. Perfect.

Air in through the nose, out the mouth in a controlled rush. Roku tried to wash his nerves into a steady flow as he adjusted his stance, centered his weight properly. He snapped out a fist and struck the dummy. The padded surface remained unblemished, fortified for a DemiShou's power level.

So he struck it again. And again. And again.

The dummy was no one.

It wasn't Vosh.

It wasn't Hodge.

It wasn't First Commander Bard.

It wasn't Shichi.

It wasn't Bryce.

All of them dead and only one by his hand, yet the target took their punishments in kind. Each and every one of them had a hand in Arad's end. Nothing absolved them of that or his failing to protect Arad from their machinations. Guilt fed into rage, and the only outlet was right here, beating their effigies until the urge eventually passed.

The room reduced to the smack of fist against padding, his rapid pulse, and his heaving intake of oxygen. Over and over and over.

"Seo Eijiro, stand down! That's an order!"

The jarring command shocked Roku back into the world. His hands ached, knuckles bloody, and the sparring dummy's seams were burst and the padding in tatters. Stepping in a daze, he turned, scowling at the interruption. A crowd had formed, human and DemiShou both, well outside his reach. A palpable tension thickened the air.

One human woman stood out from the crowd, standing closer yet still at a safe distance because Moreau's primary director, Dr. Kian Windsor, was no fool.

"Forgive me for issuing an order, Eijiro, but I guessed I needed something more dramatic to get your attention. I'm told you've been at this for over thirty minutes. Perhaps it's time to time a break?" Tall and willowy, Dr. Windsor's frail appearance belied her inner strength. Her authority was forged in a fierce intellect and gentle demeanor that disarmed the most jaded opponent. Anyone who believed her weak found themselves schooled in the most subtle ways. Roku couldn't imagine her raising her voice, which was probably why she was able to break his single-minded trance in the first place.

Despite the warnings of the center's security staff, she stepped forward at a cautious pace but without fear. They didn't need to worry. Roku respected Dr. Windsor too much to harm her. She had been his personal doctor since he woke in Moreau after being sedated on the *Ansariland*.

She oversaw his rehabilitation and therapy instead of relegating his care to a lower ranking but capable staff member. It made his integration into Moreau marginally tolerable.

With kind eyes and a sympathetic hand on Roku's arm, Dr. Windsor spoke just loud enough to keep the bystanders out of the conversation. "I think I'd like to take a walk, Mr. Eijiro. Would you be a gentleman and keep an old woman company?"

Without waiting for a reply, Dr. Windsor circled and walked through the parting crowd, proving it wasn't really a question in the first place. He nearly refused her implied demand, but the tiny voice buried under his lost memories urged him to comply with authority. People gave him a wide berth as he followed her out the door and into the courtyard.

Serene and elegant, she had tied her wavy silver hair in her standard loose bun. Her footsteps light and ethereal, Windsor glided through the unoccupied greenspace, delicate coat flowing. She'd probably requested to clear the area for privacy. If she was upset with him, it didn't show. She led the way down stone pathways until they ended somewhere near the center, he guessed, at a circular copse of trees resting behind a masonry retaining wall. She took a seat on a bench opposite and waited with a casual patience for Roku to share the space. He did.

"I don't think of you as old." Oh, Dr. Windsor had been subtly modified—humans didn't stay in their prime well past one hundred years as she had—but he'd always had the impression extending her lifespan was more about dedication to her work than vanity.

Even Windsor's laugh was artful and disarming. "That's lovely of you to say. And here I'd always pictured you as too honorable to lie. Isn't life strange when it surprises you? Even so, don't think I don't appreciate the sentiment. A lady likes to be appreciated at any age. Tell me, how are you doing today?"

Clutching the seat's edge, he forced his claws not to extend. Windsor knew exactly what state he was in. Never unkind in her observations, she still carried a sharp wisdom with her experience. The facility had notified her. Since he was under her care, his file was most likely flagged with her contact information for any odd or aggressive behavior, and his session with the training dummy certainly qualified as aggressive. Having lost control so completely shamed him, so he avoided thinking of it for now.

"I need a refill on my repression prescription."

A knowing hum sang from her. She'd seen his evasions on more than occasion. "Make an appointment. I want to check your baseline before I approve it."

"Can't I stop in at one of the clinics?"

Windsor tipped her head to look at the treetops. "You know how this works. Your customization is classified, like the others we've liberated from ApexCorp's scheme. I shouldn't have to tell you that. The fewer who see your genetic profiles, the safer you'll be. My office. Oh eight hundred hours sharp. A little flattery is not going to exempt you from the rules."

"Yes, ma'am."

Silence in the courtyard bordered on sanctuary. Little by little, Roku's anger abated, in no small part to the nonjudgmental woman sitting next to him. His files were open to her at any time, which would be more of a review since she'd authored most of them. However, she never weaponized any of her findings. Any self-recrimination he experienced was all his own doing.

"Have you seen your friends lately?"

Speaking of which...

"You mean Yosei and Pakko? I wouldn't exactly call them my friends. More like co-survivors."

The treetops no longer fascinating, Windsor shifted her attention to the flower beds in the distance. "A fair description. All of you shared a unique experience. Often people bond under such extreme circumstances in ways other people can't understand."

Roku sighed. "I'm trying hard to forget everything about those circumstances."

She turned her head to focus on another part of the garden, and he appreciated her efforts. No accusatory stares. No eye contact to wither underneath. Their conversation had more hallmarks of a mother and son talking than doctor and patient.

"No one ever forgets things like that. Not really. The best we can hope for is to make peace with it and not let it consume us. Although avoiding the topic isn't exactly the solution either." Her gaze examined the flowers at the base of the trees. "Trying to forget. Does that have anything to do with the dirty look you gave me when I called out your name in public?"

Roku grimaced. "I'm not used to that name. Seo Eijiro. I don't know who that person is."

"Would you prefer I call you Roku?"

"I don't want anyone calling me that anymore." Too many memories, lovely and horrible, were associated with it. He didn't have the strength to say it out loud, but she was aware of them regardless.

"What would you like me to call you?"

Roku paused, looking for the answer amidst a shaky inhale. "I don't know."

She patted his hand in a grandmotherly way. He continued to grip the bench, using the sturdy form to anchor him in more ways than one. Eyes burning, he cast his gaze to the treetops, hoping he might find some answers in the green.

"Yosei said she hasn't heard from you since she showed you the *Ansariland* security feed."

"Don't blame her. I insisted."

"I'm well aware. I only wish she'd waited until you were better ready."

"There is no better time. I needed to see how it happened. I needed to know how he died." Roku hadn't known there even was a security feed to view before Yosei mentioned it. She'd surreptitiously activated it when she started working on repairs in case she needed additional evidence. Torrins had disabled the feature, no doubt to hide proof of his less than charitable activities.

He'd viewed the video of Bryce ambushing Arad while Roku slept comatose, helpless from Shichi's bite. Bryce's sadistic ranting. Arad's heroic resistance. Bryce injecting him. Arad gunning her down before he succumbed to the poison. How many times had he replayed the scene?

"Did it help?"

Roku scrubbed his face against his shoulder without dislodging his hands. "Arad died saving us all. He was a man with nothing, jaded and cynical, who shared everything. Knowing he died a hero makes me proud, even if it's killing me that he's gone."

"You awoke only a few months ago as a DemiShou, and in that short time, you have been part of something equal parts wonderful and horrible. Everything from our discussions, Yosei's and Pakko Garcia's testimony, and my own research tells me a story of your Arad being a worthy man who was lost far too soon." Sympathy, not pity, wove its way between every syllable. It didn't make it any easier to hear.

Eyes burning, Roku swallowed. "Why are you saying this as if I don't already know it?"

"Because you're allowed your grief. You've earned it better than most. If you weren't so depressed, I'd say something was seriously wrong with your reaction."

"I'm not depressed."

She finally pivoted her head to face him. "If you were any further down the hole, I would have you on suicide watch."

His brow creasing left a near-blinding pressure on his eyes as he ground his teeth. "I already have a therapist."

"And I expect you to make another appointment with Dr. Mercia before he ends up on your doorstep again."

"I'm assuming you have some purpose to this visit beyond dredging up my psychiatric schedule?" He hated this line of conversation enough to growl involuntarily.

Windsor, as usual, was not intimidated. "Yes, as a matter of fact, there is. At some point, we need to decide what you'll do long term."

"I'm not ready to make that decision."

"Oh, I know. And I'm not trying to rush you either. I felt it was time to plant a seed or two. If you decide to continue living on Moreau, we need to find you employment. You don't strike me as a man who will lie back watching soap operas all day, gorging on sweets."

He huffed at the ridiculous image. "No. I can't picture myself doing that."

"I think we can help find you someplace you'll be content. And maybe someday happy."

"I can't picture that either."

Windsor sighed, her lithe shoulders dropping a fraction. "I don't suppose you can. Whoever coined the phrase *time heals all wounds* should have his eyes gouged out."

"Can I help?"

The tiniest smile brightened her whole face. "See? You made a joke. Dark and morbid, but still a joke. There's hope for you yet."

"Perhaps."

"Well, there's no need to worry right now. I don't expect you to make any significant choices anytime soon."

"Thank you."

With an effortless glide, Windsor rose to her feet. A single lock of silver hair had come loose, brushing her cheek and neck, yet she paid it no mind. As in everything, nothing fazed her composure. It made her a reassuring beacon within his dismantled world.

"In the meantime, would you come with me to the lab?"

Tilting his head, he narrowed his eyes at her. "Why?"

"I'd like to show you something." Windsor glanced down at his hands. "But you'll have to let go of the bench first."

He did.

Chapter Thirty-Two

Lightning crackled.

Darkness.

Heart jumped.

Thunder and lightning gave way to dense fog.

Wet fog. Dense like molasses. Soup.

Smothered murmurs from behind the door.

Lights stabbed into the soup. Searching. Spying. Finding a ship's way home.

Invisible spiders crawled over the skin. Inside? Outside? Both?

There's no way to scratch.

Darkness.

More overlapping voices. They're more distinct, but the effort to understand is worthless. Unrecognizable noises underwater. Breathing in the fog, thick and wet, was normal yet shouldn't be. Floating weightless in the warm soup. Fluid?

Spying lights flickered across the eyes.

Can't sleep with interruptions. Want to sleep.

Darkness.

Itch, itch, itch with no way to scratch. Feel the spiders but can't see them. On the flesh, in the flesh, always itching.

Moved a finger. Voices rose and fell. They made no sense.

Darkness.

Itches became tingles. Electric fireflies danced on every inch.

A few words were said. They still made no sense. Broken down. Reassembly.

Chimes. Signals. Constant when the voices were not.

Heartbeat.

Voices were louder. Clearer, but still made no sense. Something was happening.

The soup was leaving. Draining away. Chest heaving. Coughing up the soup until there was nothing but air. Skin felt slippery slick.

Warmth replaced by a chill.

The wall opened. It was too bright outside.

"Turn down the lights."

Multiple hands. Washed and dried. Laid down on something firm yet soft.

Voices were gentle. "Can you hear me?"

I can hear. Stop the lights in my eyes.

A hand pressed his chest. "Don't sit up yet please."

"Vitals are good. Synaptic responses are healthy."

Lights were low, but he could see. The walls in front of him were bare, clinical. Some sort of pod, tube, sat behind him, full of gadgets. Strange men and women stood nearby. Visors and white lab coats and gloves. Familiar? Why? Bryce wore lab coats and gloves.

Chirp of medical stuff. He was on a bed. Thin firm mattress. Medical table. Operating table. Like Bryce's.

No.

"Please. Stay calm."

Need to get up. Need to go. Go. Go is dead.

Gloved hands tried to hold him down. Restrain him.

No.

He growled (growled?) and shoved one lab coat away. Noisy table of tools flipped over. Other gloves gripped tighter.

"Dammit, he's strong. I don't think we can hold him much longer."

"Is Seo Eijiro still out there?"

"He's waited seven weeks. You think he's not?"

"Screw your sarcasm, Gerald. Get him in here! Now!"

More yelling and another lab coat flew with a push. The rest shouldn't be able to hold him, but he was groggy. Muddied brain. He spied doors. With a roar (roar?) he shoved them all away and leaped for the doors, landing closer than he expected.

More shouting. More chaos. Too loud. Too much noise.

Covering his ears didn't block the volume.

Flee.

The doors burst open, and the most handsome tiger man blocked the path. *Do I know you?* It made him pause, but he needed to run.

"Don't let him out!" a lab coat yelled.

He tried to dodge the tiger, but he was too fast and snatched him off the ground. The tiger's arms sparked recognition, like they were something he should know. Like they felt right. He slowed his struggles, but he needed to go. Lab coats would get him. Just like Bryce. No more pain.

"Arad. Stop. It's me. It's Roku."

He (Arad) stopped. The words surged into his head.

It's Roku. I know you.

The urges to run drained away like soup. Roku cupped his head in his oh-so firm hands. Amber tiger eyes hypnotized him, bright and sad all at once. Beautiful and strong, they nudged opened a door in Arad's head, causing all kinds of awesome thoughts and recognition to leak in.

Arad's chest squeezed with glorious pressure. "Roku."

A wet, joyous laugh choked out of Roku. "Yes! Yes! I can't believe you're here. You're so beautiful, Arad. I missed you so much."

"I was gone?"

Roku's nodded. "For a long time. But you're here with me now." His glossy eyes overflowed, tears catching in the fine hairs coating his cheeks. He was moments away from sobbing.

Arad reached up and thumbed away the wetness. "You're laughing. And crying."

"Because I'm happy. So very, very happy to see you."

Roku pulled Arad close and scrubbed his head along Arad's. It was like home. Arad pressed his face into Roku's neck, relishing the fur. A purr rolled out, and the most fabulous smell appeared. Musky and sharp, it rolled into his nostrils and filled his head, triggering a full-body shiver. He did and didn't know the scent, but he needed more. Arad nosed his way down Roku's neck, but a collar got in his way.

Stupid shirt.

The fabric parted in two easily under Arad's hands, giving him access to that broad chest. For some reason, he thought he should be hunting for wounds, but they weren't there, so it wasn't important now. He wanted the scent. It belonged to Roku. Arad craved it on him, so he rubbed his whole body against the tiger. Best application method ever.

Smells so delicious. Must taste.

"Um...uh-oh. Mr. Eijiro, we need to finish examining him."

Arad wrapped his legs around Roku's sturdy thighs for leverage. It allowed him to scrub himself against the hard planes of furry muscle and lick his way up Roku's neck. Taking more scent in, he shivered all the way into his hardening groin.

"Arad. Perhaps this isn't the right time..." Roku shuddered as he protested yet tightened his ridged stomach for Arad to better grind himself. The intoxicating scent wafting off Roku intensified.

Lab coat voices rose around them, which Arad promptly ignored.

"Geez, you think you can wait until you're back in your quarters?"

A gloved hand landed on Arad. Roku tightened his hold on Arad and let out a threatening yowl, primal and territorial. The hand vanished as fast as it came. Smart hand.

"This is exactly why I didn't want him in here. We can't assess his health like this."

Without looking, Arad reached for Roku's beltline and yanked his pants open. A wayward musing of how a kilt would be better breezed through and was lost as quickly. The column of pulsing flesh thickening in his hand was a great prize. He tugged at the length, his circling thumb and fingers being forced apart as it swelled.

"He's looking kind of healthy right now. Is this happening? Hello, we're right here."

"Oh, wow. This should not be happening in front of me."

"Dr. Windsor, what should we do?"

"From the looks of things, I'd said you give them some privacy or it's going to get awfully awkward in here."

"Kian, you're leaving?"

"I don't need to watch this show. I already know how it ends."

"All right, that's enough. Everybody out! Clear the room!"

Voices disappeared, leaving only needy animal noises between them. The swell of meat between Roku's shoulder and neck called to him. Arad clamped his jaws around it, and Roku answered with an approving trill while mirroring the bite on Arad.

Arad's frenzy grew as he used his legs to press himself up and down. Roku's pants shifted down under the bouncing movement, and his cock slipped beneath Arad, tapping the tender space under his balls and sliding deeper. Some areas were still slick with soup.

Roku's hold increased, and they spun until Arad's back was crushed against the wall. They rutted into one another harder and harder. Arad lost himself to a new craving he'd missed forever, taking Roku with him. Curling his body, Arad caught the tip of Roku's slippery knob at his hole. He'd never wanted anything more. Jaws still holding each other tight, Roku paused, his yowling muffled as Arad squirmed, determined to capture the swollen head. His weight shifted, and he sank, slippery soup, perseverance, and gravity helping Roku's tool drill its way to where it belonged.

The burn and the heat and the oh-so full screamed the words *mate, mate, mate* into every corner of his consciousness. They growled and thrust and clutched at each other. Arad smelled how needy they were, how desperate to bond, how desperate to be one.

Arad folded himself nearly in half to give Roku room to bury the entire length with each furious slam of his hips. Yowls vibrated through his flesh, setting every inch of him on fire. The heat spiked and Arad let it take him. With a reckless cry, he came, splashing between them, mixing the heady scents together. Roku roared and shoved himself in as deep as possible, trying to go deeper still as he spilled, squeezing the air from Arad's lungs in the process. They stayed locked together for so long, neither willing to let go, even as both their bodies twitched, losing their strength.

Roku carefully slid them both to the floor. Joy, rapture, and tears echoed off the walls. Arad wasn't sure if it was himself, Roku, or both as they lay tangled on the tile floor.

Each sawing breath sharpened the world more and more. Arad stretched out his arms and legs, joints popping, loving the delicious ache of muscles waking. Curious. His arms were different. Firmer. Stronger. The skin color was a different shade of brown, but it wasn't skin he was seeing, was it? A silky sheen coated his forearms and hands, but it didn't cover the new definition in the muscles. Arad rolled to the side, his eye catching a shiny metal surface.

The reflection confused him. He blinked once, twice. The reflection did the same, but by someone he didn't recognize. Roku lay behind the unfamiliar furry male with bright eyes shining at him, who he somehow knew he should be familiar with. Understanding crystalized in steps. Long threads of memories stitched themselves together into a tapestry that held the secrets to his universe.

Lightning. Darkness. Soup. Doctors.

"Arad. It's all right. You're perfectly fine." Roku placed a hesitant hand on Arad's back, his whisper filled with hope.

The door in his head creaked open, shining light on the most recent parts of his recollection.

"I was gone?"

"Yes. But you're here with me now."

"You're laughing. And crying."

"Because I'm happy. So very, very happy to see you."

The door in his head opened further, letting in a deluge. The volume threatened to explode his skull, sweeping in with every memory wanting equal priority. Crashing behind his eyes and ears in a giant tide of information and identity smothered under trauma.

Pawn takes queen.

Blood in her face, Torrins's gun in my hand.

I saved you, Roku. I kept my promise.

Is that my heartbeat? Why is it so slow?

Old thoughts twined themselves with new ideas, some less formed than others, but his all the same.

Purring. Scents. Mating. Fur.

Arad gasped as the wave settled, and it all became clear.

"I'm...a DemiShou."

Time paused. No one spoke as the revelation cemented. Roku didn't interfere as Arad crawled closer to the reflective surface.

Feline eyes circled in black were centered within fine white fur surrounded by warm sandy brown. Spotted stripes graced the edges of his face, framing it in dark walnut. The lines continued down his neck and back, marking his upper arms and legs.

He was taller, more muscular than before. Still smaller in scale than Roku, but a marked increase overall. Was his penis bigger? DemiShou designers were all a bunch of pervs. Where had he heard that before?

Ears lengthened to a point that peaked through his standard thatch of wild black locks, grown out long enough to brush his shoulders. In spite of the fur and markings, his features were less feline than Roku, but there would be no mistaking him for human.

Not ever again.

"Arad?" Roku's voice had gone timid in a way that didn't fit his fierce presence. He was terrified.

Why shouldn't he be? Arad remembered the final fight with Bryce in bits and pieces, ending with the med bed. He'd died. And now he was alive again but different. Roku had the benefit of not knowing what came before he woke up changed. It was his entire existence. Arad's life, while nothing to envy, couldn't be returned to. Not in the way he knew it.

"Arad, speak to me. Are you all right?"

Turning the palms up, Arad pondered his hands. He was convinced there were claws in there. Spreading his fingers didn't make them pop out. "I'm a DemiShou."

"Yes."

"How long have I been..." Arad couldn't finish the sentence out loud.

"Seven weeks."

Dropping his hands, Arad turned to face Roku. The memories haunted him still, shining through his eyes no matter how thankful he was to see Arad again. "I'm so sorry you had to go through that."

"I don't care. I have you back." Crawling over with his pants still half down his thighs, Roku took Arad's hands in his own. "I think you're beautiful."

"You do?"

Gaze averted to the floor in embarrassment, Roku's head bounced with an eager nod. "Yes. Very much so. What do you think?"

"I never would have asked to become DemiShou. But now that I am..." With a hand to Roku's chin, Arad nudged him to raise his head. "This is beyond awesome."

Roku's big, tiger eyes glossed with tears on the edge of falling. "Really?"

"Coming back as a Demi is worth it if I have my mate again."

Lurching forward, Roku snatched Arad in his arms. Head pressed into his shoulder, Roku let the dam break and sobbed. Body heaving, he held Arad tight as if unable to risk letting him go. That was fine with Arad.

Face hidden in Arad's neck, Roku's voice broke. "I love you so much. I don't know how I survived without you."

Picturing the sorrow choked Arad's words. "I didn't get to say goodbye."

"I'm never letting you out of my sight again."

"You promise?"

"I promise."

Arad gripped him tighter. "Okay."

They embraced until the tidal wave of grief subsided and the floor warmed under their bodies. Time passed. Lying in each other's arms, they basked in the bubble of joy surrounding them. It was almost worth dying for.

A woman's smooth voice broke into the serenity over the speakers. "Mr. Eijiro?"

Roku's eyes opened wide as reality came crashing in. Face falling in shock, he glanced around the room, finally seeing where they were, his unerring focus on Arad shattered. It reminded Arad of the time Davis had complained about the police—calling them pigs—with an officer standing behind him. The stammered backtracking was worth the price of admission.

"Yes, Dr. Windsor?" Squirming on the floor in more ways than one, Roku shimmied his pants up over his hips like he'd been caught by his parents with the boy next door.

"If the reunion with your mate has hit a lull in the action, perhaps we can allow Mr. Ansari an opportunity to get cleaned up and dressed so my team can complete his health check." Amusement colored Dr. Windsor's maternal tone while Roku figuratively paled. "He's been through a great deal, and I would like to be sure there are no lingering after-effects to his procedure. Afterward, I'd be happy to answer your questions and take our young Arad on a tour of the colony. Would that be acceptable?"

"Very, ma'am." Roku tugged ineffectively at closing his torn shirt.

Arad made no effort to cover himself and burst out laughing. He had no shame.

Chapter Thirty-Three

It was hard not to adore Dr. Kian Windsor.

Once Arad and Roku had showered and redressed, she oversaw the remaining tests to ensure Arad's health. She even countermanded her more zealous colleagues regarding more invasive testing for more passive options. As Arad's memories became clearer, lying on an examination table triggered a bank's worth of panic. Roku's protective instincts were strung so tight every doctor's safety was at risk. Windsor had been happy to scan him standing up.

True to her word, she took Arad on a tour of Moreau, stopping first at a local diner. She laughed at Arad's reaction when he ordered a standard meal portion instead of DemiShou sized. He'd underestimated his newfound lynx-human hybrid appetite. There were so many adjustments to his new body. He wasn't the same street slug anymore.

Grey District could go to hell. After setting foot on Moreau, Arad vowed to never go back.

Clean architecture gleamed in every direction, lacking zones defined by class and poverty. DemiShou and humans coexisted without the blatant bigotry he'd been used to. Little faults were visible when he searched for them—Arad's cynicism denied utopia's existence. However, the hard differences between those with wealth and those without were far more blurred than the life he'd led before this.

More DemiShou intermingled than Arad had ever seen in one place. They existed in Grey District, but the population was a sparse minority. He didn't know much about other districts, but the impression he had was that the percentages didn't fluctuate much. Here, that was not the case, and the numbers intimidated him a bit.

It was ridiculous, especially now that he was one too, but there was so much to absorb. Their proximity raised the hair on the back of his neck as well. Such as the wolf DemiShou waiter bringing them a new round of drinks.

Dr. Windsor practically giggled as she took a sip of tea. "Stop growling, Arad. He's not going to poach your mate."

"I'm sorry. It slipped out." Ducking his head in embarrassment, Arad kept a hand on Roku's sleeve and an eye on the server, who was polite enough not to mention anything. Perhaps he understood. Roku's protective streak had been in full force, refusing to allow Arad out of his sight. On top of that, they'd been in near-constant contact all day, with Arad using Roku as a rod to direct emotional lightning into the ground. He wasn't upset per se, but the newness of his body left a sandpapery roughness to all his heightened senses only Roku smoothed. He felt good, stronger and more alive than he could ever remember, but everything was a little too bright, a little too loud, and a little too close to his territory.

"The mate bond is new and fresh. Your reactions are going to be a little exaggerated around Roku for a while until it settles."

Arad glared at the waiter as he walked away. "He didn't have to stand so close to Roku, did he?"

"Now you know what I felt like after I woke on the ship." Roku covered Arad's hand with his own. "Wanting to protect you even though we were alone. Imagine if I took a spacewalk and didn't return."

"Hey. I made it back." A frisson of panic burned through the memory's resurgence, brighter than it should have been considering the outcome.

"Yes, you did. But I nearly went mad when it happened."

Arad scrubbed at his face to bring himself back to what served as normal. His feelings were purer and more potent, most likely the animal genes learning to play nice with the human. In a sort of messed-up kind of way.

"Don't get me wrong, I think this is the most awesome thing that's ever happened to me, but am I gonna be over-sensitive to everything forever?"

Windsor's smile had all the hallmarks of the comforting mother he should have had. "It will take some adjustment, but yes, you will. Every DemiShou we ever made went through the same thing."

Slumping in his chair with a sigh, Arad tipped his head to face the ceiling. "I'm going to need an owner's manual."

"We have all the support you'll need here as you transition into your new life. It's not as if any of this had been planned."

"No, it wasn't. Why didn't you tell me what was happening to Arad?" Roku asked.

The previous delight in Windsor sobered, leaving her face tinted with regret. "It was kinder not to. When the DemiShou program was in its infancy, we tested the process on medical cadavers. Dr. Felix Chakijane had a breakthrough in reversing necrosis and reanimating the donor, but the success rate was poor at best. Add in the moral and ethical equation, and we ended that direction and used what we learned to open the door to live trials. Felix took the decommissioning of the DemiShou project hard, but I had no idea he'd been recruited by ApexCorp. The files Yosei acquired from Captain Hodge outlined his new project analysis using the early research as a launching method. One hundred forty-eight body donors were listed, all ApexCorp employees having their post-mortem clauses enacted. Only thirty-two survived to be rebirthed, and some of those weren't fortunate enough to make it to the end. Arad coded twice over the last six weeks, but thankfully we were watching closely and resuscitated him."

"That still doesn't answer—"

"We didn't tell you because I couldn't give you that kind of hope only to watch you lose it again." Her delicate sigh made her whole body sag. "Arad's first death devastated you. You were displaying signs of deep depression and self-destructive tendencies. I doubted you'd survive a second. I didn't want to be that cruel when the odds were against us."

Roku voice dropped to a near whisper. "If the process failed, if Arad hadn't survived, would you have told me?"

"Thankfully, I didn't have to."

Tiny lines formed at the corner of her eyes, giving away the guilt at her decision, no matter how well intended. Roku had suffered in his absence. It showed in barely there anxious tremors when he stepped away for a moment because shadowing one another in the public restroom raised eyebrows. Or how Roku turned his head, focusing on the silverware rather than responding to Windsor's confession. It made Arad's chest ache to hear, but he refused to dwell on the unchangeable past. He was alive, bigger and better than before. Sadness was overrated, so he kept his positive mood up front and center.

"I'm not complaining, but if the chances were so low, why'd you do it?" Arad asked.

A warmth filled Windsor's eyes as her smile showed itself again. "Yosei made a compelling argument. Here we have a young man with next to nothing and nothing to gain. He finds a batch of DemiShou sleeping in chrysalis. With no idea of the potential risk or outcome, he assigns himself as their guardian. Even when the scenario turns horrible and he comes to true harm, he still strives to put their lives before his own. He brings them home, sacrificing himself in the process. It only seemed like fair payment."

Peering into Arad's eyes, Roku took his hand. "I don't think I can thank you enough, Dr. Windsor."

"We beat the odds. And seeing the two of you together makes the risk worthwhile."

Arad raised their linked hands to his lips and kissed Roku's knuckle. When they got back to their quarters, he planned to make up for lost time. But until then, he still had questions to ask the doctor since she was in such a good mood to share.

"So...why a lynx?"

"It was the name on the wall the dart hit." Dr. Windsor's words were as serious as her next sip of tea.

Jaw slack, Arad goggled. "Uh, what?"

"Oh, my, you should see the look on your faces. That was far too easy." Raucous laughter uncharacteristic of her standard demeanor shook her shoulders, and she had to set down her cup while she composed herself. "Honestly, we ran a genetic comparison between you and the templates on file. Of the three profiles that matched, the lynx appeared the most suitable. Strong, agile, smaller than Roku yet fast enough to keep up with him. You had to be based off a predator if you'd be mated to one, and I wasn't about to make you into a canine. I'm not a fan of excitable peeing."

Hopefully his new fur would hide the blush. Arad's face heated. She'd caught him so off guard. He chuckled as he compared himself to the other DemiShou visible in the diner and walking outside.

"My features have more human elements compared to Roku." It was true. The main difference was his face. He didn't have a muzzle or snout like some. Yes, he had spots, fur, and feline eyes, but his appearance could be mistaken as an excellent costume to an untrained eye.

"I was saving your life, not designing a soldier."

Arad lowered his voice so it wouldn't drift beyond the table. "I'll accept that, but isn't it illegal now to turn people into DemiShou?"

Her brow quirked as she looked over the edge of her teacup. "Yes, it is. But when I run your DNA, every database says you don't exist. So, under the circumstances, I was willing to embrace the technicality."

"I like technicalities." Arad nodded, and Roku did the same with a grin.

"I thought you might." Windsor set down her cup and put her hands together on the table in full doctor mode. "Tell me, do you remember what happened to you?"

Roku's back tensed and straightened. "I don't think we need to make Arad relive any of—"

Arad squeezed Roku's hand. "It's all right, Roku. She wants to know if my memory is intact." Once Roku relaxed a bit, Arad faced Windsor. "Mostly. More and more comes back when I think about it. Does this mean the same will happen to Roku's memory?"

A tiny frown curled the corners of Windsor's mouth. "I'm sorry, but it's doubtful. There's actual damage in his memory centers compared to yours. Felix is a brilliant geneticist, but others were more skilled at synaptic programming. I read the cryotube logs. The nanotech scrubbed Roku's memories during the synaptic phase with all the finesse of an ice cream scoop. He resisted the procedure, went into seizure, and arrested."

"But I was there and pulled him out." Recalling the day, Arad gripped Roku's hand harder.

"Yes. Your timely intervention saved him."

Brow furrowed, Arad dug up the question that had nagged him from the moment he'd found the sleeping DemiShou. "Is that what happened to Go? The wolf Demi?"

"According to the logs, it appears so."

Dr. Windsor's practiced calm had the potential to be annoying, but it helped blunt unpleasant news. The nightmare of Roku dying in the tube was something he'd fought and smothered for months.

"Except when it happened to him, there was no one to help."

No one responded to that.

They finished their drinks in quiet with Arad leaning into Roku. The solid wall of his body helped shore up his resolve as he navigated the changes to his body and environment. Fading away one day and waking up the next seven weeks later as a new species, no matter how much of an improvement, bent the mind a bit.

Dr. Windsor tapped a finger to the mini kiosk built into the table to pay, and they left to continue the colony tour.

Once outside, Arad found himself half listening as Windsor pointed out various aspects of Moreau's construction. A small transport filled with passengers glided by overhead, and Arad followed its path between the skyscraper network without the slightest traffic congestion. The amount of free space was staggering. The streets were open and lacked the overdeveloped, claustrophobic quality he'd grown up surrounded by. Buildings in Grey District were practically constructed on top of one another, and crowds were common. Wealthy or slug, the experience had been a similar version of population density. No wonder being closed in on the *Ansariland* had come so easily, so second nature.

The transport drifted out of sight, and Arad's mind drifted to his time in space, reconnecting to their previous conversation thread before the depressing news of Go's fate had snipped it short.

"Dr. Windsor, what happened to Hachi? The bull?" he asked.

Windsor glanced around to see who might be near, giving Arad a sense the information she continued to share was privileged. "Once we formulated repression meds for him so his mating instinct wouldn't endanger anyone, we woke him. He passed his physical and psychiatric evaluations, so I had him placed in Moreau security. It was what he was programmed for and made for a smoother fit into our society. We didn't want to disrupt him more than necessary. He's doing well. Rumor has it, he's a gifted card player."

"So he's okay?"

"I get daily reports. He's doing wonderfully."

Her sincere smile didn't halt the next step in Arad's thinking. "I wish I could have saved Shichi."

"Don't feel guilty about that. It's entirely misplaced. Shichi's programming was...nightmarish, and Dr. Southerland exploited it." Windsor's spine stiffened as she spoke, radiating her displeasure. "He was a custom design for a paranoid dignitary. At some point, his life would have ended the same. His death was regrettable but unavoidable, and it most likely saved many lives in the end."

"Are you only saying this to make me feel better?"

Windsor huffed. "No. I may withhold information from people when necessary, but lying lacks integrity, and I have always strived to possess that quality."

They continued touring through the prime market square, Dr. Windsor pointing out various vendors. Moreau sat off the public grid, so outside supplies ran exclusively through PlanetGenCo. Otherwise, the colony was quite self-sufficient. Many goods available were quality and handmade, and fresh-grown produce was easy to find, as people made do with available materials. Combined with all the high-end tech, Moreau's quality of life sat galaxies away from Grey District.

The unexpected comparison didn't endear it to Arad.

Roku must have sensed something. Perhaps anxiety left a bitter scent in the air because the tiger held Arad close as they walked, arm around his shoulder, sides brushing against one another. An argument could be made he was staking his claim, unwilling to risk another DemiShou sniffing around. Arad doubted that. If they were going to live on Moreau—or anywhere else for that matter—it would be together. While they hadn't had any opportunity to discuss it, they'd been through too much to contemplate any other scenario. As long as he had Roku, he'd learn to appreciate the differences that rubbed him the wrong way.

Hopefully.

Centered in the public square, a news kiosk broadcast stories and data from multiple sources, all focused on the current popular story: the ApexCorp scandal. Stock feeds, press releases, and other sordid details spewed forth, absorbed by the milling crowd. Spokespeople from Apex-Corp's legal team shouted denials and vowed to find the ones responsible for "fabricating this slander." Identities of the newly birthed DemiShou remained classified, but it would only be a matter of time before details leaked and people came looking.

Roku viewed the newsfeed with special interest. "Are we going to be watching over our shoulder for ApexCorp from now on?"

Sighing, Dr. Windsor answered as honestly as ever. "Possibly, but I'd wager you have some time to breathe. The files for Felix's program were leaked to the public, and the whole debacle has gone pandemic. DemiShou manufacturing and slavery make for poor bedfellows. No one wants to be involved. ApexCorp's stock is in freefall, and the board of directors is being indicted for conspiracy. Other corporate powers are circling. I'd read memos about possibly dismantling their power structure and selling off the assets. ApexCorp has its hands full."

"What about First Commander Bard?" Arad asked.

"Incarcerated. Court-martialed in disgrace. ApexCorp lawyers are trying to make him into a scapegoat, but the other corporations are far too excited over the blood in the water. ApexCorp has made no friends with its competitors."

"Including PlanetGenCo?"

"Especially them. No one likes their intellectual property stolen and abused."

Arad closed in on the kiosk to read the financial feed. The numbers and financial codes had meant more to him so many years ago in a life long lost, but he still read enough to get by. "Isn't this place owned by PlanetGenCo?"

"It is, but they only keep a loose oversight on Moreau. More like absentee landlords. Since the research and development of DemiShou has been shut down, it serves as a sanctuary of sorts."

Steeling himself by not facing her, Arad found the strength to ask the nagging voice whispering under all the good things Moreau had to offer. "So if I don't want sanctuary, if I decide to leave, you won't stop me?"

The lack of answer drew Arad to turn and find Dr. Windsor frozen in place. Wounded surprise colored her face, filling Arad with a stomach full of guilt.

"Arad, you're my patient, not my prisoner. You and Roku both. I would hope you would stay until we've completed all the medical assessments, but we don't have any right to keep you if you want to leave. Moreau is not a gulag."

Roku jumped in before Arad said more. "You put Pakko in jail."

"You did what?" Arad blurted out.

Windsor's raised hand stalled any further outrage. "Even if he's seen the error of his ways, Pakko Garcia was part of a trafficking scheme selling DemiShou. As director, I couldn't turn a blind eye to that. Given ApexCorp's public scandal, there would be a dangerous amount of criticism, and rightly so. However, I managed to convince the magistrates to be lenient. Thanks to his testimony and Yosei's recommendation, he received an extremely light sentence in minimum security. You'll be seeing him again soon."

"I suppose you're right." Jail time brought enough dread to Arad because in his experience, people didn't come back once arrested. He wanted to trust Dr. Windsor's word that Pakko would return.

Stopping in front of the kiosk, Windsor saddened as she read the newsfeed. "We always knew there would be consequences and prejudice when we introduced the DemiShou into the population. To help combat the backlash, Moreau was intended to be a safe haven for human and DemiShou both."

"But not every DemiShou knows about it."

Nodding, Windsor paced in a lazy arc, arms clasped behind her. "That's true. I hope to improve on that before long. We've stayed isolated outside of any other jurisdiction for protection of the colonists, so any changes will require careful planning."

Eyes narrowing, Roku apparently caught some hidden meaning. "What kind of planning?"

"I have a few ideas brewing. Let's continue our tour and I'll share them. If they sound interesting, once we clear Mr. Ansari for work, I may have an opportunity for you both."

Chapter Thirty-Four

"Scan here, sir."

Arad pressed his thumb to the portable screen, and the text turned green. The attendant tapped out a confirmation and sent it to Arad's private mail account—something he'd never believed he'd have again.

"Your clearance is complete. The window for departure ends in forty-five minutes. Have a nice voyage, Captain Ansari." With an efficient nod, the attendant collected his tablet and walked away, leaving Arad standing in front of his ship.

The *Ansariland* had never been so shiny.

Arad needed to step way back in the hangar to get the full effect. His ship sported a fresh new finish, updated exterior panels and repairs, and renovations going beyond the surface. No more carbon scoring stained the hull. No more evidence of his recent adventures. The veneer of a smuggler's craft gone, what stood in its place was classy and fit for a legitimately employed man. At Dr. Windsor's request, PlanetGenCo had paid for upgrading the *Ansariland* as compensation in lieu of an award for bravery.

A lot of things had been improved in Moreau. Arad's body. The *Ansariland*. His potential future.

He had no illusions the repairs were a bit of bribery to coax him into accepting an employment contract. He'd scrutinized every word of the deal, demanding simple language and making sure no corporate ownership of his vessel had been wormed into it. Nothing legally binding or forcing his hand. Not a bad set-up, running unique supplies between space stations and Moreau as a primary source of income. The idea made him a little giddy. He'd never held a real job for any length of time before. The workhouse didn't count. Of course, PlanetGenCo's request to hire him was more complex, but it was voluntary, even if they were convinced he'd say yes in the end.

It only took another six weeks to get to this point.

Getting Dr. Mercia to sign off on Arad's mental wellness took some effort because the doctor refused to believe being turned into a DemiShou hadn't irreparably damaged Arad's psyche. After weeks of sessions with no progress, Arad began antagonizing Mercia. Oh, the look on the man's face when Arad told him being a homeless slug would be no worse as a Demi than as a human with no options. Only it would be much more awesome. He told him burglary would be much simpler with claws and night vision, and he might not need to hustle. His customers would be sad, but he wasn't about to risk Roku going on a murder spree in a jealous rage to make a few credits.

Left frazzled over Arad's exaggerated tales of life in Grey District, Mercia gave up and cleared him. Dr. Windsor found the whole thing amusing in that polite way she handled everything in her orbit.

Now, Arad had been declared fit for duty with new clothes and a new haircut befitting his status as a cargo ship captain. Captain Ansari. He liked the sound of that.

Validating his ownership of the *Ansariland* took so long he doubted it would actually happen. Licenses needed to be confirmed and his identity needed to be added back into the grid. A near lifetime of distrusting authorities left doubts despite all of Dr. Windsor's reassurances. Receiving his documentation made him want to celebrate. The *Ansariland* was freedom no one could take away. He'd dreamed of escaping the ground since the filth of Grey District had ground unlaunderable stains into his soul. To stay or leave was his choice. Moreau wasn't a prison made of beautiful buildings for him anymore.

The colony held an appeal, but reminders of social classes lingered no matter how subtle they were here. Societal divisions existed everywhere, and perhaps Arad's past made him too sensitive to tune out even the tiniest distinctions.

With the *Ansariland* all prepped and ready to fly, he wouldn't have to.

The ground crew disengaged from the hull and cleared the bay, signifying the *Ansariland* was fueled and prepped for launch. All they needed was the captain's orders.

Arad's beaming smile could have powered an entire city for days.

Taking one last appreciative look, he jogged up the ramp and entered the ship. Bright hallways without evidence of the old, peeling paint greeted him. He'd vetoed streamlining every surface because it reminded him too much of the *Nightingale*'s pristine set-up, and living in a posh space was like a lie. A version of upper crust that had long since been scrubbed out of him. Instead, the existing walls were clean and vibrant while maintaining the industrial aesthetic he'd found comfort in.

A quick turn to the left had him heading for the bridge, following the voices. This time when he entered, the conversation didn't abruptly stop in a suspicious way.

"Arad!" Yosei squealed at an inhuman pitch sharp enough to make Arad and the new pilot, a wolf DemiShou named Julian, both wince. She bounced up and threw herself at Arad, wrapping him in an excited hug. "I was afraid you weren't coming!"

"It's my ship. I'm not leaving it behind for you lot to salvage."

She let go and hopped as she landed, her oversized smile infectious. "Did I tell you how awesome you look these days?"

"At least a dozen times, but it doesn't get old. Thank you."

For all her schoolgirl exuberance, Yosei could be discreet. She'd avoided mentioning Arad's recent conversion because it was illegal, and while Julian had come well recommended by Dr. Wilson to join the new crew, Arad wasn't ready to fold the newcomer into the secret circle. Not yet.

"Leave him alone, Yosei. The captain was outside admiring his ship before we break gravity." Julian's respectful teasing was appreciated. Being ex-military, he had the structure of rank forever ingrained into his habits, which went a long way in easing Roku's acceptance of another DemiShou on board.

"Because the *Ansariland* is the best ship in the galaxy." Arad wasn't totally joking.

Julian gave him a toothy grin. "You won't hear me complaining."

"As long as you can pilot him, I'm good."

"I can pilot anything, sir."

"And that's why we hired you. And I told you, call me Arad. Not captain or sir. I'm not military, and I'm not old."

A casual salute joined Julian's nod. "I'll do my best, sir."

Arad forced himself not to roll his eyes. Julian didn't rub his more paranoid instincts the wrong way, so he'd agreed to let him pilot the *Ansariland*. A little stiff and set in his ways, he'd likely relax once they got to know him in tight quarters. Arad wasn't too jaded yet to not give him the chance.

"I still don't see why we needed another pilot." Yosei turned and stuck her tongue out at Julian.

"Because your brilliance is better suited keeping the software at peak efficiency, and Julian's brilliance is his military piloting and navigational record. Make sure he has all the system privileges he needs."

Leaning back in his chair, Julian crossed his arms over his chest and smirked at Yosei. "Oo-rah."

Her pink hair stood straighter at the taunt. "Don't get snippy, Spot. I'll lock you in your room without your favorite chewy."

"Oy! That's speciesist."

"No, that's the truth of what I can do. As far as you're concerned, I rule here, Mr. Oo-rah, and don't you forget it." Yosei kept poking Julian in the chest. He didn't flinch, barely registering the prodding.

"Forget? I could sit on you and not even notice."

Yosei lurched in animated shock. "Making fun of my height? That's low."

"Yes. Yes, it is."

"I'm gonna airlock your kibble—"

And Arad left the bridge. The risk of being dragged into their mindless squabble... No. Not today. He had better things to do. Arad crossed his fingers, hoping their friendly banter was actually friendly, and hurried around the corner before they dragged him into the middle like the last time.

"Arad!"

Paused by the shout, Arad found his chief mechanic jogging up to him. "Pakko, what's up?"

"I wanted to catch you. Engine's all tuned up. We're good to go."

Pakko was more physically fit than before Arad's death. His incarceration stretch hadn't done him any permanent damage. Head still shaved with matching dark stubble over his jaw, he was energetic and ready to work. The darkness of the *Nightingale* hadn't weighed down his every movement.

Arad had been fortunate to visit Pakko in jail, which helped calm—but not erase—his prejudices of the prison system. He'd been well fed and hadn't appeared to suffer any harm. In fact, he looked healthier than when they'd first met. Once he recognized Arad in his upgraded body, Pakko burst into tears and begged forgiveness for not saving him from Bryce and her insanity. Arad spent a lot of time assuring him he'd never blamed Pakko for anything Bryce had done. They'd survived enough together. Arad could forgive.

"Good. We've got about forty minutes left. Is my jump drive working?"

"Hell yes. I wouldn't go anywhere with you without it." Pakko grinned yet hedged his next sentence. "But seriously, thanks for hiring me right out of jail. I wasn't sure what I was going to do next."

Parole had been granted barely a week ago with minimal stipulations. With Arad as his sponsor and a good word from Dr. Windsor, he'd been granted leave to accept a job that included interstellar travel.

"It took me weeks to get to know my ship, and you and Yosei figured out the details in a few days at most. I needed a crew that can keep us running smooth. It wasn't that big of a leap."

"Y'know, I don't think I ever had a chance to say thank you."

"For what?"

Tiny creases formed between Pakko's brows. "The *Nightingale*. Hodge. All the crap I was involved in. You didn't have to choose me for the crew." Pakko inhaled, his eyes watering.

"Nope. But we all deserve second chances."

"I won't forget that. I swear." Pakko discreetly glanced around. Even though he lowered his voice, he barked out a laugh laced with happy near-tears. "I still can't get over you getting turned."

Chuckling, Arad gave a hearty pat to Pakko's shoulder as he continued on his way. "Second chances, man. Second chances. Tell Yosei and Julian we launch in thirty."

"Aye, aye, Captain."

A fleeting wind of guilt rustled his fur at Pakko walking into the potential chaos on the bridge, but it vanished just as fast. Must have come from the ventilation system. Either way, he picked up his pace before anyone became wise.

Despite this, he made a stop at the infirmary, which now was a real live medical center under Dr. Windsor's guiding hand. Somehow the ship renovators had increased the room's footprint from the dismal closet space it had once been. In fact, he was pretty sure they'd somehow increased the overall size of the *Ansariland* in general.

He tried to picture the original wall mountings for the old, pathetic first aid kit between a pair of panel monitors running final calibration tests. Efficient work surfaces and new equipment made it a place where real help could be provided. Dr. Windsor stood in the center, inspecting a series of medical tools Arad wanted no part of.

Arad rapped the doorjamb because he had no interest in crossing the threshold. "We're leaving shortly. Are you sure you want to come along?"

"I did not arrange all of this to be left behind. Besides, you deserve to have a proper doctor on board with proper facilities equipped to care for DemiShou." New profiles had been uploaded to the med bed to prevent the "file not found" error loop that had kept it from counteracting Shichi's poison, leading to Arad's eventual death.

"Blame the crappy facilities on the previous landlord, not me."

Windsor paused, watching him with an assessing gaze. She lost none of her casual elegance as she opened a drawer and swept all of her devices inside and out of sight. A line of tension Arad wasn't aware of dissipated.

"Perhaps, but I still want to be there when we find the first of Chakijane's exiles. I'm better equipped to answer questions than most." A number of the dignitaries who purchased DemiShou from ApexCorp had gone into hiding, taking their trophy hybrids with them. PlanetGenCo, on behalf of Dr. Windsor, had made deals with corporate authorities to be the point of first contact with the exiled DemiShou to let them know they had options other than quarantine or prison. When she pitched her plan to Arad, asking to use the *Ansariland* and its crew as the ship given the mission, he was sure she was crazy.

And he immediately signed the contract.

"I can't say you're wrong. It seems an odd trip for the director of Moreau to be taking."

"Didn't you hear? I'm not director anymore."

"You quit your job?" Arad was so stunned to hear the news he almost stepped into the sick bay.

Brow cocked, she crossed her slender arms over her chest. "I set aside my position to focus on the new mission and start bringing awareness of Moreau to more of the DemiShou population. People in my position don't *quit*. We resign."

"And you're all right not being in charge?"

"You're far more intelligent than you give yourself credit for, and you're a talented strategist. Your survival techniques should be in training manuals. We may not agree on every decision, but I will defer command to you. Unless, of course, you're being ridiculous."

"I do have the security chief on my side."

"Repressing the serfs already? Your future as a despot is solid. Until that happens, I have a game of chess waiting for us. Assuming you won't cry when an old woman spanks you."

Arad's ears perked up at the mention of *chess*. "Once we're underway, you may regret those words."

"I regret nothing. Your king, however, is going to be used like a two-credit whore. Let me know when you're free."

Horrified by her trash talk, Arad left before she scandalized him further. The hallway circled past the crew quarters, then the exercise room and the lavatory, thankfully now separated by a wall. Every area was in better condition than he ever imagined possible.

Once he moved past the engine room, he stopped in front of the cargo bay and touched the lock panel. The door slid open, no longer accompanied by scraping metal on metal. Automatics lights flickered into life, and he stepped inside.

No crates formed a wall to hide anything, and he didn't need to navigate the maze. Tidy stacks of supplies lined the room with space for potentially more in the open center. The bay was barren in comparison. The first things he missed were the chimes of the missing cryotubes, a constant in the early days before Roku woke. No more reading manuals while standing watch over sleeping Demis since there was no mattress to lounge on anymore.

So much had gravitated around this room over his original time on the *Ansariland*. First it was the secret space he didn't have access to, then the home for living contraband. So much violence. So much pain connected a cadre of thieves to the schemes he'd been entwined in. He was only supposed to be the cabin boy.

How things had changed.

Arad walked over to where the cryotubes once sat, shallow scuffs on the floor the only witness to their existence beyond his memory. Hours and days spent being their silent guardian, not knowing what to expect or what would be required of him.

Massive arms surrounded Arad from behind. It didn't startle him. Roku's scent was a part of him, and his sharpened hearing had caught the tiger's soft footsteps. The days of his mate sneaking up on him had long since passed.

"Reminiscing?" Roku asked, rubbing his chin over the top of Arad's head.

"A bit. A lot happened here. Sometimes I wondered what would have happened if I'd never had the urge to come in here after I ranked up."

"Our lives would have been quite different."

"You probably would have died." Arad reached up and squeezed the hard muscles holding him tight.

Roku's chin ground Arad's hair as he nodded. "Probably."

"I'm glad you didn't."

"I am too. I wouldn't have you if I did." Roku gave Arad a sultry chuckle, pointing at the nearby drain. "I believe that's where we met."

"You mean the spot where you ravished the drug-addled captain into being your willing sex slave?"

Finding Arad's nipple through his shirt, Roku circled a thumb over the nub while pressing himself into Arad from behind. "Yes. I believe that's exactly the spot I'm talking about."

A purr rolled out of Arad at the tempting offer, but he forced himself to pull out of Roku's grasp with a regretful laugh. "Oh, no, you don't. We'll be launching shortly, and I'm not about to be caught by anyone while sneaking in a quickie before we go."

"Are you sure?" Crossing his arms over that marvelous chest made Roku's arms flex in a way Arad liked. Since Arad's conversion, Roku didn't need to hold back his animalistic nature, and the result allowed him to relax and be more playful. A wonderful change of pace. He'd also started wearing kilts again, which Arad heartily approved of, especially his penchant for not wearing anything underneath. The slit up the side exposed his thick thigh and would give Arad ample access...

"Yes, I'm sure." Arad adjusted himself. His trousers were too snug for this sort of teasing. "Later. After we get settled in, you and I will celebrate our first official day as owners of the *Ansariland*."

"Technically, you're the owner of the ship."

Arad clasped Roku's hand and drew him in close. His voice failed him once or twice before he finally forced out the words. "You're my mate. Everything I have is yours. Anything I can give you, I will."

"I would never abuse that trust."

Now that the declaration was out in the air, it all became easier. "That's why I give it to you."

Roku curled his shoulders until their foreheads touched. "I love you, now and forever, Captain Ansari."

"And I love you too, Security Chief Eijiro."

The kiss was sweet and simple, sealing a bargain they'd already made and would continue to make over and over again. Roku was patient every time, as Arad had difficulty sharing parts of himself because others had used him for their own purposes over the years. His parents. Davis. Torrins. Bryce. Through manipulation or torture, all had their agendas. Roku didn't deserve to be compared to any of them, but habits were difficult to break, and he continued to work on it every day. Not everyone got a second lifetime to compensate for the first.

Arad playfully tapped Roku's lips with a finger. "You know, my title doesn't sound so bad when I hear you say it out loud."

"Then I'll have to use it more often," Roku said as he kissed Arad's fingertip.

"See that you do."

Roku reached up and caught Arad's hand in his own and stared deep into his eyes. "I love the brightness of your eyes, Captain Ansari."

Opening his shirt with his free hand, he guided Arad into palming his chest and stroking the slabs of glorious muscle. "I love the way your fur meshes with mine when we touch, Captain Ansari."

With Arad feeling the hard flesh, Roku wrapped his arm around Arad's waist and jerked him up and on his toes, aligning their groins. "I love the way you surrender when I press myself against you, Captain Ansari."

Roku's organ bucked and snaked upward as it hardened. The pressure drew a husky gasp out of Arad. He rubbed his jaw along Arad's head and neck, making Arad gently yowl.

"I love it when you take my cock, Captain Ansari."

Arad found himself grinding into Roku as he whispered in his ear. "Roku...make sure the door is closed and serve your captain already."

And he did.

Acknowledgements

Thanks to Royce, who helped me brainstorm my way through the creation of the DemiShou, even though sci-fi is not his genre in the least.

About J. Alan Veerkamp

While spending years more focused on visual arts, J. Alan Veerkamp never let go of his innate passion for storytelling, wanting to write and draw comic books when he grew up. Once he discovered M/M fiction, a whole new world opened filled with possibilities. Why couldn't you have fantastic and dynamic sexy tales with an M/M cast? He started reading the online tales of authors like Night Tempest, Rob Colton, and Alicia Nordwell, which only fueled his need to create. Eventually he found GayAuthors.org and, with a little coercive nudge, started sharing his tales with an unexpected level of positive response. The experience and support gave him the courage to cross his fingers and aim for the world of M/M publishing.

Born and raised in Michigan, J. Alan continues to type away, wishing it was practical to use a noisy old-fashioned keyboard that clacks with each strike, if only to annoy his loving partner and spoiled miniature dachshund.

Facebook
www.facebook.com/jalanveerkamp

Twitter
@jalanveerkamp

Website
www.jalanveerkamp.wordpress.com

Other NineStar books by this author

Centauri Survivors Second Chances Chronicles

The Luxorian Fugitive

A Cook's Tale

Priest & Pariahs

Also from NineStar Press

The Luxorian Fugitive by J. Alan Veerkamp

Trying to escape his tortured past, Sergeant Liam Jacks travels aboard the transport vessel, the Santa Claus, as the security chief alongside his best friend and captain, Marc Danverse. Having survived the Civil War, they shuttle amongst the Proxima Centauri planetary cluster, trying to find some modicum of peace. Something of which Liam is in short supply.

During a stopover on the planet Luxoria, they take on a mysterious passenger. Hadrian Jamison's history is questionable and his effect on Liam is undeniable. The more they learn, the more questions they have. As they are drawn together, Hadrian's presence threatens to disrupt the quiet.

When Hadrian's past catches up to claim him, the ensuing conflict is more than any of them expected.

Connect with NineStar Press

www.ninestarpress.com

www.facebook.com/ninestarpress

www.facebook.com/groups/NineStarNiche

www.twitter.com/ninestarpress

www.instagram.com/ninestarpress

www.ingramcontent.com/pod-product-compliance
Lightning Source LLC
Chambersburg PA
CBHW020627020726
47494CB00001B/85